MW00475036

The Adventure of
the Missing Better Half

A New Sherlock Holmes Mystery

Note to Readers:

Your enjoyment of this new Sherlock Holmes mystery will be enhanced by re-reading the original story that inspired this one –

The Adventure of the Missing Three Quarter.

It has been appended and may be found in the back portion of this book.

Welcome to
New Sherlock Holmes
Mysteries

The first six novellas are always free to enjoy. If you have not already read them, click here now, sign up, download and enjoy.
www.SherlockHolmesMystery.com

All New Sherlock Holmes Mysteries are always FREE TO 'borrow' on Prime/ KU. Cut and paste 'Copland New Sherlock Holmes' into your Amazon search bar and they should all be there for you.

The Adventure of the Missing Better Half

A New Sherlock Holmes Mystery

Craig Stephen Copland

Published by:

Conservative Growth Inc.
3104 30th Avenue, Suite 427
Vernon, British Columbia, Canada
V1T 9M9

Cover design by Rita Toews

ISBN: 9781693934612

Dedication

To Larry Scott, my high school physical education teacher at Scarlett Heights Collegiate Institute in Toronto. He introduced me to the great game of rugby, for which I continue to be grateful. In addition to being an inspiring teacher, he was also a man of high personal integrity and moral rectitude. We respected him.

Contents

Acknowledgments

Like all writers of Sherlock Holmes pastiche stories, I owe a debt of gratitude to the genius of Arthur Conan Doyle for having created the immortal characters of Sherlock Holmes and Doctor Watson and the wonderful sixty original stories of the Canon.

This story is a tribute to *The Adventure of the Missing Three Quarter*.

Again, I acknowledge my high school English teachers at Scarlett Height Collegiate Institute in Toronto—Bill Stratton, Norm Oliver, and Margaret Tough. They encouraged me to read and write. For this book, I must also express my thanks to my physical education teacher, Larry Scott, who introduced me to the sport of rugby.

Early drafts of several of the chapters were shared with the Buenos Aires Writers Group and, once I returned to Canada, with the Vernon Writers Critique Group. I am again indebted to all of these fellow writers for their invaluable critiques and suggestions for improvement.

My faithful group of Beta Readers continue to make very useful suggestions for editing and improvements to all my stories, as do my wife, Mary Engelking and my brother, Jim Copland. Without their longsuffering help, my stories would be far too verbose.

Chapter One

This unusual case began innocuously enough on Boxing Day, 1898 with the arrival at 221B Baker Street of a gilt-edged envelope addressed to both Sherlock Holmes and me. Inside it was an invitation to attend the wedding of Mr. Godfrey Staunton and Miss Millicent Brocklehurst at the Church of Saint Monica on the morning of Saturday, 31 December, with a Wedding Breakfast to follow at the Langham Hotel.

"Please, Watson," said Holmes to me, "write a polite reply with any credible excuse for our not being able to attend."

He stretched out his long arm to hand me the letter and its contents but then quickly pulled back. Affixed to the back of the invitation card was a hand-written note. He peeled it off, read it, scowled, and gave it to me. It ran:

Imperative that you attend. I have been threatened and am being followed constantly. The wedding reception will be the only opportunity I have to speak to you without alerting those who are seeking to destroy my reputation. I have nowhere else to turn. For God's sake, I implore you. Please do not fail me. Godfrey Staunton

"Good heavens," said Holmes, with a sigh of resignation. "Surely he could have had sufficient imagination as to find a way to speak to me without demanding that I endure an entire wedding ritual. I have come to loathe such abuses of my time."

That made sense. Over the past twenty-five years, Sherlock Holmes had acquired a long list of former clients who felt themselves deeply indebted to him for having saved their reputations, their fortunes, and even their lives. They were compelled to demonstrate their gratitude by inviting him to their weddings or, as was the more common case, to the nuptials of their children.

Invariably, the host would draw people's attention to his presence, and for the remainder of the gathering, he would be beset by no end of people visiting at his table. They would suggest that he should have done this or that in the most recent case I had published, or ask his opinion of a recent crime that had taken in the East End, or ask him to solve the riddle of their Schnauzer who vanished two years ago come spring.

As a result, he now detested such gatherings and contrived any and every possible excuse to decline to attend.

"Godfrey Staunton?" said Holmes as he studied the note. "I am utterly in the dark as to what happened to him after we left him disconsolate beside the bed of his dear dead wife three years ago. Do you know anything about him?"

"As a matter of fact, I do," I said. Holmes had no use for the sporting news. I, on the other hand, as a devoted follower of most sports and particularly of rugby, the one I played in my youth, read those pages of the press every day. It was a rare event when I found myself in a position to educate my unique friend, and I confess that I enjoyed the opportunity.

"Young Mr. Staunton's recovery," I said, "was long and painful after that tragedy. For the first few weeks after her death, he confined himself to the small cottage they had shared, refusing the entreaties of his teammates to join them either for a round at the pub or for a social practice on the rugby pitch."

"And just how are you privy to such intimate knowledge?"

"I am getting to that," I said and continued. "Dr. Armstrong— you do remember him do you not?"

"Of course, I remember him. Kindly get on with it."

"Yes, well, I happened to run into him a few times. He said that he kept a careful eye on Godfrey. His health was sound, but there is no medical cure for a heart that has been torn apart. Only time can do that."

"Please, Watson, skip ahead to the part of your story that might have anything to do with this note."

"Quite so, yes, well, it is said that time heals all wounds. And Godfrey slowly recovered. After three months, he was observed taking walks through the town and along the shore of the River Cam. After six months, he accepted the invitation of his teammates to toss the ball back and forth as they ran a line down the pitch. Inexorably, the paralyzing gloom subsided and a full year later, having graduated from Cambridge, he accepted an offer to play for Blackheath."

"Ah, your old club," said Holmes. "That accounts for your more recent knowledge of the chap."

"It does indeed. You may be incapable of understanding, but when I read about his joining my old squad, it gave my heart a small thrill. His play on the right wing has been magnificent and widely reported. And that, my dear Holmes, led to his becoming the subject of another inescapable social phenomenon; one with which you are also not particularly familiar."

Holmes was drumming his fingers on the arm of the chair. "And just what might that be?"

I took a sip of my tea before answering.

"He was soon the object of affection of no end of tender-hearted young women who are divinely called to be the instruments of love and care and succor to a young man who has suffered such tragedy and loss. It is a common occurrence in the sporting world."

"And everywhere else on earth," said Holmes. "The fact that he was handsome, an athlete, and the heir to an enormous fortune no doubt added fuel to the fire."

"No need to be so cynical."

"I am not being cynical, merely stating a universal truth."

"Regardless," I said. "Some of my chums, old boys from Blackheath, told me that Geoffrey Staunton was swarmed by highly eligible young women. A coterie of lovely young females attended every game played on Blackheath's home pitch. Many of them even managed to follow the team when they played elsewhere across the south of England."

"Did they now? And did one of the devoted fans manage to outplay the competition and claim the prize of one of the most favored heirs in the Empire?"

"No, it was not one of those who so ardently pursued him. It was that one exceptional young woman who had no designs upon him at all, Miss Millicent Brocklehurst. I believe that the invitation we have received has come from her family."

"Correct. But now he appears to be in trouble? It is not surprising. His uncle, that misery and crabbed old Lord Mount James, must be over eighty years of age. When one of the wealthiest men in the land reaches that stage of life, it would be surprising if his sole heir did not become an object of interest to those whose motives were far from pure."

"So," I said, "you think that whatever has beset Godfrey is connected to his uncle's wealth?"

"What else could it be?" said Holmes.

"What about the game of rugby? The Home Nations Championship games will start in less than a fortnight. Godfrey was chosen for England's team."

"And a few weeks later, my dear Watson, it will all be over."

"But the whole of the British Isles—England, Scotland, Ireland and Wales—will be caught up in it. We will all be following the games."

"Then do remember to wake me up when it's over. And do return to the matter at hand. What do you know about these threats against Staunton?"

"Nothing. Haven't the foggiest. I regret to inform you, my dear Holmes, that we shall have no choice but to attend the wedding if you want to find out."

"Pity."

.

Chapter Two

nd so, on that glorious, sunny Saturday morning in late December, Holmes and I, dressed to the nines, attended a wedding ceremony held in the Church of St. Monica in the Edgeware Road. All and sundry commented on the radiant beauty of the bride, making sure to add that she was also known to have a brilliant mind.

Carriages were available to take the guests the two miles from the church to the hotel, but Holmes insisted that we walk. He began interrogating me as soon as we were out of earshot of the other guests.

"What do you know about this girl, this Millicent Brocklehurst woman?"

"I believe, Holmes," I said, "that her name is now Mrs. Godfrey Staunton. And it behooves you to regard her with the respect that her position demands."

"Any woman who is that beautiful and reputed to possess superior intelligence and who succeeds in marrying an exceptionally wealthy broken-hearted young widower must be regarded with suspicion until proven otherwise."

"Honestly, Holmes, sometimes—,"

"I am being nothing but honest. Tell me what you know about her."

"Very well. All I know is what I heard from the Blackheath Old Boys, but they say that she comes from a fine family. Her father is a Rector in a church in the Midlands and her mother an accomplished musician and poet. They named her after Millicent Fawcett, the founder of Newnham College and a hero of emancipated women throughout England. I assume you have heard of her."

"Of course, go on."

"Whilst at Cambridge, she took a first in the study of Natural Sciences and secured several prizes from Newnham College."

"I assume then," he said, "that she not only also secured young Staunton but must have bewitched old Mount James."

"That is uncalled for, Holmes. What right do have to say something like that?"

"I have the right because I am sure I am right. The miserable old miser is paying for her wedding. Therefore, he must be smitten with her."

"I couldn't say. Why don't you ask him when we get to the hotel?"

"Because, if you remember, he does not like me, and the feeling is mutual. Enough of him. How did she contrive to meet Staunton? Did the Old Boys talk about that?"

"Such tales," I said, "are not told out of school. However, I expect that we shall hear full accounts of their history during the speeches at the breakfast."

"What a horrifying prospect."

His interrogation had waned by the time we strolled down Portland and entered the imposing portico of the Langham. The doorman directed us to the Palm Court, where the mannered staff took our coats and led us to seats at one of the tables near the back of the splendid hall. Even though it was mid-winter outside, the enormous urns, supporting the palm trees and the lush green fronds affixed to the marble pillars, gave one the feeling of having entered the tropics. Uniformed waiters bearing trays of Champagne were already circulating throughout the assembled guests, and the general mixture of laughter and effusive exchanges of greetings gave one the impression of a merry and light-hearted assembly.

The young waiter who pulled out our chairs leaned toward Holmes and, grinning, whispered, "Thrilled to have you with us, Mr. Holmes. I have read every one of your stories and books."

Holmes did not reply. He silently sat down and immediately consulted his watch. I took my place in the chair to his immediate left and strained my neck to see which of London's rich and shameless were in the crowd.

On Holmes's right, a gentleman folded a journal he had been reading and stuffed it into his suitcoat pocket. Then he turned directly to Holmes.

"I am happy to see you here, Mr. Holmes," said Dr. Leslie Armstrong. "Godfrey was very much hoping that you would come."

"Once again, Sir," said Holmes, "it would appear that you are far better informed as to the reasons for my meeting with him than I am. So, I respectfully request that you enlighten me. Why am I here?"

"You were invited because Godfrey was at his wit's end and, as his intimate friend, I told him to request your help. I acknowledge that my disapproval of your profession has diminished and inviting you to the wedding seemed the most expeditious opportunity to meet with you without arousing suspicion."

"Suspicion?" said Holmes. "From whom?"

Dr. Armstrong leaned his head close to Holmes's and began to speak *sotto voce*. He uttered only a few inconsequential words when the wedding party entered the room, and the guests all stood and engaged in enthusiastic applause.

The Master of Ceremonies ascended the dais and bade the guests be seated. He was impeccably dressed in the latest style with the full armor of accessories. He spoke with all the polish and elocution of a seasoned politician who was used to peacocking himself in front of gatherings of wealthy people.

Holmes leaned his head over to my ear.

"Who is the coxcomb?" he whispered.

"His name is Baron Worthington," I whispered back. "He was a star fullback on England's squad a decade ago. Now he's one of the governors of the RFU."

"Obviously, three of the groomsmen do not like him. It is apparent by their posture. Why not?"

"Some say his arrogance led to the schism between the Union and the League."

"What else does he do?"

"An industrialist; quite successful. And the Mayor of Wakefield."

The Baron smoothly delivered effusive welcoming remarks and moved quickly to acknowledge some of the more distinguished guests who had graced the event with their presence. First off, he looked at the table directly in front of him.

"Lord Mount James," he said, "is the beloved uncle of our groom and for the past decade has taken the place of a caring father after the tragic passing of his younger brother and sister-in-law, our groom's parents. Accompanying him is his friend and companion, the lovely Lady Maynooth, whose constant cheerfulness has added such vivaciousness, elegance, and sparkle of late to His Lordship's life and is doing the same to our gathering here this morning."

He called upon the two of them to stand and be greeted by a loud round of applause. I had to admit that Mount James looked much better than I remembered him from three years earlier. He stood straight and smiled and even managed a wave to the room. The woman who stood beside him, Lady Beatrice Maynooth, was tall and slender and bore a head of silver hair beneath her stylish hat and veil. I put her age at about fifty and remembered having read of the unexpected death of her husband several years ago and her much-admired charity work on behalf of universal suffrage, land trusts, homeless cats, young refugee women, enhanced longevity, and the lifeboat society. She appeared often in the society pages of the newspapers, always reported as being charming, and seemed to have friends in every quarter of the city. Subsequent to her husband's death, she had managed to become acquainted with Lord Mount James, and they now formed an elegant couple in spite of the obvious difference in their ages.

Several other distinguished persons were introduced, and then, as a final note, Baron Worthington pointed to our corner of the room.

"And you will all be interested to know," he announced, "that England's, indeed the world's, most famous detective, Mr. Sherlock Holmes is here in our midst."

A sea of heads turned in our direction. Holmes's face turned to stone.

"But be assured," the Baron continued, "he is not here to investigate any of us for our bad behaviors or faults in manners, let alone criminal dalliances. He is here as the close friend and companion of Dr. John Watson…"

Now the turned heads were looking at me.

"…who is not only England's most popular writer but is also a dedicated Old Boy of the Blackheath Rugby Club."

This brought a cheer from some of the younger members of the crowd, and all six of the groomsmen leapt to their feet and applauded.

As the Master of Ceremonies droned on about other matters, Holmes turned to me.

"Why did all the groomsmen clap for you? They cannot all be rugby players, are they? Three of them look much too scrawny."

"They must be the backs," I whispered to Holmes.

"The what?"

"They play in the backfield. The other three, those who look like monstrous gorillas, are the members of the pack."

"Pack of what?"

"Just *the pack*. The forwards."

Fortunately, this conversation was halted by the Baron's calling on Godfrey to come to the dais and introduce the wedding party. He was nowhere near as comfortable and polished and, though utterly fearless on the pitch, seemed somewhat petrified by having to speak to over one hundred people.

He began by saying some kind words about his lovely wife and commenting on how beautiful she was on her wedding day. Every head in the room nodded and a few utterances of "hear, hear" were heard. Godfrey then turned to the chap beside him, a handsome young man with a head of curly red hair and unmistakable Irish complexion.

"My best man," said Godfrey, "has been my dearest and closest friend during the past three years. The first of those years was a very dark time for me, but Danny stood by me, closer than a brother. I am deeply indebted to him."

The crowd fell silent, punctuated by some murmurs of solemnity, knowing that Godfrey was referring to the tragic death of his first wife.

"And even though I love him dearly," Godfrey continued, "as of the fourth of February, he will become my mortal enemy!"

Here the crowded roared in laughter and gave a round of applause.

"What," Holmes said into my ear, "is he talking about?"

"Daniel O'Hearn," I replied, "is from Dublin. He plays now for Blackheath, but he was selected to play for Ireland in the Home Nations Championship. They play England on the fourth of February."

"And since Danny is a son of the sodden Emerald Isle," Godfrey was now saying, "he is much more talented than I in telling a good story. And so, I turn the pulpit over to him to give an exaggerated account of how my beloved bride and I met and our progress from that day until we said 'I will' at the altar. But I caution you, he is an Irishman to the depths of his soul, and therefore you should not believe a word of what he says."

Again, the crowd laughed and applauded as the smiling Dubliner took his place in front of the room.

He looked over the room slowly from one end to the other, spread his arms, palms facing up, and began his story.

Chapter Three

"**S**ooo ... you are wanting to know how this lovely romance began, are you now? Then I shall tell you. It all began on a sunny day in June of last year. And where? It was on the green, green grass of the Gonville and Caius sports field in Cambridge. And have any of you been there? If you have, then you will know that those grounds are to be found right next door to Newnham College. And do you know who is permitted to attend Newnham College? Ladies, and only ladies. Several hundred of them, and every one of with a beautiful face and a superior intelligence. So, is it any wonder that some lads, and I confess that includes a few who are with us today, found any excuse to show off their athletic skills on those grounds, hoping to impress some lovely lass with the brawn of their bodies, having failed to do so with the brightness of their brains whilst in class.

"It so happened that on that fateful day, a certain Mr. Godfrey Staunton, accompanied by his mates Cyril Overton—the emaciated chap at the end of the table—along with Terry Heaton and yours truly were demonstrating our exceptional skill in forward kicks that could be caught by a teammate whilst he was running at full speed toward the goal line.

"Well, didn't Cyril let fly a perfect kick. It sailed up and up and up into the heavens and descended at least forty yards down the field. Godfrey, swift of foot and with peerless skill, ran like the wind to catch it. But as fate would have it, Godfrey had his eye on the ball somewhere up in the sky above him and not on the green in front of him.

"I will never forget what happened next. He ran pell-mell into the backside of a young woman who was on her way to the Newnham library. Great and horrible was the crash thereof. Her books went flying in all directions, and she was flung, as if hit by a cannonball, to the ground. Godfrey stopped and stared at the victim of his carelessness as she was lying prostrate, motionless. We ran to the spot where she lay. She was not breathing; her eyes were wide in terror.

" 'Jaysus, Mary, and Joseph,' I said to Godfrey, 'look what you've done. You've gone and kilt her.' Godfrey dropped to his knees beside the inert body and leaned down beside her ear. He shouted the most useless words known to man. 'Are you all right?' he demanded.

"And then, to the relief of all who had gathered around, she began to gasp for breath. She turned her head toward Godfrey Staunton and said something which cannot be repeated in polite society. She struggled to get back on her feet but was wracked with pain and so Godfrey, being to the manor born and a gentleman to his marrow, put his strong arms under her and lifted her up. Although she was a tall, strapping girl and in spite of her mild protestations, he effortlessly carried her across the grounds to the University infirmary on Newnham Road.

"It so happened that the attending physician feared that one or more of her ribs might have been cracked and insisted that she remain and rest for a week.

"Godfrey promptly forgot all about his rugby practice. And what happened next is beyond human understanding. Perhaps it was guilt that made him keep asking after her every day for that next week. Perhaps it was his horror that not only had she never heard of him, but that she had no interest whatsoever in the game of rugby and had assumed that a scrum must be the vulgar name given to Scottish oatmeal. Who can say?

"Whatever the cause, it came to pass that he visited daily, and brought fresh flowers on each occasion, and stayed and chatted with her over a cup of tea. As you might have guessed, having listened to Godfrey trying to make a speech, during his first visits, the conversations were stilted and awkward. Any interest she might have had in him was much more directed to what he had in his head and heart than in his robust thighs and calves. Or, as we say on the blessed isle, more what he had in his upper floor than in his cellar.

"And what did she discover? To her surprise, she discovered that although he had worked hard to conceal it, our Godfrey had a jolly good mind. And he learned that this alluring goddess was about to complete her studies in the natural sciences and had already published three monographs in the field of ornithology."

Here he turned to the groomsmen. "That big word, my dear chaps, means the study of birds."

He returned to speaking to the roomful of guests

"By the end of the week, didn't conversations become warm and revealing. Once they reached that stage and had bared their souls to each other, there was no escape for either of them.

"The magic of love has no explanation ... Oh, what fools these mortals be ... They fell in love.

"But Godfrey had a fearful secret that he was loath to confess. Fully a month passed before he sat her down and, with downcast face, whispered to her that which he was afraid would cause her to run away forever from him. He said those awful words. He said, 'My darling, before you think of bestowing on me the blessing of becoming my wife ... before you honor me by taking my last name as yours ... I have no choice, as a gentleman ... to confess to you that ... I have ... an UNCLE.' "

The crowd roared. Some leapt to their feet. All eyes turned to Lord Mount James. At first, he looked nonplussed and offended, but there is no more powerful a weapon in the world than joyful laughter, and he could see that everyone was clapping and smiling at him. He smiled back and waved. Lady Maynooth leaned over and patted his gnarled hand with hers, to the cheers of the crowd.

Once the crowd had settled down, Danny O'Hearn continued.

"Let it never be said, nay, not for a day, that Miss Millie Brocklehurst was anything less than courageous. Upon learning Godfrey's fearful secret, she went straight away to his fearsome uncle and had a chat with the dear old fellow. Within an hour, she had not only won his heart but from that day on, Lord Mount James could be heard telling all and sundry that his nephew had finally come to his senses, although he now appeared to be marrying well above his station in life. A sentiment with which Godfrey would most certainly agree. Is that not correct my friend? And are you not the luckiest man on God's green earth?"

He directed this last question to Godfrey, who nodded his head vigorously.

Several more speeches followed and then the singularly attractive bride and groom cut the wedding cake and began to distribute small pieces of it to all of the tables of the Palm Court. Twice, I noticed that Godfrey and then Mrs. Staunton gave a look across the room to our table and appeared to be arranging their journey so that we would be visited last.

I could tell that Holmes was eager to question Dr. Armstrong but was constrained from doing so by the enthusiastic questions that were posed to him by some of the other guests at our table. There was only one brief interruption when Danny O'Hearn came down from the head table to visit ours.

"Mr. Sherlock Holmes," he said. "I am so glad that you were able to join us. I do hope you will have a minute to chat with Godfrey and Millie. I know that they are looking forward to the opportunity."

With that, he returned to his place, and a few minutes later, the bride and groom arrived at our table. When they reached Holmes and me, Godfrey leaned down from behind us and put his head between ours.

Through a toothy, wide smile, he said, "Would you please stand and chat with Millie and me a few feet back from the table?"

He also gave a nod to Dr. Armstrong, who rose from his chair and joined us.

Holmes, fine actor that he is, let out a forced chuckle, and stood, as did I. The five of us huddled, all smiles and forced little bursts of laughter as Geoffrey put his case to Holmes.

"Please, Mr. Holmes, I implore you, I am at my wits' end. Can you suggest to us a time and place when we can meet with you in the immediate future? It must be a complete secret. My every move is being watched. Can you suggest one to us?"

"Where," said Holmes, "are you spending your wedding night?"

Chapter Four

Neither Mr. nor Mrs. Staunton immediately replied. I assumed that they had not had quite *that* unsuspected and private a venue in mind.

"Uhh ...," said Geoffrey.

"At the Grosvenor," said Millie.

"Excellent," said Holmes. "Demand a room on the first floor, one that has a balcony looking out toward Victoria Station. We will be there on the stroke of midnight whilst all and sundry are distracted by New Years' revelers. Turn up your lamps twice so we can know which room you are in. I will tap on the glass door, and you will let us in. And Mrs. Staunton, might I request that you take responsibility for making sure your husband is awake at that time?"

The bride let peal an infectious laugh and nodded and promised. Then they returned to the head table.

Once the ceremonies were over, Holmes and I departed. As soon as we were standing outside the hotel, I turned to him.

"Merciful heavens, Holmes. Have you no sense of decency? There cannot be another man in England who would be so inconsiderate as to even think of meeting with a young man on his wedding night."

"Precisely," he said as he lit a cigarette and began walking in the direction of Baker Street.

I said nothing.

He continued. "I shall come to your house at half-past eleven. Please dress in dark, comfortable clothing and plimsolls. Meanwhile, I shall begin to make discreet inquiries into the affairs of Lord Mount James."

He left me standing on the pavement and walked toward the City.

I returned to my home and, at eleven-thirty that night, a small closed carriage stopped in front of our house. Dressed in black from head to toe, I climbed inside and was greeted by a similarly attired Sherlock Holmes.

"I have the feeling," said I, "that we are about to become cat burglars."

"A reasonable feeling," said Holmes.

"The lowest balconies," I said, "are at least eighteen feet off the ground. Just how are we going to scale the walls of the Grosvenor and climb on to them?"

"You will follow me and do what I do."

That was the only instruction he gave me.

Grosvenor Place and Buckingham Palace Road were dark and deserted and, in the stretches of road near a street lamp, the fresh-fallen snow sparkled like diamonds in the silence. We arrived at the Grosvenor, but the driver did not stop. He drove on past it, did a complete circle around the block and then stopped at the curb in a darkened stretch some distance from the main front door.

"As I expected," said Holmes, "there is no one lurking around the hotel. We shall not be seen."

When we stepped out on to the pavement, Holmes turned and spoke to the driver.

"Freddy, would you please hand down the ladder?"

The driver reached behind him and fed down to Holmes a ladder that was about ten feet in length. On closer examination, I could see that it was a two-piece extension ladder that, when entirely pulled out, would reach at least as far as the bottom of the balconies.

"This does seem," I said, "a bit extravagant. Is he in that great danger?"

"I cannot be certain that there is no one observing from the lobby. Better to err on the side of caution."

For the next ten minutes, we huddled silently in the cold darkness waiting for midnight. Somewhere in the distance, I heard a clock tower sound the hour, and a glow appeared in the windows of a room four down from where we were standing. The glow vanished and then reappeared and vanished a second time.

"That's it," said Holmes. "Time to climb."

He moved like a cat in the night, walking quickly to the balcony and setting up the ladder. He pulled silently on the rope until the ladder was fully. Effortlessly, he climbed up, used his arms to pull his body onto the edge, and swung his long legs over the railing. I followed and, with some assistance from Holmes's outstretched hand, did likewise. He then reached down and pulled the ladder up behind us,

A quiet tap on the balcony door was followed by its silent opening.

"Quick," whispered Mrs. Millie Staunton, who had appeared, dressed in her night clothes and covered in a dark silk dressing gown. "Come inside. I'll wake him up."

In the limited light from the low lamps, I watched as Millie went to the washstand and put a thimble-full of water in a cup. She came over to where her husband was sleeping soundly and tossed the water in his face.

"Wake up darling rugger boy," she said in response to his startled arousal. "We have company."

"Oh, huh? Who? What the ...? Oh, yes. Sorry, just catching forty winks. Mr. Holmes and Dr. Watson. So good of you to do this."

"Yes," said Millie, "I am afraid that we are in a tight spot, and I admit that I am rather concerned."

"Then please," said Holmes, "explain your situation as precisely and concisely as you can. You may assume that I am fully cognizant of the intricacies of Lord Mount James's holdings and affairs."

"Uncle Jimmy?" said Geoffrey. "What's he got to do with this?"

Holmes was momentarily speechless. "Are you saying that whatever has brought distress into your life has nothing to do with your being the scion and heir to his estate?"

"Good heavens, no. The old boy is as healthy as a horse. He'll be around for at least another decade. No, this is all about the Home Nations Championship games starting next weekend."

I said nothing, although it is possible that inwardly I might have smirked.

"Are you telling me," he said, "that you have demanded a secret meeting with me over a rugby game?"

"Yes. Nobody can know that we're meeting with you or there will be the devil to pay," said Staunton.

"But you play Rugby Union, do you not?" said Holmes. "There is no money involved. Unlike League play, you receive no pay and admission is free. Amateur sport is free of gambling. Wherein lies the possible connection to criminal behavior?"

Staunton looked at Holmes in disbelief.

"Why, Mr. Holmes, I thought you knew things. Where have you lived? It is about the betting. The money bet on the Championship games on the outside is beyond belief."

"Is it indeed?" said Holmes. "How much is expected to be bet?"

"All told, over a million pounds. And that does not include what is under the counter. Altogether it's enormous."

"Well now, that changes things," said Holmes. "Kindly state your case and explain why it is that you require my services."

"Well, Sir," said Staunton, "it started just over a week ago."

"Ten days, to be precise," said his lovely wife. "On the Thursday before Christmas."

"Yes, well ten days then. I was selected to play on England's National Team."

"My congratulations," I said. "That is indeed an honor."

"Right, thank you, Doctor. Me and Cyril Overton, my old teammate from Oxford, and Danny were all selected along with a splendid group from right across the nation. You should see our forwards; our 1,2 and 3 chaps are giants. They are all over seventeen stone. In the scrum, they're like a locomotive. With the locks behind them, nothing can stop them. The Scots, Irish, and Welsh players are just runts of the litter. My mates from Blackheath, Percy Royds, and Bob Livesay, are with me in the back. Together we're—,"

"Darling," interrupted Mrs. Staunton, "I believe Mr. Holmes needs to know about what happened in the pub more than about who is on the team."

"Yes," said Holmes. "I have no doubt England has a superb team. Wherein lies the problem?"

"The problem is," said Staunton, "that some blackguards are trying to bribe me to throw the game."

"Very well," said Holmes. "Tell them to go fly a kite. You are not in need of a single farthing. You are the heir to one of the wealthiest families in the country. You are receiving an allowance from your uncle and, beginning in a few days, the two of you will be living in one of his houses in Chelsea. Is that not all true?"

"Yes, it is. But how did you know that?"

"It is my business to know things. And I know that as a prospect for offering a bribe, you must be one of the poorest bets possible. Just refuse."

"It is not that easy, Mr. Holmes. They have also threatened me," said Godfrey.

"With what?"

"Look at this," said Godfrey. He walked over to the dresser and from his wallet extracted a note. He handed it to Holmes, who then passed it onto me. It ran:

Do not underestimate our determination to make you agree to our demands. Do you remember what happened to Jimmy Pike in April 1893? We fixed him bloody well. The same will happen to you if you do not do as you are told. Your future is at stake. On the Tuesday following your wedding, you will receive further instructions from us.

"Who is Jimmy Pike?" asked Holmes.

"Jimmy Pike?" said Godfrey. "Have you never heard of him? He was one of the best forwards ever. Played for St. Helens Recs. He could hold the line in the front row or the back row or even as Lock. Made the Home Nations team. And—,"

"Thank you, Mr. Staunton. Now Watson, if *you* will, tell me what happened to him."

"The reports," I said, "were not terribly revealing but it appears that he was attacked during the championship games. It was said that somebody took a hammer to his kneecap. Whoever did it was never caught. But Pike descended into desuetude and never played again."

"Ah, yes," said Holmes. "I vaguely recall some mention of that incident. A brief report on it was elevated from the sporting pages to the news section. Yes ..."

He then closed his eyes and held up his hand to indicate he wished us to be silent. Slowly he moved his head from right to left, giving a barely perceptible nod every inch or so. When his chin had reached the spot above his left collar bone, his eyes popped open.

"Fraudsters," he said. "The threat is confected. Whoever sent that note had nothing whatsoever to do with the assault on James Pike."

"But Mr. Holmes," said Godfrey, "how can you know that? No one ever found out who these people were."

"The attack on Pike took place in the spring of 1892, not 1893. I assure you that no criminal forgets the exact time, date, and place of a crime he committed and for which he was never even suspected let alone arrested. Such events, and there are fortunately very few, are carried in his memory as a source of pride, every bit as much as your memories, Mr. Staunton, of the games in which you were singularly triumphant. I would ever go so far as to wager that Dr. Watson can recount his successes on the pitch for Blackheath even though they were a quarter-century in the past. Is that true, Watson?"

"I scored," I said "a grand total of nine tries, thirteen penalty kicks, and, sixteen drops. I can give you a detailed account of every one of them."

"Precisely," said Holmes. "And you, young man, may take whoever made this threat against you with a grain of salt. It was not sent by any serious member of the criminal class."

"But Mr. Holmes, they do not have to be criminals. Any thug-for-hire with a hammer could destroy my playing days for the rest of my life. I cannot take that risk. You have to help me find whoever it is and stop them."

Holmes pondered his plea for a moment and then replied.

"Given the amount of money that is in play, I concede that a high level of risk is possible. However, there is an exceptionally simple solution."

"What?" demanded Godfrey. "Tell me."

"Were you the only three-quarter considered for selection to England's national team?"

Of course, not. Joe Davidson is the Reserve Back. Charlie Wilson from Percy Park was right behind him."

"And if you were injured the day before the first game," said Holmes, "what would happen?"

"Joe would come in from the Reserve Bench, and Charlie would be called up to replace him. Either of them is a brilliant player. Splendid chaps. Run, kick, pass, tackle; they can do them all."

"Excellent. Then the obvious solution to your problem has no need of my time. You will announce later this week that you are incapacitated and cannot play. The entire business will be over."

In the soft glow of the lamps in the hotel room, I could see a look of dismay come over Godfrey's handsome young face. He opened his mouth and for several seconds struggled for words.

"No, Mr. Holmes, no. You don't understand. I cannot do that. It's not possible."

"Young man, it most certainly is possible. It is not only possible, it is the obvious course of action that will frustrate the plans of whoever these fearful thugs might be while protecting you from harm."

"You do not understand, Mr. Holmes."

"Godfrey, darling," interjected Mrs. Millicent Staunton, "it's only for a few games. You can try again next year. You don't want to risk not being able to play all next season for Blackheath, do you?"

"Millie, sweetheart, I just cannot do it. It is not possible."

"You can," snapped Holmes, "and you must. May I remind you, unkind though it may be of me to do so, that three years ago, when you had a good reason to be absent from a game in which your presence was critical, you chose to let your team lose and did what personal duty demanded of you. This time, you can easily be replaced with only a marginal inconvenience to your team."

"I can't."

"Then I cannot help you. If you are besotted with the importance of mere sport, then I am not the person to ask for assistance. I bid you goodnight Mr. Staunton, and I wish the two of you all possible happiness in your married life together. And a prosperous new year. Come, Watson."

He moved quickly across the room and out the door. I followed him down the stairs and out through the front door and onto the pavement. He shouted for one of the cabs that spend the entire night by the door, and we clambered inside.

"Holmes," I said."

"What?"

"You forgot your ladder."

Chapter Five

It was nearly one o'clock in the morning when, with a ladder strapped to the top of the cab, we returned to 221 B Baker Street. As we were pulling up to the door, Holmes bade me goodnight and requested that upon reaching my home, I provide the ladder a place of rest for the night, to be attended to the following morning. I agreed, and he opened the door to depart, began to step out, and then stopped.

He was staring directly at a figure huddled in his doorway, covered in a blanket. The cap the fellow wore was easily recognizable. He was one of the couriers employed by Scotland Yard.

"Would you be so kind as to wait for just a minute, Watson?" said Holmes.

I got out of the cab as well, and we approached the messenger boy. He was wrapped in a blanket that had earlier been on the bed I used to sleep in upstairs. Mrs. Hudson must have given it to him to protect him from the cold.

Through his shivering, he looked up at us.

"This is for you, Mr. Holmes. Inspector Lestrade said it must be delivered to you no matter what time you returned."

"Thank you, young fellow," said Holmes. "You have done your duty. Now hop on your bicycle and let the inspector know that I am on my way." He took the envelope and pulled out a shilling from his pocket.

"Just a minute," I interrupted. "Lestrade has already been waiting for a while. He will not die if the boy does not get back to him straight away. Come now, son. Mrs. Hudson will make up a cup of cocoa and let you warm up before going back."

Two minutes later we had both returned to the same cab and were on our way through the cold, dark, deserted streets of London to the Embankment.

"Did Lestrade say what the situation was?" I asked.

Holmes nodded and handed me the envelope. I opened it and read:

Come immediately to Scotland Yard upon receiving this. I have a dead man on my hands and no explanation.

Riding in a cab through London in the very witching time of night is enough to render even a resolutely unsuperstitious man somewhat unsettled. The streets were now void of any human activity. The vagabonds and beggars had all found shelter from the cold and the only movement we observed once we reached the Embankment was the silent dark shape of the odd barge as it pushed its way up the Thames.

A solitary electric light marked the door of Scotland Yard, and the cab stopped in front of it. Holmes stepped out quickly and bounded up the steps to the entrance, leaving me to pay the driver.

"Hey there," the driver shouted at me as I turned to follow Holmes. "Don't forget your ladder. I've no use for it."

With each of us bearing an end of the ladder, Holmes and I entered Scotland Yard.

"Where have you been?" said Inspector Lestrade when he saw us. "I've been waiting over an hour. And why in heaven's name are you bringing me that thing?"

"Explanations can wait," said Holmes. "How may I be of assistance to you?"

"He's down in the morgue," said Lestrade as he turned and descended a set of stairs.

At that time of night, all of the regular staff of the police morgue were off duty save one older chap who went to wheel out the body Lestrade requested.

"He was brought in earlier this evening, just past eight o'clock. Neighbors found him lying on the pavement, not breathing, no pulse. Stone, cold dead. No bullet wounds, no knife cuts, no vomit from poisoning. Just a large bump on the side of the head. Take a look at him, Doctor. What's your conclusion?"

Now in front of me was the body of a young man. His face was turned away from me, exposing a large, dark hematoma on the side of his head, with the bruising discoloring much of his forehead and upper portion of his cheek.

"He's had a blow to the sphenoid," I said right off. "The temple, as it's better known. Hard enough to rupture the middle meningeal artery and cause an epidural hematoma. Likely rendered him unconscious immediately and with no one to get him to a hospital, he would have died within the hour. It's not a common cause of death, but it does happen every so often. This injury could have been caused by a blow from a weapon, a blackjack, for example. Or it could have just been from a fall. Every week, somewhere in England, someone falls and bumps his head and dies. Foul play is not usually involved."

"So I am told," said Lestrade. "Happens to older folks most often, right?"

"Right," I said.

"And how many times have you seen it happen to a nimble-footed rugby player?" said Lestrade.

He turned the dead man's face around as he spoke.

"Merciful heavens!" I cried. "That's Danny O'Hearn. We were with him just this morning."

"Right," said Lestrade. "So I am told. His wallet was in his pocket, and it only took a couple of hours of diligent police work to learn what he had been doing earlier in the day. Seems he was at a wedding breakfast at the Langham and seems that the name of Sherlock Holmes was on the guest list. And over the past twenty years and more, it seems that when a body appears and there is a direct connection to Mr. Sherlock Holmes, then there is good reason to suspect that something more than a trip and a fall is in play. Right, Mr. Holmes?"

"Right, as always, Inspector," said Holmes.

For the next hour, assisted by cups of coffee provided by the night staff of the Yard, Lestrade, Holmes, and I sat in Lestrade's office and went over such data as we had concerning Danny O'Hearn. When we had concluded, Lestrade looked puzzled.

"Something about this makes no sense," he said.

"And why is that?" asked Holmes.

"You believe that there might be a connection between the threats and bribe offers to Godfrey Staunton, and the murder of Danny O'Hearn, and all the money being bet on the Home Nations Championship."

"Yes, it is a reasonable probability."

"So, one the one hand, whoever is behind this wants England to lose, and so they try to bribe and threaten Godfrey Staunton. But on the other hand, they go and kill one of the key players for Ireland, making it more likely that Ireland will lose. Unless we have some fanatical Scots or Welshmen running around London, there is no logic to it. Not that I can see."

"I assure you, Inspector," said Holmes, "that there is a perfectly logical explanation."

"You don't say. Well then, tell me what it is."

"I did not say," said Holmes, "that I knew what it was, only that there is one. When I discover what it is, I promise to inform you."

On hearing that, Lestrade got up, harrumphed, and left us.

Courtesy of one of the drivers who was on night duty, we were taken home in a police carriage, leaving a ladder in the hall outside Lestrade's office as a gift to the constabulary.

Upon our reaching 221B, Holmes asked, "As your good wife is out of the city for several days, would you mind staying over in your old bedroom. I believe you still have a fresh change of clothes in the closet and I would appreciate your assistance first thing in the morning."

"Where are we going?"

"Back to the Grosvenor to be the bearers of some tragic news, and to let a certain young couple know that I have changed my mind and will now agree to accept them as my clients."

Chapter Six

Given how much of the night had already passed before I fell asleep, I had been expecting that our next day would not start before nine o'clock. That was not to be. At half-past seven, I felt Holmes's friendly hand shaking my shoulder.

"Come, Watson. We have company, and I am in need of your presence. Please make yourself respectable for an elegant young woman."

After attending to necessities quickly, I entered the front room of 221B to find Mrs. Godfrey Staunton sitting, impeccably attired, and sipping tea. The great-hearted Mrs. Hudson was fussing over her with trays of delectable if fattening breakfast pastries.

Instinctively, I looked around, expecting to see her husband, but he was not there.

"Good morning, Mrs. Staunton," I said. "Are you alone?"

"Yes, Dr. Watson. My husband was sound asleep when I departed, and I expect he will still be in that condition when I return. It is necessary that my conversation with you and Mr. Holmes be confidential."

I had been in medical practice for long enough to know that secrets between husbands and wives were universally not a good idea for a happy marriage and that one taking place on the first day after the wedding did not augur well.

"At ease, my friend," said Holmes, reading my mind one more time. "I have no doubt that Mrs. Staunton's motives are solely for the good of her husband. I have asked her to wait to speak to me until you were present. Now then, Madam, please state your case for your visit."

She gave Holmes a questioning look but then confidently placed her gloved hands in her lap and looked directly at him.

"I have come to beseech you to reconsider your refusal to help Godfrey. He believes that the threats made against him are credible and, for reasons that may make no sense to you but that create an imperative for him, he must continue to play for England."

"Granted," said Holmes. And that was all he said.

Now the woman furrowed her brow and stared at him.

"What," she demanded, "do you mean, 'granted'?"

"I mean precisely what I said. Your request is granted. I agree to take on the cause of your husband and the issues related to the Home Nations Championship. I will devote to it my utmost energy and will spare no actions to bring the criminals to justice."

The poor woman was stunned.

"There is," Holmes continued, "one condition."

She was silent for several seconds and then gave a tentative "Yes?"

"You must disclose to me fully and completely, the reason or reasons why your husband is so obsessed with continuing to play when his withdrawal would be such a far more sensible course. Will you do that? Anything you tell us will be kept in strictest confidence."

"Yes," she said. "I can do that. After you departed from the hotel last night, I insisted that he explain his reasons to me. Perhaps I should say that I demanded them. I told him that I and our future family are now a part of any action he takes and he can no longer act in whatever way he sees fit, regardless of how noble his motives may be."

"As you," said Holmes, "had every right to do. And his answer?"

"He said that he was afraid to tell me as it was directly connected to his first wife. He was trembling as he spoke and said that he feared that I would feel a jealousy, a sense of competition from her memory with our marriage and his loyalty me."

"And do you?" asked Holmes.

"As God is my witness, no! What sensible wife would ever have such feelings? He was quite clearly committed to his marriage and his love for her. Such a man is rare to find today and I count myself one of the luckiest women in England to now be loved by such an honorable man."

"I could not agree more," said Holmes. "Very well then, what did he say?"

"He said that as Lilian was dying, she turned to him and said that she was leaving this life in peace knowing that she had been deeply loved and cared for by her husband and that she had only one last request. She said, 'I will be up in heaven looking down, and all I ask is that you live a life that will fill me with pride and admiration. And I want you to promise me that you will not only be a good and honorable man, but that you will be a hero to all of England and win the Championship for our country.' "

She stopped speaking and struggled to keep her sobs and tears back.

"That," she whispered, "is why he has to play. He vowed to her that he would. To take the easy way out of his current troubles, no matter how sensible, would be to deny who he is as a man … as a man who keeps his word."

Again, she stopped speaking. Holmes said nothing either, so I spoke.

"Mrs. Staunton," I said, "I agree that you are most fortunate to have such a wonderful man as your husband. And, if I might be so bold as to add, he is exceptionally fortunate to have found such a fine woman as his wife. With the help of Sherlock Holmes, I assure you that these current troubles will be resolved and I can see nothing in your future except joy and blessing together for years to come."

"Thank you, Doctor. You are very kind."

"Yes indeed," said Holmes, "you do have that gift. And if I may, my friend, a brief minute in confidence."

He rose and walked away from the front room toward his bedchamber. He expected me to follow, and I did. Once inside his room, he closed the door.

"Thank you, my friend. Your words were exactly what she needed to hear. You are, as I have observed over the years, far more capable than I am with these delicate matters. And now I have a further request."

I knew what he was going to say.

"You need me to tell her the tragic news about Danny O'Hearn."

"Precisely. Would you please? I fear I would make a horrible, insensitive mess of it. So, will you? If not for my sake, for hers?"

I nodded. If there is any skill a doctor acquires after many years of practice, it is finding the least devastating way to speak to someone about the unexpected death of a loved one. So, I took a deep breath, collected my thoughts, and returned minus Holmes to speak to Mrs. Staunton.

Drawing on such experience as I had, I sat across from her and first gave a brief warning that I was about to deliver some bad news, and then, without equivocation or euphemisms, I told her about the death, apparently by murder, of her husband's closest friend.

I watched as shock set in. Her eyes widened, her face paled, her hands and lower lip began to tremble, and her breathing shortened.

"No. No!" she screamed and then dropping her had into her hands, she collapsed into uncontrolled sobbing. After several minutes, her body stopped convulsing, and she lifted her head and looked at me. Her lovely face was disfigured by her tears, and her eyes were bright red.

"Godfrey will be devastated," she said. "He and Danny were like brothers. They were so close. It will break his heart."

"Yes," I said, "I am sure it will. And unfortunately, Mrs. Staunton, it is you, as his wife and the one bound to him for better or for worse, who will have to tell him. It will be one of the most difficult things you have ever done, but you will get through it, and it will pass. Prayers for divine grace and strength will be necessary."

Once again, her face paled, but this time she did not begin to weep. Instead, she grasped the arms of her chair and squeezed them until her knuckles turned white. After several controlled breaths, she looked directly at me.

"Thank you, Doctor. I can do it because I have to. Please thank Mr. Holmes for his offer of help. I now understand why he changed his mind. If I can be of assistance, I am ready to do so."

I assisted her down the stairs and hailed a cab. As she rode away, I could not help but recall the times at a hospital when I had sent a husband or a wife off to bring the tragic news of the death of a loved one, all too often a child, to his or her spouse and family. There could be no more desolate journeys in life than such a cab or omnibus ride.

I climbed slowly back up the stairs to the front room, where Holmes was waiting for me.

"Thank you, my friend," he said. "I am sure that such a task never becomes easier even if carried out many times."

I gave a shrug of forced nonchalance.

"We do what we have to do. What happens now?"

"A visit to Lord Mount James, I fear. I am not at all convinced that his wealth does not have a role to play in this affair."

Chapter Seven

About an hour later, our cab stopped in front of a substantial home on Phillimore Place in Kensington. The houses in this neighborhood are amongst the most exclusive in London, and the one belonging to Lord Mount James was once, not long ago, two separate, detached houses that had been combined to form one of the most expensive in the city.

"Have you been here before?" I asked Holmes when we were standing in front of it.

"Yes. You may recall that three years ago he told me that I could charge my expenses to him when searching for Godfrey."

I laughed. "I remember that he said he could offer you a fiver or even a tenner."

"Precisely. And I have a sufficient bent to my character that I came around with receipts for seven pounds six."

"Did he pay it?"

"He was outraged and questioned every item. In the end, we settled for a fiver."

"Was it worth it?" I asked.

"Oh, yes. I had heard about his wealth and his collections and wanted to see his lares and penates. The place was packed with rows of Gainsboroughs, Lawrences, Constables, and an impressive selection of Sir Joshua Reynolds. The plate he had sent away for safekeeping had all been brought back once any threat had vanished. And the Bechstein Grand could have overpowered an orchestra in the Royal Albert."

"Indeed?" I said. "I would have thought the old miser would be living as an ascetic."

"Ah, and there you have hit upon one of the great divides between the truly rich and the rest of us."

"In what way?"

"Those rich who continue to become richer know that it is not only permitted, it is wise to purchase assets, provided you only acquire those items, whatever they may be, that do not depreciate in value with the passage of time. Such items ascend in value at a rate well beyond the most reliable of stocks and bonds. Such have been the assets acquired by Lord Mount James."

"I cannot wait to see them," I said. "What time is your appointment?"

"I did not make one. Why should I?" said Holmes.

"Why should you? He is a nobleman, a Viscount, I believe, and one of the richest men in England."

"And when have you ever observed me to be deferential to either of those categories?"

I signed in resignation. "I will always be looking for signs of progress, Holmes."

"And will always be disappointed. But come, the element of surprise is always to the benefit of the one responsible for its delivery."

We were greeted at the door by a highly starched and aloof young butler who, upon learning that we had no appointment, left us standing in the rather austere vestibule, having been given singularly forceful instructions by Holmes.

"Kindly inform his Lordship that Sherlock Holmes wishes to speak to him concerning possible threats to his properties."

Holmes had the faintest twinkle in his eye. "That should do it, Watson. Mark my words, he will appear within five minutes. Good thing he has a handsome new butler. The old one did not find my presence to be at all desirable."

Lord Mount James appeared at the top of the grand staircase within less than one minute.

"You again!" he barked. "The last time you told me something like that, I had to remove all of my plate straight away and pay to do so, only to find that it was a complete waste of time. And you, Doctor, told all of London that I was a crabbed, gouty old miser."

He descended the stairs quickly, so quickly that I had to comment on it.

"My goodness, your Lordship," I said. "Obviously I was wrong. Your vigor has improved wonderfully since I last saw you walking.

That brought a smile to his face.

"An improved observation on your part, Dr. Watson. And yes, I do indeed feel far better than I have in years. I really should have Perkins here toss the two of you out onto the pavement, and I would if it were not for the presence of the exquisite individual who is following me. Allow me to introduce you to the splendid cause for my health and good fortune."

He turned and glanced back up the stairs. Descending them gracefully was Lady Beatrice Maynooth.

She was attired in a simple but elegant (and I knew to be very expensive) charcoal grey dress that did not quite cover her ankles. Her silver hair was mostly gathered on top of her head except for long ringlets that descended in front of her ears. Her erect bearing was queenly, and her eyes, fixed on us, did not once stray to her sure footing as she navigated the stairs.

She approached Sherlock Holmes and extended her hand at a low enough level to require that Holmes bend over slightly to grasp it. Then she turned to me and repeated the gesture.

"This divine Lady," said Lord Mount James, "came into my life as a godsend nearly six months ago and has been visiting me almost every day. She has been the Dr. Pangloss to my Jeremiah."

"My goodness, your Lordship," she said, "Voltaire is so vulgar. I insist ... I demand a more elegant classical reference."

"See what she's like. Giving me orders all day long. And like the strictest of martinets, no sooner had she started paying visits, than she immediately gave orders to my kitchen staff to remove all organ and game meats from my diet, and next went the delectable shellfish, and finally, over my vociferous objections, all beer and wine and spirits. And then she insisted that I consume copious amounts, a veritable Niagara, of fresh spring water. Within a month, my gout had all but disappeared. We take vigorous walks every day come rain or shine, and I swear that I am a new man."

"And," added Lady Maynooth with a confident smile, "with not just a healthy body but a positive, youthful mind as well. One must always look on the bright side, mustn't one."

"Indeed, one must," said Holmes. "It is a pleasure to hear of your improvement, Sir."

"Thank you," said Mount James. "But that does alter the fact that it is not at all a pleasure to see you, Mr. Holmes. And I heard after the fact that you were a guest on my shilling at the Langham. I have no idea how that was permitted."

"You nephew insisted on it, and it is concerning him that I have come to speak to you. There have been threats made against him that could, I fear, be extended to both you and Her Ladyship."

The nobleman scowled. "Heavens! Such a villainous suggestion. Who would dare do such a thing? Very well, Mr. Holmes, come and sit down and inform me concerning such inhuman rogues."

He led the way into the large front parlor. As soon as we entered, I could see Holmes darting his eyes around the room, and I did likewise. Except for a few strikingly modern works of art, the walls were bare. Unless the Bechstein Grand had been taken upstairs, it too had vanished. The wallpaper had been removed from the walls and replaced by white paint with stunning effect.

"Ah, Mr. Holmes," said the old fellow, "I see you are taken by my change in decor. It has also been by the hand of this exceptional Lady. If I am to move and act like a younger man, it is necessary that I think like one. I have gotten with the times. All that old clutter has been sent away, and a modern spirit has moved in. What was it, my Lady, that Ruskin and Hunt and those critics called my dear old Joshua Reynolds?"

Lady Maynooth chuckled. "They referred to him as Sir Sloshua. We are much better off without him."

"Yes, yes, that was it. Well, I wasn't going to have Sir Sloshua hanging around anymore. And the poet, Browning—you are familiar with him, I am sure, Dr. Watson, even if Mr. Holmes is not—he so succinctly told us that 'less is more.' Quite clever, eh? Less is more. Nothing now but the most tasteful of the *avant-garde*. And we have added the latest of scientific invention. Do you know what that is, Mr. Holmes?"

"I can think of several items that have been hailed with that description."

"Right. Well, we have one. A telephone! Right here in my home. The good lady organized that one as well. What do you think of that, Mr. Holmes?"

"How wonderfully modern you have become, Sir. However, I am more concerned at present with your nephew than with your modern conveniences."

"Right. Very well. Now then, do be seated and tell me what problems my nephew has visited upon me this time. Dear me, I thought that Millicent had straightened the boy out. However … not the case, right?"

As Holmes explained the bribery offers and even the threats of physical injury made against Godfrey Staunton, His Lordship's eyes appeared to glaze over in boredom.

"Please, Mr. Holmes. Godfrey is quite capable of looking after himself. He can run like the wind, and if he chooses to turn and fight, he is as strong as an ox. He is constantly in the company of teammates who frankly are oxen. Wherein is the danger?"

Then Holmes reported the murder of Danny O'Hearn. Lord Mount James ceased being nonchalant. His face turned as white as his neckcloth.

"Oh, no!" said Lady Maynooth with a gasp of horror, shaking her head and wringing her hands. Her face visibly paled. "That is dreadful, just dreadful."

"Dear God," said Mount James. "He was such a vivacious young chap. Who are these monsters that would do such a thing?"

"I do not yet know," said Holmes. "But I am determined to find out. And I fully expect that they might escalate their actions if Godfrey continues to refuse their demands."

"What worse could they do?" said the old man.

"They could seriously injure him or those close to him. That could include Mrs. Staunton, yourself, Sir, or even Lady Maynooth."

"No! Oh, dear God. That is unthinkable. There must be something you can do?"

"I am giving this case my full attention, and Scotland Yard is also. I suggested to Godfrey that he withdraw from the team and simply not play—,"

"Oh, no," interrupted Lord Mount James. "He will never do that. He cannot. He gave his word."

"Ah, so you are familiar with his pledge to one he loved so dearly," said Holmes.

"Of course, I am. I was there when it happened."

That was news to both Holmes and me. We both knew that his Lordship was nowhere near the deathbed of Godfrey's first wife.

"I beg your pardon, Sir," said Holmes. "You were there?"

"Yes. When his mother and father died, I was beside them with Godfrey. His father, Geoffrey, was my little brother, the child of my father's old age and at least twenty years younger than me. I helped to raise him and loved him dearly as only an older brother can. When he and Elizabeth were stricken with the influenza and near death, he looked at me and asked me to promise to look after Godfrey, and I have. He has not been spoiled in the least, but I made sure that he had all the training and discipline necessary to become a responsible young man."

"And did his father ask Godfrey for some promise as well?"

"He did. My brother Geoffrey was an enthusiastic sportsman and had spent hundreds of afternoons and weekends teaching his son how to run, and kick, and tackle. They went to the games every Saturday. With his dying breath, he asked Godfrey to promise that he would be the best rugby player he could possibly be and would set as his goal playing for England in the Home Nations. Godfrey has no choice but to play, and I would never think of asking him to do otherwise."

Holmes nodded slowly and solemnly, gave me a short look and nodded again.

We took our leave soon after this conversation. Noon hour of New Years Day, 1899, found Homes and me walking along a stretch of pavement in Kensington looking for a cab.

"I must say," I said, "young Mr. Godfrey Staunton is under exceeding pressure. Do you think his mettle is up to it?"

He did not immediately reply. Instead, he lit a cigarette and walked in silent contemplation until we reached the corner of Kensington High Street. There he stubbed out the cigarette and turned to me.

"When you were in Afghanistan, did you not see countless young men, almost all of whom had far less discipline and rigor bred into them that Godfrey Staunton, rise to the occasion and put their lives on the line for their country?"

"Almost all of them did so. Some exhibited heroism that was beyond belief. And far too many sacrificed their lives."

"I suspect that had Godfrey been there with you, he would have been one of the heroes."

Chapter Eight

The cab ride back through the Gardens and Hyde Park took a full half-hour even with the absence of traffic. As soon as we arrived, Mrs. Hudson met us at the door.

"There's a young fellow waiting to see you," she said. "He's been here for some time?"

"I hope," I said, "that he took some tea and one or two of your excellent scones whilst waiting."

"I brought them out to him, but I do not think he has touched them. He's done nothing but pace back and forth since he arrived."

We ascended the stairs, entered the room, and gave our greetings to Godfrey Staunton.

"Please, Godfrey," said Holmes, "sit down and have some tea. It will help you to relax before we start to talk."

"Sure, thank you," he said. He sat down, took one large bite of the scone, swallowed it and, ignoring the tea, began.

"As soon as I woke up, Millie told me that she had been here to see you."

"She was," said Holmes, "and I congratulate you on marrying an outstanding young woman. She is most impressive."

"Sure, she really is. I know. She told me that you had agreed to take on my case."

"Excellent. I have indeed done that."

"And she told me about Danny," he said. He laid the scone back on the plate and stood up and started pacing again.

"Then I left her in the room," he said, "and I ran here from the hotel. I was distraught. It is only about a mile, and a hard run helps me clear my head."

"And what did you conclude?" said Holmes.

"First, I wanted to thank you for agreeing to help me."

"I am also assisting Scotland Yard. This has become a criminal matter, and I fear that more criminal acts are a possibility."

"Sure, well, so do I. Something could happen not only to me, but to Millie, or another one of my teammates."

"Or," added Holmes, "to your uncle or his companion. I need to disclose to you that we have just paid a visit to him to talk over the matter."

"You did? Well, that's good, I suppose. He will likely hire some guards to protect the two of them and his house. In the past, he has hired Lascars and Africans. He says they are by far the cheapest and scare the daylights out of any would-be thief, especially at nighttime."

"I expect," said Holmes, "that he will make good use of their assistance. Please sit down."

He did and took a gulp of the tea.

"Right, well that brings me to what I had to talk to you about."

"Go on."

"It all came to me whilst I was running over here. You are going to need some assistance as well."

"I am generously supported by Scotland Yard as well as by Dr. Watson."

"Yes, but you are going to have another helper...me."

"That is a courageous offer, but I am afraid that—,"

"No. Listen to me, Mr. Holmes. We have to take the offense, that's how you win a match. We have to force the play. We have to do something to make these monsters act and not leave the next play up to them."

Holmes gave the young man an intense look and a faint smile.

"That is an interesting and possibly a useful idea," he said. "What did you have in mind?"

"I will be the bait."

"That is not a useful idea."

"No. Listen to me. Here's what we can do. I am going to go to the press and give an interview. I'm going to say that I am going to honor my dear friend by playing like I have never played before. That story will go all over the country. The newspapers love stories that involve murder and revenge and honor. They do, don't they?"

"Now, that is true."

"And then I am going to walk the streets in public, maybe even give little speeches and make myself a target for those blackguards. And you and Dr. Watson and maybe a couple of coppers are going to be on my heels all the time, but hidden. You understand? Never let me out of your sight and be ready to tackle as soon as they make their move. It will work, Mr. Holmes. I know it will."

Holmes lit another cigarette, and now he began to pace the room.

"It is," he finally said, "an imaginative strategy. However, it does place your future at great risk."

"I know it does, Mr. Holmes. I know it does. But I have no choice. I cannot let them stop me. I have to play."

"I understand and appreciate your obligation. You also have an obligation as your uncle's sole heir to apprise him of your actions."

"I will. He will not care as long as he never has to pay a ransom to get me back."

"Likely true, but I must ask something else. How will your wife react to your plan?"

"Oh, I hadn't thought of that."

"Then start thinking about it. Now."

"Sure. Right."

He took another bite followed by another gulp.

"Right. I've thought about it. She will demand that she accompany me at all times. She's like that."

"Precisely," said Holmes.

Chapter Nine

The Sporting Times

Wednesday, 4 January, 1899

Will Ireland Finally Defeat England?
One Man Is Pledged to Stop Them

The Irish National Rugby Team promises to do on the pitch what Parnell could not do in Parliament—best the English. One man, playing Right Wing for England's team will do everything in his power, and his power is impressive, to stop them. What makes the contest, the Home Nations Championship, singularly noteworthy is that both the Irish team and the England three-quarter are motivated by the same cause: the honoring of the life of one of the most popular players in the Rugby Football Union.

On Saturday evening last, the body of Mr. Daniel Patrick O'Hearn was found on a street in the Leadenhall neighborhood. Scotland Yard has reported that it is investigating his death and that it has been classed as being under suspicious circumstances. Mr. Sherlock Holmes, the famous detective, has been called in to assist in the investigation.

O'Hearn's death came as a shock to the entire Rugby Union. Danny, as he was known by one and all, was not only one of the best Number Eights in the Union, he was popular with everyone, no matter what team they played for.

"Danny always had a friendly laugh and ready smile," said Baron Worthington, one of the Directors of The Union. "He was a terror on the pitch but a most convivial chap in the pub after the games. No one could tell a story like Danny. We will miss him terribly."

His life will not be allowed to pass in vain. Another star player, Godfrey Staunton, Danny's teammate on Blackheath, has vowed that he will lead England's team to triumph in the Home Nations Championship as his way on paying tribute to his closest friend.

"Just hours before he died," said Staunton, holding back his tears, "Danny was the best man at my wedding. I cannot begin to say how devastated my wife and I are by his death. The only way I have to honor his memory is to let it be an inspiration to me every time I step on to the pitch. My next games are in the Home Nations, and so I will play like I have never played before, knowing that Danny's spirit is with me."

Daniel O'Hearn and Godfrey Staunton were not only the closest of friends, they played together for the past year for Blackheath. However, O'Hearn was not an Englishman. He was born and bred in Dublin and had been selected to hold the Number Eight position for Ireland's national team in the upcoming championship games. Members of that team have also promised to honor his memory by winning the cup, and they must defeat England to do so.

"Sure and Danny played for Blackheath," said Connor Murphy, the captain of the Irish, "but he was an Irishman through and through. He was one of us, and we claim him as our inspiration."

Will an irresistible force meet an immovable object on the rugby pitches of Great Britain? The games will be played in London, Dublin, Edinburgh, and Cardiff over the next two months. Thrilling reports of each match will appear in *The Sporting News* as every rugby player gives his all on field, inspired by the example of Daniel Patrick O'Hearn.

Charles Parnell died in the arms of Kitty O'Shea, his great goal never achieved, and his life and death, some say, in vain. Godfrey Staunton and all the Irish players are determined that Danny O'Hearn's life will not go the same way.

The following day a similar article appeared in the *Daily Chronicle* and the *Telegraph*. And then on Friday, the day before the first game of the Home Nations Championship, it ran in the *Times*.

Mr. and Mrs. Godfrey Staunton made numerous appearances at receptions and interviews related to the games. They walked arm in arm along the Strand and around Piccadilly.

Holmes and I followed them at a distance, accompanied by two young police constables dressed in plain clothes.

Nothing happened.

No one tried to pass him an envelope containing a threat, let alone attack him. It was as if the actors in the criminal conspiracy had exited the stage.

On the Thursday evening, Holmes and I sat by the blazing hearth in 221B sipping our after-dinner brandy. I was reading a recent *Pink'un* that had been issued for the games, and Holmes was reading confidential files he had received giving the details of Lord Mount James's holdings. When he put the file he had been reading down on the side table and pulled out his pipe, I could tell that something was not sitting comfortably inside his brilliant mind.

"Something curious?" I asked.

"Might be better to say, insufficient data. His Lordship owns considerable assets throughout Great Britain, but over the past decade, he has invested heavily in South African securities, Argentine railways, and the new Bakerloo line. He stands to reap an enormous fortune if they all pay out, making him one of the richest men in the entire world."

"And if they fail?"

"Impossible to say at this juncture. Time will tell. He has never failed in the past. But enough of him, what intellectually stimulating material are you encountering in your *Pink 'un?*"

I ignored the jibe and handed over *The Sporting Times.*

"You need to take a look at this. If this entire enterprise with Godfrey is all about the betting, then the game has changed."

"What do you mean?"

"The odds have changed," I said. "A week ago, the bookmakers were giving even on both England and Ireland, with Scotland and Wales both at three to one. But with O'Hearn off the team, it has gone all topsy-turvy. They are now quoting four to one against Ireland winning the cup."

Holmes took the cheap colored newspaper from me and spent the next few minutes reading it over.

"Yes!" he suddenly exclaimed, snapping his fingers at the same time. "That's it."

"What's it?"

"The murder of Danny O'Hearn was not about weakening the Irish team; it was about increasing the payout if they won. Today, a winning bet would return more than twice what it would a week ago. Yes, if it is all about the betting, then we may expect whoever is behind this to continue to try to increase the odds against Ireland and then to try to fix the games so that they win."

"Then," I said, "you do not believe that Lord Mount James's wealth is involved after all?"

Holmes did not immediately respond. He took out his pipe, loaded it up with tobacco from the familiar Persian slipper and took several slow puffs before saying anything.

"I am not yet ready to exclude that possibility. My years of trying to understand the criminal mind tells me that there must be a connection. At the moment, however, it is still shrouded in a fog."

Chapter Ten

The first game of the championship series was scheduled for Saturday, 7 January. The English squad was up against the one from Wales, and the game was to be played in Swansea at the famous St. Helen's stadium. We would travel there from Paddington on the Friday afternoon before the match.

That left Friday morning of 6 January as the last opportunity for Godfrey to be seen in public, with the hope of tempting whoever was part of the criminal conspiracy into the open. Accordingly, he and Mrs. Godfrey Staunton attended a team breakfast at the Reform Club on Pall Mall, to which the governors of Rugby Union and the Press had been invited. Never ones to turn down a free meal, reporters from all of London's newspapers as well as from a sprinkling of the major dailies from other cities were packed into the dining room.

Godfrey made a point of strolling around the room, greeting the reporters and making predictions about the upcoming game. I admired his skill in doing so. Whereas he had been uncomfortable in front of a room full of wedding guests, he was now in his element as long as the conversation was restricted to his beloved game.

As he walked through the room, he stopped briefly for a chat with Baron Worthington and then moved on to engage the Press. He alternated between giving one reporter a jovial smile and a slap on the back, and the next one a somber, morose comment when invoking the memory of Danny O'Hearn.

The early afternoon edition of all the papers quoted him. There was no question that he was going to play his heart out for England. It was as flagrant a defiance of those who had threatened him as one could imagine.

But again, nothing happened.

There were no notes passed to him; no staged accidental bumping into him on the pavement with threats whispered in his ear.

Nothing.

Mid-afternoon on the Friday arrived, and Holmes and I were in a cabin on the GWR from Paddington to Swansea. By the time we passed Reading, we had the cabin to ourselves. Holmes was busy giving himself a quick course in the gentleman's game of Rugby. At one point, he looked at me and shook his head.

"There are thirty men on the field," he said. "How does anyone keep them straight."

"The color of the uniform and the number on their backs. That will tell you their team and position. And then you merely have to look at the program you will receive at the gate and match it up with their name."

"And what if we should run into one of them in a pub this evening? How then?"

I reached into my suit jacket pocket, withdrew a package of cigarettes, and extended it to him.

"Time for a Capstan," I said.

He gave me a blank look in return.

"What in the world are you talking about?"

I gently peeled back the top of the package and withdrew a small card.

"Ah ha," I said. "I now have Tom McGown to add to my collection. He's playing for Ireland. Do you not take the cards out of your cigarette packages? Given how often you consume tobacco, you could soon have a full set of all four international squads."

"I have better uses for my time that collecting minuscule pictures of castles, and ships, and glamorous actresses."

"As do I, but both of England's major purveyors of tobacco, Wills and Players, are inserting a full run of rugby squads in conjunction with the Home Nations Championship. Every member of every team will have a card. I started collecting them back in December and will happily give you the dozen or so I now have. Your tobacco use is far greater than mine, so if you start now, you will have them all by March, and then you will have your own personal picture of every player. The reverse sides of the cards are printed with data about the player: number of caps, position, points scored, home club, age ... all sorts of useful information, especially should one be in the habit of wagering on a game."

"You may keep your collection," said Holmes. "But, speaking of wagering on the games, how do they decide who will be the final winner?"

"Whichever squad wins the final game in March."

"Yes, of course, but how is it determined which of them gets to play in the final?"

"Ah, that is a bit complicated. It is a combination of wins and losses and points scored for and against."

"And what," said Holmes, "are the sporting types predicting for this game?"

"Oh, England is going to win," I said. "The only argument is by how much."

By six o'clock that evening we had passed through Cardiff and were rolling our way on to Swansea when the door to our cabin opened and Godfrey Staunton stepped inside, quickly closing the door behind him.

"Good evening, Godfrey," I said. "How's your squad doing back there in the lounge car."

"They are well. None of them know I came to see you. Only Millie. The others think I went to the loo."

"Then do sit down," I said, "and tell us what is on your mind."

"They are on this train. I know they are," he said.

"Who?" demanded Holmes.

"The thugs who are going to try to make me stop England from winning."

"More precision, please."

"In the third car. I walked past them twice. There are two large men who are thugs for sure, and I overheard them talking. They're Irish."

"Oh, yes, those two," said Holmes. "I observed them as well. But you failed to notice the small crest on their jackets. They both play for Trinity in Dublin. I suspect that they are coming to watch the game. It would be more accurate to refer to them as rugby fans than thugs. Although it is possible that the difference is minimal."

Godfrey looked quite put out.

"Mr. Holmes, I will have you know that rugby fans are not thugs. Only football fans."

"If you say so."

"But what about the chaps sitting back in third class?"

"What of them?"

"There's half a dozen of them, and they are all enormous and look quite fearsome. I overheard them talking too."

"And what were they talking about?"

"I could not make it out. But I could tell they were from Glasgow. As Scottish as bagpipes at a funeral."

"And have you," said Holmes, "ever seen a Scotsman in a private cabin? Where else would you expect to see them gathered if not in the cheapest car on the train."

"Oh, yes, I suppose you're right. I guess I am just on pins and needles."

"Then use all that stimulation to focus your thoughts on winning the match."

"Oh, right. I suppose I should do that."

"And we shall cheer you on," said Holmes. "We are aware of and understand your feelings of obligation toward the Championship games. You have our complete sympathy and support."

Godfrey looked perplexed but then shrugged.

"Thank you, Mr. Holmes, and let me assure you that you do not know the half of it."

With that, he opened the cabin door and departed.

I turned to Holmes. "So, you do not believe that any of your criminal quarry are on the train?"

"On the contrary. I am certain they are here and equally certain that they appear to be as inconspicuous and common Englishmen as we do. We are not dealing with complete fools."

At seven o'clock, we pulled into Swansea Station. We stepped down on to the platform and, after waiting for our valises, walked to the exit at the far end. Godfrey Staunton was standing there, waiting for us.

"I cannot stay and talk," he said. "I have to catch up with Millie and my squad. But a porter gave me this just before we stopped."

He handed Holmes an envelope and then turned and walked smartly out of the station.

The envelope had no markings other than Staunton's name. Holmes opened it, read the typed note inside, and handed it to me. It ran:

Very foolish of you to involve Sherlock Holmes and Scotland Yard. They cannot protect you. You must do as we say or endure the consequences. You may defeat Wales but not by more than five points. Otherwise, it will be the last game you ever play.

"What do you make of it?" asked Holmes.

Although he had asked for my observations for over twenty years, I still hesitated. It still rather chaffed when he used my lack of deductive acumen merely as a spur to encourage his. Nevertheless, I did my best to oblige.

"Whoever sent this clearly knows Godfrey's every move."

"Correct. Go on."

"And they are quite knowledgeable about the game tomorrow and the scoring for the Championship."

"Excellent. Keep going. What can be observed other than the content of the message?"

"It is high quality writing paper. Whoever sent it is not without means."

"Very good. Keep going."

I held the envelope up to my nose and sniffed.

"No apparent odor. Must have come right out of the box."

"Anything else?"

I could not think of anything.

"Look," he said, "at the quality of the print."

I did and observed that the type was rather faint and uneven.

"Either the writer," I said, "needs a new ribbon or his fingers are weak. But those letters that are solid are cleanly legible. So, it is likely a relatively new model."

"Excellent, Watson. There is hope for you yet. It was typed on a Remington from the 1895 lot. Now, let us find a cab to the hotel. Tomorrow will be a full day and we need both a decent dinner and a full night's rest."

A cab took us and our luggage the few blocks from the station to the select Morgans Hotel. The hotel dining room was reputed to have an excellent menu, and we were not surprised to find it crowded with fellow travelers who had come to Swansea for the rugby match.

Holmes, by habit, scanned the room, looking for anyone that might be of interest to a seasoned detective. The scowl on his face indicated that he had spotted several.

"This place is lousy with the excrescence of Pall Mall. I recognize seven already who spend every evening at the card tables, only two of whom are known to be honest players. I suspect that they may be the only ones of such character in the room."

"Godfrey," I said, "did inform us that the games would be one of the greatest opportunities for betting this year. The vast majority of we sportsmen who like to place a small wager on a match are scrupulously honest and fair. One or two, mind you, whose integrity, you doubt a bit."

"Really, Watson? Perhaps a decent dinner will clear your mind."

We were only part way through a superb supper of Atlantic Cod when a perfectly dressed and coiffed gentleman approached our table.

"Mr. Sherlock Holmes, is it not?" said Baron Worthington.

"It is indeed, Sir," said Holmes.

"I am surprised to see you here. I knew you were a friend of Godfrey's, but I had no idea that you were such a fan of rugby that you would travel to Swansea just to watch a game."

"As am I to see you. One would have thought that you would be sticking close to Wakefield given the difficulty your mill is facing from the competition in Leeds."

The Baron was taken aback but recovered immediately.

"An effective manager must hire competent staff who can mind the store whilst he is away."

"Quite so. And I hear that you are standing again for mayor in the upcoming election. How is the campaign going? Any problems from that young fellow, Sir Norman? Quite the looker, if you can believe the Press."

"A handsome face," said the Baron, "will not get a man elected, at least as long as we are sensible enough not to grant suffrage to women."

"A sea change that is on its way," said Holmes. "But do allow me to wish you success in your campaign, and do not let us keep you from your dinner. It is not nearly as delectable when eaten cold."

He gave Holmes a cold stare, nodded, and went away.

"Goodness gracious," I said. "You were positively rude to him. There was no reason for that."

"No? Then tell me, do you trust him?"

"I have no reason not to. He was an outstanding fullback and is now a governor of the Rugby Union."

"And held the record for incurring penalties during his years on the pitch."

"Holmes, you have suddenly become much more knowledgeable about the game."

"Every new case demands the strenuous application of research. Would you like my opinion on which team to bet on tomorrow?"

"Absolutely not. I am a loyal Englishman, and that is where I shall place my wager."

"Pity."

Chapter Eleven

One thing that must be said for the rugby fans who thronged into the St. Helens stadium: they had to be rugged and unafraid of the cold and damp. During the first week of January, the temperature in the middle of the day seldom reaches fifty degrees. Sunlight is limited to just over eight hours and, to top it all, Swansea holds the record for being the wettest city in Great Britain.

The hotel thoughtfully provided warm wool blankets to all the guests attending the game and had barrels full of umbrellas at the ready should it look like rain. Fortunately, the day, though far from sunny, was not the worst that could be expected in this corner of the nation. So, we followed the crowds down Oystermouth Road and into the stadium. Our seats were close to the mid-field line and up enough rows to give us an excellent view of the game. We took our seats, wrapped ourselves in blankets, and purchased the first of many cups of hot tea from one of the vendor boys.

"Which one is Godfrey?" asked Holmes when the teams had come onto the field. He was holding a set of field glasses to his eyes and trying to see the faces of the players.

"He's the right wing for England."

"That was not helpful in the least, Watson."

"The red and white shirts and he has number 14. All right wings have that number."

"And how was I supposed to know that?"

"You said you had been doing your research on rugby."

"Only those aspects that touch on criminal enterprise."

The referee called the squads to order, sounded the opening whistle, and the game was on.

The Sporting Times
Sunday, 8 January, 1899

Wales Trounces England in First Game of Home Nations Championship

Favoured English Internationals Upset by Crafty Welshmen

Taffy was a Welshman; Taffy was a thief,
Taffy Played 'gainst England and sent them home in grief.
England went to Taffy's house; the game became a farce
At 26 to 3, Taffy kicked John Bull up the ... shin.

Yesterday, England's Internationals played against Wales and suffered a devastating loss.

The first ten minutes of the game, held in the St. Helens Rugby Football Club grounds, was all England's and it looked as if the favored team was going to match the odds and come away with a fine victory.

On three successive plays, England's captain, Arthur Rotherham passed the ball out to George Gibson who sent it along smartly to the right wing, Godfrey Staunton. Three times in a row, Staunton, playing like a man possessed, broke through the Welsh line and, as he was being hauled down, passed to Percy Royds, his teammate from Blackheath. On the third time, they made this move on Wales, Royds scampered past the Welsh defense and went in for the try. England was up by three to nil.

But there it ended.

The Taffies regrouped and shut down every effort by England. They took control of the game and never surrendered it.

First Willie Llewellyn, the winger from the second tier Llwynypia Club, scampered across for a try. It proved to be the first of four he would score before the end of the match.

"It were a brilliant performance for a young lad gaining his first cap," said Billy Bancroft, Wales's captain. Bancroft, the fullback with the "magic toe" added four more points with his accurate conversion kicks.

To top it off, "Huzzey was hustling," bragged David Jones, the part-owner of the host St. Helen's Club. Viv Huzzey, on the right wing, dove across England's line and touched the ball down for two more tries later in the game.

Somewhere during the second half, England ran out of steam and was off the boil for the entire final twenty minutes. Only Godfrey Staunton appeared to have the drive to fight a losing battle all the way to the finish, but his determination and drive for every possible inch were not enough.

The final score: 26 to 3 was a shock to rugby fans throughout Great Britain. Bookmakers will be offering different odds from now on.

The next match in the Championship games is on 4 February when England crosses the Irish Sea to Dublin and has an opportunity to redeem themselves.

We are still betting on England, but not so much as we were two days ago.

Chapter Twelve

The common practice after almost any rugby match is for the players, wives, lady friends, and assorted fans to descend on a local pub and spend the evening in song, stories, laughter, and general disorderly conduct.

Such a celebration did not happen on 7 January, 1899 for England's Internationals.

For certain, the Welsh team celebrated long into the night, and the pubs of Swansea did a roaring business.

England's players and fans merely faded back to their hotel rooms. Most ordered room service.

Holmes took advantage of the time to insist that Mr. and Mrs. Staunton join us for dinner at the Olde Cross Keys, an ancient enterprise that had stood in the shadow of Swansea Castle since the year 1326, if you could believe the sign above the door.

I arrived in advance of Holmes, who had said that he would be delayed whilst pursuing his search for more data.

Seated at a table in the corner of the pub were Mr. Godfrey Staunton, his wife, Millie, and his close friend, Dr. Leslie

Armstrong. As I approached them, Millie greeted me with a smile. Godfrey merely looked up at me for a moment and then returned his gaze to the cutlery in front of him. Even in that brief glance, I saw that his eyes were puffy and reddened. Once I had given them a cheerful greeting and sat down across from them, I was able to look again at his face. He appeared utterly disconsolate.

In my tripartite role as a doctor, a man old enough to be his father, and a Blackheath Old Boy, I laid my hand on his wrist.

"Young man," I said, "you gave it your all. You played your best. That is all that anyone can ever expect of himself or his teammates."

Dr. Armstrong gave an approving grunt, and Millie placed her delicate hand gently on his other wrist. Godfrey merely looked at me as if he were a stricken puppy.

"But we lost," he whined. "We lost horribly. I have never in my entire life lost *that* badly. *Twenty-three to three!* That is humiliating. It is not enough that I tried hard. We needed to win."

"There are," I said, "more games to come. You can still win the championship."

"But we should have won this one. If only ..."

He prattled on for another minute with one instance after another of *if only*, bemoaning the particular action he chose on the pitch when another one might have let him break free to touch the ball down and score a try.

"Enough, Godfrey," I said, trying to be kind but firm. "None of those would have made a spot of difference. Stop for a minute and think. If you had pitched out to Rotherham instead of trying to crash through their line, they would have stopped him dead in his tracks."

A lifetime of watching rugby matches allowed me a whiff of authority, and I proceeded to contradict every one of his *if onlys*.

He nodded sullenly and then muttered, "I suppose what galls me the most is thinking that those blighters who threatened me are now all chuffed, believing that I gave in to their threats and threw the game."

"No one who watched you," I assured him, "would think for a minute that you deliberately let your team lose. The taffies were all over you in spite of your kicking and clawing for every inch."

He looked up at me like a beaten whelp. "I do hope you're right, Doctor. Losing that badly was horrible enough, but it would tear me apart if I thought that anyone, *anyone*, believed that I did not have the spine to stand up against some thugs."

I moved the conversation away from the debacle of the afternoon and on to strategies for the next game. Godfrey, as with all sportsmen, was easily distracted with meaningless banter about games and players past and present. We had just moved on to the Irish national team when Holmes arrived. He looked somewhat puzzled and was holding a *Pink 'un* in his hand.

I gave it a look and asked, "And where have you been that you needed *that*?"

"At one of the pubs near the stadium. The punters were well into their cups and had no idea who I was. They were full of loud opinions but did manage to impart some useful data."

"Such as?" I asked.

"There was some consensus amongst the louts that the odds of one of the teams taking a Triple Crown had changed now that England no longer had any chance. But it was expected that the bookmakers would be offering fifteen to one for Wales, and twenty to one for either Scotland or Ireland."

"That seems reasonable," said. "What do you think, Godfrey?"

He nodded his agreement amidst generous gulps on his ale.

"Thank you," said Holmes. "Now, would one of you mind confirming for me what a Triple Crown is?"

I gestured toward Godfrey, and he obliged.

"In the Home Nations Championship, a Triple Crown is awarded when the winning team successfully defeats all three of the other teams, not losing a single game."

"And is that a rare event?" asked Holmes.

"Not rare and not common. Maybe one-half of the years in the past. England had been favored to win it this year, but that hope is now dashed. Odds are against any of the other three teams doing so."

"Thank you, that is more or less what I thought."

Our supper soon arrived, and the conversation turned back to the great sport of rugby, of which Holmes, to my surprise, had acquired a decent knowledge in the past few days. The banter, along with three more pints of ale lifted Godfrey's spirits and the gloom of an hour ago seemed to have vanished. Sufficient alcohol does rather have than effect.

It also has another predictable result, and Godfrey rose to excuse himself for a trip to the loo. As he walked away from our table, I observed a telltale look in Holmes's eyes. He was staring directly toward the bar and clearly disturbed.

"What is it?" I asked.

"I have been glancing in the mirror behind the bar since I sat down. There are three rather unsavory chaps a few tables away who have been watching us. They looked directly at Godfrey as he stood and walked away."

"They must recognize him," I said. "Probably saw him at the game."

"It was not," said Holmes, "the friendly look of adoring fans."

"Most likely," said Dr. Armstrong, "then that they are Welshmen."

I chuckled my agreement, but Holmes was having none of it.

"Then they should have been gloating," he said. "And furthermore, they were on the train from London, and by their speech, they're Cockneys, not taffs. I would not be surprised if they get up to follow him."

I could not see them without turning myself around, but Millie was sitting so that she was looking directly at them. I saw her eyes widen as she lets out a short gasp.

"They're following him," she said, "and they're big, all of them."

"Come, Watson," said Holmes, once the thugs had their backs to us. "I hope you have your service revolver."

I nodded, and the two of us quietly stood.

"Don't let them hurt Godfrey," pleaded Millie as we squeezed past her.

"Not to worry," said Holmes. "They won't lay a glove on him."

He was positively grinning as he spoke and it was then that I noticed that his familiar walking stick was gone and in its place was a seriously sturdy Penang lawyer.

"Where did you get that?" I whispered as we stepped quickly to the hallway that led to the men's loo.

"Traded a punter for mine."

"Was he drunk? It's worth three of yours."

"Totally soused."

A muffled cry came from the hallway and, as we turned a corner, some twenty feet in front of us, two of the thugs were kneeling on top of the prone body of Godfrey Staunton. One of them had his fist in the air, ready to start delivering blows to the head.

"Halt!" shouted Holmes. "Get off him this instant! Let him go."

Three heads snapped toward us.

"Well now," said one of them, "if it isn't the famous Mr. Sherlock Homes comin' to the rescue. We was told to let you have one as well if you got in our way."

One of them stood up and joined the fellow who was already on his feet. The third one stayed down with his knee on Godfrey's head.

The two on their feet began moving toward us. One quickly pulled a small knife from his pocket, and the other extracted a blackjack and began to twirl it slowly.

Holmes raised his newly acquired stick and smiled at them.

"Ah, a fair fight, I must say. By the time I'm done with you, you will be locked up in a jail cell. Are you with me, Watson?"

"No. Not necessary."

I pulled my service revolver out of my pocket, aimed it at the closest man and cocked the hammer.

"There is not going to be any fight," I said. "Drop your weapons. Now!"

For a moment, the two men who had been advancing toward us froze. I lowered my revolver so that it was unmistakably pointing at the nether region of the anatomy of the chap who was closest.

"I will not," I said, "shoot to kill you, but you risk living the remainder of your life minus your manhood."

A look of terror came over his face and, in a flash, he turned and ran away from us down the hallway toward the back entrance to the pub. His two colleagues sprinted after him. I could have fired and wounded one if not two of them in the buttocks but doing so seemed not quite fair cricket whilst a man was running away.

"My dear Watson," said Holmes, flourishing his Penang Lawyer, "you spoiled my fun. I was prepared to disarm them and give them a jolly good whack on their heads."

"Discretion, Holmes," I replied and rushed to see about the well-being of Godfrey Staunton. He had pulled himself up and was standing on his two feet by the time I reached him.

"Those miscreants," he said. "They attacked me from behind. I could have put up a good defense if they'd had the decency to fight face-to-face."

"That, young man," said Holmes, "is not how thugs intimidate their victims. Now, are you injured?"

"Only my pride, and perhaps a bit of a scrape on my face."

"Did they say anything to you?" asked Holmes.

"The only thing they said to me before you arrived was something like 'Here's a new play, lad. It's what happens to people who won't do what they're told.' I'm afraid that my reply was rather rude."

"What did you tell them?"

"I said that they could take their new play and shove it up their arses. They did not seem to appreciate the prospect. But then you two showed up and interrupted our friendly conversation."

"Did you," asked Holmes, "see what they looked like? Could you identify them?"

"Only one of them, but you must have seen all three."

"Indeed, I did, which means that they will not attack again."

"Are you sure of that?" asked Staunton. "Are you saying that I am safe now?"

"Of course not. Having been seen openly, those particular thugs will be replaced, and quite possibly by ones who are more dangerous."

I suggested that the three of us return to our table in the pub. Staunton demurred, reminding me that he had been on his way to the loo for a good reason and would rejoin us presently. When Holmes and I appeared at the table *sans* the young husband, Mrs. Millie Staunton and Dr. Armstrong looked alarmed.

"Where's Godfrey?" demanded Mrs. Staunton. "What happened?"

"Those English boys attempted to engaged him in fisticuffs," said Holmes. "That is all. He will be along shortly."

Staunton returned two minutes later and, in response to his wife's request, gave a full and factual account of what had transpired. He did not refrain from repeating Holmes's conclusion that another attack by more dangerous men was a possibility. Mrs. Staunton raised her hands to her face as she listened to him.

"Godfrey," she said, "you cannot let this go on. They could hurt you terribly. You do not have to continue to be on the team. You do not have to do this."

He looked at her, his face glowing in tender concern.

"Yes, darling, I do. You know I have to."

The two of them said nothing for several seconds, and then she quietly nodded her head.

"Yes, my love, I know you do."

She turned to Holmes. "What can we do? How can my husband be kept safe?"

"When is the next game?" he asked.

"Not until the fourth of February," said Staunton. "We're playing Ireland in Dublin."

"Since you have only been married for such a short time," said Holmes, "I strongly suggest that the two of you leave directly from here for a pleasant honeymoon. Do not tell anyone where you are going, although I recommend the south of France at this time of year. Montpellier is a delightful place I can assure you. There is a Cook's office near the Swansea docks, and ships leave daily for the French coast."

Mrs. Staunton had lost her earlier look of concern and was now beaming back at Holmes.

"Oh, what a splendid idea. Don't you agree, darling?"

"But we do not," her husband replied, "have anything packed for three weeks."

"France," said Holmes, "has shops."

"But I do not have the funds available," said Staunton. "I am dependent on Uncle Jimmy until I'm twenty-five. He would never agree to anything so extravagant."

"Your job is to look after your wife and enjoy yourselves. I shall pay a visit to Lord Mount James and make sure that funds are forwarded to the *Société Général* on *Rue de la Loge*. You may use my name when asking for Aramis, the director of the branch. Now, both of you, go and pack. There is an overnight ferry leaving at midnight."

Chapter Thirteen

Having returned to London the following day, I joined Holmes for supper at 221B. Mrs. Hudson had prepared a delicious meal of pressed duck—somewhat too rich and French for a regular diet—and the two of us sat and enjoyed it along with a bottle of fine Madeira. Holmes chattered on about everything and nothing and, my curiosity having gotten the better of me, I demanded to know what his next steps would be.

"I have an appointment tomorrow with Lord Mount James and would be very grateful if you would accompany me."

"Are you assuming," I asked, "given that he is not fond of you, that he would agree to any request you made that required him to part with a farthing? What makes you think the presence of a doctor would be useful?"

Holmes laughed. I failed to see the humor.

"Oh, my dear Watson, of course, you will be useful. He will behave himself, yes. But it has nothing to do with your being a doctor and everything to do with your being a widely-read author. If he is as obnoxious as he was the last time we had dealings with him, he knows that you will record his words and actions and make them known to all of England, just like you did before."

"But I disguised his name. I called him *Mount James* and there is no such person in Great Britain. I will do so again should I have reason to write an account of this case."

"And will you again so accurately describe him—shabbily dressed, jerking and twitching, full of gout, miserly, one of the richest men in England—that everyone in London will know who it must be? I am quite certain that he will be very guarded in what he says."

At a mid-morning hour on Monday, 9 January, Holmes and I paid another visit to the Kensington home of Lord Mount James. Again, Holmes had refused to request an appointment, and we were ushered into the library by an arrogant butler. We waited there for a full fifteen minutes before Lord Mount James entered, with Lady Maynooth by his side.

"Crikey," he said. "What did you two scalawags do to Godfrey."

"I beg your pardon, Sir?" said Holmes.

"I never thought he would throw the game. But you two must have bewitched him and convinced him to take the coward's way out."

"I assure you, we did nothing of the kind."

"Well then, who did? Who got to him?"

"No one got to him. He played quite valiantly."

"Posh," exclaimed the old fellow. "How could they lose by twenty points if he was playing fairly. Impossible."

"On the contrary, your Lordship. The entire English team gave it their all and were beaten fair and square. We watched the game and can attest to that fact. You may consult the scribblers in the sporting press, and they will say the same thing."

"And since when did Sherlock Holmes believe what was written in a newspaper?"

"Their efforts were also observed by those who have threatened him."

His cantankerous Lordship was speechless and glared back at Holmes with a blank face.

Holmes then coolly and succinctly recounted the altercation in the hallway leading to the loo and the decision to have Mr. and Mrs. Staunton run off to France until the next game. Lord Mount James listened attentively, as he did so, his countenance changed, and he appeared to be persuaded that his nephew had indeed stuck to his vows and played his heart out.

"Thank you, Mr. Holmes, he said. "I do indeed feel much better now knowing that my nephew behaved in a manly way."

He was not, however, at all pleased when Holmes informed him of Godfrey and Millie's escape to France and the need to send them funds.

"A honeymoon in France! Utterly profligate. Don't look to me for a penny—not a penny. English people, if they must, can have perfectly good honeymoons in Blackpool."

"He would not be safe there, your Lordship," said Holmes. "Whoever has threatened him seems to have agents all over the country. He could be readily found and attacked again."

"The boy is as strong as an ox. And quite a good pugilist. His father taught him that skill as well. He is perfectly capable of looking after himself."

"But Mrs. Staunton, Millie as she has become known to you, is also in danger."

"Then he can look after her as well. Even if she is attacked, what's the worst that could happen to her? A few bruises maybe, right? She's young and healthy. She would recover. Out of the question!"

"I quite understand your position," said Holmes, with a mischievous twinkle in his eye. "Perhaps you are not aware that if assaulted in a horrible way, a young woman's tender body is at great risk of becoming infertile and no longer capable of conceiving and bearing children. Her future son would be the only heir to your estate and the sole means of carrying on your name. He will be your *de jure* grandson."

The old fellow said nothing and then slowly walked over to the window of the library and looked out for a full minute. It was a reaction I had observed countless times during my years as a doctor. When suddenly faced with the prospect of a grandchild, the hearts of even the most misery aging men or women turn from stone to putty. His Lordship slowly clasped his hands behind his back, turned, and walked back to face us. Lady Maynooth sidled up to him and slipped her hand through his arm. She leaned in toward him and spoke softly in his ear.

"Jim, darling, it would not hurt to do our part. As long as we know that they are indeed using the money to go to France."

He scowled and uttered something close to a grunt.

"I suppose," he said, "I could spare a few pounds to ensure that Millie is safe. What is the address of the bank to which some funds can be wired?"

"If you will entrust the funds to me," said Holmes, "I will promise that they will be forwarded in complete confidence and secrecy and that I will not shave off so much as a farthing for my services."

"Right. Very well. I would not object to your keeping a fiver or even a tenner. I am a firm believer that a laborer is worthy of his hire. Mind that you send me the records of the transfers. Books must be balanced. Right. Jolly good. Now, off with you."

Chapter Fourteen

O n the Saturday of that week, the fourteenth day of January, I dropped in again at 221B on the pretense of being concerned for the health and well-being of both Holmes and Mrs. Hudson. In truth, I had heard nothing from Holmes and was itching to learn what had happened to the young couple and to the investigation into the murder of Danny O'Hearn. Holmes welcomed me warmly and immediately fetched the bottle of sherry off the mantle.

"My dear Watson," he said, "I expect that this will satiate your curiosity."

He handed me an envelope, post-marked *Palavas-les-Flots*, and addressed to him by a feminine hand. I opened it and extracted a document in French that I recognized as a record of a bank transfer.

"His Lordship," explained Holmes, "kindly forwarded a hundred pounds, which I, in turn, sent on to the bank in Montpellier. The paper from the bank confirms that it was received by Godfrey. I shall send it along to the old boy in due course. The letter with it is much more satisfying to read."

I unfolded the letter. It was written in the same woman's hand as the address on the envelope. It ran:

My dear Mr. Holmes:

How can I thank you? Your suggested honeymoon on the Mediterranean has been a dream come true. We arrived here on Sunday evening after taking the ferry to Marseille and then a short train ride to Montpellier. We stayed in the city for only one night and then took the delightful little train south to the coast. Cook's had booked us into a perfectly charming small cottage that looks out over the sea. I could not have imagined a more perfect place to spend a honeymoon.

The weather is too cool for bathing, of course, but it is mild enough for Godfrey and me to stroll arm-in-arm along the beach and the Boulevard. It is not the season for tourists from Paris or London and thus the plethora of fine, small restaurants—every one of them boasting their gastronomic specialty and particular wine from a select vineyard—are almost empty. The men and women working in them are friendly and greet us enthusiastically, in English! So unlike Paris.

But I am sure you are not interested in how we are indulging in the pleasures of the flesh. I wanted to confirm that we received the funds from Uncle Jimmy that you discreetly forwarded to us. The amount received will be more than enough to last us until we come home.

My dear husband at first seemed terribly on edge and kept looking around to see if we had been followed. We were not; unless a couple of nasty Englishmen have donned tams and learned to speak French. I am joking, of course. We are completely safe, and by this afternoon (Wednesday, 11 January), Godfrey finally relaxed and even drank one more glass of wine than he usually permits himself (or maybe two).

I must sign off now and haste to get this in the post. Again, from the bottom of my heart, I thank you. Do give our warmest regards to Dr. Watson. I will send a separate note to my family as well as to his Lordship and Lady.

Very truly yours,
Millicent Staunton (Mrs.)

I could not help but smile and chuckle to myself as I read her letter, and I expected that Holmes would be doing the same.

He was not. When I looked up at him to return it, he was frowning.

"Good heavens, Holmes, why the sad face? Come, come now. How many times over the years have you been thanked so effusively for bestowing such a lovely benefit on young lives?"

"I should have insisted on their not communicating with anyone other than me. Every additional individual who knows of their location puts them at risk."

"My dear Holmes, any girl from a good family is going to send a note to her mother assuring her that the honeymoon is going well. That is what they all do."

Holmes sighed. "You are no doubt correct, but not every young couple busying themselves with making the beast of two backs is a potential target for those seeking untold amounts of ill-gotten gain. An exception would have been in order, but that is now water under the bridge. You might also be interested in this item."

He pulled a sheet of paper out from under a disheveled stack on the side table and handed it to me. The letterhead indicated that it had come from Scotland Yard. The message was written in the now-familiar hand of Inspector Lestrade. It ran:

Holmes. Regarding death of Daniel O'Hearn. Latest.
Yard has interviewed residents and shopkeepers throughout East End. Using minimal coercion, officers secured names and descriptions of most likely suspects. These match yours from incident in Swansea. Large males, all cockneys. Bulletins have been issued for arrest of George Cornell, Ronnie Kray, and Billy Hill. N.B. – all sources were adamant that the three were well-known as

thugs hired for extortion but had never committed murder. Put that in your pipe.   Lestrade.

"What did you make of this?" I asked.

He did not immediately reply. Ever so deliberately, he took out his pipe, filled it with tobacco, tamped it down, lit it, and began puffing.

"Given what is at stake, it is likely that more than one team of thugs has been engaged. More data is required," he said.

Over the following two weeks, I called in on Holmes several times, and each time our brief conversation was the same. I asked what, if anything he had heard about our newlyweds on their honeymoon.

"Not a peep," he said. "It would appear that they have other things on their minds. I expect them to return just in time for the next game in the Championship. I am planning on going to watch it, and I do hope you shall be able to come along with me. It will be on 4 February in Dublin."

I refrained from reminding him that I knew perfectly well when and where the next match would take place.

"And what about Lestrade?" I then asked. "Anything from him on Danny O'Hearn and those three thugs?"

"Nothing of late. It appears that the three from Swansea have gone into hiding. They must have been informed by someone that their identities had become known."

"Whoever is behind this," I said, "seems to have spies everywhere."

"Precisely. Your powers of deduction are showing signs of life. Well done."

The quiet period of tranquility ended sharply on 31 January. At four o'clock in the afternoon, a breathless bicycle page rushed into my medical practice and handed me a note from Holmes. It ran:

See attached. Come at once and be prepared to offer protection to our foolish young couple.

Chapter Fifteen

I then read the short letter that accompanied the note. This time it had been written, none too neatly, in a masculine hand and ran:

Mr. Holmes: We are on our way back to London and should arrive London from Dover at 5:00 pm 31 January. Although our honeymoon has been splendid, I do not feel good about missing the practices with the England International team. This will give me a few days to join them before departing for Dublin for the match.

I know you think I am far too suspicious, but I believe that someone has learned where we are hiding. Three days ago, I spotted two men who appeared to be loitering around the café where Millie and I took our breakfast. I had not noticed them before, and I have been constantly on the lookout for any unsavory characters. They were there again at supper last night at another café several blocks away. They were wearing berets and scarves and trying to look French and smoking Gauloises, but I saw that their boots were Trickers – something any Cambridge man can spot – so they must be English. They were not big chaps like the ones in Swansea, but they had the look as if they might as soon cut your throat as look at you.

I hope I am wrong, but if not, then it looks like someone at the bank must have tattled, and I will make sure that no one knows or sees us leaving France early.

I did not mention them to Millie as I do not want to worry her if there is no need, but I wanted you to know. We have notified Millie's mother of our plans to return, and I sent a wire to Uncle Jimmy but have said nothing about these two thuggish fellows.

Can you arrange to meet me after I return home and advise me what best to do? We will soon be living in one of His Lordship's properties in Chelsea.

Godfrey

I scribbled a note back to Holmes, letting him know I would meet him as soon as possible and gave it to the boy with the bike to rush over to him. I hastily shut down my office and called a cab. I was always eager to oblige Holmes when he asked for my help even at times when I thought his fears and reaction were a bit over the top.

He was standing on the pavement outside 221B pacing and smoking as my cab pulled up. A copy of Bradshaw's was tucked under one arm and his Penang lawyer under the other.

"Poor Godfrey," I said to him. "The lad must be terribly tense. He's seeing an assassin behind every *lampadaire*. Just because a man wears English shoes, it does not mean he is an Englishman. The factories in Northampton send their shoes all over the world."

"No, Watson. No Frenchman who smokes foul, cheap French cigarettes can afford select English footwear. Most wear cheap boots made for the working class. The French are like that. Godfrey's observations are astute and his fears reasonable."

He jumped inside the cab and directed the driver to get us to London Bridge Station post haste.

"The five o'clock SER train from Dover comes into London Bridge. If young Staunton was precise with his times, that is the train they will be on."

In the busy afternoon traffic, the cab hurried its way along Marylebone and then south through Bloomsbury. It stopped in front of the London Bridge Station with ten minutes to spare before the arrival of the Dover train. Holmes led me to a small tobacconist's shop on the concourse in front of the platforms.

"We shall," he said, "have a good view from here of the passengers as they descend the train."

"It should be easy," I said, "to spot a young couple returning from their honeymoon."

"Good heavens, Watson, we are not here to accost them. We can find them later at Mount James's. We are looking for the two men who found them and are most likely now following them."

"How will you know who they are?"

"Their boots."

"Holmes, Trickers is one of the most popular shoemakers in England. A score or two of men will be wearing them."

"Very well, then, two men with those shoes and also scarves and berets."

"Berets? Really, Holmes? If they are Englishmen, don't you think they would have doffed anything that would make them look like a French dandy?"

"Very well, then. Shoes, scarves, wiry, and looking as if they would happily cut your throat."

"You do know that I do not have my service revolver in my pocket."

"Why not?"

"I am not in the habit of taking it with me to my medical practice, and you requested that I come immediately from there."

"Yes, that is correct. An oversight on my part. But you do have your walking stick."

"It is not the best weapon against a cutthroat with a knife."

"Then you best be quick with it."

According to the chalked notices on the station board, the SER from Dover was expected on time. At five o'clock on the spot, it pulled into the second platform and disgorged its load. Mr. and Mrs. Staunton were easy to pick out in the crowd. Handsome couples walking together with the arm of a beautiful, tall young woman through that of a handsome, athletic gentleman stand out anywhere. They were stylishly dressed, much more so than they had been in Swansea. Mrs. Staunton appeared utterly *dégagé*, as would be expected having spent a honeymoon in the south of France. A porter followed them, pushing a cart bearing three shiny new steamer trunks.

"Are you not," I asked Holmes, "going to greet them?"

"Of course not. If there is anyone following them, it would be a signal for them to flee."

Holmes had propped himself against the corner of the tobacconist shop and had his spyglass up and steadied. From the angle at which he was holding it, I concluded that he was inspecting the boots of the male passengers.

"There they are," he said. "Follow them but keep well back."

Two men, *sans berets* but with scarves wrapped around their necks in the French style were walking about ten yards behind the Stauntons. They were wiry fellows, and although I could not tell what they had on their feet, Holmes apparently could.

He was off at a quick pace. We moved in behind our two suspects and followed them out to the pavement. A queue of passengers had formed out on London Bridge Street and were hopping into the waiting line of cabs. The Stauntons were well ahead of us as well as the Trickers chaps with a dozen or so passengers between us. With each loaded and departing cab, the queue moved forward, and a driver soon jumped down from his cab to assist the Stauntons and load their luggage inside and on top.

Holmes leaned over and whispered to me. "Be ready to move."

That made no sense. We were still behind our suspects, and there were several passengers ahead of them.

The cab with the Stauntons pulled away, and the cab behind pulled up and opened its doors. The two men in front of us stepped forward and jumped the queue to the door of the cab.

"*Permettez nous,*" one of them shouted in English school-boy French. "But *nous sommes* in a very big hurry. *Pardon*, but we must have *ce taxi.*"

The rightful passengers looked very offended but said nothing and did not attempt to stop them.

Sherlock Holmes did. He moved quickly up to the door of the cab and placed his cudgel across the opening just as the first *faux* Frenchman was stepping up and in, catching him across the abdomen.

"We shall have none of that here," announced Holmes in his most arrogant and haughty impersonation of well-starched English nobility. "Whilst that may be the way you Frenchies behave in Gaul, that is just not done here in England. Now get back to your place in the queue and wait your turn."

"Here, here," was heard from the curious crowd who had inevitably come closer to observe an altercation. Two or three of them gave a polite round of applause. The chap who had been blocked from getting in the cab first glared at Holmes and then cast a glance at the cab bearing the Stauntons as it turned to corner on London Bridge Street and was about to vanish from sight.

"Bollocks to you," he shouted at Holmes. "Stand back, you bloody flapdoodle, or I make you pay for it." He looked again down the now-empty street and attempted to grab Holmes's stick and thrust it out of the way. Holmes was much too quick for him and bracing the tip of his stick against the far side of the cab door rapidly leveraged it out against the fellow's stomach. It forced him back off the step, and he tumbled backward onto the pavement, landing unceremoniously on his backside. Cheers and claps went up from the growing crowd.

He was on his feet in a second with a very dangerous knife in his hand.

"Get back you bloody toff, or I'll slice you good," he shouted at Holmes. Gasps and cries came from the onlookers. Whoever the fellow was, he had no appreciation for Holmes's skill in single-stick and the heavy end of the Penang lawyer landed hard on his wrist, evoking a scream of pain and an uncouth oath.

"Look out!" someone shouted. "The other Frenchie has a knife."

Indeed, the second man was running toward Holmes with a gleaming blade held in his hand. I was not in position to give his wrist a whack with my walking stick as Holmes had done, but I managed to snap it up and deliver a glancing blow against his face.

What happened next could have been predicted whenever any group of Englishmen sees one of their own under attack from a knavish Frenchie. Out of the crowd, at first half-dozen men, followed by a second lot rushed forward and threw their arms around all eight limbs of the nasty enemies. It was one of those things that unites the English. The band of vigilantes ranged in age from boys in their teens to elderly old fellows, and their class from working men in their caps and rough jackets to gentleman in evening dress. Nothing like a spat with the French, I thought, to unite the nation.

Within a few seconds, the two assailants were pinned to the ground with a total of sixteen men—two to each limb—holding them and a few other chaps who had been farther back in the queue jockeying to find an empty spot around the immobile bodies so they could pitch in and do their bit.

A constable appeared and, although provided with a garbled account enthusiastically given all at once by several bystanders, discerned sufficient to blow his whistle and call for the police wagon that was customarily parked beside every rail station in London. He was assisted by far too many would-be heroes in affixing a set of darbies to the miscreants and loading them into the police wagon.

Three more police officers had appeared and encouraged the pressing crowd to step back.

"Who witnessed this?" demanded one of them.

"That man there," shouted someone in the crowd pointing to Holmes. "He's the one who put those cheese-eating surrender monkeys in their place." Murmurs of approval and admiration followed.

"Right then, you, sir. What's your name?"

Holmes stepped up close to the constable and whispered in his ear.

"My name is Sherlock Holmes. It would be useful if I were to accompany you and take these men to Scotland Yard."

"Sherlock Holmes!?" said the constable much too loudly. "My lucky day if I do say."

The front line of the crowd heard his every word, and soon the name of Sherlock Holmes was being whispered throughout the assembled mix of passengers who were now ignoring the waiting cabs and the cab drivers, who were becoming impatient. I listened to hear if perhaps someone might speak my name as well, but it was not to be.

The two men were locked into the back portion of the wagon, and we joined the constables in the front section. We drove through Southwark and across the Westminster Bridge, arriving at Scotland Yard as Big Ben was striking six.

"Is Lestrade," I asked Holmes, "going to want to question these louts?"

"I am sure he will as soon as we tell him that they may be linked to the murder of Danny O'Hearn."

"Will he get anything out of them?"

Chapter Sixteen

Inspector Lestrade was on his way out of the Scotland Yard building as we stepped out of the police carriage. He looked at us and sighed.

"What is it this time, Holmes? It better be something worth my time. The missus will have my supper waiting, and I don't like eating it cold."

Holmes gave a quick answer, making reference to the murdered rugby player. That was good enough for Lestrade who then instructed the attending constables to lead the prisoners from the carriage and into a holding cell. Once they appeared, however, Lestrade stopped the process.

"Hold on there a bit," he said. "If it isn't Eddie Biddle and Willie Moffat."

"From the Worthington bank gang? Surely not," said Holmes.

"Cousins," said Lestrade. "Their families are choc-a-block with the criminal class. These two have already been guests of Her Majesty at Wandsworth, and they might be again soon."

"You can't send us away for a having no more than a little set to in the queue at the station," said one of them.

"No? Well then, best we find out what else you lads have been up to."

He called three of his constables over to confer with him. I could not tell what was being said, but the three of them were all nodding, noting their understanding of his orders. One was positively grinning. As soon as the colloquy had ended, the constables manhandled the miscreants into the building.

"Now then, Holmes," said Lestrade, "get into my office and deliver your report and try to be concise. My supper is waiting."

Holmes did as he had been bidden and over the next twenty minutes provided a candid and succinct account of what had transpired in the life of the Stauntons and the incident at the station. I scribbled notes as he spoke.

"Do you," asked Holmes of the inspector upon completion, "have any queries?"

"Of course not," said Lestrade. "I am quite certain that you have given me a full account of everything you want me to know."

"Splendid, then do not let us keep you from your dinner with your good wife. Allow us to wish you a pleasant evening."

"You're not going anywhere. Not quite yet. Just wait here for another ten minutes. Doctor, there are a few novels on the side table that you might enjoy. And Holmes, I expect that you will go into your impression of the Gautama."

He gave no reason, and he turned his attention to a file that had nothing whatsoever to do with our case.

I picked up a newish novel by an American writer that had received excellent reviews since it appeared just over a year ago. It was set in their War Between the States and quickly proved to be as depressing as the reviews had warned. Holmes closed his eyes and placed his hands together under his chin, his fingers tented. He stayed that way for a full ten minutes while Lestrade and I read.

At just past the ten-minute mark, a constable came to the open door and gave a quiet knock on the frame. Lestrade looked up at him, nodded, and using his chin directed him to come in. He was one of the three who had led our queue jumpers into the building, and his face was now flushed and his brow lightly glistening with sweat.

"Very well, Billingsley. Tell us what nuggets of information you gleaned from our prisoners."

"Yes, Inspector, Sir. Biddle and Moffat are a couple of tough Johnnies, and it took a little extra persuasion to coax statements out of them but thanks to the electricity you had installed down in that cell, they eventually became cooperative."

"Right, and what did they tell you?"

"Not so much as I know you would like to hear, Inspector, Sir, but we, the three of us that is, agreed that they did not know any more than they told us. If we had kept up persuading them, we knew they would just start making up stories to get us to lay off."

"I trust your judgment, Billingsley. Now, what did they tell you?"

"Well, as you know, Inspector, Sir, Biddle and Moffat are in the business of providing services for hire. Quite the fearsome duo they are, and feared too and rightly so. They have been known to rough up some gents rather badly. Not above breaking bones or cutting flesh or using the ends of their cigarettes to make a party either stop or start doing what they or their employers want done."

"Right, now resist the urge to explain what I already know and get on with it."

"Of course, Sir. They admitted that they had been hired ten days ago to go and find a Mr. and Mrs. Staunton somewhere in the south of France."

"Who hired them?"

"They do not know names. And believe me, Sir, on our honor, we tried to get that out of them, and they were consistent. If we had kept pushing, they would have just made up names to get us to curtail our efforts."

"They must have said something."

"Yes, Inspector. They said the chap they met with was in a hurry because the three men he hired previously had been identified and he needed new services straight away. But all they said was that he was well-dressed, a right polished gentleman, a veritable esquire, they said. Youngish, a finely tailored suit, new hat, ... a rich-looking toff is what they called him."

"Right, that describes about five thousand men in London and more being excreted every year from Oxford and Cambridge. Move along then, what were they hired to do?"

"That they did tell us, after a bit of persuading, mind you, Sir. They were told that Mr. and Mrs. Staunton were somewhere close to Montpellier and they were to go there and find them and follow them back to England. They were quite clear on that. Said that they were told in no uncertain terms not to do anything criminal whilst in France as it would cause an international incident, so none of that over there."

"But when they came home to England? What then?"

"They were to find Godfrey Staunton and cut him a few times. Not enough to stop him from playing but enough to make him know that his enemies were to be taken seriously. Seems he was not doing that and they wanted to convince him to do so."

"But they didn't."

"Well, no, Inspector. They said they had followed him all the way from France and were about to follow him to wherever he and Mrs. Staunton were staying and deal with him there but then Mr. Holmes appeared and put an end to that. And you should know, Mr. Holmes, that they did not speak kindly about you."

Holmes smiled, somewhat smugly.

"Anything else?" demanded Lestrade.

"There was one more thing they said, Inspector, Sir."

"Very well, out with it."

"They said they were told that one of them must hold a knife to Mr. Staunton's throat whilst the other tied him to a chair and then with him watching they were to do some nasty things to Mrs. Staunton. You know, slap her and twist her arm and such. Threaten to break her fingers and so on. Nothing that she would not recover from, but just to give Mr. Staunton a taste of what they could do to her if he did not cooperate."

"Merciful heavens," I exclaimed. "I thought you said the man who gave them these instructions was a gentleman. Such behavior is unthinkable. And you say he was an Englishman? Great Scott."

"It would not, Doctor," said Lestrade, "be the first time it has been done."

"By some low-life no doubt, but the constable said the instructions were given by a well-dressed, refined gentleman."

"Saying such things," said Lestrade, "is beneath contempt but unfortunately not against the law."

"Does that mean," asked the constable, "that we have to let them go?"

Lestrade appeared to ponder that one for a short while.

"Where's Connor, the janitor?"

"He's working in the refectory, Sir."

"Right. Take him downstairs but where he can't be seen and give him two shillings to sit for an hour and let out no end of screams as if he's being branded with a hot iron and tell him to shout curses at you. He's Irish. They are all quite practiced at both of those acts. After an hour, pay a visit to the cell with Biddle and Moffat. Let them go, but let them think that whatever was happening around the corner from them is what will be done to them the next time."

"Jolly good, inspector, Sir. We shall get right on that."

The constables departed, and Lestrade turned to Holmes.

"Whoever is behind all this appears to have rather extensive contacts in the criminal class. Finding thugs who will travel to France and do your bidding at the drop of a hat is not an option available to many."

"I concur with your deduction," said Holmes. "I suspect that we are beginning to pull on the edges of a web that extends well beyond the punters and sportsmen of London."

"And who knows who else beyond the Stauntons they have already wrapped their tentacles around."

"Again, I concur," said Holmes. "I shall be available to assist Scotland Yard with its investigation if my services are so requested in the future. Now, however, I must devote my attention to the protection of my clients."

Lestrade nodded his agreement. "Might I assume, Holmes, that you will now be on your way to have a friendly chat with Mr. and Mrs. Staunton?"

"Correct as usual, Inspector. Do you wish to come with us?"

"No, I shall go home to a supper that by now is cold. Let me know what happens over in Kensington."

Chapter Seventeen

It was a relatively short cab ride from the Embankment and along the Mall and through Knightsbridge to Lord Mount James's home. It had gone eight o'clock by the time we arrived there and, as it was only a few weeks past the winter solstice, darkness had descended.

"Good evening, Perkins," Holmes said to the butler who opened the door. "We urgently need to speak to Mr. and Mrs. Staunton. Would you be so kind as to tell me the location of their new residence?"

"They're here," replied the butler. "They are dining with His Lordship and Lady."

"Splendid. Kindly inform His Lordship that Sherlock Holmes wishes to speak to them on a matter of great importance. And no, I do not have an appointment."

I detected a quick flash of anger in the young man's eyes before he fixed his gaze on the night sky and spoke to the empty distance behind us.

"His Lordship does not appreciate being disturbed whilst dining. I suggest that you return later. Shall I make an appointment for Friday next, Mr. Holmes?"

"A better time would be at forty-five minutes past seven o'clock this evening."

The butler looked confused. "But that time has already passed."

"It has? Oh, dear, then I must be late already. That will not do."

Without another word, he strode out of the foyer and towards the dining room, I followed him, ignoring the protests of young Mr. Perkins.

The dining room of the Mount James city house had also been refurbished in a thoroughly modern style. Gone was the clutter the ancient family portraits, paintings, coats of armor that give an air of ancient privilege. In their place, on the spare white walls, were four somewhat smudged prints of landscapes and peasants in the recent French style and two large, framed photographs of scenes from what I assumed were marketplaces in Turkey, or maybe Algiers. Sitting beneath them, around the dining table, were Mr. and Mrs. Staunton, Lord Mount James and Lady Maynooth. They appeared to be enjoying their desserts when Holmes and I entered the room, and they looked up at us. The Lord and Lady were pasty in complexion, as was normal for the English nobility in the depths of winter, but the young couple glowed with a radiance that had been acquired by a honeymoon in the south of France.

"You two! Again!" snapped Mount James. "Have you no manners at all? Now, what do you want?"

"An urgent report," said Holmes "that has serious implications for the health and welfare of all of you. Do you wish to hear it?"

"Of course, we do," said Mrs. Millie Staunton as she stood up. "Please, let me get your chairs, and you can join us for tea."

Lord Mount James looked as if he were about to burst a blood vessel in rage and would have much preferred if the two of us had been left standing, like lowly privates delivering a report to their commanding officer.

Lady Maynooth placed her jeweled hand on his wrist and cooed.

"Your Lordship, we mustn't be upset. It is not as bad as it would have been if they have arrived during the soup course."

Godfrey Staunton was already up and, as would be expected of an attentive young husband, had stepped in to help his wife.

Once we were seated, Mrs. Staunton poured us a cup of tea and passed over a plate with some dessert pastries.

"Tea first, gentleman," she said. "then your story."

We obeyed. Once a few sips had been enjoyed, Holmes began his account. He started with the receiving of the note from Godfrey Staunton, at which point he was interrupted by Mrs. Staunton.

"Godfrey," she said to her husband. "You never said anything to me about seeing those men."

"Of course not, darling. I did not want you to be upset."

"Godfrey. That is not acceptable."

Being present in the midst of a tense moment between a husband and wife is always awkward, particularly if followed by several seconds of chilly silence. The four non-participants in the exchange suddenly found one of the paintings on the wall more interesting than it deserved. Several times, Godfrey seemed as if ready to respond and then swallowed his words. Finally, he smiled and nodded.

"You are entirely correct, my dear. In future, I will not conceal anything from you."

Mrs. Staunton smiled back and then turned to Holmes.

"Please, Mr. Holmes, continue."

In his customary concise and precise manner, he recounted the events of the day, concluding with his warning that the threats against both Mr. and Mrs. Staunton had escalated and that their situation had become more parlous. When he had finished, an atmosphere of silence and apprehension descended over the room.

Holmes broke the tension with a question to Godfrey.

"Your schedule between now and the next game? What are your plans?"

"What? Oh, yes, right. Well, tomorrow we have a team practice at the Rectory Field in Blackheath. Then on Thursday, we travel to Dublin via Liverpool. Friday, we practice at Lansdowne Park, and then Saturday is the game. Do you think we will be followed again?"

"Difficult to say. There is only a short window of opportunity for whoever is behind this plot to find and hire yet another set of thugs. Nevertheless, Dr. Watson and I shall come with you and will be prepared to offer protection. If I have the least inclination that we are being watched, then, immediately before boarding the ferry back to Liverpool, we can exchange our tickets and travel south and come back to England by way of the Rosslare to Fishguard ferry. It is a small boat and offers no quarter for any passengers to blend in with the crowd."

Lord Mount James harrumphed his approval. "Sounds like a good plan to me. And do not forget, Master Godfrey, you cannot let those bog-trotters win. I expect to hear a report of your brilliant play."

"I will do my best, Uncle."

"We know you will," added Lady Maynooth, smiling sweetly.

Chapter Eighteen

Two days later, Holmes and I entered Euston Station and boarded the early morning train to Liverpool. England's team had seats in the second-class carriage, and the rest of the train was packed with Liverpudlians returning to their home city and jabbering away loudly in a language that bore only a remote resemblance to English. It was impossible to seek out a couple of dangerous thugs in the midst of them. Holmes had said that he did not think it likely that we would be followed to Dublin, and I assumed he was right.

We disembarked at the Lime Street Station and hired a cab to take us and our baggage the few blocks down to the Royal Albert Docks at Merseyside. There we clambered aboard the ferry that sailed across the Irish Sea to Dublin. Whereas the bulk of previous passengers on the train were from Liverpool, the majority on the ferry were Irish. But like the Liverpudlians, they were speaking loudly in a semi-intelligible form of English, made worse by the combination with Gaelic.

I had brought several recent novels with me and found a comfortable place to sit and read for the six or so hours it would take to get to Ireland. A chap from Bromley by the name of Herbert Wells had released a sensational book every year for the past several, and the populace was quite keen on his, admittedly, strange and perverse tales. *The Island of Doctor Moreau* was enough to give one nightmares.

For the better part of the journey, Holmes paced. He constantly walked around the sitting rooms and the bar and even ventured a few times out into the freezing winds of the outer decks. It was only once we were in sight of land that he came and sat down beside me.

"See any suspicious types?" I asked him.

"Reasonable deductions cannot be made from observation when all most all Irishmen qualify as suspicious types."

"Come now, Holmes. At least a quarter of these chaps are members of the Catholic clergy."

"Especially them."

A cab took us from the docks at Dublin Port and into the city. Because of the game on the weekend, most of the decent hotel rooms had already been booked, but Cook's had found us a place at the Ormond Hotel on the north bank of the River Liffey. It was not exactly a house of ill-repute, but neither was it far from it. We were assured, however, that the food and ale were decent and, as it was the supper hour, we found our way to the bar after depositing our baggage in our rooms.

No sooner had we sat down that two no-longer-young but still-buxom barmaids sauntered over to our table. Miss Lydia Douce and Miss Mina Kennedy introduced themselves, smiling at us through their seductive wet lips. Being always a gentleman, I politely introduced ourselves to them and engaged in a few minutes of pleasant banter. At first, I assumed that they were Gaelic strumpets, but their actions proved that they were merely employed because of their expertise in assisting male patrons to part with the contents of their purses. After quizzing the two of us with rather prying questions, they apparently came to the disappointing realization that Holmes and I were worth no more than a pint of Guinness and returned to chat with a brash popinjay on the other side of the room.

Several minutes later, after our pints of stout had arrived, that chap came over and sat down across from us. He had a cigarette in his mouth that he did not remove to talk. Instead, he tilted his head to the side so that the smoke might not ascend directly into his nostrils. The cigarette bobbed up and down as he spoke to us.

"So, you have come to Dublin, have you? Well, welcome. Here for the rugby match are ye? Are ye willing to place a small wager just to make it a bit more interesting?"

Holmes gave him a stern look. "I do not believe we have been introduced, Sir."

"Haven't we? Well, you don't say. Well now, we'll have to fix that up, won't we? Hugh Boylan's the name. But all the fellas inside the Pale just call me Blazes Boylan."

"Why?"

"Hey there, Mina," he shouted across the room. "Tell this sassenach here why everyone calls me Blazes Boylan."

She rolled her eyes and shouted back. "Because there's a part of your anatomy that's always on fire. Pity, it's not your brain."

Boylan guffawed loudly and slapped his thigh.

"Isn't she just a fine floozie? And you, my good man, can call me whatever you want. I am at your service as a top-drawer promoter of concerts, pugilistic contests, and any other event that will draw a crowd. And on the side, a reliable manager of the wagers of sportsmen. And who might I have the pleasure of speaking to this fine evening?"

"My name is Holmes, and this is my friend, Dr. Watson, and I assure you that the pleasure is all yours."

"And are ye willing to be a chancer on the match?"

"If we so chose to do so, we shall place our bets at the stadium."

"And I would be willing to wager that you will place a bet for England and let me tell you that you will be losing your money if you do."

"And how is it that you are so sure of that, Mr. Boylan?"

"If you are wanting to know, my good man, I will tell you. All the punters over in England believe that Ireland will suffer from the tragic loss of Danny O'Hearn. But our National Team has excellent reserves. We've brought Tommy Ahearne, the Bulldog from Blarney, up from Cork to fill his place. The squad is back at full force."

"Is it now?" said Holmes.

Blazes Boylan prattled on about rugby and, I must say, he was surprisingly well-informed. Part-way through his lecture, Miss Mina Kennedy appeared at our table, bearing two plates of potatoes and Irish stew, accompanied by bowls of giblet soup. As she was bending over the table to place our dinners in front of us, I could not help but notice Boylan's brazen leering as he looked down her blouse. She gave him an icy look, and he just laughed.

Seeing that Holmes and I had become more interested in our dinners than his wisdom, he departed but not without a few more vociferous comments on the upcoming match.

Having traveled all day, I was hungry and quickly tucked into the meal in front of me. It is difficult to cook a potato badly but, sadly, the same cannot be said about a stew. What was on my plate appeared to be a concoction of the inner organs of beasts and fowls.

Holmes was picking away at his supper and sighed. "God made food, the devil the cooks."

We agreed to seek out an alternative bar on the morrow.

"But what," I asked Holmes, "did you think of the insights into the match offered by Mr. Blazes Boylan?"

"I believe that here on the sodden isle, they have a name for chaps like him. Rugger bugger isn't it?"

"He is indeed, but is he right?"

"My dear Watson, that is not the question. What we must ask is whether or not he is in league with the network of agents who have threatened Godfrey Staunton and, no doubt, expect him to throw the game. His appearance at our table seemed a bit too convenient to be explained by chance."

"So, you are saying that you do not trust Mr. Boylan?"

"Do you?"

Chapter Nineteen

The following morning, Holmes and I departed the Ormond Hotel early enough to give us time to walk across Dublin to Lansdowne Road and find seats in the stadium. For an hour, we watched England's team practice, which is to say that I watched the field whilst Holmes held a set of field glasses to his face and constantly scanned the seats and stands for anyone whom he might consider suspicious.

Sitting in the cold on a hard board does become a tedious ordeal, and after an hour of doing so, Holmes stood up.

"No one," I asked, "of interest to spy on?"

"Nothing but players' wives, reporters and a few of the governors of Rugby Union. I am sure," he said, "that I can find more profitable ways to spend my time."

"You might enjoy watching the boys practicing out on the pitch."

"Becoming chilled with a blanket wrapped around me and watching a troop of grown men run around in short pants pretending to be so stoical that they are not afflicted by the cold, strikes me as an abuse of my time. I shall see you for dinner."

I stayed for another half-hour before likewise succumbing to the elements and coming to my senses. I had not been to Dublin before and, needing to occupy several hours, took the opportunity to stroll through Dublin's fair city. I began by walking east from the stadium the few blocks over to reportedly scenic Sandymount Strand and the view it afforded of the Irish Sea.

Scenic it was, but not particularly hospitable in early February. I imagined that on a sunny day in August, it would be populated by no end of young men and women in their bathing costumes, with shirts and skirts blowing in the ocean breeze; but not today.

My route back into the center of the city took me past a building I had encountered in the medical literature, the Holles Hospital, and then to the grounds of Trinity College. I stopped there long enough to take a look at the Book of Kells and then give a nod of homage to some of the writers who were my idols. Congreve, Burke, Swift, and Goldsmith all came to my mind. No doubt there were many more that I did not remember.

The ocean breeze had given me a bit of a chill so, on coming across a chemist shop under the name of Sweny, I entered and purchased a small bottle of the popular Heroin Cough Suppressant made by the German, Bayer, and then, wanting a warm place to relax for a while, entered the National Library and curled up in a large leather armchair with a strange tale, *The Picture of Dorian Gray,* that an American had asked Oscar Wilde to write at the same time he asked me to send him a new story about Sherlock Holmes.

By the time I finished the short book, I had developed an appetite and found a small pub, *Davy Bryne's,* a block away on Duke Street. They were offering a discounted price on a lunch of gorgonzola sandwich and a glass of burgundy, so I sat and enjoyed it.

In Temple Bar, I noticed a poster that I thought might interest Holmes if we were to have any time free. It advertised an event tomorrow evening in Mayer's Opera House: *Molly Bloom – Soprano*, singing arias from William Wallace's *Maritana*. Curiously, the small print at the bottom claimed that the event was managed and promoted by Boylan Productions.

I crossed the Liffey and returned to our hotel. Holmes showed up to the Ormand at dinner time, and we walked a block to the other side of the river and found a pleasant pub, *The Brazen Head*, where we both enjoyed a beef and Guinness stew. Holmes seemed highly distracted and slowly ate his dinner without uttering a word. Finally, I chided him for his lack of civil behavior.

"Come now, Holmes. Stop acting as if you were the last boy to be picked for the team. What happened today that has made you so disconsolate?"

"Nothing."

"Holmes, that is the answer of a twelve-year-old. I am your friend, and I asked you a civil question."

He looked at me somewhat blankly.

"That is the truthful answer. Nothing. I spent the entire day after leaving the stadium making inquiries in every hotel, every bar, every café, anywhere and everywhere in Dublin where the Irish punters gather instead of going to work. There was not a single whisper of attempts to fix the game or manipulate the odds and the wagers. Nothing."

"It is not completely impossible that the good Catholic citizens of Dublin do not engage in the deadly sin of greed. You might consider that as the reason."

His face betrayed his profound contempt for my suggestion.

"To the best of my knowledge, this sodden isle is not known for its moral rectitude or its abstaining from any of the seven sins. It is possible, I do admit, that the Irish punters simply lack the funds to place significant bets and therefore cannot enter the realms of the prodigal wastrels. Yes, I suppose that is possible. But I cannot escape the improbability that whoever is behind the threats and assaults on Godfrey Staunton would ignore this match."

"They must have known that there was no chance of England's losing to Ireland, even if Staunton were to do his utmost to throw the game. Of that, I am quite certain and have placed my bet accordingly."

"I suppose that we shall just have to go and watch and see what happens."

The Sporting Times

Sunday, 5 February, 1899

Ireland Upsets Favoured England in Home Nations Championship

England's Finest Dominate the Game but Stubborn Irish Defence Keeps Them Out of Touch

"Janey Mack, we done the English langers in!" shouted Louis Magee, the captain of the Irish national team when the final whistle blew to end the game. "My word and willywigs! And didn't we turn those Tommies into knackered toffs!"

The game ended with a score of six to naught for Ireland. Late in the match, G.G. Allen fought his way through the English defense, to score a try. Then, with minutes left on the clock, Ernie Fookes fouled and Ireland's captain, Louis Magee launched a penalty kick through the uprights, sealing Ireland's victory.

But that was not the way the game began. The bookmakers had set the odds in England's favor, and for the first three quarters of the match, it appeared that they had been spot on. Time and time again, England took control of the ball and, led by the ferocious runs of Godfrey Staunton, moved the play well past Ireland's 25-yard line. The crowd of several thousand gathered in Dublin's Lansdowne Road stadium—almost all of them shouting *Erin Go Bragh!*—held their breath. Their National Team did not disappoint. The Lads from the Emerald Isle formed an impenetrable wall and stopped the English from scoring.

"So, those Limeys ran into the Pale of Ireland!" exulted Mr. Daniel Tallon, the Lord Mayor of Dublin. "And this time weren't the Irish keeping them out and beyond." It was reported that even His Grace, the Most Reverend William Walsh, the Archbishop of Dublin was overheard shouting highly unecclesiastical cheers every time that his boys held the line. Rumors that he muttered promises of three years less in Purgatory every time a Clover tackled an English back should not be believed but are being celebrated in Temple Bar nonetheless.

"We gave it our best shot," said Arthur Rotherham, England's weary captain, "but those fire-crotches were blazing." "They were playing for the memory of Danny O'Hearn," acknowledged Godfrey Staunton, England's star three-quarter. "His brave spirit was all through them and, try as we might, we could not overcome their determination."

Ireland now moves on to Edinburgh to play Scotland, a fortnight from yesterday. England's next match is against Scotland on 11 March.

"The Crumpet-Stuffers will have to trounce the Porridge-Wogs if they hope to stay in the rounds," noted Tommy McGowan, Ireland's colorful Number Eight. "If they can't, then we're on our way to a Triple Crown."

Keep watching and reading The Sporting Times to follow the Home Nations Championship and the ever-changing odds.

Chapter Twenty

That evening, the roar from Temple Bar could be heard from across the river well into the small hours of the morning, and I despaired of ever falling asleep. Bleary-eyed, I rose at seven o'clock on the morning of Sunday, 5 February and met with Holmes and Mr. and Mrs. Staunton in a pleasant restaurant above a bookstore just past the north end of the Ha'penny Bridge.

Godfrey Staunton was markedly more chipper that morning than he had been after the mortifying loss to Wales.

"We played up and played the game," he said as he consumed an Irish breakfast that consisted half of recognizable food and half of bacon fat. "I have to hand it to them. They were playing for Danny. One has to admire their spirit. They earned their caps. Now all I want to do is to get back to Blackheath and practice with the team. If we are on top of our game, we should have no trouble besting the Scots. As soon as we're done here, we shall be on our way to the port for the first ferry back to Liverpool."

"I think not," said Holmes.

"Good heavens, why not?" said Godfrey.

"I suspect that you have been followed and are still in danger."

"But nothing has happened."

"Correct. Any event that is reasonably expected to occur and does not is reason to arouse suspicion. And that is why I expect that danger still lurks."

"What then," asked Mrs. Staunton, "do you want us to do?"

"The best course of action is to appear to be going to the Docks but then to stop at the train station and quickly board the one leaving for Wexford and then to return to England by way of the ferry to Fishguard. We will take the train from there back to London. It will require several more hours than traveling directly, but it will be the safest alternative."

Before Godfrey could express his palpable frustration with such a delay, his lovely wife spoke up and forthwith agreed.

We met at the Ormond at ten, and a cab took us east from the hotel toward Dublin Port. At Amiens Street, we turned a hard left and sped toward the Connolly Station.

"Shall I run in and purchase the tickets?" I said.

"Not necessary," said Holmes. "I have already done so, as well as for the ferry. If we move with alacrity, we shall board both within minutes of their departure. If anyone is following us, they will have a difficult time boarding at the same time as we do."

The first hour of the journey from Dublin to Wexford runs along the coast and affords many scenic views of the Irish Sea. I was content to enjoy it, but Holmes was soon up and out of his seat and wandering the length of the train. After we had passed Arklow, he returned to our cabin and took out his pipe.

"Any undesirables on board?" I asked.

"As this train goes all the way to County Cork, there are many men who fit that description but none that looked out of place."

"You mean none that looked like English thugs who are following us?"

"Precisely."

"Excellent. Then do try to relax and enjoy the remainder of the journey."

"I am certain," he said, "that I shall be able to do exactly that when we have safely returned our young charges to Kensington."

The train stopped in Wexford and disgorged about half of its passengers before departing for Rosslare Harbour, the ferry port for Wales. A handful of new passengers boarded and found their seats, and we departed for the short distance over to the docks. Once again, Holmes strolled up and down the train making mental notes on every passenger in his unique mind.

"None that strike me immediately as suspicious. There are a few who are dressed respectably and are likely coming on the ferry with us. The rest of the chaps appear awfully Irish and must be on their way through to Waterford and Cork."

"Goodness, Holmes, you sound as if you are disappointed that our travels will be uneventful."

"We still have the ferry crossing to endure. At sea, all things are possible."

It had gone four o'clock when we arrived at Rosslare Station, conveniently situated adjacent to the port, and made our way down the pier to the ferry. It was a much smaller boat than the one we came on from Liverpool, and I expected a rougher crossing, at least until the winds subsided after sundown. No more than a hundred passengers boarded and, as there was no such thing as private rooms, the four of us took seats amongst the general population in the front cabin. It was not heated, but the windows protected travelers from the winter wind.

Once away from the harbor, the boat assumed the rhythmic ascent and descent that ships at sea experience as they cross an expanse of open water. We sat in seats close to each other, saying nothing. Godfrey, understandably exhausted, had slid downward in his chair and rested his head on the chair back. He was soon sound asleep. Holmes was busy reading a monograph on some esoteric aspect of blood chemistry, and I was jotting notes about the past few days but feeling disappointed, thinking that this case would turn out to be a tedious exercise and not worth publishing.

Millie Staunton was sitting across from me and for a while appeared to be trying to read a novel by Francis Hopkinson Smith. I glanced up at her every so often and thought that she was looking rather wan. After being at sea for just over an hour, she got up, wrapped a blanket over her shoulders, and walked toward the door of the cabin that opened to the outer deck. I was concerned that she had become seasick and, a minute later, followed her out.

She was standing at the rail, looking out over the dark ocean. Even in the moonlight, I could see that she looked sickly and pale. With one hand she was clasping the blanket tight around her torso and, with the other, firmly grasping the rail.

It was a relatively mild night given the time of year, but I was worried that she might catch a chill, as often happens when one is feeling ill.

"My dear," I said, "only another two hours and we'll be back on *terra firma*. This rolling sea plays havoc with the most determined of tummies. Would you like a little laudanum to settle your stomach?"

She shook her lovely head. "Thank you, doctor, that is very kind of you to be concerned for me. But I love the sea at night and have traveled many times on ships in much rougher waters."

Then, ever so slowly, she turned her head and looked directly at me. A smile of unmistakeable joy had spread across her face.

"I am feeling under the weather, but it has nothing to do with being at sea."

For a split second, I was confused, and then I grinned back at her.

"Ah ha! And might the reason have anything to do with the arrival of a bouncing future scrum-half in about eight months from now? A nine-pounder on the way."

She laughed merrily. "Possibly. Or maybe it will be a lovely princess, although not likely to be petite and fragile."

"My dear, that is wonderful. I'm sure that Godfrey is thrilled beyond words."

"Oh, my goodness no. I haven't told him yet. He has been so obsessed with his games and his team. I'll wait until we have the privacy of our hotel room tonight and away from everyone."

"That sounds entirely fitting," I said, feeling a glow of happiness for the two of them welling up inside me. "It might help if we walked around the deck. It will not make your queasiness go away, but it might distract you from the discomfort."

She agreed, and for the next hour, we circumnavigated the outer deck at least twenty times before going back inside. It would have been much more enjoyable to chat with her if she could have talked about anything other than her wonderful husband. Not that I disagreed with her, and I acknowledged to myself that I was witnessing the signs of a loving young marriage. However, even a few minutes on a subject other than the glories of her magnificent spouse would have given a welcome respite.

When we went back into the enclosed front cabin, Godfrey was still sleeping, but Holmes was nowhere to be seen. He remained that way until the purser came through announcing that we would be arriving at Fishguard pier in another twenty minutes. He reappeared, holding a sheaf of paper in his hands. I could see that it was full of his illegible scribbles and was clearly not the monograph I had seen him reading earlier.

"Captain Jack Bucket," he said, "is a splendidly convivial fellow and thanks to your sensational stories, knew exactly who I was. He was kind enough to furnish me with a list of the passengers, and whilst you were attending to the needs of our young mother-to-be, I was checking off every bloke on board."

I wanted to demand how he knew the condition of Mrs. Staunton but refrained from doing so and asked, "And did you find any who might be a threat to the growing Staunton family?"

"No. Not one. There are only thirty other men on board, and every one of them strikes me as a minor public servant, an accountant, a school master, or an aspiring member of the clergy; Catholic, Church of England, reformist, and otherwise."

"Excellent. Then we're safe. All we have to do now is find a decent hotel for the night and then catch the morning train through to London."

"The hotel is already booked."

Chapter Twenty-One

The Hope & Anchor Inn was a short walk from the pier and appeared to be a favorite of weary travelers. We checked in at the front desk, took our room keys in hand, and agreed to meet in fifteen minutes in the dining room for a late supper. Holmes and I came back down at the agreed-upon time and then sat and waited another ten minutes for Mr. and Mrs. Staunton. When they appeared, she was clutching his arm with both hands, and he was wearing the silliest, widest grin I could imagine ever seeing on a young man. They appeared to be divinely happy.

Holmes requested that the serving staff bring a round of Champagne and, once it had arrived, proposed a toast to the young family. The three men at the table stood and emptied their flutes, but Mrs. Staunton merely raised the glass to her lips and did not imbibe.

Holmes, as was his habit, took his cigarette case from his suit pocket.

"Pardon me, Mr. Holmes," said Godfrey Staunton, "but I have to ask you not to engage in tobacco use in the presence of my wife."

"Oh Godfrey, darling," said his wife, "Mr. Holmes is on the far side of the table. It won't do any harm."

"Nevertheless, one cannot take chances. Cigarette smoke can be harmful to our baby."

"I agree," said Holmes as he put his case back in his pocket. "I shall assume that from now on, I am charged with the protection of three clients, not just two."

Mrs. Staunton laughed and replied, "Well, for the next few minutes, you will only have one client to attend to. Two of them are excusing themselves briefly and shall return forthwith."

She stood and departed from the table in the direction of the ladies' loo. Holmes immediately took out his cigarette case and quickly lit one and began, somewhat furtively, to enjoy his short window of freedom.

"I do believe," he said, "that I should have told the dear lady not to hurry herself and to take her time. Rushing one's tobacco is no less a discomfort than rushing one's visit to the lavatory."

He leaned back in his chair and enjoyed his cigarette in an exaggerated languorous fashion. Mrs. Millie Staunton did not rush back.

After five minutes, Holmes, having finished with his cigarette, turned to Godfrey Staunton. "Do thank your lovely wife for her consideration."

"I will."

Ten minutes passed, and Mrs. Staunton still had not returned; then fifteen minutes. Godfrey had begun to be uneasy, glancing several times in the direction of the hallway leading to the lavatories, as if by doing so he might speed up the process. After twenty minutes, I gave a look to Holmes, and I could see the concern in his eyes. I rose and walked over to one of the waitresses, a well-fed lady of a certain age, and asked her if she would go into the ladies' loo and check on Mrs. Staunton.

"Sure and I can do that, love. A shilling says she found another lady in there and they are pouring their hearts out to each other."

Well, I thought, that was a distinct possibility.

The waitress returned a minute later.

"You are certain, are you, that she went into the loo down the hall? Might she have gone back upstairs? Prefer the privacy and such? There's no one in the loo down here."

Godfrey leapt to his feet. "I'll check our room," he said and almost ran from the dining room and quickly ascended the stairs.

I looked again at Holmes. His earlier look of concern had descended into alarm, and his complexion was distinctly paler.

"Maybe she is upstairs," I said.

"Good heavens, Watson, please think. Godfrey knew he could check their room because he has the key in his pocket. That can only mean that Millie does not. Unless you think she kicked the door down, she cannot be upstairs."

"Are you thinking—,"

"Yes!"

He rose quickly from his chair and ran out of the dining room, past the front desk and into the street. A second later, I heard him blowing loudly on the police whistle that he always carried in his pocket. Then I heard his voice shouting for the police.

While he was doing so, Godfrey Staunton came back down the stairs.

"She's not there," he said. Using Holmes's logic, I could have told him that but instead took him by the arm.

"Something may have happened," I said. "Holmes has called for the police. You and I must start immediately to search the hotel. I will search the kitchen and rooms on this floor. Go back up the stairs to your floor and pound on every door and demand to know if anyone has seen her. If any of the guests strike you as suspicious, force your way into their rooms and apologize later. Now go!"

The poor fellow's eyes had gone wide with terror, and I feared that he might be paralyzed by the fright. But he recovered in a trice and this time ran like the right wing he was through the dining room and bounded up the stairs three or four at a time.

I went first into the kitchen, then the pantry, then the storage room, the loos, and the hotel office. Each time I shouted at whoever was there, demanding to know if they had seen Mrs. Staunton.

No one had.

Having covered the interior of my floor, I ran outside to where Holmes was barking orders to the local constable.

"Officer. Straight away. Now! Organize a troop of citizens and begin a search. You are looking for two quite strong men walking with a tall, young woman between them. Send someone immediately to the station and demand that no train leave Fishguard until it has been searched—,"

"Oh, come now, sir," the officer replied. "You are at the port where the boats go back to Ireland. Every month or two some poor young lassie runs off in panic rather than accompany her husband back to the land of the bog-trotters."

"She was not going to Ireland," Holmes said, now barely refraining from shouting. "She was just in Ireland and is coming back to England."

"We get a few of those as well. Any English husband who would make his wife spend time in Ireland isn't worth staying with. Just relax, now, sir, she'll show up."

I could tell that Holmes was ready to dress the officer down in no uncertain terms, but we needed his help, and so he labored to explain the recent history of Godfrey and Mrs. Staunton to a doubting policeman. He must have gotten through to him. The officer blew on his whistle and sent the first several men who appeared off through the village to fetch other reliable fellows from their homes.

Within fifteen minutes, about a dozen sober and sturdy yeomen had assembled and were given instructions to search the town and stop any two men and a young woman who appeared to be hiding or who might attempt to board the late train.

"How," I asked Holmes, "can you be sure that it must have been two men who abducted her?"

"Could you manhandle Millie all by yourself?"

I knew the answer to that one. "Not a chance. Unless they were strong men, it might take three—,"

I was interrupted by the pounding of steps behind me. Godfrey Staunton had come running out of the hotel, breathing quickly.

"She can't have gone far," he said. "None of her belongings are gone from the room."

"Did you check all the rooms on the floor?" I asked.

"Every one. Some folks had already gone to bed for the night and were none too happy with me, but they all cooperated. Two of the older women laughed and told me to go to bed and not to worry, that my wife would be back in bed with me come the morning. Do you think they might be right, Mr. Holmes?"

"No."

"But all of her things are still here."

"Even Wales has shops."

"What are you saying, Mr. Holmes? You can't believe that she has run off and left me and all her things."

"No, Godfrey. I fear she has not left of her own accord."

Chapter Twenty-Two

For a moment, Godfrey Staunton looked utterly bewildered, and then a look of terror and panic swept across his face.

"No! Somebody has taken her? It can't be. Who would do something like that?"

"The same people who attacked you, I am afraid," said Holmes. "They have progressed to more drastic measures and taken your wife."

"No! We have to find her!" he shouted, looking wild-eyed. "I'll ... I'll break every bone in their bodies."

"We have to find her and her captors before you can do that," said Holmes. I could tell he was wanting to keep Godfrey from exploding and madly running off in all directions. I could also tell that he himself was exceptionally agitated.

"The most likely place she would have been taken," said Holmes, "is one of the cheaper hotels close by. Watson, could you and Godfrey start by calling at the Cardtref Hotel. It caters to sailors and stevedores and offers rates for the frugally inclined. I shall go in the other direction to the Bay Hotel."

"No!" protested Godfrey. "I can cover a hotel on my own, so can Doctor Watson. That would be a better play."

It was clear to me that Holmes did not want Godfrey running all over the village on his own advertising our quest to anyone and everyone. But Godfrey had a point.

"And what if," said Holmes, "you find her and run up against her captors? What if there are two of them? Or three? You would be of no use to your wife. Better there be two of you and, if necessary, the doctor is armed. So am I."

I grunted my affirmation, and Godfrey reluctantly nodded.

"Meet back here in twenty minutes," said Holmes as he turned toward the pier.

"Let's go then," said Godfrey, tugging at my arm. We set off smartly into the village, but it was immediately evident that I was a middle-aged gentleman unaccustomed to placing a tax upon my legs and Godfrey Staunton was a star three-quarter who could run like the wind for an hour without tiring. He was soon a block ahead of me, and I could see him turning right into the High Street and sprinting toward the Cardtref Hotel. By the time I reached the intersection, he was running back towards me.

"She's here, Doctor. She's here. Come, please, quickly."

"You saw her?"

"No. But I demanded that the front desk tell me if two men had checked in recently, along with a young woman they were forcing to accompany them."

"And they saw them? Forcing her?"

"Yes, well, no, not exactly. The clerk said that two low-life chaps had entered only a few minutes ago and they had a woman with them and she had one arm draped over each or their shoulders. He said she acted as if she were drunk. They must have drugged her."

"Ah, yes, chloroform, no doubt," I said as I accelerated my pace from a canter into a gallop for the remaining half block.

The clerk at the front desk gave a sly smile when I asked about the recent arrival of two men and a woman who appeared to be drunk.

"Tally ho, Sir," he said, smirking, "you can knock on room 214. Just upstairs on your left. I'm sure they will be glad to let the two of you in."

That, I thought, was highly unlikely. Ignoring their comment, Godfrey and I quickly climbed the stairs. I would have approached the door cautiously, listening with my ear against it before deciding how to go about surprising them, but Godfrey was in front of me. He raced to the door and pounded on it.

"Open up this minute," he shouted to the door. "Open up, or I'll break it down."

From behind the door came a raucous laugh and it soon opened. A young man who looked as if he were a member of Her Majesty's Royal Navy was standing there. He gazed at us and broke into a wide grin, grabbed Godfrey by his sleeve, and pulled him into the room.

"Oh, ho. Two toffs to join us. Come on in there, gents. She's wanting four pounds, so it will cost you a quid apiece." He then turned toward the woman, who looked buxom, slatternly, and somewhat inebriated. "That good by you, Duchess?"

"Ooww, no. A quid and six each. What do you think I am?"

It was now my turn to grab Godfrey's sleeve, and I did so, turned around, and departed back into the hall.

"Sorry, Doctor," sputtered Godfrey. "I didn't stop to think. So sorry. As soon as I heard that it was two men and that the woman seemed drunk, I assumed it must be the blackguards who took Millie. Terribly sorry."

"It is quite all right," I said. "Your brain is on fire and somewhat addled. Perfectly understandable. Now, let us go back and find Holmes and see if he has discovered anything."

Godfrey Staunton was crestfallen and began the trek back to our meeting place slowly. His pace quickened as his imagination returned to his wife.

"We have to find her. We have to find her before they do anything to hurt her. If anything happened to Millie, I could never forgive myself."

"You have nothing to forgive, young man. You have acted honorably and are up against a very determined gang of criminals."

"I could have just gone along with their demands. Then this would not have happened."

"And you would live the rest of your life with that shame," I said, and then I delivered the *coup de grace*. "Is that how Millie would have expected you to act? And what about your parents, or Danny, ... or Lilian?"

He stopped in his tracks and glared at me. Then a tear slowly emerged from his left eye, and he hung his head.

"You're right. They would all demand that I play up and play the game, especially Millie. She's like that. Where is Mr. Holmes?"

Chapter Twenty-Three

olmes was waiting for us on the pavement outside our hotel. I sensed that Godfrey was about to confess to his folly, and so I spoke first.

"Nothing to report. What about you?"

"Nothing in the hotels or pubs between here and the pier," said Holmes. "The local constable tells me he has spoken to every annoying busybody and nosy gossip in the town and no one reports seeing Millie being dragged or carried anywhere. He has posted four good men at the train station to watch and apprehend anyone leaving on the late trains who seems the least suspicious."

"She must be somewhere," said Godfrey. "She must be. Where else can we look?"

"If she is still in Fishguard," said Holmes, "it will be reported soon. This place is small enough that no one's actions can be hidden for long. I suspect, therefore, that whoever has taken her will try to spirit her out of here as quickly as possible."

"How? Where would they go? Back to Ireland?"

"The ferry," said Holmes, "is docked until tomorrow morning. So, she cannot have been taken back there. As the locals are watching the station, the only other possibility is by coach. The livery is a block away on Windyhall."

The words had scare left his lips before Godfrey was on the run again. Five minutes later, we caught up with him just as the door to the livery master's was opening, and a sleepy-looking fellow in his bedclothes was looking at Godfrey in a none-too-friendly way.

"Two blokes and a young lady, you say. Yes. As a matter of fact, I did rent a carriage and two horses about an hour ago now. Said they were off to Swansea. Said they would leave the horse and carriage at Driscoll's Livery. Paid in full, they did. Not tight-fisted. No, not a bit. In a right good hurry, they were. Had to be in Swansea in two shakes of a dead lamb's tail's what they said. A bit mysterious, I thought. You can see in the register that the lady signed and gave a false name."

"It is imperative that we find them," said Holmes. "Might you have another carriage and horses to let to us straight away?"

"That I can do. Come on into the stable. It's like pigs' feet at the moment, but you can have your pick of the mares."

"What name did she give," asked Holmes.

"Signed as Mrs. Victoria Regina," said the liveryman with a laugh. "Not very wise. Dumb as a calf if you ask me."

"Or," muttered Holmes, "as clever as a vixen, leaving an obvious clue for us to follow."

Holmes and I followed the fellow into his stable, but Godfrey hung back and instead of coming to look over the horses moved over to the desk just inside the stable door. He pulled out the register and opened it.

As Holmes and I and the liveryman were approaching the first stall, Godfrey called to us.

"Don't be bothering with the horse and carriage. It's not Millie."

We quickly came over to him.

"How can you be sure?" asked Holmes. "Writing the name of the queen strikes me as just the type of clue that Millie would leave us."

"It is, that's true," said Godfrey. "But this is not her writing."

"Are you certain?"

"We have exchanged hundreds of notes and letters. This is not her at all. Look at how sloppy it is. Millie has an obsession with neatness. She could not write so poorly if she tried. No, it's not her. I am sure of it."

Chapter Twenty-Four

As we walked back to our hotel in the darkness, none of us spoke. We could hear the sounds of laughter coming from the pubs and the occasional horn of a ship out on the Irish Sea. Upon entering the lobby, Holmes looked at Godfrey and me.

"It is highly unlikely that Mrs. Staunton is still here in Fishguard. It stands to reason that she has departed, most likely on one of the late trains. Whoever is behind this scheme is clever enough to have smuggled her onto a train without being spotted by the local constabulary. I suggest that we all, and particularly you, Godfrey, try to sleep as soundly as possible. We shall leave for London in the morning."

"You think that is where they will take her?" asked Godfrey.

"Where else?"

Holmes was about to expound on his conclusion when he was interrupted by a call from the chap behind the front desk.

"Mr. Holmes, Dr. Watson, Mr. Staunton. I have a letter here. It's addressed to the three of you."

Godfrey dashed across the lobby and retrieved the envelope and then rushed back to us, tearing it open as he came.

He read it and as he did so, his fists clenched and his knuckles turned white. I was sure he might rip the letter in two before he had finished reading it, but he took a deep breath to control his rage and handed the letter over to me. I held it so that Holmes and I could both see it. It was typed on a plain sheet of paper and ran:

Dearest Messrs Holmes, Watson, and Staunton:

By the time you read this note, Mrs. Staunton will be long gone from Fishguard, and you will have wasted your time searching for her.

She is being held as our prisoner because you, her stubborn husband, Godfrey Staunton, have refused to comply with our requests.

As a result, we have had no choice but to take such action as required to force you to do what we need to have done.

The next game in which you will play for England will take place on 11 March in London and will be against Scotland. That game must be won by Scotland and you, Mr. Staunton, must see that it happens. We require that you advise us of your agreement with our demands at your earliest convenience.

Until you do that, your wife will continue to be unavailable to you. She is currently being treated with respect and civility and is in no danger. However, with each passing week, the treatment she receives at our hands will deteriorate. If you respond within one week, no harm will come to her. If you refuse to respond then with each passing week, some type of injury will be visited upon her person. If you do not comply at all, then she will be returned to you following the 11 March match, but shall will no longer have been exclusively "yours."

We suggest that you govern yourself accordingly.

Further instructions will be delivered to you care of Lord Mount James's residence.

You have been warned.

There was no name or signature attached. Godfrey Staunton had begun to pace back and forth across the hotel lobby, and I detected his muttering of several vile and ungentlemanly curses as he did so. He stopped and glared at Holmes.

"Who sent it, Mr. Holmes? You are supposed to be such a brilliant detective. I've read about your so-called deductive powers. So, tell me. Who sent it? Who are these monsters?"

For a moment, it looked to me as if Holmes might respond with a sharp rebuke, but he refrained and merely gave a sympathetic nod to the distraught young man. Then he returned his gaze to the letter in his hand and scowled.

"This was typed on a recent model of a Royal typewriter with a fresh ribbon," he said.

"There must be several thousand fitting that description in London alone," I said as I watched him rub his thumb over the lines of print on the page. From his pocket, he pulled out his glass and examined the document more closely. His scowl deepened.

"It was not typed during the past hour."

"What?" I asked. "Earlier in the day? Before Millie disappeared?"

"No. The condition of the paper and the ink marks indicates that it was prepared several days ago. Perhaps as long as a week."

"But that's not possible. We only just arrived here on the ferry. The lady vanished no more than two hours ago. How could anyone have known?"

"Indeed, how could they."

Chapter Twenty-Five

I slept poorly that night. On several occasions, whilst I was awake, I could hear the slow footsteps of someone pacing back and forth in the hallway outside my door. Godfrey was not sleeping at all. At six o'clock in the morning, he knocked on my door.

"I've been down to the station. The first train back to London leaves in forty-five minutes. If we move quickly, we can catch it. Would you mind waking Mr. Holmes?"

He was already awake, and I had the distinct sense that he had not slept much either.

"You look as if you have spent the night pondering," I told him.

"I have," he said. "It was a foolish blunder on my part to have entrusted the reconnaissance of the trains to the local constable and his henchmen. You would think that they could have easily seen two men who were not from around here and who were assisting a young woman that seemed to be drunk or drugged. But the only explanation now is that they failed to do so and our quarry is long gone."

"Where would they go from here?"

"Until I have evidence otherwise, I am assuming London. There are two routes from here to there. One train travels north through Wales and over to Birmingham. The faster route is south by way of Cardiff and the Severn Tunnel."

"Which one leaves next?"

"The southern route."

The three of us took a quick breakfast and made haste to the station.

"We should," said Godfrey, "have posters put up at all the stations. I will get that done as soon as I get back to London."

"No, Godfrey, we should not. The last thing we want is for the English populace to bombard us with a hundred dubious sightings. I have already contacted Scotland Yard, and they will follow their standard procedure of sending confidential telegrams to all of the publicans, the hotel desks, the station masters and the livery operators along every route between here and London."

The young man did not respond immediately but stood and gazed at the waiting train.

"No doubt, you are right, Mr. Holmes. Nevertheless, I shall also do whatever I think is necessary. With all due respect, Sir, you were contracted to provide protection from whoever these people are, and now my wife has been kidnapped and threatened with unspeakable harm. Therefore, I am requesting that you continue your efforts as you see fit, but I shall do whatever I see fit to secure the safe return of my wife."

He climbed aboard the train but did not join us in the same cabin, nor did he speak to us when we changed trains at Cardiff Central and boarded the GWE to Paddington.

With the opening of the Severn Tunnel a few years ago, the time required to travel from Cardiff to London had been cut down to four hours. Several times during the journey, I stepped out of our cabin to walk the corridor and stretch my legs. Each time I did so, I encountered Godfrey Staunton pacing back and forth. I was tempted to tell him to try and relax but thought better of it. He seemed to be stretched tighter than a drum and was not about to be at ease.

Neither was Holmes. Although he remained in the cabin, he did not cease to either peruse the note we had received or to close his eyes and enter his private world of intense concentration. Only once did he unfurrow his brow and enjoy a cigarette.

"I cannot make sense of it, Watson," he said in between puffs. "There is no doubt that Millie is no longer in Fishguard. But she could not have been taken away on the ferry or by coach. The only possibility would have been the late train, but it was being watched."

"Could her abductors have paid off the fellows who were watching for them?" I asked.

"A remote possibility. The constable assured me that he selected only reliable chaps. Husbands and fathers every one of them; the type who pass their weekends not in the pubs but either in church or teaching the local lads how to play cricket."

Chapter Twenty-Six

It was late afternoon by the time we arrived back at Paddington. Godfrey Staunton, who had not spoken to us whilst on the train, was waiting for us to step down on to the platform.

"Mr. Holmes," he said, "I am confirming that I wish to continue to retain your services and expect you to report any progress to me. However, I will also be carrying out my own pursuit of whoever has taken Millie. I bid you good-day, Sir."

Without waiting for Holmes's response, he abruptly turned and promptly marched off down the platform toward the exit.

"Not a very sporting attitude," I said. "I would have expected better from a Blackheath Three-Quarter."

"My dear Watson," said Holmes. "I cannot fault the young man in the least. He requested my assistance in protecting him from criminals who wished to use him for their nefarious purposes. His best friend is now dead, and his dear wife abducted. His inevitable conclusion is that I have failed him, and

I have. Failing my clients is not a situation I greet with any degree of equanimity. Therefore, I now have three tasks facing me. I must rescue Millie Staunton, bring those who commissioned the murder of Danny O'Hearn to justice, and thoroughly discomfit those who are seeking ill-gotten gain by attempting to fix the outcome of these rugby matches. I shall be highly occupied with these tasks for the foreseeable future. Any assistance you can provide me with would be appreciated."

We hailed a cab at the station and drove to Baker Street. Holmes invited me to join him for supper and, as my wife was still abroad, I agreed.

Mrs. Hudson greeted us upon our arrival and, after kindly welcoming me back to 221B, turned to Holmes.

"A boy came by an hour ago and delivered a letter for you, Mr. Holmes. I have left it on your coffee table."

I climbed the stairs and entered the parlor ahead of Holmes and picked up the envelope and handed it to him. I noticed his name had been typed on the envelope, but it bore no postage mark of any kind. Even to my untrained eye, the texture and color of the paper and typeface looked similar to the note we had received in Fishguard. Holmes took the envelope and opened and read the letter. Without making any comment, he handed it to me. It ran:

```
Sherlock Holmes:
    You are strongly advised to cease and
desist in your attempt to interfere in our
engagement with Mr. and Mrs. Staunton. Your
refusal to abide by this advice will result
in severe consequences to both of them. It is
imperative that you govern yourself
accordingly.
```

It was not signed.

I handed it back to Holmes, who had taken his glass from his suit pocket, and he spent the next several minutes examining it. He concluded his inspection by laying the note on the coffee table and running his thumb over the typed message. Then he looked at me with a smug smile on his face.

"It is always useful when my adversary freely gives me clues that assist in my pursuit of a case."

"What are you talking about?"

"Unlike the note we received in Fishguard, this one has been typed within the past hour or two. You notice how the ink smudges just a little when I rubbed my thumb over it. The previous note did not. There remains a significant indentation in the paper from having been struck by the typewriter. Again, that was not the case last evening. And, it was delivered by a boy and not by the postman."

"And what does all that prove?"

"That whoever is behind this odious scheme is directing it from London and is in the city now. We can also be sure that he has the means to know our every move. That narrows the radius of my search considerably."

"Fat lot of good that does. You cannot put Mr. and Mrs. Staunton at risk by continuing this case, can you?"

"Of course, I can. I shall merely have to do so in a clandestine manner whilst appearing not to."

I assume that was what he did, as I heard nothing from him for the next two weeks. On the Saturday, the 18th of February, the next match in the championship series was played in Edinburgh between Scotland and Ireland. The Scots had been favored to win, but to the surprise of the punters, Ireland prevailed, touching down three tries against a single penalty score by Scotland.

I was reading the account of the match in the afternoon paper the following day and wondering if the same syndicate of criminals had managed to have that game fixed. In the middle of my pondering, a knock came to my door. A boy handed me a note.

It was from Holmes, with an urgent request that I come at once to 221B, and bring my medical bag with me.

"He's lying down on the bed in your old room," said Holmes as I arrived in the front room.

"Who is?"

"Godfrey."

"What's wrong with him?"

"You are the doctor, not me. Please check him over and let me know if we need to take him to hospital."

Chapter Twenty-Seven

I entered my old bedroom and immediately caught my breath. Lying supine on the bed was our young man. Not only was he dressed in a working man's clothes, but his face was swollen, bruised, and bloodied.

"Good heavens," I exclaimed. "What in the world happened to him?"

"I do not know," said Holmes. "A half-hour ago, someone rang the bell on Baker Street, and a moment later, Mrs. Hudson came running up the stairs to fetch me. Godfrey was lying on the pavement in front of the door. He was conscious but utterly dazed. The two of us managed to haul him up the stairs and put him in the bed, but then he lost consciousness."

I carefully loosened his collar and shirt buttons, opened his shirt, and examined his torso. As far as I could tell, there were no broken bones or damage to his internal organs. I broke open a small vial of smelling salts and held it to his nostrils. The desired effect was achieved, and he opened his eyes.

"Godfrey," I said loudly and clearly, "can you hear me?"

He nodded.

"Tell me where you are injured."

He nodded again, and I gently applied pressure to various parts of his body. Each time I did, he shook his head. After concluding my quick once-over, I looked up at Holmes.

"Nothing that won't get better soon enough. Just a thorough beating, I'd say."

I then spoke to Godfrey, who appeared to have regained the use of his faculties.

"What happened to you?"

"You should see the other chaps. Hardly laid a glove on me." He forced a smile, and both Holmes and I chuckled.

I opened my doctor's bag and took out my small bottle of rubbing alcohol and some gauze.

"This is going to hurt," I said and began to daub the abrasions and cuts on his face. Several times his eyes involuntarily winced, but he said nothing.

"Try sitting up," I said when I had finished cleaning the wounds on his face.

In obvious pain and with his teeth clenched, he slowly raised his torso and forced his legs to turn toward me until he was sitting on the edge of the bed.

"Just help me get to my feet," he said, "and I will be all right."

I was not at all sure of that, but put one of his arms around my neck and assisted him to his feet.

"Thanks, Doc. I can make it into the parlor."

Using the dresser and the door frame for balance and support, he staggered out of the bedroom and sat down in the closest chair.

"Sorry," he said, "to have been a bother to the two of you."

"You are still my client," said Holmes. "So, there can be no talk of bothering, but an explanation would be in order."

I had gone over to the hearth and poured a generous glass of brandy for Godfrey. When I offered it to him, he declined.

"Thanks, Doc. But I'm not touching any type of alcohol until I find Millie. I cannot afford to have my mind dulled."

"Given your present condition," said Holmes, "one would tend to think that at some point during the past few hours, your mind was far from being sharp."

"Yes, well, I suppose so. I got a bit carried away I guess you could say."

"Apparently so. Your explanation, please, Godfrey," said Holmes.

"Right, well, I had to start somewhere in my search to find my wife. So, I went to the London Bridge station where you had told me that those two thugs had followed us, and asked around for the local constable, the one who was on duty when you brought those two fellows in. The shopkeepers and porters directed me to the police officer, and he told me that the two fellows who had been following us and who you disarmed and brought in were named Eddie Biddle and Willie Moffat. He also said that both had been released by Scotland Yard and could often be found lollygagging around at *The Hoop and Grapes* pub in Aldgate."

I looked at him in disbelief. "And *you* went *there*? What were you thinking?"

"Right, well, I suppose some might say I wasn't thinking very well at all, but I have been going out of my mind. And I reasoned that those two must know something. So, I went over to Aldgate and began to ask for them."

"Dressed as a gentleman?" I asked.

"Oh no, I might have been acting impulsively, but I was not altogether stupid. I did my best to look like a working man and casually dropped in and ordered an ale. Then I started to ask around. You know, talk with the chap beside me about rugby—that's always a good way to get a fellow to start—and then move on. Well after chatting with several fellows over the course of the evening, I asked one of them about Biddle and Moffat, and I was told that they usually came in in the early afternoon seeing as they had business to conduct in the evenings."

"And today," said Holmes, "you returned there and found them."

"Right. That's what I did. All I could think about was that they had to know something about who was behind trying to bribe me and then taken Millie and I was going to find out. I had to. So, I put on these clothes again and combed my hair in a different way and went back to the pub, thinking that they would not recognize me."

"Forgetting, I assume," said Holmes, "that the two of them had spent over a week watching your every move whilst you were in the south of France."

"Yes, well, I said I was thinking; I did not say I was thinking brilliantly."

"Go on."

"As soon as I entered the pub, I started chatting with a young lad and slipped him a shilling and asked if he could identify Biddle and Moffat for me and he points to a table where the two of them are sitting having their ale. So, I got myself a glass as well from the bar walked over there and asked politely if they would mind if I joined them."

"And," said Holmes, "they knew who you were instantly."

"Yes, I suppose you could say that. And they were more than a little hostile. Said that because of some obnoxious twit at the station, they lost a fine piece of work in getting paid just to follow Millie and me and send in their reports. Well then, we had a few words between us. That was all."

"The condition of your face," said Holmes, "would indicate that your exchange went well beyond a few words. Kindly complete your explanation."

"Right, well, then they started to make some rather rude remarks and vulgar jokes about their observation of Millie and me engaging in the sort of activities that you would expect of a young couple on their honeymoon."

"Rude and vulgar does not account for your face. Keep going."

"Well, one of them, Biddle, I think it was, made a highly unacceptable comment about Millie based on what he had observed whilst acting as a Peeping Tom. That was the last straw as far as I was concerned. I could not care if they insulted me, but a husband cannot sit idly by whilst a bloke insults your wife. So, I threw my ale in his face. And that was when the fisticuffs began."

"Which you obviously lost," said Holmes.

"No. Not at first. I have learned the manly art of self-defense and must say that I am quite an excellent pugilist. Of course, I abide by the Marquess of Queensbury rules."

"Which your adversaries did not."

"Correct. Not at all. I landed some excellent punches on both of them even if it was a fight of two against one. But then they summoned the help of some of their friends in the pub, and several of them grabbed onto my arms and pinned them behind my back so that I could not block their punches. That put me at a distinct disadvantage, but I am also quite good at delivering dropkicks, and I placed one right between the uprights of Moffat's legs. That enraged them, and they began to pummel my face and body until I was losing my consciousness. I do recall that they said some nasty things about you as well, Mr. Holmes. Then they must have thrown me out onto the pavement, stuffed me inside a cab, and told the cabbie to deliver me to your address."

"And how did they know to send you here?"

For several seconds, Godfrey Staunton looked befuddled and said nothing.

"I have no idea," he finally said. "But someone seems to know about every step I'm taking."

"To whom have you spoken about what happened to Millie?"

"No one. Well, almost no one. I told the other lads on the Blackheath team. They're all my friends, and I trust them. I met again with that inspector at Scotland Yard and brought him up to date. Uncle Jimmy, of course."

"You spoke to Inspector Lestrade?"

"Yes. That was his name. Not the friendliest chap I ever met."

"What did he tell you?"

"He said that I was a damn fool to be trying to solve things myself and that I should leave it to Scotland Yard and Sherlock

Holmes. And that if I were to meet with you to remind you that your client in this case is Scotland Yard and not me."

"Not surprising. However, I consider both you and your wife as well as Scotland Yard to be my clients in this matter. And since you have paid me a visit, voluntarily or not, I shall bring you up to date on what I have been able to accomplish."

He walked over to his desk and retrieved a file.

"Since our last conversation, I have also been making inquiries concerning whoever might be behind this gambling conspiracy. My entire network of discreet contacts has been alerted, and it appears that I may have provoked a response. Please read this."

He handed Godfrey a page from the file. Godfrey read it and handed it on to me. It ran:

Mr. Sherlock Holmes:

You first crossed our path on the 31st of December when you attended the wedding. The following day, you incommoded us by agreeing to use your arrogant and limited talents to assist Scotland Yard in their investigation. On the 7th of January, you seriously inconvenienced our negotiations with Mr. Godfrey Staunton. You have manipulated him with the result that he has turned down our reasonable offers. Your presence in Dublin and Fishguard hampered our plans and made it necessary for us to remove Mrs. Staunton from her husband so that he will be forced to come to his senses and cooperate with us. Your continual persecution of us must end else unfortunate and irreparable harm shall come to Mrs. Staunton. You must drop it, Mr. Holmes. You really must, you know.

The final hurdle in our enterprise is the match between England and Scotland on 11

March. England must lose that match. Godfrey Staunton must make sure of that.

Your response and that of Mr. Staunton confirming agreement with our demands may be posted in the Agony Column of The Telegraph.

The Scrum Team

Chapter Twenty-Eight

"**I** recognize this message," I said. "It is very similar to the conversation you had with Professor Moriarty eight years ago. The remains of his evil network must be behind it."

Holmes sighed and looked at me with familiar condescension. "Please, Watson. I think not. It is much more likely that whoever is making these threats has read your account of that conversation and is using it to mock me."

"Oh, yes, I suppose that is possible. Very well, at least we cannot fault them for their reading habits."

"Unless they stole their copy of the Strand rather than paying for it."

"That would be unscrupulous, do you not agree, Holmes? I must say—,"

"Gentlemen!" interrupted Godfrey. "Please. These people are threatening my wife. This is not the time to be quibbling over magazine sales. I have to respond to this. Now."

"Not exactly," said Holmes. "I already have. Here is a copy of the note I posted in the newspaper."

He handed a second sheet from the file to Godfrey who read it with his hands trembling in rage. He then forcefully placed it in my hands. It ran:

```
Scrum team: Prior to any demands being met,
proof is required of good health and
condition of your asset by means of live
telephone conversation. Subsequent
cooperation will then be possible.
```

"Do you," Godfrey asked, "think that any harm has come to Millie?"

"Highly unlikely."

"Then why did you ask? Why are you demanding proof if you don't think anything has happened to her?"

"Every communication between our side and theirs provides an opportunity to gain data on their position and tactics. The more often we are in contact with them, the more they expose their strategy and identity. I assume that your English team sends spies to observe the Scots, Irish, and Welsh during their practices, do you not?"

"Well, of course, we do. You always have to anticipate your opponent's next play."

"Precisely."

"Well then, Mr. Holmes, what's happened?"

"This piece of correspondence arrived at my door yesterday." He handed Godfrey the third sheet of paper from the file. It ran:

```
Sherlock Holmes: Will call you in due course
prior to the game against Scotland. Call will
be placed to the Mount James residence on
```

WRKGDN 1027. Mrs. Staunton will be on line.
No further communication until then.

"But that's still weeks away," said Godfrey. "We cannot just sit around until then."

"Quite correct, young man," said Holmes. "Between now and then, I shall be acquiring data and expertise in the hidden world of betting on sporting events. Our adversaries inhabit that sphere, and I expect I shall be able to limit the circle of their possible identities if not reach a conclusion as to who they are."

"And what am I to do?"

"Attend your team practices and do everything you can to make sure that your chances of winning the championship are vastly improved from what they are now."

"That's not possible. I cannot just sit idly by when Millie is held captive."

"You can, and you must. Belligerent actions such as you have been engaging in will only increase the possibility of harm being brought upon Millie. Now, as you appear to have recovered adequately from the beating you were given, kindly be on your way and over to the Blackheath sporting grounds. Your practice begins in an hour from now. Good day, Sir."

Holmes stood up and retreated into the bedroom, leaving Godfrey alone with me in the parlor.

Godfrey said nothing for some time and silently looked at the door through which Holmes had departed. Then he turned to me.

"That man is impossible," he said. "Does he have no feelings whatsoever?"

I was tempted to laugh and say that I understood his reaction to Holmes all too well. A look at Godfrey's face, bruised and battered, forced me to give a serious reply.

"Sherlock Holmes does have feelings, I assure you. They are many and deep, but he forces them into submission when engaged upon a case."

"But Doctor, surely you understand. You are a sportsman, and you are a married man. You know I cannot just sit idly by. I am going mad."

"Then permit me to offer some advice," I said.

"Please, do. I am at my wit's end."

"Hard work is a universal mask for pain and anxiety, especially if it is constant and physically demanding. You need to do what you were told and attend every practice of your team. You cannot think about your wife whilst you are tackling a charging hooker."

"I'll do that. Sure. But practices only last the morning. What do I do for an afternoon and evening? I cannot sleep sixteen hours. It's not possible."

His eyes spoke of his desperation whilst his knuckles had whitened, and every sinew and muscle of his exposed athletic torso had become taut. I weighed my words carefully.

"In your studies at Cambridge," I asked him, "did you read Maximianus?"

"What? Who?"

"Maximianus. The poet."

"You mean the one they call the last poet of Rome? He wrote a few elegies. Yes, I had to read him. Why?"

"In his Second Elegy, he offers the advice I would give you, which, by the by, happens to be one of the principles by which Mr. Holmes governs his behavior."

"Right. So, what is it?"

"*Plus ratio quam vis.* And it means?"

He shrugged his powerful shoulders. "Something like *more reason than force.* Yes, I remember it now. *Reason over force.* That's it. Right?"

"Exactly. Now then, Godfrey, you have been given an inordinate amount of force in your body and your energy. But you have also the exceptional good fortune of being born with an excellent brain. My advice to you is that you use such time as you have when not on the practice pitch or getting sufficient hours of sleep, to think. Use your mind the way Mr. Holmes does and *think.* If you are going to be staying with your uncle, then you are within a few blocks of Kensington Gardens and Hyde Park. Go to one of the benches there and sit and think. Force yourself to review every aspect of knowledge you have as to what has taken place so far and attempt to discern the connections behind them. That is what Sherlock Holmes does. That is what you must do. Can you do that?"

He shrugged again and offered a sheepish smile. "I suppose I could."

"Not *could,* Godfrey. *Must.*"

Chapter Twenty-Nine

He departed, looking somewhat befuddled. I could only hope and pray that what I had said might keep him occupied and out of Aldgate until Holmes, using his own magnificent brain, deduced a solution to this case. A solution did not appear.

A few days later, at the end of my working day, I met up with Holmes in his lair on Baker Street, worried that I might be interrupting his investigation but hoping that he would be glad of my visit. He was sitting in silence and puffing on his pipe.

"Ah, Watson," he said. "Do come in. How good of you to drop by."

"I am not disturbing, you, I trust," I said.

"Not at all; not at all. You have always been terribly useful to me. Your insights into a case are inevitably simple-minded, but in their hopeless originality, they invariably lead me into greater use of my imagination. I cannot thank you enough."

That was not my preferred way to be welcomed but nonetheless I agreed to join him for a glass of sherry and to listen to his account of what he had been doing.

"I have been turning over stones and discovering the hideous creatures and activities lying beneath them."

"What stones? What creatures?"

"Sporting events, of course. The bigger the event in the press, the more corruption associated with it."

"Come now, Holmes. You are exaggerating."

He chuckled. "A skill I learned from you, my dear friend. No doubt there are countless games played on football, rugby, and cricket pitches throughout Great Britain that are as honest as the day is long. But the money that flows back and forth on the major games and tournaments is beyond belief."

"Is that all you have been doing? Investigating betting on matches?"

"Of course not. I have been poking my nose into every aspect of the lives, private and public, of every player in this game. The Lords of Rugby union, the coaches, the players, the leading punters ...up to and including our distressed newlywed couple and their families."

"And what have you found?"

He did not immediately reply but re-lit his pipe and puffed several times.

"A veritable deluge of data, most of which is irrelevant and unspeakably boring. The problem is sorting the wheat from the chaff."

"Anything more on that Baron Worthington fellow? You did not exactly take a shine to him."

"He has his fingers in many pots, but so far nothing I could find that is beyond the edges of the law."

"So, he is honest after all?"

"Either that or smarter than I first gave him credit for."

"What about the phone call you demanded?"

"Ask me about that later."

My questions appeared to send him back into his shell, and I departed back to my home. When I arrived, Godfrey Staunton was waiting for me.

My wife had provided him with a cup of tea and had enjoined him to sit and relax until I arrived. But it had been to no avail. He was pacing back and forth through our parlor and dining room.

"Merciful heavens, Godfrey. What's happened?" I asked.

"I have had a most disturbing afternoon. Threatening, when I came to think about it. I had to come and talk to you."

"I am listening. But I cannot do so properly if you continue to pace. Now sit down, collect your thoughts, and tell me what happened."

"I followed your advice. I have been playing hard every morning at practice over beyond Greenwich. I run there every morning from Uncle Jimmy's house."

"You run? Why, that's at least ten miles."

"Almost eleven. I start whilst it is dark and get there by half-past nine in time for the practice. And then I run home. You were right. Doing that has kept my mind clear of all the horrors that come raging in."

"And," I said, "put you into leaner form than I have ever seen in a Three-Quarter."

"Well, thank you, Doctor. It has not hurt. I'm better on the pitch than ever. But it is not the mornings that became a problem. It was the afternoons. Or, I should say, this afternoon."

"Yes."

"I did what you said. I put on warm clothes and took myself over to the Gardens. There's a bench that lets me look out over the Long Water. It is quite conducive for reflection and contemplation."

"I'm sure it is. And something happened there this afternoon?"

"Right. I was sitting there, lost in thought, and this young woman walked up to the bench. She was pushing a pram, and as she was not dressed as a maid or looking like a nanny, I assumed that she must be the mother of the infant in the pram."

Chapter Thirty

"There are," I said, "many such young mothers who enjoy taking their babies for such an outing. Good for both mother and child. Nothing unusual about that but apparently this encounter was highly unusual. Go on."

"Right. It was a pleasant, sunny afternoon and she stopped by the bench and asked, very nicely, if I minded if she sat down as well. Of course, a gentleman cannot say no to such a request, so I said 'by all means,' and she did so."

"And then," said I, "she began to chat with you."

"Right. That's what she did. At first, it was just about what a fine afternoon it was. And then we started talking about babies and children. I was careful, of course, not to say anything about my current travails, but I acknowledged that my wife was expecting our first child and I was eager to learn about being a responsible and loving father. She was delighted with my curiosity and became quite chatty."

I sensed he was withholding some significant details and, pretending in my mind to be my astute friend, the detective, I began my quest for more data.

"What was she wearing? Describe this woman to me."

"Wearing? Well, she had on a bright red wool coat with a fur collar and a scarf from Burberry's. It was warm, as I said, and she had loosened her scarf and opened her coat. Her neck was exposed, as was her upper chest. I assumed that she must be nursing her baby and found sweaters with high necks to be impractical, but I truly know nothing about such matters."

"I also asked what she looked like."

"You did? Well, yes, I suppose that is part of describing someone."

Here he hesitated, as if reciting his words to himself before uttering them.

"I suppose you could say that she was exceptionally attractive. Yes, very attractive. One of the most stunningly beautiful women in all of London, if you must know. She had a trace of an accent from somewhere in Europe, but I could not place it."

"And how did you respond to her?"

"Oh, I was a courteous gentleman. I always am."

"Godfrey, how did you respond to her *as a man?*"

He visibly blushed and looked at the floor.

"That is part of the reason I had to come and talk to you. The longer I looked at her, the more I felt ... well, you must know ... I suppose you could say I felt a fire in my loins."

I nodded and uttered a doctorly response. "Um-hmm, yes, go on. And did she by any chance twist her head away briefly, fully exposing her neck?"

"She did."

"Um-hmm, and did she stroke her neck lightly with her hand, stopping and resting her fingers just below her throat."

"That's exactly what she did. How did you know? It was the same as Millie does when she is feeling … how shall I say … you know … *amorous*."

"I do know. And, by any chance, did this woman from time to time look away from you as if lost in thought and slide her tongue lightly over her upper lip quite unconsciously?"

"Yes! That *is* what she did. Several times."

I was on ground that was familiar to me as a man now well into his fifth decade on this good earth but *terra incognito* to the young adult members of the male species.

"And, might she, by chance, have begun to speak in a low but confidential manner about the joys of being a young mother?"

Godfrey was staring at me in disbelief.

"Umm … yes … we did chat about that."

"And your reaction? In your mind? And in your loins?"

He shook his head and again looked down at the floor.

"I am ashamed to admit it, but I have never felt so physically attracted to any woman before in my life. Not even to Millie. In my mind, all I could think about was taking this woman and ravishing her. I'm sorry. It is humiliating to admit it. But that is what I felt and thought."

"You are not the first, and you will not be the last, Godfrey. It has happened to all of us. Now, go on with your story. Did she ask if you were hungry?"

"Good lord, Doctor. Yes. how could you have possibly known that?"

"Man's two appetites are closely linked. Go on. How did you answer."

"Truthfully. All of a sudden, I felt famished and said so."

"Keep going."

"She said that she lived only a few minutes away, on Bayswater, and said that her cook had prepared some excellent meat pies for her and her husband and that they were just out of the oven and would I like to come and have one. She seemed so honest that I agreed. I confess, I felt safer once I was standing and walking. My body's response to her was not so noticeable once I was on my feet."

"And then what happened?"

"Her home was where she said it was. We arrived there in less than five minutes and went inside."

"Did she knock?" I asked.

"Umm...no. Now that you ask. I suppose I should have noticed that."

"Your mind was addled. Go on."

"Once inside, she tossed her coat on the chesterfield and quickly pushed the pram down the hall to what I assume was the nursery and vanished into the back of the house for about two minutes. When she returned to me, she was bearing a tray of meat pies and set them down on the coffee table in the parlor."

"Bending over toward you as she did?" I said.

"Yes ... and I do not have to admit where I was looking, do I? Then she stood up, minus the tray and I saw that she was wearing a tight-fitting dress that was surprisingly low-cut. She could have stunned any audience in the West End. I didn't know what to say, so I asked about her cook and the meat pies. She bent over again and lifted one of the pies and held it out to me.

The smell of it was wonderful, and I was about to take a bite when I came to my senses."

"Did you now?"

"I did. I realized that I was alone inside a private home without a single servant present and had utterly compromised myself and my reputation. I muttered some sort of thanks and turned and fled out the door."

"With the meat pie in hand, I hope."

"Uh, yes, well, I was starving after all."

Chapter Thirty-One

I laughed and gave him a hardy slap on the back.

"Well done, young Godfrey Staunton. Well done."

"Doctor, I did not behave well at all. Had I stayed … I refuse to imagine what would have happened next."

"Indeed? Then let me tell you. You would have spent the afternoon violating your marriage vows and not only borne the shame of your actions for the rest of your life; you would have exposed yourself to blackmail of a kind that you could not have resisted."

"You believe she was part of the network that has been after me. She seemed so completely honest, so wonderfully friendly.?"

"Answer this question. In the entire time, you were together, how many times did the baby in the pram cry? Or even make a sound?"

It was as if I had hit his head with a hammer. He slowly shook his head.

"Not once."

"Dolls have a way of doing that."

"I was being entrapped."

"Without question. You don't have to be Sherlock Holmes to see that."

"I almost gave in."

"But you did not. Your honor prevailed. Well done."

"What do I do now?"

"I assume you have eaten the meat pie."

"I couldn't let it get cold."

"I agree. Now then, write down the address you were taken to on Bayswater. Holmes will want to see it. And then go back to your home and take a cold bath. Have some supper and spend the evening reading a boring book. Anything by Lord Bulwer-Lytton would be just fine."

He departed, and I joined my wife for supper, regaling her with my account of Godfrey's afternoon adventure. As soon as we had finished dessert, she smiled at me and stroked her neck, landing her fingertips on her Suprasternal Notch.

On 18 February Scotland's International Team played Ireland's in Edinburgh. Scotland had been favored even though they had yet to play a game in the tournament. Billy Donaldson, their Three-Quarter on the left was one of the fastest runners in the Union. And their pack, red-bearded monsters every one of them, were as fearsome as William Wallace was reputed to have been. But the stalwart Irish team held them to one three-pointer penalty. Against that feeble effort, Eddie Campbell, Colin Reid, and Jim Sealy all fought their way into touch for tries, although none were converted. The final score was three for Scotland and nine for Ireland.

The odds on the championship then changed. Back before the first match, the bookmakers were offering thirty to one against Ireland winning the Triple Crown. Those odds had now fallen to three to one. Unless England utterly trounced Scotland on 11 March, Ireland only had to beat Wales to win the Crown.

Two days after the game in Scotland, Godfrey came around to my house. He was looking superbly healthy and fit, and his much-abused face had recovered and was once again handsome and shining. He had a letter in his hand that he immediately thrust into mine.

"What do you say, Doctor. Is this chap on the level? Or is he just another muck snipe from the press?"

The letter bore the embossed name of *The Evening Star* and had been sent to Godfrey by one of their reporters, Walter Durnan. It ran:

Dear Mr. Staunton:

By this letter, I am requesting the honor of conducting an interview with you on the Home Nations Championship and specifically on your opinion, as an expert in the game and one of its finest players, on the recent game in Edinburgh.

The readers of *The Evening Star* are, to a man, enthusiastic supporters of Rugby Union and many are dedicated fans of you and your fellow players on Blackneath. Whilst I am one of your most loyal fans, I would not for a second, claim anywhere near your depth of knowledge and insight into the game. That is why we need you to give us your wisdom, earned over the past three seasons playing in Rugby Union.

The Evening Star, as you know, is one of London's leading newspapers with a daily readership of well over one hundred thousand.

Need I bring to your attention the publicity that your chatting with us would add to your fame and career. After appearing in our pages, you would be assured of loud and riotous cheers every time you stepped onto the pitch for any team in Greater London.

To be totally candid, I will be forthcoming and inform you that my story will make reference to the great adversity that you have overcome and by doing so it will present you as a strong moral example to the boys of our nation who are following in your footsteps.

Might I suggest meeting this Thursday at noon in the Churchill Arms on Kensington Church Street?

I await your reply. I remain,

Yours truly (and loyal fan)

Walter Durnan

"He's flattering you," I said.

"They all do that when they want an exclusive," said Godfrey. "But is he on the up and up?"

"You have some doubts else you would not be here. What are they?"

Godfrey pursed his lips and forced a long breath out through his nose.

"I don't want anything about Millie to appear in the press."

"He says nothing about her. His allusion appears to be to your loss of Lillian."

"Oh, yes, I know. But look; he did not even spell the name of my team properly."

"Possibly a typographical error."

"Possibly, but suspicious all the same. And I have not been playing three seasons for Blackheath, only two."

"Then he is not one of your true fans," I said. "But that does not mean that he has malicious intent. He just wants to score another byline and rise above his peers in the Press. I believe they all do that as well."

"Yes, yes. I know. But how did he know to suggest meeting in Kensington? A bit too convenient, isn't it? He knows where I am living."

"He knows where Lord Mount James lives."

"Maybe. But I smell a rat. I may be wrong. It could be a big help to my career. I cannot be paid for my play now, but there's money to be had by writing a book or giving lectures. Fame does not hurt on that score. It would help our bank account until I turn twenty-five. I could even afford to pay Mr. Holmes to keep on working on our case until all the munz-watchers who had a finger in doing this to us were in prison. What do you think, Doc?"

I thought.

"Here's my suggestion. Agree to meet with him. But arrive there early and sit in a booth. Sherlock Holmes and I will sit in the booth behind you so we can hear every word. Make no promises or agreements to whatever he says before you discuss it with Holmes and me afterward. If you are not happy with where he goes, you can send him off a note straight away."

"And say what?"

"Holmes's favorite way of dealing with reporters: you say to them, 'I immensely enjoyed speaking with you and assure you that seventy-five percent of what I said to you of God's truth. The remaining twenty-five percent is pure fiction. Have a good day, Sir.'"

"Is that really what Mr. Holmes does?"

"Not all the time; only when necessary. He is a firm believer in playing the Press to his advantage."

Chapter Thirty-Two

Holmes liked my strategy and enthusiastically agreed to join me as an eavesdropper to Godfrey's interview. At his insistence, we disguised ourselves. He donned his familiar dog collar and straggly wig and became an Anglican cleric. I pasted on a false mustache and sideburns and put a workingman's cap on my head and looked entirely out-of-place in Kensington. Holmes, however, was confident that we would not be recognized and that as long as we ordered a decently priced ale or glass of spirits, the pub would happily serve us.

We were in our place by half-past eleven and Godfrey arrived a few minutes later and sat in the booth immediately behind ours. As Holmes's suggestion, he ordered his lunch shortly after arriving so that it would be in front of him before the reporter came, eliminating the likelihood that Mr. Durnan would suggest moving to another table.

The plan worked, at least in that Durnan arrived at five past noon and made his way over to Godfrey's table and sat down. Both Holmes and I cast glances at him as he passed our table. I had met many chaps from Fleet Street over the years but did not recognize this fellow. From the look on Holmes's face, neither did he.

Walter Durnan was of average height and girth and dressed in a manner that could be described as stylish but highly affordable. I would have put his age somewhere between mine and Godfrey's and noted that he might have done a better job of shaving before leaving his home in the morning. He was holding a lit cigarette in his one hand and his notepad in the other.

"Halloa Mr. Staunton," he said as he sat down across from Godfrey. "Awfully good of you to meet me on such short notice. I can imagine that your life must be frightfully busy, and I do want you to know how much I appreciate and respect your time."

I could not see Godfrey's physical response, but his stiff upper-class reply was of one to the manor born.

"Very well. I was rather famished after this morning's practice, so I ordered my lunch immediately I arrived here. If you go up to the bar, they will take your order."

"Hey-ho, I will do that."

His accent identified him as a Mancunian but with minor refinement such as is acquired in a university that is considered second rank. He walked up to the bar and placed his order. In doing so, he allowed Holmes and me to get another look at him. He kept looking at his notepad as he strode past us, and I could see his lips moving as if he was rehearsing his lines.

"A jolly fine day for still being February, wouldn't you say, Mr. Staunton?"

"It is normal for this time of year, yes."

"Normal? Why on my way here, I passed at least a half dozen lovely bits of jam all strolling *sans* their winter coats. The spring does bring out the best in our English girls, don't you agree?"

"I had not noticed."

"No? Ah, such a shame. But now that you are a married man, you cannot allow your eye to wander. Am I right, Mr. Staunton, heh-heh?"

"The ring on your finger says that you are also married," said Godfrey.

"Oh, yes, well, of course, just because a man is married it does not mean he has lost his roving eye, now does it, heh-heh?"

"It does for me."

"Right, well, that was not what I wanted to speak to you about anyway."

"Good."

"We're here to talk about Rugby, aren't we. What did you think about the game on Saturday? Never expected that the Irish would trounce the Scots like they did, did you?"

"I would hardly call a score of six to three a trouncing."

"No? Well, heh-heh, right you are. Jolly good. What about the game coming up? Another match up in Edinburgh, right? This Saturday, right? Who are you putting your money on to win that one? The Welsh? The Scots?"

"Mr. Durnan, I have the impression that you are not a reporter who writes about rugby, are you?"

There was a pause before Durnan answered.

"How very astute of you, Mr. Staunton. You are quite correct. I am here today as a representative of the owners and senior editors of *The Evening Star*. Our interest is in selling newspapers, and to do so, we have to have stories that will capture the hearts and minds of the average reader. Therefore, we are always on the lookout for a story that we describe as *gripping*. And your story, Mr. Staunton, what with the tragedy of losing your first wife, overcoming your grief through the grand Etonian quality of *perseverance,* and rising again to the top of your sport, is just the type that both the punters of the nation and their wives cannot get enough of. We shall start the series of stories next weekend and shall continue it right through until the next rugby season."

"Mr. Durnan, I see nothing in it for me other than hours having to answer your questions."

"My dear chap, there is fame and fortune. You will soon have an income of your own beyond anything you could ever hope to achieve and well before your age advances to the day you can claim your inheritance."

"I will have you know, Sir, that there is no money in rugby. At least there is none in Rugby Union. It is strictly a sport played by amateur gentlemen. I shall never accept a farthing for my efforts on the pitch."

"Oh, my dear young man. Of course, you cannot be paid for your play. But after we make you the great hero who triumphed over adversity, the captains of industry and commerce will be pounding at your door, all begging you to endorse their products. The chaps at Players Tobacco will pay a fortune for a photo of you puffing on one of their cigarettes. Those Irish brewmasters who claim their dark beer is good for you are desperate to expand their sales in England. Who would be a better spokesman for their brand? And that is only the beginning. A lecture tour would follow. Towns and cities all over the British Isles would invite you to come and speak, and the people would gladly pay dearly for a ticket to listen to your inspiring story. You would not only be rich and famous; you would be admired, adored. Your name would be on the lips of every schoolboy in the land, and they would look up to you. It is a brilliant opportunity. What do you say, young man?"

Now Godfrey was quiet for a minute. His voice when he responded sounded puzzled.

"But how would that work? Yes, my wife died, and it was terribly sad and, with the help of my dear friends and my new wife, I have struggled to overcome my misfortune. All true, but that is in the past. My suffering on that account is over."

"Ah, but you will continue to meet future disappointments and disasters and continue to show your pluck and carry on through adversity and failure and again and again snatch success from the jaws of defeat."

"What future disappointments and disasters? What do you know of my present situation that would lead you to expect that a disaster was in my near future?"

Holmes and I caught each other's eye, and we nodded at each other. Godfrey was showing his mettle and was coolly drawing this Fleet Street agent out into the light. Good on him. If this so-called reporter knew anything about Millie, he might be led to give it away.

His response was not what we expected. "Why the All Nations Championship, of course. You and your team were the favorites to win and are facing a crushing defeat. It is a terrible disappointment to you, but you will again recover have a grand come-back in the summer and fall with Blackneath."

"Black*heath.*"

"Oh, yes, yes, of course. That is just the name we in the Press call it. Anything to the east of Whitechapel and especially on the south shore is considered *beneath* the rest of the city. Just our little joke amongst ourselves."

"I fail to see the humor. And it is not at all a foregone conclusion that England is going to lose."

Durnan laughed. "Oh, ho, come come now. Surely after your first two games, you do not expect to end up on top? That is just not possible."

"I beg your pardon, Mr. Durnan, but it *is* possible. Should we have a high scoring win against the Scots and Ireland lose to Wales with low points, then our victory could still happen."

"I regret to inform you, Mr. Staunton, that such an outcome, even if highly improbable, must not be allowed to happen. No, no. It would ruin our entire series of stories. Our readers are not about to embrace a young man who is merely a wealthy widower and has gone on to live happily ever after. No, no. You must alternate between suffering and loss and joyful success. You know, meeting triumph and disaster and treat those two imposters just the same. A win in the All Nations would just not do."

"I assure you, Mr. Durnan, that on this Saturday, I will be playing to not only to win but to keep England's chance for the Championship alive."

"Please, Mr. Staunton, don't be foolish. Think of what you would be giving up. Fame fortune—,"

"Honor, integrity, and my conscience!"

Chapter Thirty-Three

"Expensive and unnecessary luxuries in the life of a young man. Compared to fame and fortune, hardly worth mentioning."

"To me they are, and I believe that this conversation should now be terminated. Good day, Sir."

We could not see over the back of our booth what took place next, but Walter Durnan did not get up to leave. Instead, we heard a condescending sigh and the striking of a match. It was followed by a stream of tobacco smoke ascending to the ceiling.

"Very well, Mr. Staunton. We have made you a generous offer. If you will do whatever it takes to make sure that England does not win by more than three points on Saturday, you will be generously rewarded. I suggest to you that the alternative would not be in your interest."

"And why not?"

"Did you attend the theatre often four seasons back, in 1895?"

"Yes. And what does that have to do with anything?"

"Did you happen to attend Mr. Wilde's *The Importance of Being Earnest*?"

"Yes."

"Jolly good. Well, if I might paraphrase a line from Lady Bracknell: *To lose one wife may be regarded as a misfortune; to lose two looks like carelessness.*"

His comment was followed by a moment of silence during which Holmes and I again gave each other a look, this time with our eyes widened, not sure of what would happen next. The threat was thinly veiled, and I did not expect Godfrey to take it sitting down.

A loud curse from Godfrey was soon heard along with the banging of furniture and crashing dishes. I leapt to my feet, my worry that Godfrey, in his distress, would give away my disguise, overruled by my concern over what he might do to the ratbag from Fleet Street.

By the time I had moved from my seat in the booth behind Godfrey and Durnan, Godfrey had reached across the table, grabbed the fellow by his lapels, and—strong arms being useful in such a situation--lifted him out of his seat and laid him across the table. The plate of fish and chips and mushy peas suffered serious damage as an unfortunate bystander to the incident.

Godfrey's face was two inches from Durnan's, and his one hand was around his throat.

"You ...," he was saying, adding several profane and vulgar words that I will leave to your imagination, "tell me what you know of Millie or, so help me, I'll rip your arms out of their sockets and then mangle your face to a pulp."

"Let...me...go, you fool," Durnan was gasping.

Holmes moved quickly to place his hands on Godfrey's wrists.

"Now, now, boys," he said in his most gentle and ministerial tones. "This won't do between two Christian gentlemen. Peace, please."

His efforts were overridden by the burly barkeep who had rushed over to the table.

"Enough of that in here!" he bellowed. "You chaps are in Kensington, not the Isle of Dogs. Let him up and take your nonsense outside."

He was of sufficient size to grab one of Godfrey's arms, the one which was being used to strangle Durnan and wrench it away. That gave Holmes the chance to wrap both his arms around Godfrey's other arm and pull him back. Durnan got up from the table and used his handkerchief to remove the mushy peas from his face and jacket.

"You'll pay for that, Staunton. If you won't play with us, then be prepared for the consequences. I could have made you a hero. Now, you will be painted as a pariah ... a philanderer ... a cheat ... a malingerer. By the time we're done with you, not a club in England will touch you. And your dear Millie will be turned into a whimpering whore."

With that, he turned and ran out of the pub. Holmes, the barkeep and I all held onto Godfrey else he would no doubt have run the blighter down and visited life-long injuries to his person.

We forced a seething Godfrey to be seated and offered him a brandy, which he refused. After several deep breaths, he seemed to have gotten himself under control.

"That blackguard knows something about Millie," he said. "You should have let me hurt him until he squawked."

"Which," said Holmes, "he would not likely do, except to tell you lies. But we know now who he is and it will not be difficult to investigate his network of associates. Your temper was justified but not useful in the least."

Godfrey looked chagrined and slumped into his seat. "And now he's going to libel me in his newspaper. I should have just strangled him."

"And sent yourself to prison for years to come," said Holmes.

"Yes, I suppose you're right. But what can I do now about what he's going to write about me?"

"Easily thwarted," said Holmes.

Both Godfrey and I looked at him in disbelief.

"How?" asked Godfrey.

"The idea of the suffering hero who has overcome adversity is an excellent idea for a story. We shall take it immediately to *The Telegraph* and arrange to have it published straight away. If there is anything a newspaper will not do, it is to appear to be a day behind their competition is publishing a story. To be seen to have been beaten is humiliating. They would lose readers and face within the denizens of Fleet Street."

"But I'm not a suffering hero any longer."

"Since when are the facts allowed to get in the way of an account that will attract both the punters and their wives. The only difference between our story and Durnan's will be that ours shall end with whatever happened in the Championship and will paint you as made of the stuff that built the Empire."

"Can you truly arrange all that?"

"I am owed some favors by several front-page reporters. I will arrange for an interview at first light tomorrow morning. It will be on the streets of London by the early afternoon edition."

Chapter Thirty-Four

During my break for lunch the following day, I ran out from my medical practice and purchased the early afternoon editions of both *The Telegram* and *The Evening Star*. I do not know how Holmes managed to do it, but there on the front page of *The Telegram* was a flattering photograph of Godfrey Staunton in his rugby uniform, looking like some sort of cross between Hercules and Adonis. The story was extensive and carried on to later pages. It told of Godfrey's loss of his parents and of his beloved first bride, Miss Lillian. The pathos of the language was enough to bring a tear to my eye, and I already knew all about it. By the end of the article, he seemed to be exalted into the ranks of David Livingston, Lord Nelson, and James "The Mighty Combatant" Figg all rolled into one.

One the front page of *The Evening Star*, I saw a boxed highlight in which I read the following:

The Evening Star Investigates: A member of England's International Team is a Fraud. Learn all about this scandal beginning tomorrow.

As Holmes had predicted, there was no story the following day, or the next.

On Friday, 3 March, I dropped in on Holmes to catch up on what had become of Godfrey.

"He departed this morning," Holmes said, "along with most of his teammates to Edinburgh to watch the match between Scotland and Wales. He is still extremely distraught over Millie, but Lord Mount James, Lady Maynooth, and I all agreed that it would be better for him to be with his mates than sitting and stewing here in London."

"I'm not surprised," I said, "that he is stretched tighter than a drum. Do you perceive that Millie is in true danger?"

Holmes was quiet for several seconds before responding. "I think not. We are dealing with clever people who know that their power, and it is significant, resides in their threats more than in their actions. If anything were to be done to Millie, they know that Godfrey—and I would help him to the best of my ability—would track them down no matter where they fled and that he would be merciless to them once he had found them. They do not wish to live with that fear. All they want is their money. That is my conclusion."

"I suspect that your conclusion is cold comfort to Godfrey."

"You are utterly correct on that one."

"What happened to the phone call you arranged through the Agony Page?"

"Nothing yet."

"Was it just a blind?"

"Not likely. But it is a card that is not likely to be played before the final hand. I expect to receive notice on that matter sometime next week, following the match this weekend."

The account of the match that weekend appeared in the late edition of the newspapers on Saturday. The story had been rushed into print, and details remained sketchy. To the surprise of all fans of the game of rugby, Scotland defeated Wales in the highest-scoring match of the series. The Caber Tossers, led by Douglas Monypenny and Henry Gedge, allowed the Taffies to cross into touch twice and kick two converts but in return, they put twenty-one points on the board. While the game itself must have been quite exciting for those who traveled north to see it, the true significance was that it opened the possibility for England to have a fighting chance at winning the championship if they defeated Scotland by a wide margin in the match schedule for 11 March. I imagined that Godfrey and his mates talked about how to play the upcoming match as they traveled back to London on the Sunday after.

It was as they were on the train that Sunday morning that I received a note from Holmes requesting that I come immediately to Baker Street.

Chapter Thirty-Five

"What is it?" I asked after hurrying up the stairs and entering the front room.

He was already pulling on his coat and hat and pointed back down the stairs.

"I will tell you as we travel. Quick now, we have to get a cab to Kensington."

Once inside and bouncing our way south and then along Bayswater Road, he explained.

"I had a note an hour ago telling me to be prepared to receive a telephone call at eleven o'clock this morning at the Mount James residence. Mrs. Staunton will be permitted to speak to us."

"But Godfrey's not here. He's somewhere to the north on a train."

"I am sure the timing was deliberate."

"But why would they do that?" I asked.

"I suspect two reasons. In the first place, it will be far more distressing to Godfrey to know that Millie has been heard from and that he was not able to speak to her. It will render him, I expect, more vulnerable to their threats against her."

"And the second?"

"He would know immediately if it were Millie on the other end of the call and not someone pretending to be her who is prepared to say whatever the rogues behind this scheme tell her too."

"Will you be able to tell?"

"I am working on that problem."

He said no more and closed his eyes and vanished into his mode of intense concentration until we arrived outside of the Mount James home on Phillimore Place.

"Are they expecting us?" I asked.

"I sent a note off to them. I am sure they will be prepared for the call."

To my surprise, we were greeted at the door by Lady Maynooth. She graciously welcomed us and bade us enter.

"As it is a Sunday morning," she said, "I have given the staff some time off. Had we known you were coming, I would not have done so. But please, gentlemen, give me your coats and make your way to the library. His Lordship is waiting for you there by the telephone."

"And will you be joining us?" asked Holmes.

"Yes and no," she said, smiling beautifully. "I had the men from the telephone company splice in another line to my bedroom. I shall be listening from there and will not be saying anything unless asked. It will be so good to hear directly from Millicent and know that she is safe and sound." She motioned with one hand to the hallway that led to the library and then hung our coats in the vestibule closet.

"Good morning, Lord Mount James," said Holmes as we entered his library. He was seated at his desk, fully dressed in his morning suit. A recent model of a telephone, imported from Sweden, sat on his writing pad in front of him.

"Pull up a chair on either side of me," he said. "I will relay what is said and, if you so insist, will pass the handle over to you so you can speak directly. Right, now sit down. The call should come through in five minutes."

I could tell that Holmes would have preferred to be the one controlling the call, but it was Mount James's home after all, and he asserted his right of property owner. The three of us then sat in silence, waiting for the telephone to ring. "Your Lordship," said Holmes, "kindly remember that it is important to keep the call going as long as possible and to extract as much data as we can concerning their location."

"It was not necessary to inform me of that, Mr. Holmes. I will conduct the call as I see fit."

At precisely eleven o'clock, the telephone rang. Mount James picked up the combined transmitter and receiver unit.

"WRKGDN 1027; Mount James here," he said. He listened for a moment then shouted. "You will have to speak up, man. You sound as if you are calling from Borneo...Yes, Sherlock Holmes is here...No, I will tell him whatever you want to say to him...Oh, very well then."

He handed the unit to Holmes.

"Whoever it is says they will only speak to you." He harrumphed his reaction.

"Holmes here," said Holmes, taking the unit but leaning his head over toward me so that I might be able to listen in.

"Yes, this is Sherlock Holmes. But you will have to speak up."

With my ear pressed against the shielded side of the receiver, all I could hear was a constant buzz of static.

"Put Mrs. Staunton on," Holmes shouted. "Hello, yes, is that you, Miss Millie ... I am sorry, my dear, but Godfrey is not here. He is traveling back from Edinburgh...Yes, I know you are desperate to talk to him, but the time of the call was set by your captors. Please confirm that you have not been harmed...Excellent. I have Doctor Watson here. He is going to ask you some questions about your health."

Holmes handed me the telephone, and I held it to my ear. The static was loud, and although I could hear the words from the voice on the other end of the line, there was no way I could be sure that it was Millie. To make matter worse, she must have been calling from near a railway station as her voice was drowned out by a series of train whistles and I had to ask her to repeat what she had said. I asked her the standard questions that a doctor poses to a young woman who is expecting a child. Such questions concern a woman's bodily functions and do not bear repeating, but her answers assured me that whoever was on the other end of the line was in good health and had been well fed and not treated abusively.

"She's in good condition," I said to Holmes as I passed the telephone back to him.

"My dear," Holmes said loudly, "we must have some proof that you are indeed Mrs. Millicent Staunton...Yes, please tell me something that only you would know...yes, perhaps something confidential about Godfrey...Did you say he has two moles above his left nipple that look like eyeballs of the man-in-the-moon?... That is quite fascinating, but it will not do. Godfrey has been in locker rooms with hundreds of unclothed men, any one of whom could see his bare chest... yes, something else."

"Ask her," barked Mount James, "about the birds."

"The birds?" said Holmes.

"Yes, for pity sake. The girl is a blessed ornithologist. She's brilliant. Whoever is holding her could never have found someone that knows every species in the entire bloody nation."

"Mrs. Staunton," Holmes shouted, "can you please tell me which unusual species of birds you have observed during the past two weeks."

There was a long period of silence.

"Ah ha," said Mount James, "if she cannot answer that then it is not Millie."

Holmes eyes then lit up, and he mouthed the words, "She's back."

He quickly pulled out a notepad and pencil from his pockets and held the telephone against his ear with his shoulder.

"Yes...go ahead...I am listening."

Holmes scribbled what must have been the abbreviated names of eight to ten birds on his pad. I could not decipher what any of them were.

"Excellent," he said back into the telephone. "I am convinced that you are indeed Mrs. Staunton. Now, is there a message you want me to give to Godfrey?... Yes, of course, I will tell him that you love and miss him but that you are well. Yes ...concerning the demands that have been given to him for the game? What of those?"

Her next words were screamed loudly, so much so that I could hear them from my side of the receiver.

"Tell him never to give in to these bastards! Tell him to play the best game he has ever played!"

Those words were followed by a cry of pain and something that sounded like, "Give that back to me!"

Then the line went dead.

Chapter Thirty-Six

The three of us sat and looked at each other, saying nothing. Finally, Lord Mount James broke the silence.

"Very well, then, Mr. Sherlock Holmes, the famous detective, tell me what you learned. One of your brilliant deductions if you please."

"Ask me tomorrow."

Mount James was about to respond when he looked up and towards the door of the study. We could hear the sounds of Lady Maynooth approaching.

"Splendid," said Mount James, "here comes Beatrice to tell us that aren't we lucky, things, after all, could be much worse."

The old fellow obviously knew what to expect. Lady Maynooth, looking as if she had just stepped out of a fashion magazine, entered, smiling serenely.

"Oh, wasn't it good to hear Millie's voice? It was such a relief. Thank you, Doctor, for assuring us of her good health. And wasn't that wonderful at the end when she was shouting? Such a spirited young woman, isn't she? Don't you agree, Mr. Holmes?"

Holmes gave her a condescending look. "Why yes, of course."

"Now, I suppose," she said, "you are going to go to the telephone company and have them tell you where the call came from. The Royal Mail is in charge of all phone calls, aren't they? They must know something like that."

"I fear not," said Holmes. "The level of static on the line and the faint volume of her voice indicates that the call was re-routed through at least two or more exchanges before arriving here. It will be impossible to tell its point of origin."

"Oh, that is a shame. Nevertheless, I am sure that a brilliant detective like you will sort it all out."

"I shall let you know when I do. Now, kindly excuse us. We have some work to do. I assume Godfrey will arrive back in London later this afternoon. Please tell him to contact me straight away upon his return. And a good day to both of you."

We fetched our own coats and hats and departed from the house. Once out of the pavement, Holmes lit a cigarette.

"Would you mind, Watson, walking back instead of hailing a cab? The brisk air will help me focus my thoughts."

"Happy to. Shall I share my insights as we walk?"

"Please, don't."

He clasped his hands behind his back, leaned slightly forward and strolled all the way from Kensington to Marble Arch, saying nothing. At Hyde Park corner, he turned to me.

"It is Sunday, and Mrs. Hudson will have gone to church. I shall have to find a restaurant if I want any lunch. Will you be so kind as to join me?"

"Not if your conversation is to be as vacant as is has been for the past half-hour."

"I shall be the soul of wit, I assure you."

We found a small pub just off Oxford Street and, true to his word, Holmes was pleasant and chatty, making all sorts of witty observations on the political events of the day and not adding a word about the current case. Having finished with a glass of Claret, we rose and walked back to 221B Baker Street. Mrs. Hudson had returned by then and greeted me warmly.

"Oh, Dr. Watson, how lovely to see you again. Do come in and I shall put on the kettle. And, oh, Mr. Holmes, there's a note came for you a few minutes ago."

There was a small envelope on the coffee table. Even without inspecting it closely, I could tell that it was of the same order as the notes we had previously received regarding Godfrey. I picked it up and handed it to Holmes. He read it, furrowed his brow, and handed it to me. It ran:

Mr. Holmes: You are advised in the strongest way possible that it would be exceptionally unwise of you to inform Godfrey Staunton of the unfortunate outburst by his foolish wife during your conversation with her. You should also warn him that if he does not finally conform to our demands, his wife will most certainly be restored to him, but her face and bosom will be beyond recognition. Vitriol is at hand.

I gasped. "These people are inhuman."

Holmes took the note back from me and said nothing. He perused it carefully, and then a faint smile flickered across his face.

"They have just removed all doubt that it was truly Millie on the telephone. And it is highly likely that they are here in London."

"How can you tell that?"

"It is only two hours since we concluded the call and a note has arrived here already. They cannot be all that far away."

That seemed reasonable, but I had to ask, "What if they made another phone call to a contact in London?"

"An excellent question, Watson. I shall take that under consideration."

"Are you going to tell Godfrey about all of this?"

"Yes. I believe I shall. He may be overly passionate and impetuous, but he is above all an honorable man and he is Millie's husband. If he took the Flying Scotsman from Edinburgh, he would be in London by this evening. His Lordship and Lady Maynooth will tell him about the phone call, and I expect that he will appear here very early tomorrow morning. It would be good if you could be here when he arrives. You seem to have a congenial rapport with him."

.

Chapter Thirty-Seven

The following morning, Monday, the sixth of March, I rose before sunrise and made my way over to Baker Street. As Holmes's had predicted, not long after I arrived, there came a furious ringing of the bell accompanied by a pounding on the door. Mrs. Hudson hurried to open it, and five loud thumps were then heard as Godfrey leapt up our seventeen steps. He burst into the room, looking flushed and perspiring and began to speak at a high volume.

"Uncle Jimmy and Lady Maynooth told me about the phone call. What happened? Are you sure it was Millie? Are you sure she has not been harmed?"

"Yes, on both counts," said Holmes. "Now, please sit down, and we shall give you a full account."

Godfrey dropped his athletic frame into one of the armchairs and for the next several minutes gripped the arms tightly but remained in place and suppressed any outburst. I began our account by giving a verbatim account of my inquiries into Millie's health. Godfrey listened and nodded as I spoke.

"Thank you, Doctor," he said when I had finished. "That is reassuring. Was there anything unusual in what she said? Anything that you might not have expected to hear? Anything that might contain a clue?"

I slowly repeated each answer Millie had given me, and the three of us parsed each line. But nothing stood out beyond what I had heard a thousand times from young mothers-to-be in my doctor's office.

Godfrey then turned and looked at Holmes. "And your account, Sir?"

Holmes also repeated the conversation concluding with Millie's shouted demand at the end. On hearing it, Godfrey smiled ever so slightly.

"That's my Millie. Isn't she something?"

"She is indeed," said Holmes. "There is, however, a further development. You need to read this, and please try to control your reaction."

He handed Godfrey the note that had been waiting for us when we came to Baker Street the previous afternoon.

Godfrey read it I watched the blood drain from his face. He threw the note on the table and leapt to his feet and began to pace the room while uttering many unrepeatable oaths and curses. But then he stopped at the far end of the chemical apparatus table and placed both hands on the edge, spread out, and dropped his head and shoulders. He remained in that posture for a minute and then came and sat back in his chair.

"We have to find her," he said.

"We do," agreed Holmes. "Given the alacrity with which this last note arrived, I suspect that she must be here in London."

Godfrey shook his head. "Not likely."

"Why not?"

"No. Millie knows London. If she were here, she would have screamed blue murder until half the neighborhood came running to her door. Either that or she would have jumped out of a window. She's like that. No, they must have taken her somewhere remote; somewhere that she has no way of escaping from."

"England," said Holmes, "has a thousand such remote locations. It will be complicated to narrow them down."

This time it was Godfrey who closed his eyes tight and pushed his closed fists together in front of his sternum. Suddenly, his eyes popped open, and his head rose.

"The birds," he said. "Show me the list of the birds."

"I only noted abbreviations," said Holmes. "It was a means to make sure it was her. Your uncle suggested it. I asked a question that only a trained ornithologist could answer."

"She's not just a birder," said Godfrey. "She is brilliant. Smarter than the three of us together. She is. Believe me. Please, Sir, write out the full names of the birds she said she saw."

Holmes now closed his eyes and reached into his memory. One by one he wrote down the exact name each bird. When he had finished, he handed the list over to Godfrey who in turn handed it on to me. On it were the following names:

European White-fronted Goose, Dunlin, Widgeon, Ringed Plover, Manx Shearwater, Gadwall, Whimbrel, Black-tailed Godwit, Berwick's Swan.

Chapter Thirty-Eight

"I haven't heard of most of these," I said.

"Neither have I," said Godfrey. "She could have named off some that were more common, but she chose not to."

"You suspect," asked Holmes, "that there is some message hidden in her selection?"

"I cannot tell, but it's possible. She's like that."

"I confess," said Holmes, "that scholarly ornithology is beyond my ken."

"Mine as well," said Godfrey. "But are you familiar with the name of Henry Dresser?"

"The zoologist?"

"Yes, that fellow. He's the expert. Millie studied with him for two summers. If he's not off in South America, you could find him over in Hanover Square at the Zoological Society building. If we sent a note now, we could likely secure a meeting with him by tomorrow."

"An excellent suggestion," said Holmes, "with one minor adjustment. *We* will not be meeting with him. *You* will be attending practice with your teammates at Blackheath. Doctor Watson and I will have a chat with him as soon as possible."

Godfrey did not look pleased with Holmes's caveat, but he shrugged and acquiesced.

"But you will tell me anything you learn from him. You must do that."

"We shall," said Holmes. "And if you leave here now you should be able to get all the over to Blackheath in time for your practice."

Godfrey stood up and walked toward the door. Before passing through it, he turned back to us.

"Do you truly believe that we are dealing with people so vile that they would throw vitriol on the face and breasts of a beautiful young woman just because I refused to go along with their demands?"

"Godfrey," said Holmes, "I think it highly unlikely but, in truth, I cannot give absolute assurance. I have several suspects, but I do not yet know who these people are. They may be pretending. They may be not."

He departed, descending the stairs slowly, one at a time.

"We do not have much time left," I said to Holmes. "England's final game is this Saturday."

"Could they," asked Holmes, "run up a high enough score against Scotland to still have a chance at the championship?"

"It's possible," said I. "They did not put up a very good show against Wales and Ireland, but after all, they are English, stalwart lads every one of them. My money is still on them."

Chapter Thirty-Nine

A meeting with Mr. Henry Eeles Dresser, the author of the multi-volume set of books on the birds of Europe, was arranged for the following day in the late morning. Godfrey did not participate as he was at the team practice over on the Blackheath field and Holmes and I traveled the short distance to Hanover Square and the impressive building that housed the Zoological Society of London. We walked through the lobby and down the halls, past innumerable stuffed animals from all over the globe, matched by almost as many skeletons and colored maps. Up on the third floor, we were met by a tall, thin mustached gentleman who had a pith helmet on one corner of his desk and a butterfly net propped up against his small-mammal-laden bookshelves. His finely tailored suit reminded any visitor to his menagerie that he had also been a highly successful captain of the import-export trade markets and had made a fortune as a young man running the Yankee blockade and supplying goods and armaments to the Confederate States.

"Mr. Sherlock Holmes a-a-and Doctor Watson," he said, rising from his chair. "The-the-the world of global zoology is not known as a warren of crime so I must say I find your visit rather perplexing. Please, please, do be seated. A-a-a cup of tea perhaps? I brought back some lovely cases of Silver Tip from Ceylon."

He rang a small handbell and an elderly woman, looking every bit as anti-diluvian as the specimens we had passed, appeared with a tray of tea and biscuits.

Mr. Dresser chattered on about the world's tea in a manner that made it clear that he was a renowned expert on any subject one wished to discuss. Finally, he got around to demanding that Holmes explain the reason for his visit.

"I understand," said Holmes, "that you helped supervise the studies of a young female student from Cambridge, a Miss Millicent Fawcett. Is that correct?"

"Miss Millicent. Yeh-yeh-yes. A brilliant young woman. Much smarter than any of the boys in her class. Yes, positively brilliant. Not one of the boys could tell a Goldfinch from a Chaffinch, but Millicent could nail it every time. Yes, we had a delightful field trip, oh, it must be three years back now, out to the Romney Marsh. Bit of miserable weather we had but none the less, Millicent was as gung-ho as any boy I ever supervised from Cambridge, or from our other university, and didn't she just pull on her wellies and go sloshing through the bogs until she—,"

"She is in trouble," interrupted Holmes.

Mr. Dresser lost his look of arrogant aplomb immediately. "Oh no. What's wrong?"

Holmes succinctly explained the events of the past several weeks, including the latest note we had received. Dresser's face looked deeply horrified.

"Good heavens, I hope you can do something, Mr. Holmes. This is terrible. But what in the world has it to do with me?"

"During the phone call, in order to assure us that we were indeed speaking to her, it was suggested that she name the birds she had observed. She did not immediately respond and then she listed off nine, none of which are usually on the lips a casual citizen. This is the list. What can you tell me about them?"

He handed the list to the esteemed ornithologist. He glanced at it quickly.

"These are all birds that make their habitats near water; all found around shorelines and marshes."

"But where in England are they found?"

"All over. From the Hebrides to the Lizard. Their location may change with the season but almost all of them winter here in the British Isles rather than migrating."

"*Almost* all?"

"Yes, yes. The Manx Shearwater departs in the early fall and flies all the way to South America. An amazing species. They live for up to fifty years, and by the time they die, they may have flown for several million miles during the lifetimes. Yes, yes, a truly magnificent species."

"There are none around England now?"

"No, no. Mind you they will come back in April, again from Central and South America. Some as far away as the Argentine."

"Miss Millicent reported having seen this bird last week."

"The Manx Shearwater? Here in February? Not at all likely. Almost impossible."

"*Almost?*"

"Well. Yes, I suppose it is theoretically possible. There are always a few of them who winter in the Severn Estuary and can't be bothered crossing the Atlantic. Yes, yes, there is a small colony of them there but only along the marshes of Severn Beach up to Frampton. Unless she was there, she could not have spotted them."

"Is it an easy bird to confuse with any other species? Similar markings perhaps?" asked Holmes.

"Uh-uh. Of course, to the untrained eye, one waterfowl looks like the next. Yes, yes. Terribly easy to get them mixed up. Even the schoolmasters at Eton are doing it all the time and turning their pupil's knowledge into a pig's breakfast. Shameful what they do, if you ask me."

"Would Millie have made such a mistake?"

"Miss Millicent? No, no. Not her. No, never. She's the best of the lot. No, not possible."

"Assuming then that she is not deliberately misleading us, are you saying that she must be somewhere north of Pilning?"

"North of Pilning, you say? Yes. That would be it. Within that stretch of twenty miles. Mind you, it is one of the finest habitats for waterfowl in all of the British Isles. All those other birds on the list winter there and a couple of dozen more I can name. There's—,"

"Sir, that has been very helpful. I can see why Miss Millicent enjoyed her studies with you so much. You may have saved her life."

"Who? Me? Well, I do hope I have been of some use. Awfully fond I was of her. Brilliant mind. An exceptional young ornithologist, I must say. Happy to help. We birds of a feather, as they say."

We thanked him profusely and hustled our way back out of the building as quickly as possible. As soon as we were out on the pavement of Brook Street, Holmes walked on the double to the nearest tobacconist shop and asked to see their copy of Bradshaw's.

"Confound it," he muttered, placing the guidebook somewhat forcefully back on the shopkeeper's counter. "We've have missed the last train for the day to Bristol. The next leaves early tomorrow. Can you meet me at Paddington at half-past seven tomorrow morning?"

I assured him that I could, and we both walked back to Baker Street, commenting more than once on the cleverness of Mrs. Millicent Staunton.

Chapter Forty

"Were there any other clues?" I wondered aloud.

"Not in what she said to me," said Holmes. "You are quite certain there was nothing in her report to you about her health."

"Nothing. Her answers were utterly standard."

"No other noises? Clicking her tongue? Smacking her lips? Giving a whistle?"

"I heard a whistle," I said, "but it was not from her."

"Then where was it from?"

"It was a train whistle."

"Good heavens, why didn't you say so?"

"What good would that have done? You hear distant train whistles all over England. They are designed so that the sound carries for miles."

He walked on in silence, then acknowledged my point. "Yes, that is correct."

After another block, he came back to the whistle.

"Describe the whistle."

"Describe it? I already said it was a train whistle."

"No, Watson. Think, please. What was the pitch? Was it one long blast? Several short ones? How many? Try to remember."

I reached back into my memory. "Now that you ask, there was a change in the pitch. You know, a Doppler effect; isn't that what they call it?"

"Precisely. Now was it changing from a high pitch to a lower pitch or lower to higher?"

"From higher to lower. But the change was not all that great. That means the train was approaching, doesn't it? But not coming directly at you, right?"

"Yes. Anything else? Long blasts; short blasts?"

I wracked my brain and tried to think back. "Neither long nor short. But the higher tones I heard first were odd."

"In what way?"

"It was as if they had a hollow timbre to them; a bit of an echo. Then that ceased, and they sounded like the usual train whistle."

"My dear Watson, this appears to be a time when you have actually been of some use to an investigation."

I was quite taken aback.

"And just what do you mean by that remark, Holmes?"

"You have just informed me as to Millie's location, or at least jolly close. The Manx Shearwater sighting told us that she was somewhere along the Severn Estuary. The train whistle, as you described it, could only have been from a train emerging from a tunnel and moving toward Millie. There is only one place that could have occurred and, to my chagrin, we passed directly by it within a few hours of Millie's having been abducted."

"We did? Where?"

"At the East Portal of the Severn Tunnel, just before the train passes the station at Pilning. We came that way on our journey back to London from Swansea two months ago."

"And she has been there all this time?"

"That we do not know. But it is quite certain that she is there now."

"But the train whistle can be heard for miles? Where are you going to start?"

"Ask me tomorrow."

But that time we were walking north on Baker Street toward 221B. Up ahead, I could see a man standing in front of our door. He was looking in our direction. A moment later, he started running toward us.

"Merciful heavens," I said. "It's Godfrey. What is he doing here?"

The young three-quarter was sprinting and was soon upon us.

"Quick," he gasped, "Get in a cab. We have only a few minutes before we have to be there. I waited until the last minute, hoping you two would show up. I'm so thankful you did. But we have to get going."

He waved down a cab, opened the door before the driver could descend, took my arm and then Holmes's and almost threw us inside. Then he shouted the destination to the driver.

"White's! On St. James! A sovereign if you can gallop all the way."

The whip was laid to the haunches of the mares, and we jolted and bounced our way back down Baker Street.

"Why are you taking us there?" asked Holmes. Whites, as most readers will be aware, is the oldest gentlemen's club in London and one of its most prestigious. Its members are exclusively Tories who are in high positions of government, industry, commerce, the church, or the nobility.

"This came for me this morning," said Godfrey. He handed Holmes an envelope on which was affixed a regal-looking coat of arms. It seemed familiar to me, but I could not place it until Holmes opened the note inside. The coat of arms appeared at the top and underneath in an embossed Tudor font I could read *Secretary of Her Majesty's Privy Council*. On the next line was the name *The Honourable Clarence FitzClarence*.

"Oh, my!" I said. "This one takes the cake."

Readers will recall that in one of my earlier accounts of the adventures of Sherlock Holmes, I observed that Holmes's brother, Mycroft, sometimes *was* the British government. Whatever position Mycroft Holmes held, of course, was due to his omniscient knowledge of the workings of Whitewall and Westminster. The Secretary of Her Majesty's Privy Council, on the other hand, was officially the head panjandrum of the entire administrative apparatus that ran the British Empire. Indeed, thousands to his bidding sped and posted o'er land and ocean without rest.

The man himself who currently held this loftiest of Mandarin titles, Sir Clarence FitzClarence, was the second son of a second son of some Irish peer and, lacking inherited wealth and title, had ascended to his perch by dint of blazing genius and unrelenting hard work. Yet he was said to be able not only to walk casually with Kings but to possess the common touch that rendered all who met him instantly attracted to him.

Chapter Forty-One

Than he should have sent a note directly Godfrey was beyond belief. But here it was in front of me, addressed to Mr. Godfrey Staunton by name and, to my enormous surprise, it was copied not only to Sherlock Holmes but to me as well. The short note read:

My dear Mr. Godfrey Staunton:

Please forgive this last-minute request, but if you can possibly do so, would you kindly come to my office at three o'clock this afternoon?

It is entirely understandable if you cannot do so, and a later date would be possible, although not nearly so advantageous.

Given the turmoil that has recently been visited upon you, you may wish to have your associates, Mr. Sherlock Holmes and Dr. John Watson, accompany you.

I shall be waiting for you at White's. The porter will direct you to me.

Thank you in advance for your response to my request.

Yours very truly,

C F-C

"We should," said Godfrey, "be able to make by three. I am so glad I was able to catch the two of you. I have never met with anybody so highly placed before. Have you, Mr. Holmes?"

"One or two. They are not nearly as intimidating as their letterhead suggests."

"What do you think he wants?"

"I haven't the foggiest. However, his reference to your turmoil indicates that he is aware of Millie's abduction, and one can only assume that the requested meeting has something to do with it."

"Requested?" I said. "If you ask me, it is more like a command performance."

For the next few minutes as we hurtled our way through Marylebone and Mayfair, Holmes and I attempted to soothe the nerves of a highly agitated Godfrey, all the while wondering ourselves what was in the offing. Informing him of what we had learned from our meeting at the Zoological Society was somehow delayed.

White's, as all informed Londoners know, is one of the oldest and most exclusive—some would say pretentious—gentlemen's clubs in the Empire. It is inhabited by the *crème de la crème* of the Tory establishment. Through its unmarked door at 37 St. James Street, those few, those favored few who control the destiny of a third of the globe, come and go.

"Good afternoon, gentlemen," said the porter as we entered the *sanctum sanctorum* of imperial power. "Sir Clarence is expecting you. And please allow me to note that it is a pleasure to welcome three such distinguished Englishmen to our premises. In spite of our members' attempts to conceal them, copies of the latest editions of the *Strand* and the *Sporting News* are constantly smuggled in, and the accounts of your various exploits are thoroughly enjoyed. Come now, this way, please."

He led us through the front room in which were seated a dozen or so men whose names were continually in the press. Godfrey was walking beside me and after glancing to the chairs in front of the bay window, leaned over and whispered to me.

"Isn't that—?"

"Yes," I whispered back, "that's Bertie, and he is chatting with Bob Cecil. Please do not stare at them."

We were led up two flights of stairs to the third floor and along an ornate hallway to a private meeting room.

"Sir Clarence," said the porter after opening the door. "Your guests."

The gentleman seated in a high-backed leather armchair on the far side of the small room put aside the file and pencil he had in his hands and rose to greet us.

"Ah, Mr. Sherlock Holmes, Dr. Watson, and Godfrey Staunton, how very good of you to accommodate my unforgivably inconsiderate request and make time to join me."

He was of the same vintage and Holmes and me but was the picture of conservative elegance. He stood about six feet, had a military bearing, and bore broad shoulders and a narrow waist. There was nothing unusual in the fashion of his clothes except that they were, even to my untrained eye, exceptionally well-tailored and of Saville Row bespoke quality. Every hair on his erect head was set in place, and his eyes, mouth, and jaw radiated a congenial self-confidence. He did not walk toward us to shake hands but gestured instead to the sideboard on which were laid several crystal glasses, monogrammed plates, and a tray of afternoon delicacies. I am no *chef de cuisine*, but I assumed by looking at the spread that we were being offered tidbits of partridge, pheasant, quail, and grouse, spread on an assortment of wafers of various sizes and textures.

"Please, gentlemen," Sir Clarence continued. "It is the most I can offer as my penance for disturbing your afternoon. Do help yourself. The sherry is excellent, and I confess I have already imbibed, and the kitchen here is famous for its seasoned game meats."

I was somewhat hungry and helped myself to a wafer and a glass of sherry. Holmes refrained. Godfrey took the food but filled his glass with water. Sir Clarence chatted pleasantly as we were devouring the tasty appetizers.

"Have you been before to White's? No? None of you? Well, we'll have to see about that. I think it's a splendid place for England's star Three-Quarter, our best-selling author, and our most famous amateur detective to come and relax."

"Really?" said Godfrey. "I should like that a lot. But am I not a bit too young for membership?"

"Oh, goodness, not at all," said Sir Clarence. "Why William Pitt the Younger was only twenty-one when he was inducted. And His Lordship's title and estate will come to you when he passes on to his eternal reward. Years pass so very quickly, don't they? And what about you, Mr. Holmes? You have earned world renown for your brilliant detective accomplishments. A man like you would fit right in here."

"I fear that not only would I never want to belong to a club that would have me as a member, but that your members would not take kindly to having a detective in their midst who has an unfortunately insatiable sense of curiosity."

FitzClarence roared with laughter. "You mean we might all end up in front of a magistrate if you were here and eavesdropping?"

"Precisely."

"I'll have to give you that one, Mr. Holmes. I can only imagine how much livelier the gossip around our dining room tables would be if any one of our esteemed members were hauled away in irons. I am afraid that is an event that will have to remain in my imagination. However, that was not the reason for my asking the three of you to join me this afternoon. Please, make yourselves comfortable, and I will explain the urgency of my request."

The three of us sat across from him, and he smiled warmly at each of us in turn, again thanking us for coming on short notice.

"Mr. Staunton," he began, "I was just recently informed about the dreadful situation you are in with regards to your lovely wife. Is she still missing?"

Godfrey had not expected that question, but he handled himself well and responded. "She is, Sir. But we are working together to find her and rescue her as quickly as possible."

"Yes, yes. Quite so. I understand that both Sherlock Holmes and Scotland Yard are on the case, but I did want you to know that I have put the word out through all branches of the government of Great Britain, in strictest confidence of course, that they are to report any possible sightings or clues. The entire military, the customs men, the public works supervisors ... everybody ... several hundred thousand good men and women are all now alerted. I am sure that we shall find her and return her safe and sound to her husband."

"Oh, well, that … that is very generous and thoughtful of you, Sir. I cannot thank you enough. It has been quite a strain these past few weeks."

"Of course, it has. I cannot imagine what you have been going through. Had it happened to my Eugenie, my loving companion and helpmate for these past thirty years, the paragon of a virtuous woman, I would have been utterly beside myself. I could not possibly have borne up the brave way you have."

"It has been hard, Sir, but I have had some wonderful friends to help me. Mr. Holmes and Dr. Watson here have been rocks, and Dr. Armstrong has been like a caring father. My teammates have been absolute princes, every one of them."

"You are blessed," said FitzClarence, "to have such fine friends. Of course, it takes a good man to have good friends. And you do have a bit of a reputation for being of a gem yourself. Your playing your heart out in the Home Nations in spite of what you have been going through has been noticed and, I must say, most highly admired."

"I have tried to do my bit, Sir, but it hasn't helped much. We were humiliated by the Welsh, and even the Irish team got past us."

"Oh, yes but any man who has played rugby—and I did do myself for a couple of years whilst at Oxford—any man knows that some days you win, some days you lose. The thing is that you play your best, even when enduring great adversity. The game must go on, as they say. And that story about you a few days back in *The Telegraph,* the one that Mr. Holmes helped to arrange, it really did not do justice to your perseverance and courage. You deserve all the praise and adulation you are receiving."

Godfrey blushed and looked down at the floor. "Uh, well, that is very kind of you to say so, Sir."

"That story, along with what we have heard about you and your play and now your current situation is what led to my request for you to come here this afternoon."

"Yes?"

"There is some considerable urgency to the matter. I assume you know what sporting event will be taking place in Paris next summer?"

Chapter Forty-Two

"Y ou mean the Olympic Games?" said Godfrey.

"Yes. And four years later, they will be held in America, and then, in 1908, we are hosting them here in London. That last date has not yet been announced, but the agreements are in place."

"That's excellent to hear, Sir, but—,"

"But what has that to do with you?"

"Well, yes, sir."

"The Olympic Association for Great Britain, which of course includes most of the Empire, is made up of a doddering bunch of old fuddy-duddies. Yours truly included. We had all come to the conclusion that we need a new face, a fresh face, a young face to be what the British people see when they think about the Olympics."

"You ... you don't mean me?"

"Indeed, I do."

"Well, that would be quite all right, I suppose. You can use my photograph if you think it would help. Blackheath, my home team that is, already has it on some of their posters. So, sure you can go ahead and use my face if you think it would do any good."

"Oh, no, my dear Godfrey. It is not your photograph we want; we want *you*."

"Me?"

"Yes. We want you to come on to the Olympic Committee of Great Britain as the Second Secretary. Lord Beauclerk will continue in his role as General Secretary as you would expect. He's frightfully efficient in that role but no good at all in front of a crowd or the Press. Can't get a sentence out without stuttering. That's why we need you. There's a meeting next week in Paris to plan for the games, and the Press will be all over it, and we need a strong, fine, young Englishman to represent the spirit of the Olympics to the English public. And, it goes without saying that your wife would travel with you."

"I ... I suppose I could do that. I was a second on the debating team from Cambridge. Public speaking is not my forte, but I can manage when I have to."

"Speaking is only the tip of the iceberg. We are forming an administrative network that will help to organize all types of sport across the nation, and eventually the Empire. We shall be starting with those twenty or so sports that will be competing in Paris, but each year we shall be adding new sports until every imaginable form of athletics is included. We shall look after the finances, the training, the facilities, the rules, the preparation of coaches and judges, the international tournaments. Young men and women will enter at the bottom of the pyramid and be funneled up to the top.

The best in the nation will then go on to the Olympic Games and the international tournaments. *That* is where we need you. Overseeing all that enormous web of programs is what we need a young, energetic, athletic man to be in charge of. If we are to succeed in Paris and St. Louis, we have to start now. Today. So, do you see why we decided to act quickly? That is why I needed you to come this afternoon. What do you say, Mr. Godfrey Staunton?"

Godfrey looked as if he had been struck by a bolt of lightning.

"I...I was not expecting this. Would it be all right if I thought about it for a day or two? I have the game this weekend, and I have to prepare for it."

"I'm afraid, Godfrey," said FitzClarence, "that time is of the essence. We have to move very quickly if we are to have a new Second Secretary in place in time for the meeting in Paris next week. I do apologize, but I have no choice but to request that you give me your answer now. The powers that be already have another chap waiting in the wings who they will ask if you do not agree."

Godfrey looked over at Holmes.

"Golly, Mr. Holmes, what do you think?"

"The world of amateur sport," said Holmes, "is not in my purview. You would be better to ask Dr. Watson."

The young man then looked at me.

"Dr. Watson?"

I thought it was a magnificent opportunity and said so. For a young man who had not yet reached his quarter-century on this earth to be offered an opportunity to be part of such a visionary movement as the Olympic Games and at the same time to influence millions of young men and women to pursue the grand spectrum of sport was beyond anything a young athlete could ask or imagine.

"Think of it, Godfrey," I said. "Years, even decades of youth from throughout the British Empire can be encouraged to engage in the brotherhood and sisterhood of sport. And you can be an influence upon them. It is an opportunity that is once in a lifetime. If it does not work out as you had hoped, you can always resign, but if this is your one and only opportunity, you should grasp it with both hands."

After saying those words, I wondered if I had let my enthusiasm and my passion for sport get the better of me, but Godfrey merely looked at me and nodded.

"Right. That does make sense, Doctor. But I wish Millie were here with me. She's always so sensible. This will affect our life together."

"Your wife," said FitzClarence, "will be returned to you shortly. We shall see to that. If at that time, you discuss the matter with her and you change your mind, that is quite acceptable."

"Oh, thank you, Sir. Then I would gladly accept your offer. And I am sorry, but I cannot even think about it until next week. I have the final game for England on Saturday, and I have to try to focus my thoughts on it until it's over."

"Yes, yes, of course, you do. Mind you, at the level of the Olympic Association, we do not concern ourselves with rivalry between England, Ireland, Scotland, and Wales. At the Olympics, we all compete under the same flag. The divisions within our sceptred isles are completely inconsequential. But we understand that you have an obligation and we respect that. Just please do not exhaust yourself in any way that would require you to forfeit the trip to Paris. If that were to happen, we would have to replace you with our second choice. Oh, do be careful."

"Yes, I will. I can promise you that."

"Splendid."

I thought that Godfrey was walking on air as he descended the stairs back to the ground floor of White's and out on to the pavement of St. James Street.

"Can you believe it, Doctor," he said to me. "They are going to get Millie back and make me the Second Secretary, and we will have a life of traveling the world and engaged in the international brotherhood of sport. It is a dream come true."

"Yes," I said, "you are very fortunate. However, please come back to your senses and listen for a minute. There is something Holmes, and I learned earlier today about Millie's whereabouts, and we are determined to find her."

"Oh, that is awfully good of you, Doctor, but my mind is so much more at ease now. Mr. Holmes, you and Scotland Yard have worked hard, I am sure, on my behalf, but Millie is still a captive. Now, I have thousands of people who are going to help to find her. So, it really is not necessary for you to continue."

"Godfrey," I said, "now listen." I then briefly explained our reasons for concluding that Millie was being held somewhere along the Severn Estuary. He listened politely, although in a rather desultory manner.

"Thank you, Doctor. May I suggest that you immediately pass that information along to Sir Clarence's office. I am sure that their resources far outnumber those of yourself and Mr. Holmes. I am enormously relieved that the entire force of the British government will be assisting me. I am, of course, deeply appreciative of the efforts you and Mr. Holmes have rendered to date even if they have not been productive. But you do not need to trouble yourself any further. I am quite certain that Millie's life as well as mine and those of our soon-to-be-begotten children are in good hands. Good day, gentlemen."

With that, he turned and walked toward the nearest cab and rode off. Holmes had stood by throughout my conversation with Godfrey, saying nothing. He was nonchalantly smoking a cigarette and gazing down St. James toward Pall Mall and had ignored Godfrey's comments entirely.

Chapter Forty-Three

"Holmes," I said, "did you hear what Godfrey just said?"

He appeared to ignore my question entirely and kept gazing off into the distance.

"How did they do it?" he said.

"How did *who* do *what*?"

"Whoever this cabal of criminals are behind Millie's abduction and the manipulation of the bets on the games, somehow managed to get to one of the highest offices in the land and corrupt him."

"What are you saying?" I demanded. "Do you believe that so respected a civil servant as Sir Clarence FitzClarence has been corrupted? You think that his offer to Godfrey was not genuine?"

"My dear Watson. The good Lord gave you a brain. Kindly try to use it. Of course, the offer was fraudulent. I do not follow sports at all, and even I could name a half a dozen chaps who would be far more appropriate for appointment to the Olympic Association's leadership. You could, I am certain, name two dozen. Why not invite Arthur Gore? He just won Wimbledon, did he not? Or Bob Fitzsimmons, the boxer? Godfrey has nothing to his name except two international caps and one dead wife. The entire thing is a setup."

"But why?"

"Honestly, Watson, open your eyes and look at it. Godfrey resisted temptation directed to his physical and animal appetites. He sent the scoundrel offering fame and fortune packing. And so, they have come at him with the most dangerous temptation of all. Power. And not merely power in its raw and forceful dimension, but power disguised as the ability to fulfill his own most noble desires. And it appears that this time, they—whoever *they* may be—have won. His mind will no longer be on winning the next rugby game; it will be on his trip to Paris. The Home Nations Championship has become inconsequential to him. His play this Saturday at the final game for England will be lackadaisical. Scotland will win the match. Ireland will go on to win the cup, and those who have manipulated the betting will go home with a fortune."

"But he will be the Second Secretary of the Olympic Association. That is a splendid opportunity for a young man like Godfrey."

"Oh, please, my dear friend. Do not be hopelessly naïve. The most fickle status in the world is a political appointment. It can be given one day and snatched away the next when it is no longer useful to those who control it. If Godfrey plays in such a way that the game is lost then, if he is lucky, he might get his trip to Paris but not a jot more. His usefulness will have been used up."

"So, what are you going to do now?"

"*We*, my friend, for I am in need of your assistance, are going to hurry down to Bristol and try to rescue Millie."

"You don't believe that Sir Clarence will honor his word to find her."

Holmes did not answer. Instead, he gave me a withering glance that said, without speaking, that I had been duped.

We walked back up to Baker Street in silence, but when we arrived, Holmes asked if I would mind staying the night so that we could leave early the following morning. I agreed, and we passed a quiet evening together. He was lost in thought, and when he spoke, it was only to repeat his befuddlement at how this confederacy of criminals could have extended their tentacles to one of the most protected of public offices.

At nine o'clock, I got up out of my chair and announced that I was retiring for the night. If we were to be up and out early in the morning, I was determined to get adequate sleep. I had just turned toward the bedroom when suddenly there came a tapping on the Baker Street door, followed by a ringing of the bell.

Holmes and I looked at each other, and both shrugged. I was not expecting anybody, and neither was he. As Mrs. Hudson had retired for the night, I headed for the stairs. At the bottom, I opened the door and in the dim light was greeted by a man with a square, massive face, thatched brows, and a determined jaw. When he removed his hat, I recognized Dr. Leslie Armstrong. Standing behind him was another man, a head taller and several inches wider in the shoulders. It was Godfrey Staunton.

"Good evening, Dr. Watson," said Dr. Armstrong, "kindly accept my apologies for such a late call. Is Mr. Holmes in? I hope he has not already retired for the night."

"No, no. He's still up. Please, come in. Hello, Godfrey."

Godfrey responded with a muttered greeting but did not look at me. I led them up the stairs and into the parlor, where Holmes was standing and smiling warmly.

"Ah, how good of you to drop in this late in the evening," Holmes said. "Please, let me take your coats and be seated. Some brandy, perhaps, to warm your hearts on cold night."

Dr. Armstrong began again to apologize, but Holmes cut him off.

"Not necessary. Not at all. I was expecting you, just not quite so soon. Please, gentlemen, make yourselves comfortable and begin your account of why you have come to see me."

"Godfrey has something he has to say to you," said Dr. Armstrong.

We now looked directly the young man who only a few hours ago had become Holmes's former client. He looked rather embarrassed and kept his gaze to the floor.

"After we parted this afternoon," he said, "I went straight away to Uncle Jimmy's place to tell them about all that had happened. He was somewhat skeptical, saying that it was unearned, but Lady Maynooth was very cheerful and quite thrilled. Both of their reactions were what I had expected. But then this evening I went over to Dr. Armstrong's house and, well, I suppose you might say that he slapped some sense into me."

"Metaphorically only," said the doctor.

"Yes, well, he told me in no uncertain terms that when something seemed too good to be true, it invariably was. And then he named off exceptional sportsmen from every sport in the Olympics who were much more deserving and every bit as attractive on a poster as I was. And then he told me that I was being used as a political pawn. And then he said that I should not count for a minute on Millie's being found. And then he called me some rather unpleasant...but I fear justified...names for having dismissed Mr. Sherlock Holmes. So, Mr. Holmes, I am here to apologize and to ask that you accept me again as your client and help find my wife."

"Godfrey," said Holmes, "you are a fortunate man to have two people in your life who love and care for you enough to tell you the truth even when it is not pleasant to hear. One of them is here with you and tomorrow morning, first thing, Dr. Watson and I are off to find the second one, your exceptional and lovely wife."

"You mean you were going to keep on the case anyway?"

"Of course, I was. May I remind you that it was Millie who hired me, not you, and I shall keep looking for her until I find her and return her safely to her husband's arms."

"Well, then I have to come with you."

"No. That is out of the question."

Godfrey looked startled and even somewhat angered.

"If you know where she is, then I have to come and help."

"I know only the general location where I expect she is being held. I must be frank with you; it is not yet a certainty."

"But then you need all the help you can get. I must come."

"Again, if I may be frank, your presence would be more trouble than help. Besides, you have an obligation to play your match the day after tomorrow."

"The game, the Championship does not matter compared to finding Millie. You have to let me."

"Godfrey, answer this question honestly. If Millie were on the other end of a phone call at this minute and asked if she thought you should forfeit the game and come with me to look for her in a location that was not certain and on the questionable chance that you might be of some assistance, or that you should attend your team practice tomorrow and play your heart out of England on Saturday...what would she say."

"You're not being fair, Mr. Holmes. You know what she would say."

"Do I? Best you tell me."

"She would tell me to get up off me arse and go and play the game and leave the detective work to those who knew what they were doing. She's like that."

"And you are lucky that she is."

Godfrey stood and nodded to Dr. Armstrong.

"We'll be on our way. Thank you for being so committed to helping."

"It is what I do and who I am," said Holmes.

Godfrey was pulling on his coat when he turned again to Holmes.

"About that threat they made...you know...about the Vitriol. Do you truly believe that anyone would do something so vile and evil?"

Holmes did not answer immediately. I could sense that he was choosing his words carefully.

"It is highly unlikely as they would not do anything until the game was over and their nefarious plans had already come to naught. There would be nothing then to gain. However, I do know, from my years of dealing with the criminal mind, that there is always a possibility that some might act in abject cruelty just for the sake of spite and revenge."

"Please, Mr. Holmes, don't let anything happen to her."

"That is my calling. Yours is to make her proud of you by winning the game."

"And you will promise to let me know everything you find out. Immediately. Everything. You have to do that."

"You have my word."

The two of them descended the stairs and departed into the night.

Chapter Forty-Four

Five o'clock the following morning found Homes and me at Paddington, boarding the first train of the day to Bristol. The GWE ran an express with only a half dozen stops, and we expected to be at our destination within three hours. For most of the journey, I read and Holmes paced. After pulling out of the station at Bath, he came and sat down.

"Do we have any idea how many men might be holding her?" I asked him.

"A minimum of two, possibly more, as they would have to watch her in shifts."

"Armed?"

"Most likely. You have your service revolver? Good. I have my Webley."

"There's only two of us. That's not much if they have four or five."

"I sent a note to Lestrade. He agreed to have four constables available to assist us if we have to storm some barricaded hideout."

"Will they be armed?"

"They will be police officers on duty and will have billy clubs."

That was not reassuring.

At just after eight, we crossed the River Avon and ten minutes later arrived at Bristol Temple Meads.

"Can we find a cab to Severn Beach?" I asked.

"Not yet. That will be our second stop," Holmes replied.

"Would you mind telling me what our first stop is?"

"The post office; their telephone records."

His methods made sense. The Royal Mail controlled the telephone services in this part of the country. They would have the records as to which house, flats, stores, and offices had telephones. It was not likely that more than a handful had them in the small neighborhoods close to the Severn. All we had to do would be to find and observe them methodically and then make our move.

The central office of the Royal Mail was housed in an elegant stone building facing Queen Square. The doors opened at nine and we entered. I took a seat in the waiting room, and Holmes quickly approached the most senior-looking man behind the counter. I watched as they chatted briefly and then the two of them vanished into the inner sanctum of the edifice.

I waited patiently for a half hour. At the three-quarter mark, I was up and pacing. By an hour, I was fretting, imagining that during all the time that was passing, the danger to Mrs. Millicent Staunton was becoming greater.

Finally, after an hour and a quarter, Holmes re-emerged bearing a large, folded piece of paper.

"What in heaven's name took you so long?"

"The Royal Mail is run by public servants," he said. "They do their jobs effectively but rigidly according to the manuals they have been issued. A request from a private detective for the location of telephones in a specific neighborhood is not a matter that is routinely handled. To begin with, they had no reason to believe me when I said that my name was Sherlock Holmes."

"But they've heard of you, haven't they?"

"Of course, they have, thanks to your sensational stories—which I must confess, have occasionally come in useful. But anyone could walk into the Bristol Post Office and say they were Sherlock Holmes. However, I am indebted not only to you but also to your friend, Mr. Sidney Paget, for his very good likeness of me he has drawn for the stories in the *Strand*. One of the young assistant clerks had read and re-read all of your stories and could vouch for my looking exactly like Paget's portraits of me."

"Yes, but what happened then?"

"The chap who is in charge of opening and closing the records room, and the only one entrusted with the key, does not start his shift until half-past nine."

I sighed. "But you did get what you needed."

"Yes. I brought an ordnance map with me, and they were able to mark on it all of the places where telephones are now installed between Chittening and Oldbury. We can go over it in the cab. It is an hour's drive to from here to our start."

It was difficult to find a cab that was willing to take us an hour away from the city. I ended up offering a cab driver two pounds for the full day if he would look after our needs until the evening. He agreed, and we climbed in and set out at a quick trot toward the shore of the Bristol Channel.

Holmes spread his map out across our knees and indicated the area of our search with his pencil.

"The waterfowl Millie listed are only along the south shore. The train whistle you heard could only have come from a train emerging from the eastern portal of the tunnel. Up and down a shoreline, a train whistle can be heard for up to three miles; over land, less than two. Therefore, we are searching within this elongated rectangle area, stretching three miles along the shoreline in either direction for the portal, and back a mile or so inland."

"Very well," I said, "And are these places marked 'X' the ones that have a telephone?"

"Precisely. There are forty of them."

"Good heaven's Holmes. By the time we get to the Channel, it will be noon. Sunset is just after six. The game is tomorrow. We don't have enough time."

"Then we must use our time to the utmost efficiency. We can rank all these places according to their probability."

"Something like *eliminate the impossible...*?"

"Not exactly. More like *start with the most likely, and ignore the less.*"

As we bumped and bounced our way out of Bristol and along the Portway leading to the Channel, Holmes ticked off one location after the other.

"A local police office? Not likely. A chemist shop? No. No also to a wharf warehouse where they unload fish, an office of a barrister and solicitor, an estate agent's establishment."

"What about this place?" I asked, pointing to a small hotel that fronted onto the water.

"Thank you, Watson. A reasonable place to keep someone captive, especially in the winter season when no one is taking their holidays."

It took the better part of the hour, but by the time we reached Chittening, we had restricted our most likely locations to eight. Our first stop, the Berwick Lodge, the one I thought was a small hotel, turned out to be a substantial red-brick manor house that was surprisingly elegant with an excellent restaurant. Neither of us had had anything to eat since our early pastries purchased at Paddington, and the menu offering lobster, guinea fowl, or stone bass was sorely tempting but, alas, there was no time. The manager assured us that there were no long-term guests and displayed the telephone log showing that no call had been placed to London or anywhere else during the time we had been speaking to Millie.

We departed and moved on. By the time we reached our next possible location, a full hour had passed. The Plough Inn sat on a country road south-east of Pilning and, during the winter season, catered primarily to the local population. The barkeep was chuffed beyond words to have a visit from Sherlock Holmes and seemed terribly disappointed that he could not claim to have any young woman being held hostage in his establishment.

"There's four rooms to let upstairs, that all," he assured us. "Doors are open. Go take a look." We crossed him off the list and moved on.

It was the same story at Shirley's Café at Severn Beach. Miss Shirley, a jovial, friendly lass who appeared to have enjoyed her delicious baked goods perhaps more than might have been good for her, happily showed us her living quarters behind the café. Except for her slobbering, friendly dog, it was empty.

"You might give the Tea Cottage a look in," she suggested. It's only two blocks up the shore. Usual, it's boarded up during the winter, but I have not been past it for several weeks. You never know, now do you."

It was still boarded and, on close inspection, proved not to be inhabited.

Our list had now been reduced to four somewhat probable locations. The problem was that our time before dark had also been reduced. It had gone four o'clock before we stopped at our fifth prospect, The King's Arms. It was another small, village pub with three rooms on the second floor. All three were inhabited by older men who had spent years on the fishing boats in the Channel, but neither they nor the owner nor any of the patrons had any knowledge of any recent men from outside the village who had been living in the area for the past few weeks.

"No men," said one of the portly women who was enjoying an ale along with her equally portly husband. "But there's a new woman up in Redwick who comes into the post office and the food shops quite regular like. She's in a cottage that backs onto The Pill. That's the only new face around here this winter."

"Do you know," said Holmes, "if the cottage has a telephone?"

"Funny you should ask," she said. "I saw the boys putting a line in there back in November. Odd place to have a telephone, if you ask me, seeing as there is one at the post office and it can't be more than fifteen minutes' walk from the cottage."

We returned to our waiting cab and gave directions to the driver.

"It is next on our list," said Holmes, "but if the only person seen coming and going is a single woman, it is not an overly likely prospect."

By the time we had made our way out to the sea wall and back down and long inlet known as The Pill, the sun was nearing the horizon. We had not much more than an hour and a half left of sunlight. As we drove inland along Severn Way, I could see a small, two-story house set back a hundred feet from the road and backing onto the water. From a distance, it appeared to have a small fence and garden in front of it and rows of elm trees along the drive.

"Do we know who lives there?" I asked Holmes.

"The name registered on the telephone exchange is Hughes, but that says nothing. That name is a dime a dozen throughout England."

We were approaching from the north-west and had a clear view through the cab windows of the front and one side of the building. At about fifty yards from the drive, Holmes pushed my head aside, stuck his head out, and shouted.

"Driver! Stop! Here, now!"

Chapter Forty-Five

The cab slowly and halted and Holmes bolted out the door.
"Watson, the field glasses!"

I scrambled and fumbled and pulled them out of my valise and handed them over to him. While I was joining him on the roadway, he inspected the house. Then he handed me the glasses.

"Please observe the window on the second floor; the one closest to the back of the house."

I raised the glasses to my eyes and focused them.

"That is odd," I said. "It looks as if the window has bars across it."

"Now, look at the smaller window that is to the right."

The adjacent window was of the size and dimensions that many houses would put in an indoor lavatory. It also had a set of bars across it.

"It looks to me," I said, "like some sort of prison cell. Should we go and knock and find out?"

"Good heavens, no. Not yet. If this is the place where Millie is being held, we do not want to give away our presence. If it is not, then a closer inspection will not hurt."

"Except for the time," I said.

"Quite so. We can cut through the adjoining field and try to get closer."

Holmes had the driver pull the cab back around and up against a copse of trees. Then he and I walked through the field that ran between the roadway and the water. It was not exactly a field. This close to the water caused there to be numerous marshy spots and puddles. By the time we were at the edge of the property, our boots were covered with mud, and we had sloshed and stuck and come unstuck for at least a third of the way. The house was on a small rise of high ground surrounded by lands that were at an elevation just above the reach of the high tides that swept up the Channel. It was plain to see why no other houses had been built close to it.

From our new vantage point, we had a view now of the back of the house and the north-west side. There was another window on the rear of the house in the same corner room, and it likewise had bars across it. While Holmes trained the glasses on that window, I kept my eye on all of the other windows in the back and side of the house. The draperies were only partially drawn, and I could see dark shapes moving back and forth across the openings.

"How many are there?" Holmes asked.

"Hard to say. I can see two distinct shapes now. Oh, there's a third. What about you?"

"I am homing in on the upstairs window. It appears that there is one person in that room and sitting in a chair."

We kept watching. I spotted a fourth body. Then Holmes sputtered triumphantly.

"Ah ha. There she is. It is a body that is as tall as you or me and has a distinctly female shape. She's being kept behind bars. We've found her. It's Millie."

I gave him a pat on the back. "Bravo, but now what do we do? Shall we storm the door?"

"No. The risk would be too great. We have to assume that they are armed and even with the element of surprise, the chance of Millie's being harmed, not to mention our being shot, is beyond an acceptable level of possibility. No, I shall wire Lestrade and have him order a small squad of police officers to join us at first light tomorrow. Once they see that they are surrounded with no chance of fighting their way out, we shall have them."

"Where to now?" I asked.

"Back to Bristol. I need to send messages off to Lestrade."

"Then why not just stay at that Berwick Lodge? It's much closer and, if you recall, they have a telephone. You could phone Lestrade. And we might get two hours more sleep before our assault tomorrow morning."

"Watson, that is an excellent suggestion. You truly are useful at times."

The cab dropped us off at the elegant local hotel and the driver, other than scowling at the mud now on the floor of his vehicle, thanked us for our patronage. Holmes quickly stepped inside to the front desk and arranged for an immediate phone call to Scotland Yard. He met me a few minutes later in the lobby looking somewhat satisfied.

"Lestrade informs me that he will have a large police carriage here tomorrow morning at five o'clock along with six armed constables and a ramming pole. We should be at the house by five-thirty and able to overwhelm the house and the guards. This long and trying mission appears to be coming to a successful completion."

"Are you going to send a note off to Godfrey?" I asked. "You did give him your word that you would keep him up to date immediately anything transpired."

"You are right. I did. I shall send off a telegram this evening."

That night, I slept little. There is a feeling that comes over a man when he knows he is about to march into battle. I first felt it during my days in the Afghan War and have known it again many times as I took my place alongside Sherlock Holmes, and we faced down the forces of evil. That night, I felt it again. Come the morning, we would, Lord willing, surprise our enemy and rescue the lovely young mother-to-be who had now been held captive for over a month. If, by chance, they were prepared or could take up their positions with alacrity once they heard us at their door, there was a risk that gunfire would be exchanged.

Before putting out the light for the night, I cleaned and loaded my service revolver and laid it on the bedside table.

Chapter Forty-Six

Whe hotel staff, as requested, gave me a knock up at half-past four. First light had not yet broken, and I bathed quickly and dressed in the lamplight. In the lobby of the hotel, Holmes was waiting for me but said nothing. On the stroke of five, a large four-wheeler police carriage rolled silently up the drive of the hotel. The only sound was from the snorting and pawing of a magnificent pair of police horses.

There were six quite imposing constables in the wagon with us. Holmes had prepared a sketch diagram for each of them showing the layout of the property and the house. As we traveled, he went over his plan of attack, showing the points of entry to the building, the likely places where a guard might be encountered, and, most importantly, the room on the upper floor where Mrs. Staunton was being held. Two of the constables were designated to rush to the room and secure it so that no harm could come to the prisoner.

It took forty-five minutes to go from the hotel to the house on The Pill. By the time we were making our approach back up from the mouth of The Pill River, dawn was breaking. Within fifteen minutes, the sun would rise over the horizon, and all residents of the house would likely be awake. If we could barge in whilst some of them were still asleep, it would make the mission much easier.

We stopped just before the end of the drive and briefly debated trying to walk stealthily overland or to race down the driveway with the wagon. Given our experience with the muck and mire, we chose the latter.

The senior constable gave the command, and the driver laid his whip to the haunches of the horses. They reared and bolted into action. Within a few steps, they were at full gallop and thundered their way down the driveway. The driver reined them in and, applying the brake, skidded the carriage to a stop. The first two constables burst out of the door, leapt over the steps and onto the porch. In unison, they hurled their bodies toward the door, landing their powerful shoulders against it. The latches shattered, and the door burst open. The men rushed inside, pistols drawn, ready to disarm any guards that stood in their way.

On their heels came the next two men. They flew through the door, along the hallway and up the stairs to the prisoner's room. The last two followed them and began to sweep every room in the house, shouting at the inhabitants to come out with their hands in the air. Holmes and I hurried in behind the final pair.

As the constables were clearing the lower rooms, I could hear the two who had gone upstairs kicking down the door to Millie's room. The first two fellows, having not encountered any guard, then leapt up the stairs and began to kick in the doors of the various bedrooms, lavatories, servants' quarters, and closets.

Something was terribly wrong. The house was empty.

Dishes and food from the last meal eaten there were still on the dining room table. Unwashed pots and pans and food containers were all over the kitchen. Some articles of clothing still hung in the closets and a few sheets and towels drooped from the clothesline that was now visible from out the kitchen window.

"Hate to tell you, Mr. Holmes, Sir," said one of the men, "but it looks like someone snitched on you. Somebody put a fire under the backsides of whoever was here, and they're gone. I'd say they must have beat it out of here just about dessert time by the looks of things."

Sherlock Holmes is not given to cursing or uttering profanities, but I could tell by the look on his face that several such expressions were racing through his mind.

"What time," he asked, "did the late train leave from Bristol last night?"

"That, Sir," said another one of the men, "would have been the eight o'clock, assuming they were going toward London. If they left here by seven, they could have made it."

"When is the first one this morning?"

"It's already gone, Sir. Pulled out at six. Just a few minutes ago."

"And the next one?"

"At half-past eight. You can make it with no need to rush."

"There is a telephone here," said Holmes. "One of you, please, call the train station and if there is any chance that the train has not left yet, have the station master hold it and look for a gang of men and a young woman who most likely has been drugged."

"Won't do no good, Sir," can a reply. "The telephone is in the kitchen, and I already checked it. The line has been cut."

"And if you don't mind my saying something, Mr. Holmes," said the youngest constable, "might I add an observation?"

"Please, yes, whatever you want. Go ahead."

"Well, Sir, it's like this. We have to go into a great many houses, at least one or two a week, and I think the older chaps here who've been on the force much longer than I have will back me up on this, Sir, but it doesn't look to me like it's a gang on men you're looking for. If you look around this place, Sir, in the lavatories and the bedrooms and the closets, there's not a single piece of anything that would belong to a man. Everything in this house, everything I've seen so far that is, belongs to a lady. This has been a house full of women. Entire like, only women. You chaps agree?"

Grunts and words of agreement came from the others.

For a moment, Holmes looked stunned, and then he sat down and leaned back in one of the armchairs and lit a cigarette.

"Of course. Yes. That is why we could not stop them in Fishguard. We were looking for men, and they used women instead. They must have been waiting for her in the loo and then jumped on her, used chloroform, and took her to the station, right under our noses."

"Could they do that?" I asked. "Millie's quite the strapping girl. It would take at least two men to restrain her."

"Or four young, strong women," said Holmes. He then turned to the team of constables.

"Officers, let us make use of the time before we have to leave. Could you go through this house and pack up anything that might give any clue as to who we are dealing with? Clothing, perfumes, scraps of paper, books, anything. There may be some connection back to the criminal conspiracy behind this."

"Begging our pardon, Mr. Holmes, Sir," said the same young constable. "But you might like to start with the envelope and the perfume bottle on the sideboard."

"Why there?"

"Well, Sir, mostly because the envelope has your name on it."

Chapter Forty-Seven

Holmes jumped to his feet and walked across the room. He tore open the envelope, read it, and handed it on to me. The contents were written in a woman's hand and read:

My dear Mr. Sherlock Holmes: Did you honestly believe that we were so incompetent that we would not know of your arrival at the Berwick? How very naïve of you, Sir. Your persistence, however, has become somewhat of a nuisance to us. Therefore, we are leaving the fate of Mrs. Millicent Staunton in your hands.

You must contact her husband as soon as possible this morning and remind him of our final demands. While it is acceptable for England to win the match with Scotland, the margin cannot be by more than five points. Given Mr. Staunton's commanding skill on the team, there is no question that he can deliver this result.

If our demands are met, Mrs. Staunton will be delivered to her husband within fifteen minutes of the end of the match and, as both she and the child in her womb have been well-cared for, she will be lovely and radiant and healthy when she meets him.

However, if he dare deny us, we will still deliver her to him within fifteen minutes but he might not recognize her. Also, there can be no guarantee of the well-being of her unborn child.

If you doubt our word, you might like to sample to contents of the bottle that was sitting beside this letter.

We urge you to govern yourself accordingly. Let me remind you that circumstances rule men; men do not rule circumstances.

"Constable," Holmes said to the youngest officer, "would you mind taking the glass stopper out of the bottle and very carefully, keeping your nose well back from the mouth, describe the perfume in it?"

The lad walked over to the sideboard, undid the stopper and, from a few inches away, took a sniff.

"Holy smoke!" he shouted and jumped backwards. "It's sulphuric."

"Pour, if you would," asked Holmes, "a few drops on the wood."

The constable picked up the bottle gingerly and slowly dribbled a small amount on the surface of the sideboard. Immediately we could hear the sizzle erupting and saw the yellowish fumes rising. An acrid stench soon filled the air.

"It's Vitriol, Mr. Holmes," the constable said. "Vitriol, and a strong concentration it looks like."

"That is what I feared."

Over the next fifteen minutes, the constables collected and deposit numerous articles that had been left behind in the house. The items of women's clothing, gathered from several bedrooms, indicated that those who were holding Millie captive were not emaciated.

The item that broke my heart was a bundle of unopened letters. There were nearly thirty of them, all addressed to Godfrey Staunton at the address of the couple's new home in Chelsea. They had never been mailed.

"How utterly inhuman," I said as I leafed through them. "Millie wrote every day to Godfrey with the promise from her captors that they would put her letters in the post. And they lied to her."

More useful, it turned out, was a sheet of paper on which someone had written sloppily in pencil the same words that appeared in the letter to Sherlock Holmes.

"They made a first draft," I said, "before writing out the final one to you."

"No, Watson," replied Holmes. "The contents are not merely an almost illegible scribble. Many of the words are abbreviated. They took dictation over the telephone. This entire affair is being orchestrated from other location; London most likely."

"Can you find out?"

"If we leave here within a few minutes, we shall have enough time before we board our train to run into the Central Post Office and ask to see their log of calls."

"You also need," I told him, "to send a note to Godfrey informing him of all that has happened."

"I was hoping that you would not remind me. It would better if I could claim to have forgotten."

"You never forget anything, Holmes."

"Nevertheless, telling him about the Vitriol and the letters is not going to help him play his game."

"Can you not wrap whatever you say in abundant words about his pledge to Millie and what she would wish him to do?"

"Excellent advice, my friend. I shall attempt to do so."

It took just over an hour for the magnificent police horses to trot us quickly back into Bristol. Upon arriving at the Queen Square, we thanked the constables, bade them goodbye, and entered the central office of the Royal Mail as the doors were opening. This time it took Holmes only a few minutes to obtain the data he needed.

"The switchboard confirmed that they connected a call last evening to the Hughes residence up by Redwick. It came from the post office on Ecclestone Place in Belgravia."

"Isn't that the one," I said, "close to Victoria?"

"It is, which means that any of a thousand people passing through Victoria could have placed the call, but at least we know that our adversaries are not impoverished Eastenders."

"And are you now going to send your telegram to Godfrey?"

He gave me a bit of a look. "Oh, yes, of course. I had almost forgotten. Thank you so very much for reminding me."

"And you do know that you cannot leave out either the Vitriol or the letters."

"Again, Watson, you cannot imagine how grateful I am for your bringing them to my attention."

I knew he was annoyed with me but, after all, a promise is a promise, and a husband has a right to know everything that pertains to his wife and yet-to-be born child.

Chapter Forty-Eight

O nce we were ensconced in our cabin on the train to London, Holmes drew his long legs up under his body, placed his hands together under his chin with fingertips touching, and closed his eyes. For nearly half-an-hour, he held that pose, slowly moving his head back and forth from one side to the other and then raising and dropping it in a series of parallel vertical lines. It was as if he was tracing a grid of some sort in his mind. As he did so, a scowl appeared on his brow, and with each passing minute, it deepened.

Finally, he opened his eyes and pounded his clenched fists on his thighs.

"It's no use," he muttered to himself.

"What's no use?" I asked.

"Years ago, when I was living in Montague Street, I walked all the streets and laneways of the city, forcing myself to memorize every building, shop, intersection, office, and square of the city. It was a hobby of mine to have an exact knowledge of London."

"I have duly noted that in one of my stories. What has that to do with Millie?"

"In the letter they left for me, they explicitly stated that Millie would be delivered to Godfrey within fifteen minutes after the end of the game. That can only mean that whatever place they are now keeping her must be quite close to the Blackheath rugby grounds. I am wracking my memory to recall which hotels and pubs are within a fifteen-minute walk from the pitch. But it has been twenty-five years since I walked those streets and they are not coming back to me."

"You might have asked me for my help."

He gave me an odd look. "My dear friend, I am sure I have no memory whatsoever of your knowledge of London surpassing mine."

"Then allow me to remind your memory that I played two years for Blackheath and following every practice and every home game, my teammates and I visited every pub within a short walk of our pitch. Would you like me to name them all? Perhaps their locations as well?"

"Were not those days a quarter-century back for you as well?"

"Yes, and for the past twenty-five years, I have faithfully attended many games played by my old team and have either celebrated victory or consoled my soul over defeat in the pubs and cafés of the neighborhood. Would you like to know the current prices for Guinness and a steak and kidney pie?"

"Those will not be necessary, and your expertise in this matter clearly surpasses mine. What I want to know is where, within fifteen minutes of the Blackheath grounds, could one find a room to rent on a temporary basis in which to hide an abductee."

"The Angerstein Hotel. It is at the intersection of Woolwich Road and the avenue leading to the Blackwall Tunnel, halfway between the Blackheath pitch and the Thames. They serve excellent bangers and mash."

"Surely, that is not the only place."

"It is if you want a room for a night or two and meals sent up. Anything else is a half-hour away either over in Greenwich or up to Royal Arsenal. If Millie is being held within fifteen minutes of the grounds, she'll be in the Angerstein."

"Excellent, Watson ... truly excellent. Now, all we have to do is determine how we are going to get her out of there and over to the game before it ends. Any suggestions on that one?"

"The barkeep is a decent chap. I'm sure I could request his assistance."

We entered the station at Reading at eleven o'clock and changed trains for one that would take us to Waterloo. From there, according to Bradshaw's, we could catch a Southeastern train for the Westcombe Park Station, three blocks away from the Angerstein. If the trains were all on time, we could make it there by two o'clock. The game was scheduled to start at one and would last for the regulation eighty minutes of play plus a ten-minute half-time break. The referee might add additional time, but it would be unusual if it were more than ten minutes.

Our time was running out.

English trains are not as fervently punctual as the German ones. Of course, they are marginally better than the French and much better than those in Spain and Italy. Our trains that day came close to running on time. It had gone two o'clock when we alighted at Westcombe Park. From there we ran up Westcombe Hill Road to the hotel.

"The front door faces Woolwich," I shouted to Holmes.

"Where is the service entrance?" he asked.

"Around the back, off of Combedale. It will be faster if we go directly to the front desk."

"There may be sentries posted. Best not to take the chance."

We worked our way through a mews behind the hotel and up to the service entrance. I approached a young fellow who was bringing out a load of kitchen waste and held out a pound note.

"Young man, please tell Mr. Bunsby to come here on the double. It is exceptionally urgent. There will be another pound for you if you can get him here straight away."

The lad took the note and ran toward the door leading from the kitchen to the bar. A minute later, he returned holding—pulling would be a better word—on to the thick, tattooed arm of Jack Bunsby, the congenial barkeep of the Angerstein.

"Johnny Watson!" bellowed the barkeep. "Good heavens, what are you doing back here by the kitchen door? Get in and sit down. Haven't seen you here for weeks. Why aren't you over at the game? Good heavens, man. What's all this about?"

I introduced him to Sherlock Holmes.

His mouth dropped somewhat open. "Oh, dear, what's going on? If you're bringing Sherlock Holmes in through the kitchen, there's something in the wind."

I explained to him our reason for visiting and asked if, by any chance, a group of five women had registered last night.

"Well, Johnny, you'll have to ask the front desk about registration," he said. "But I just sent lunches for five up to room 207. And they weren't wanting no fish and chips or beef pies. No, none of that for them. It was soup and fruit and vegetables. No dessert neither. The likes of a lunch that no self-respecting Englishman would ever order. Five women if you ask me."

"We would like to visit that room, if we may," I said. "It would be awfully helpful if you could come with us. If they refuse to open the door, we may need your help using your passkey."

"That's all right, Johnny, but what if they are not the totties you be looking for? What if they're honest, paying patrons."

"We shall apologize profusely, retreat immediately, and send up some tea and scones to appease any indignation."

"That should do it. Very well, come with me."

"Just a moment," said Holmes.

"What is it this time?" I asked.

"Mr. Bunsby," he said to the barkeep, "could you take a moment to acquire a set of bolt-cutters from your serviceman? And a small sharp knife from the kitchen staff?"

"Aye, I can do that. You're thinking your lady might be tied up?"

"It is a possibility. In truth, it is quite probable. And, if I may, please tell me if there have been any unusual customers today in the restaurant or at the bar."

"Small crowd today what with the game on down at the grounds. All are regulars, except for the two blokes sitting by the door. They come in this morning, ordered their breakfasts, and have been sitting there ever since. Ordered ale and sandwiches at lunch but have otherwise been quiet and not disturbing anyone, so I let them sit there."

"No strange behavior?"

"They have a view of the staircase from where they are sitting and seems they keep taking looks up, but they haven't never moved out of their chairs except maybe to use the loo. That's all. Don't seem like particular dangerous or unsavory types, if you ask me."

I moved to the door that led to the restaurant and slipped my head around the corner. I could see the two men Jake Bunsby had referred to. I did not recognize them. Both were clean-shaven and reasonably dressed as gentlemen. Two glasses of ale with only an inch remaining in them were on their table. Beyond concluding that they were waiting and putting in time, there was nothing to distinguish them. I reported same back to Holmes.

"Best that we evade them all the same. We can take the servants' stairs up to the second floor."

The three of us made our way through the service rooms of the hotel to the back stairs and walked quietly up to the second floor and on to room 207. Jack knocked on the door. There was no answer, so he knocked again.

"Yes. Who there?"

"Kitchen," said Jack. "Coming to collect your dishes."

"A minute."

Chapter Forty-Nine

The door opened a minute later, and two young, dark-haired women faced us, each holding a pile of dishes in their hands and barring our entry to the room. Holmes immediately strode forward, pushed them aside and entered the room.

"No!" shouted one of them. "Cannot to come in."

I followed Holmes and Jack, somewhat hesitantly, came behind me and closed the door behind him.

On the far side of the room were two more women and, sitting in an armchair, her hands and feet bound and a gag across her mouth, was Mrs. Millicent Staunton.

I withdrew my service revolver and swung it in an arc around the room, pointing first at one of the women and then the other. They did not appear to be defiant in the least. The color was draining from their faces, and fear was written all over them.

"Do not move," I commanded them.

Holmes grabbed the paring knife from Jack and rushed over to Millie. There were no chains holding her in place, but she had strong cords around her ankles and wrists. He first undid the gag and then started on the ropes with the knife.

"It's about time, Mr. Holmes," said Millie but, to my surprise, there was a cheerful lilt to her voice.

"Have you been harmed?" said Holmes. "Do we need to get you to hospital?"

"No. I have been cared for, and I would much prefer that you take me to my husband."

"Excellent. Jack, go downstairs and out through the back and find a police officer. These women are to be arrested and taken straight away to Scotland Yard."

"Oh, no," said Millie. "Let them go. They are merely pawns and are acting under duress. I have heard their entire life stories, and I bear them no ill will whatsoever. Let them go."

"Mrs. Staunton," said Holmes, "even if they appeared to you to have little choice in what they have done and treated you with respect, they have committed a various serious crime, and they must know something about who is behind this entire enterprise."

"No! They do not. Let them go. I will explain. Now, please can we get moving out of here? We are only a few minutes from the Blackheath grounds, and if we hurry, I can be there in time watch Godfrey. Please, Mr. Holmes. Now!"

Millie turned to the four women, who were holding on to each other and visibly trembling, and said something to them in a language that sounded like Latin. I could not catch any of its meaning except at the end she clearly stated the address of the house she and Godfrey had moved into in Chelsea.

"Did you just tell them where you lived?" I asked her, incredulous.

"Yes. I told them to come and see me tomorrow."

"Mrs. Staunton—,"

"I'll explain later. Now, please. We have to get out of here."

Jack led the way out of the room and toward the main staircase. Seven of us—Holmes, Millie, the four women who had been holding her and me—were right behind him. We ran along the corridor to the top of the stairs and then stopped.

At the bottom of the staircase, looking up at us, were the two blokes who had been sitting in the restaurant.

"You folks," said Jack, whispering, "use the back stairs. I'll have a bit of a chat with these two."

We turned around and rushed toward the servants' stairs. The last thing I saw was Jack walking down the stairs as the two men began walking up.

"And just where might you two lads be going?" he bellowed at them.

After that, all I heard was the sounds of a scuffle and some loud curses, followed by what must have been a body rolling down the stairs.

From the back door of the hotel, our troop ran south for a block on Combedale and then out to Westcombe Hill Road. Holmes and I were nowhere near as fast on our feet as were had been when much younger, but we kept going. Millie had hiked up her skirts and was running after a fashion while holding on to the sides of the dress with each of her hands. The other four had no such inhibitions and had quickly tucked the hems of their dresses up into their waists and, with bare legs flashing in the afternoon sun, were running like farm girls chasing a heifer.

A half a minute later we were parallel to the Westcombe Park station. Millie stopped and, breathless, shouted at me.

"Do you have any money?"

I was momentarily speechless but sputtered back. "Of course, I have some money. What in the world for?"

"Give me some, quick!"

I struggled to pull out my wallet.

"Quickly!" she shouted.

I opened my wallet in front of her, and she immediately grabbed two five-pound notes from the billfold, turned around and ran over to her erstwhile captors. She said something to them again in a Latinate language and pointed to the station. The four of them turned and ran toward it.

Millie shouted at Holmes and me. "Come on, the grounds are just up ahead." Her steps were halted by a loud shout from half a block away.

"Stop where you are if you know what's good for you!"

The two blokes from the Angerstein were running toward us; both were holding a knife in their right hand and a blackjack in their left.

"Run on," I ordered Holmes and Millie. "I can hold these bounders."

I planted myself in a contrapposto stance firmly in the middle of the pavement and raised my walking stick above my head.

"Get out of our way, old man," one of them screamed.

"You will stop this instant," I said in return, "or I shall have no option but to give you a thorough thrashing."

They looked at each other and then back to me as if I had just escaped from Bed'lam.

"You stupid fool. Get out of our way. We're after the girl."

"And you shall not have her!"

Chapter Fifty

"**D**o you want to have your gut stuck like a pig? Now move."

"What? Are you afraid to engage in battle?" I said, waving my walking stick, stepping forward with my left foot and slipping my right hand into my pocket.

"You asked for it," they yelled and came at me with knives flashing.

I dropped my stick until the closest one was about ten feet away. Then I pulled my service revolver from my pocket, pointed it at his quadricep, and pulled the trigger. The was a loud bang followed by the chap falling onto the pavement, grabbing his leg, and screaming in pain.

"Unfortunately, my dear fellow," I said, "so did you. And now you." I continued, pointing my gun at the second man. "Unless you want one in your leg as well, help your partner to his feet and call a cab and tell the driver to take you straight away over to the Brook

Hospital. It is only a few minutes from here on Shooters Hill Road. Did you get that? The Brook on Shooters Hill. Well, don't just stand there, help him up, and call a cab."

He gave me a very queer look but did as I told him. I turned and started running to the Blackheath Rugby Grounds. Within another two minutes, I could hear the roar of the crowd, and I hoped that it was for Godfrey scoring yet another try.

The bleachers and the stands were cheek to jowl as I elbowed and excused my way through the masses and toward the edge of the pitch. My first glance out to the open field revealed both teams walking off and toward their respective benches.

"What's going on," I asked a chap who was standing in the aisle. "I just arrived here. What's happening."

"The referee's allotted extra time," he said. "Fifteen minutes."

"Was that what the cheer was for?"

"Aye. It gives our boys all that time to try to put points up on the board."

I then looked over to the scoreboard and was horrified. After eighty minutes of play, the score was five to naught for Scotland.

"Merciful heavens," I gasped. "What happened?"

"It was going all for England until our Right Wing was carried off."

"Godfrey Staunton?"

"Is that his name? If he's our number 14, then that was him. Kept trying to walk by himself but couldn't do it. Had to come with the stretcher."

I pushed on toward England's bench. I could see Holmes and Millie standing behind it, waiting for the players to assemble before going into their dressing room for the break. I pushed and pardoned-me until I reached them.

"Where's Godfrey?" Millie was saying to anyone who was within hearing range.

"Millie!" came a shout from an enormous player. Underneath the dirt, I could make out the face of Cyril Overton.

"Millie! Oh, you're safe. Oh, Godfrey will be so relieved. You're safe. Oh, thank God."

"Cyril, where's Godfrey?"

"Down in the first aid room. Come on; I'll take you to him."

"What happened? Is he all right? Does he have to go to hospital?"

"No, he's alive, just not walking. He was playing the game of his life. Good Lord, he was crashing all over those jockies. They held him at five yards, and he twisted to toss the ball out to me. I would have had a clear dive into touch but one of their pack hit him from the side and buckled his knee, and his toss went all dizzy, and their Fly-half caught it and had the open field to run it all the way back to our in-goal. Come on; I'll take you to him."

In the wake of the enormous prop, we worked our way through the seething mass of humanity and down into the corridor that ran behind the bleachers. The fans had rushed down from their seats and stands to try to grab a glass of ale and a warm meat pie before the ten-minute break ended. Cyril bulled his way through them, separating the crowd with his one arm and hand while holding the other behind his back and firmly grasping Holmes's wrist. Holmes did the same for me, and I did likewise for Millie so that we would not become split apart in the mayhem. Our human chain snaked our way forward until we reached a large shed, the door of which was marked *INFIRMARY*.

Chapter Fifty-One

C yril pushed it open. Peering past him, I saw a player in his muddy uniform sitting on a cot with one leg down, and the other propped on a cushion. A large bandage had been wrapped around his knee. A nurse was at one end of the bed, and a man stood at the other.

"Godfrey! My good man!" said Cyril as we were dragged in. "look who's here."

Godfrey Staunton looked up and screamed. "Millie!"

He leapt off the cot, took two steps toward her but his face contorted with pain and he hopped on his good leg past the three men until he was upon her and they threw their arms around each other.

They were both clutching the body of their loved one fiercely. Godfrey was standing on his one leg and holding the other back in the air behind him. He tottered unevenly, and Millie turned to keep him upright. I could now see his face. Tears were streaming down it, and his eyes were squinted tightly as if in pain combined with profound relief.

After what seemed like a very long time, the couple loosened their grips and Godfrey turned to Holmes and me.

"Mr. Holmes, Doctor, thank you, thank you."

"Save it," said Cyril, "for later. We have fifteen minutes of added time thanks to you. There's a set of crutches by the counter. Start hobbling and you can watch the rest of the game. I have to get back to the team. We'll meet up when it's over."

"Can you catch them?" said Godfrey. "You can still win."

"We'll do our best," said Cyril as he made his exit back into the crowd out in the corridor.

The man who had been standing at the end of Godfrey's cot now came over to Holmes and me.

"Once again, Mr. Holmes, you have proved yourself," said Dr. Leslie Armstrong. "I may have to approve of your profession after all."

"As long as the criminal classes of Europe do not," said Holmes, "I shall be grateful."

Godfrey and Millie were understandably eager to be with each other, but that would have to wait. Loving *tête-à-têtes* could take place later. For now, the final fifteen minutes of the match was about to start. As soon as the crowd had thinned, Godfrey hobbled on his crutches, and we followed him to a reserved seating space behind England's bench.

A whistle was blown, and play was underway. England took possession and raced down the pitch. Herb 'The Octopus' Gamlin went tearing across the grass and pitched it back to Ernie Fookes, who in turn tossed it to Percy Stout. They had crossed over the Halfway line and were approaching the twenty-five-yard line when he ran up against Hadrian's Wall, as the Scottish Pack called itself. The attack died, and Scotland moved it down back into England's zone. England regained possession in their technical zone, but five of the fifteen minutes had been lost.

The fans, friends, and family members who surrounded us were screaming, hoping that volume and enthusiasm would somehow cause their team to evade complete humiliation and put at least a few points on the board.

Once again, the English ran their line into Scotland's zone. This time it looked as if they would be close enough to at least kick one through the goalposts. But to the horror of the crowd, a wiry Scottish back, Jimmy Gillespie, hauled down Art Rotherham just as he was preparing to drop the ball in front of his right foot.

Back and forth went the play as the clock ticked down the final minutes. When it showed only two minutes left, I could feel the energy of the fans fading. There was still that hope that springs eternal within the human breast, but it was dying.

Then it died. The final whistle blew. England had lost its last chance in the Championship. Scotland had won by a score of five to naught. England's players stood and quietly shook each other's hands, thanking one another for the camaraderie and fellowship of the past two months. Had they all been members of the same club, they could have promised to see each other again at the start of the next season, but they were not. They had been picked from more than a dozen clubs across the nation to play for England. A few might be chosen again next year and earn another set of caps, but most would be replaced by the next crop of earnest young players.

A reporter, followed by a photographer rushed up to Arthur Rotherham, the team captain. He immediately started to ask questions and, the instant the photographer indicated he was ready they posed, but the reported pulled a large wooden spoon out of his jacket and held it in from of Rotherham. A look of anger swept across the player's face, and I would not have been surprised if he had given an uppercut to the smirking face of the reporter. He held himself under control and turned and walked away.

"They gave us the wooden spoon," sighed Godfrey. "How utterly humiliating. The booby prize. That's what they give in the public schools to the team that is the worst in the season. Those fools from the press who wouldn't know a scrum from a try think they're so smart and can ridicule us. I wish we could have them out on the pitch for even five minutes. They'd be carried, every lousy one of them, off in a stretcher."

However, if wishes were horses…, so, we plodded our way along with the throngs of quiet fans through the stadium and out to the pavement of Charlton Road and took our place in the queue waiting for the next cab in the line. Upon reaching the front of the line, Millie turned to us.

"Again, Mr. Holmes and Doctor Watson, thank you. You put yourself at great risk to find me and return me to my husband. Would you be so kind as to allow us to show our appreciation by coming as our guests for dinner on Friday?"

"We shall be delighted to," I said, eagerly. "Now, mind you make sure your husband rests his leg. No trying anything too vigorous until it has healed."

"Of course, Doctor. Let me write out our address at our new home."

"Not necessary," said Holmes. "You are living at 106 Britten Street, are you not?"

"Why, yes. How did you know that?"

"Less than an hour ago, you gave it to your captors."

We climbed into the cab behind them, and Holmes gave the driver his address on Baker Street.

"Well done, Holmes," I said as we approached the Blackwall Tunnel to take us under the Thames. "Puts paid to another case successfully completed."

"It does not."

Chapter Fifty-Two

"**W**hy not? The wife has been found and restored to her happy husband."

"Allow me to remind you, my friend, that Danny O'Hearn was murdered and his killers are still at large. On top of that, there is a wickedly clever criminal conspiracy operating freely in London who have orchestrated murder, beatings, and kidnappings all to manipulate the betting on the games. If Ireland wins the Triple Crown, they stand to reap a fortune of ill-gotten gain."

"Oh, yes, quite so. Are you going to start after them straight away?"

"No. I shall wait until the week following this one. At that point, I expect that I shall have an easy time dragging them before the bar."

That made no sense whatsoever to me, but it was all the answer he was prepared to give.

On that Friday, the seventeenth of March, I took a cab to Baker Street immediately I had finished my day at my medical practice. Holmes was waiting for me, and together we rode south into Chelsea.

We stopped at an elegant red-brick terrace house adjacent to St. Luke's Gardens and were greeted at the door by a surprisingly young butler. Once inside, a maid who could have been in no more than her teens took our coats. I caught her eye, and she quickly looked away from me.

"Holmes," I whispered.

"Yes, yes. She was one of them."

"What is going on?"

"I am sure we shall find out."

The house, while not itself new, had the look of having been only recently furnished. The few pieces of art on the walls were prints of paintings by the cadre of recent English artists who titled themselves the Pre-Raphaelite Brotherhood. It occurred to me that the brilliant and energetic Mrs. Staunton had already turned her hand to decorating her new home.

Millie came rushing down the hallway to greet us, followed by Godfrey who had wonderfully progressed from his crutches to a labored hop and step with the heavy use of a cane. Being as I am, a doctor, I could not help but notice that her cheeks were somewhat more rounded than they were at her wedding, although her complexion was somewhat wan, as is common for a woman who is into the second month of her pregnancy.

They led us into their parlor, where Dr. Leslie Armstrong, looking as grim, ascetic, self-contained, and formidable as ever, rose to greet us.

For several minutes we exchanged some pleasant badinage about the weather before I demanded that Godfrey state his opinion on the game the next day between Ireland and Wales, the final game of the series that would determine who would be declared the winner.

"Well, I confess, it's a toss-up, it is. Scotland trounced Wales, but Ireland beat Scotland. Going on that record, I would have to give the nod to Ireland. And as they are still playing for the memory of Danny, I have to cheer for them now that we are out of the game."

"It should be a near run thing, whoever the winner is," I said. "I hear that several thousand fans have already come across the Fishguard ferry and invaded Cardiff."

"Yes, I read that in the *Pink'un* too. Can you imagine? They're saying that there could be 40,000 in the Arms park, half of them Welsh and half Irish and all of them drunk before noon."

My chat with him about rugby might have gone on, to the patient boredom of the rest of the room, had we not been interrupted by another young maid bearing a tray of sherry and warm pre-dinner treats. I looked up at her and then, somewhat in shock, looked over at Holmes who gave a slight nod.

Millie had noticed our reaction.

"Yes, gentlemen, we needed staff for our new home, and I hired all four of them."

"An explanation," said Holmes, quite sternly, "is required for what is, by all standards, a most unusual act on your part."

"Then I will have to give you one, won't I. Very well then, in order of their ages they are Catina, Imanuela, Laminita, and Tatum. They are sisters, all separated by not much more than a year. The youngest is sixteen, the eldest twenty-one. They come from a fine family who used to own large orchards outside of Bucharest. Their father was not only a successful grower but also a respected man of letters who had been elected to the City Council.

Several years ago, he and a large group of his colleagues sent a petition to the Emperor, requesting that Romanian citizens be granted all the same rights and privileges within the empire as Hungarians were. The following year he and all his colleagues were charged with treason and put in prison and there they remain. Their estates were confiscated, and their families were thrown into penury."

I had read about these events in the press. They had led directly to an influx of immigrants to England who were either running from persecution or seeking opportunities that were impossible in their home country.

"There were," continued Millie, "seven children in the family. These four are the oldest. The younger ones are still at home. Last year their hardship became unbearable, and their mother told the four of them that they had no other choice but to leave Romania and flee to England for their own good and, Lord willing, to send whatever money they could spare, back to the family. They are industrious, hard-working young women, and I am delighted that they can serve in our home."

Here she stopped speaking as if to say that her explanation had been completed. Holmes was having none of that.

"Mrs. Staunton, these industrious women as you call them, kidnapped you and held you hostage. Why are they in your home?"

"Oh, yes, I suppose I should explain. Well, if you must know, when they came to London, they spoke very little English and could only find intermittent day labor. They lived in a single room near Spitalfields and could hardly feed themselves. They were at the point of having to sell their bodies in the taverns of the East End when a man approached them and claimed he had an opportunity for them to earn a pound a day each plus all their living expenses. All they would have to do would be to abduct a certain

271

woman, hold her for several weeks without doing her any harm, and then release her."

"The certain woman," said Holmes, "would be you."

"Yes. Me. Well, they knew that it was not entirely a legal activity, but it was far better than working over in *The Ten Bells*, so they agreed they would undertake it on trial and, if the payment was reliable, they would keep going. Otherwise, they would release me. So, they agreed and were sent with detailed instructions to Wales where they found us, waited for me in the lavatory, grabbed my arms, and subdued me with chloroform."

"My dear lady," said Holmes, "that is a serious criminal offense."

"Oh, yes, but they apologized to me before doing so and have told me how sorry they were a dozen times a day since. But please, let me get on with my story, if you want to know what happened."

"Go on," said Holmes.

"When I regained consciousness, I found myself in a quite pleasant room with a comfortable bed and writing desk and an adjoining lavatory. The sisters brought me several changes of clothes from the shops in Bristol—,"

"You knew where you were?" said Holmes. "Surely they did not tell you."

"Oh, no, all I had to do was to look out the window at all the waterfowl flying back and forth, and I knew straight away that I was looking out over the Severn Estuary. Except for the times when Catina walked into the village to buy supplies and wire money to their mother, all five of us were confined to the house all day. We had nothing else to do, so, being women, we did as all women do. We chatted."

"And when," asked Holmes, "did you acquire fluency in the language of Romania?"

"I didn't, at least not at first. But all four of them went to school as did I, and we all had to learn Latin. Were you aware that Romanian is the closest present-day language in Europe to ancient Roman Latin?"

"No. Carry on."

"As we had hours to spend together, we redeemed our time, and they taught me to speak Romanian, which came quite easily because of my school-girl lessons in Latin, and I taught them English. They were exceptionally eager and diligent students, and now all of them, especially the youngest, Tatum, are reasonably fluent. We quite enjoyed helping each other, and I have to confess that we became quite friendly."

"Madam," said Holmes, "these women are not your friends. Are you aware that they sent a message to your husband threatening to disfigure your face and bosom with Vitriol? Are you aware that not one of the letters you lovingly wrote to your husband was ever put in the post? How can you possibly call them friends?"

"Oh, Mr. Holmes, you are thinking, if I may say with no disrespect, like a man. Women who share times of adversity become friends. They told me about the Vitriol, and I begged them not to write about it, knowing how it would torment Godfrey, but they told me that they had been given no choice. So, I insisted that they would let me insert a famous quotation from Herodotus, the Father of Lies. I did not expect that Godfrey would spot it, but I did hold out high hopes for you, Mr. Holmes."

"In vain."

"Yes. But I tried. As to the letters, they told me right off that they could not possibly let them be mailed, but I wrote one every day to my beloved husband for my own benefit. Thinking about him fondly with my heart becoming terribly sentimental helped me endure the weeks without his kisses and embraces."

"I have," interjected Godfrey, "now read every one of them. Several times over. I confess that they are now stained with my tears—,"

"The pathos is duly noted. Go on, please, Mrs. Staunton," said Holmes.

"There is really not much more to tell you. I made the phone call and was devastated that I could only speak to you, Mr. Holmes, and not Godfrey, but you were clever enough to ask me about the birds, and I was lucky enough to recall the Manx Shearwater. They received another phone call last week after which it was all a mad panic to get out of the house and catch the train to London. The girls again apologized—they were sobbing if you must know—for using chloroform on me, but I was bundled up and taken to Woolwich. The next thing that happened was when you and Dr. Watson burst into the room. Oh, I thought the four of them were going to die of fright. I felt so sorry for them. I—,"

"Thank you, Mrs. Staunton. Your account has been most illuminating. Is there anything you can tell me that might help to identify who was behind this series of crimes?"

"No."

"Nothing at all?"

'No. You are free to cross-question them if you like, but I have tried and tried over this past week, and there is nothing more they can tell you. Would you like to speak to them?"

"No. I suggest that we move to the dining room and see if they are as capable of seducing English sensibilities by their cooking as they are by kidnapping."

Chapter Fifty-Three

Dinner was a pleasant enough affair. Millie and Godfrey talked on about their plans for the house, about rugby, about names and schools for the coming child, about rugby, about contemporary English painters, about rugby, and about the general state of the Empire and which of the colonies had emerging rugby teams.

Holmes made a valiant effort to engage in the conversation as did I. Dr. Armstrong said little and seemed even more taciturn than I recalled his having been in the past.

At nine o'clock, we departed and hailed a cab. On the way home, Holmes posed a question to me.

"My dear Doctor, you are by far more of a sporting man than I am. Tell me, how long after a bet is won would the wager be paid out?"

"If the bet is placed at the site of the game, say at the pitch, the track, or the oval, it would be paid on the spot immediately at the end of the match."

"And if it were placed elsewhere, at a tavern or the office of a bookmaker?"

"Within a day or two."

"Never more than a week?"

"Good grief, no. By then the next game is about to take place, and a new round of bets are in order."

"Thank you, Doctor. That has been very helpful. Would you mind coming around to 221B on Sunday afternoon, nine days from now? Your assistance would be beneficial."

"Certainly, but what are you going to be doing between now and then?"

"I shall be intensely occupied."

The late editions of the newspapers the next day carried the news of the final game in the Home Nations Championship. Before one of the largest and most unruly crowds in the history of the game, the Irish National team had defeated the Welsh by one try; the only try that was scored during the entire game. Throughout the game, the fans had constantly pushed their way on to the pitch, and the referees and officials had to stop the game to force them back. On one of the plays, the Irish brothers, Mick and Jack Ryan had not merely tackled the Welsh captain, Billy Bancroft, they had tossed him right off the pitch and into the benches of spectators with the result that his ribs had cracked and he had to withdraw from the game.

The mood that evening in Cardiff would no doubt have been sullen, but the entire sodden Emerald Isle must have erupted with joy. For Ireland had not only won the Championship, they had secured the Triple Crown. All three of the other countries had been defeated without losing or tying a single match. Whoever had placed a bet on Ireland back around the New Year, when the odds against a Triple Crown were absurdly high, was now a rich man.

Later that night, whilst sitting by the hearth in my home, I took out the ticket I had held on England, tore it into pieces, and threw it into the fire.

Twice the next week, I had sent a note over to Holmes suggesting that we might meet for a meal or a quiet glass of brandy and twice he politely declined and reiterated his invitation for Monday, the 27th of March.

I appeared as requested, wondering what he had been up to. Upon entering the front room of 221B, all I could see on the floor were pages and pages of paper with writing on them and at least one hundred piles of small pieces of paper neatly laid out in rows on the dining table.

"Wonderful timing!" said Holmes when I entered. His greeting might have been enthusiastic, but his appearance was dreadful. He looked as if he had not bathed, shaved, changed his clothes, or eaten more than a few mouthfuls during the entire week. The ashtrays, on the other hand, were full and overflowing.

Chapter Fifty-Four

"**H**olmes! What is the meaning of this?" I demanded.

"The result of the application of logic combined with intense and concentrated labor. It is a rather reliable way to achieve one's ends, don't you agree? And now that you are here, you can help me complete the task."

"I shall do nothing of the kind. I am not going to lift a finger until you go and bathe and shave and sit and eat a meal. And do so without a single cigarette."

He was surprised at my giving him orders and for a moment appeared ready to argue, but he gave a sheepish shrug.

"If you insist. There is time enough now and to spare. Kindly ask Mrs. Hudson to prepare supper, and I shall retire to make myself more acceptable."

"And no more tobacco."

"Of course not, and if by chance you should smell cigarette smoke coming from the lavatory, be assured it could not possibly be me."

I rolled my eyes, and he excused himself. I looked around at the ordered chaos in the room. For a brief moment, I was tempted to pick up one of the piles and try to make sense of it but decided that such an effort would be an exercise in futility. So, after requesting that the long-suffering Mrs. Hudson bring us a light meal, I took yet another fantastic novel by H.G. Wells off the rack and settled in.

I became thoroughly engrossed in the story and had reached the point when the invaders from Mars were descending upon the earth when Holmes reappeared and I had to leave Planet Earth in peril. He was looking one hundred percent better and seemed positively chuffed with himself. Over a delectable supper of smoked salmon and dark bread, he asked me about the events in the news of the past week. He had not read a paper in the past five days.

After dessert and cognac, he lit a pipe and relaxed back in his chair.

"Well, Watson, are you ready?"

"For what?"

"To catch our criminals."

"Holmes."

"It is really quite straightforward. A lengthy process but entirely logical. Whoever was behind the web of crimes must have placed bets on Ireland to win the Triple Crown. And by their efforts combined with luck and Godfrey's injury, they were, against all odds, successful. Therefore, I have collected data on all bets paid out over five hundred pounds since the end of the final game."

"From whom? Bookmakers never disclose who won and lost bets. That is utterly forbidden. You could put one of them on the rack, and they would still never tell you."

"Oh, my dear Watson, not the bookmakers; the banks. I had Lestrade's office requisition from every bank in greater London the record of deposits made during the past week. On those sheets of paper around the floor are the names and amounts of every deposit over five hundred pounds made at any bank."

"There must be hundreds of them."

"Several thousand, in fact. Thus the required hours to record them and sort them out. The summaries now appear on the dining room table. Every slip bears the name of the depositor, and every small pile is lined up in alphabetical order. 'A' is in the upper right-hand corner, and 'Zed' in the lower left."

"And what are we looking for?"

"My dear Watson, no one upon receiving a payment for a wager in excess of five hundred pounds keep his winnings under his mattress, does he?"

"No, of course not. He puts it in the bank."

"Precisely. Now, I expect that whoever was behind this monstrous but brilliant caper has likely won well over fifty thousand pounds. Does that seem a reasonable conclusion?"

"Maybe more."

"Excellent. It also stands to reason that these clever criminals are too smart to put their winnings all into one account at one time. Agreed?"

"Right. And?"

"Now, with my having sorted through the reams of data and put it all into order, all we have to do is go through the piles and extract any names that have made multiple significant deposits in various banks.

"And what are we supposed to do with them?"

"We shall examine them together. Those that we agree are not in the least anomalous we shall pass on. Those that strike us as being irregular shall be further set aside. By midnight, I expect that we shall have winnowed the lot from thousands down to a score or less. Now, my friend, to work."

I began at the pile of names that started with the letter 'A' and looked at each slip briefly. As might be expected, I encountered an abundance of Allens, Andersons, Adamses, and Abbots. All of these had different first initials, used different banks, and deposited different amounts. Nothing requiring more scrutiny in the As.

The Bs had a much larger volume to start with. There were five entries under the name of T. Brown that were made at three banks all in the City. All were for amounts over £1000. These I set aside.

"Holmes," I said, "shortly after delving into the 'C' pile. There's a fellow here by the name of G. Cadbury. He has made deposits of well over £10,000 in three different banks, all in the City."

"Mr. Cadbury is a Quaker who makes and sells chocolate and earns a fortune by doing so. He does not gamble. You may ignore him."

The Ds had a few deposits made by men whose last name was Davis and then, surprisingly, several under the name of H. Diaz. I brought the latter to Holmes's attention.

"Mr. Herman Diaz arrived in London twenty years ago from Goa. He has a jewelry business in Halton Garden. He is quite legitimate and quite rich. Give him a pass."

On the letter E, there was Eastman, Eddington, Edgecombe, and no end of Edwards. Then I stopped.

"Holmes."

"Yes, Watson. What this time?"

"Is Elpis a common English family name?"

"Not at all. I cannot think of anyone I have known by that name."

"Well, you don't know everybody in England, do you?"

He stopped, laid down the slips he had been working on, closed his eyes, tented his fingers under his chin, and retained that pose for a full three minutes."

"Elpis does not appear on any register in any major city in all of England. It is a name of Greek extraction and is found in Greece and the surrounding countries. It is not known in England. Have you found one?"

"One? No, not one. Fifteen at last count. A Mr. Elpis has made deposits of £5,000 in fifteen accounts in banks throughout the City, Belgravia, and Mayfair."

Holmes stood up quickly, knocking his chair over behind him. He sped over to me.

"Let me look at them."

I laid the slips I had pulled out of the pile in front of him. He picked them up and leafed through them.

"Well done, Watson. Well done, indeed. I think you have found our man."

"Thank you. Happy to be of service. But how are you going to locate him? Will his address be on file at one of the banks?"

"Unlikely. I expect he has been clever enough to disguise his residence or place of business."

"Might one of the tellers remember him? Amounts that large do not happen every day. We could start tomorrow to make the rounds of all the banks."

"An excellent suggestion, my useful friend."

I smiled, enjoying his acknowledgment of what I had accomplished.

"Or maybe not," he then said.

"Why not?"

"Patience, please. Let me think."

Yet again he closed his eyes. He held that pose this time for five minutes and then suddenly popped his eyes open and gasped.

"Ha! Oh my, yes! That's it. It all fits. It all fits."

Chapter Fifty-Five

"**W**hat fits?"

He was out of his chair and pacing, almost prancing down the length of the room and back.

"Watson, please be back here at ten o'clock tomorrow morning. We have to pay a call."

"On whom?"

"On Elpis. Now, do go home to your good wife and get a decent night's sleep. I shall see you tomorrow. Please, no more questions. Have a good night, my friend."

Before I could demand an explanation, he departed the front room, walked smartly to his bedroom and closed the door.

At ten o'clock on the Monday morning, I arrived at Baker Street. Holmes was waiting for me on the pavement and hopped into the cab.

"Phillimore Place, Kensington," he called up to the driver.

"Why are we going there? Are you going to bring Lord Mount James along with us?"

"He has proven useful in the past. He may again."

"All he did was to tell you to ask about the birds."

"Without which we could not have found Millie."

We soon arrived at the Mount James home and gave a knock to the door. The same handsome but arrogant butler opened.

"Oh, you two again," said. "Fine, come in. If you want to see His Lordship, you will have to wait until he returns."

"We can do that," said Holmes. "Kindly let Lady Maynooth know we are here. I believe she finds our conversation amusing."

"Yes, she does, endlessly," said the butler. "I'll let her know."

He led us into the spacious parlor. To my surprise, the Bechstein Grand had returned along with some excellent original oil paintings on the wall. We sat for fifteen minutes, after which a maid I had not seen before arrived bearing an outstanding plate of morning delicacies. I commented on them to the maid.

"Please, give my compliments to the cook. But you are new here, are you not?"

She gave a one-inch curtsy. "I am, Sir. I came with the cook. He is new here as well."

"Then you are both an excellent addition to this house."

"Thank you, Sir. Her ladyship has been very generous to us."

She retreated to the kitchen. Two minutes later, whilst my mouth was stuffed with a slender piece of breakfast sausage surrounded by a roll of French pastry, Lady Maynooth appeared in the doorway. I chewed quickly and forced a swallow.

"Good morning, Your Ladyship," I said as I rose, hoping that I was not drooling sausage juice.

"Good morning, Dr. Watson. Good morning, Mr. Holmes. Welcome on this lovely spring day. I am so sorry that His Lordship is not here at the moment. He received a notice first thing this morning that he was needed at a meeting in the City, but he should be returning within the hour."

"I must admit," said Holmes, "that I knew he would not be here. I was the one who had him called for the meeting."

That comment startled me, and it appeared to do the Lady even more so.

"And why did you do that, Mr. Holmes?"

"If you must know, my lady ... or should I be calling you Madame Elpis ... or would you prefer the Roman title, say the Goddess Spes? Or shall I just call you by the more common name in English; Miss Hope?"

Chapter Fifty-Six

She was giving him a hard look but softened her countenance and gave Holmes a thin, sweet smile.

"Please, Mr. Holmes, sit down. Have I told you before that I find conversations with you to be wonderfully amusing?"

"May I understand your comment to mean that you are prepared to carry on a conversation?"

"With the great Mr. Sherlock Holmes? Why, of course, I am. What more fascinating way to pass a morning? But I should warn you in advance that I will neither confirm nor deny anything you might say to me or about me."

"What I will say to you that you cannot deny is that you are an utterly heartless woman. You have put a fine young man through utter hell over the past two months."

She laughed and, I must note, that it did not seem to be forced.

"Oh, my dear Mr. Holmes. Of course, I can see that Godfrey went through hell ... and back again. He is now much more devoted to, besotted with might be a better term, dear Millie than he ever could have been. Back in December, his love for her was contrived at best. Now he burns with passion. Did you wish to thank me on his behalf?"

"I have observed his pain and anguish. There has been nothing whatsoever contrived about his feelings."

"Feelings? Oh, Mr. Holmes. His feelings were devastated up to the minute he spent the night in his lovely wife's tender embrace with her perfect woman's body and slightly bulging little tummy pressed against him. He has recovered and now the silly boy probably thinks of himself as the luckiest man on God's green earth. The doctor here will confirm my medical conclusions, won't you Doctor Watson."

I could not deny what she said. "Such treatment is said to be a universal cure for almost any ailment that could afflict a man under thirty years of age."

"Thirty? Really Doctor? Not beyond?"

"Forty. Well, maybe fifty."

"Oh, Doctor. Might I suggest that it still works at eighty?" Again, she laughed.

That was more information than I needed to know, and I turned the conversation back to Holmes.

"Lady Maynooth," he said, "there is nothing funny about a man who is dead. Danny O'Hearn is not going to recover. Ever. His blood is on your hands."

"I was horrified and terribly distressed by his demise, Mr. Holmes. However, you have not a shred of proof that I had anything whatsoever to do with it. Whatever accusation you make is merely your conjecture. It will not even bring Scotland Yard to my door, let alone stand up in court. And you know that, don't you, Mr. Holmes?"

"Scotland Yard? The courts? I have no need of them. I shall simply put all the evidence I have gathered about you together and hand it over to the press. After the series of stories they run about you, you will be despised throughout all of England. You will be removed from all your charity activities, banned from the theatre and the better restaurants, and likely spat upon on the streets of Belgravia."

That threat appeared to strike a nerve, but she recovered immediately.

"And what newspaper, what reporter would ever publish such a piece? They are all my friends, and they owe me endless favors."

"I would take it to the *Evening Star*. They have a reporter there, Walter Durnan, do they not? He might like it."

Again, she let out a peal of spontaneous laughter.

"Come now, Mr. Holmes. He is particularly my friend; my fondest on Fleet Street."

"No, my dear lady. He is not your friend. He is only your fair-weather friend. He is as vile a selfish snake as ever slithered through the excrescence of London. When it better serves his purpose to vilify you than maintain a false friendship, he will cast you into the street and kick you like a wounded cur. And you know that, don't you, Lady Maynooth."

"Yes, I suppose I do. But what would you gain? You would still not have solved any crime. Your murderers would still be at large. I would still be a wealthy woman, and if worse came to worse, I could move to Australia where everybody has a shameful past. Most of them brag about it."

"That may be true," said Holmes. "But I am very certain that you do not want to have to decamp from Kensington and move to

Sydney. So, I will assure you that I am prepared to play my card if I have to."

"But you would also be prepared to negotiate a settlement, a compromise, perhaps."

"That is possible."

"Oh, now that sounds much better. So much more amusing than threatening each other. Very well, then, let us proceed but I shall speak only in hypothetical terms and shall never, as I have already said, admit nor deny anything. Your turn, Mr. Holmes. Your first card, please.

"The names of those who killed Danny O'Hearn. You must turn over their names to me. That is not negotiable."

"Oh, fret not, Mr. Holmes. I am prepared to do that, but I will require a commitment in return."

"Name it."

"Complete confidentiality. Your word that whatever is said will never leave this room."

"Provided you answer all my questions truthfully, I agree."

Yet again, she burst into laughter. I had to admit that her laugh was loud and exuberant and almost infectious.

"Mr. Holmes, of course, I shall answer everything truthfully. You are a man of your word, and you have just given me my freedom. I no longer have to conceal anything as whatever I say you can never repeat, now can you? I would say I just won this round, would you agree, Dr. Watson?"

I thought for a minute, and it struck me that she had indeed. It would not even become a case of her word against Holmes's. His word would never be spoken.

"Oh, and Dr. Watson," she continued, looking at me, "that goes for you as well. I fully expect to see my story in the *Strand*, but you will disguise it, as you have done with so many of your accounts of Sherlock Holmes so that no one will ever know who was truly involved. Agreed, Doctor?"

I nodded my agreement. She then turned to Holmes.

"Before you begin your interrogation, you really must tell me how you deduced everything. I am simply dying to know. Men with superior intelligence are so rare and so enjoyable, and you are the first I have met in a very long time. Please, Mr. Holmes, out with it."

Chapter Fifty-Seven

"The names of the killers first."

"Oh, yes, of course. But I can say truthfully, that they had no intention of killing poor Danny. He was such an amusing boy. They were only supposed to give him a serious but temporary injury; only enough to drive up the odds against Ireland's winning and, of course, sending the odds against a Triple Crown into the stratosphere. It was so terribly unfortunate that Danny turned his head at the last minute and the blow struck him on the temple and he died. Hearing about it made me utterly distraught."

"I do recall your reaction and accept that it was genuine. Their names, please."

She took out a piece of writing paper and a pencil and wrote.

"The names of the two men are at the top. Underneath them are the names of two women who would be thrilled to be rid of them from their lives and would be prepared to testify in court that those men had bragged about what they did to Danny."

"Addresses would be useful. Please add them. Use your Royal typewriter if it is easier."

"I would give you the addresses if I could but, with regret, I cannot. They can be found on any given day in some pub in the East End."

"There are a hundred such establishments. I do not have a month to go knocking on their doors."

"Then, I shall suggest a far more efficient way. One of them, with the other assisting him, is still making regular visits to the Brook Hospital on Shooter's Hill. Some nasty fellow shot the poor man in the leg. The hospital will give you the time and date of the next scheduled visit."

"Thank you, my next demand—,"

"Not fair, Mr. Holmes. You went first last time, My turn now."

"Go."

"How did you do it? I thought I had covered my tracks so well. Come now. Tell me. I am just dying to know."

Now it was Holmes's turn to give a thin, condescending smile. He leaned back in the chair and crossed his arms over his chest. It was, I admit, a not entirely attractive part of his character that he enjoyed reveling in his moment of triumph and explaining to those who were lesser mortals how he defeated them by the force of his intellect.

"It took some time, of course. There is not a single family named Elpis in England. The name had a Greek ring to it, and therefore I had to send my memory back through the accounts in the press of the Greek wars of independence. Nothing there. So, I went all the way back, to Homer. Was there an Elpis in the Iliad or the Odyssey? I scanned every page of both epics in my mind and came up empty. Then I moved on to Hesiod, and there you were. Elpis was the mythical phenomenon we know by the name of Hope, the only thing left to mankind after Pandora opened her box and let all the other blessings and miseries loose in the world. Yet Elpis was more than mere Hope. It was expectation, optimism, the ability to see silver linings behind clouds, the willingness to believe that everything happens for a reason. Now then do you recall to whom Lord Mount James compared you?"

"I do. He said that I was Dr. Pangloss to his Jeremiah. How foolish of the old boy."

"Precisely. And you objected to being associated with such a blackguard as Voltaire, suggesting that he give you a better moniker, a *classical* one, if I remember your words. There is only one classical parallel to Pangloss, and you have taught yourself to act as if you were indeed Elpis, always bringing hope and optimism to all you met. Once that connection was made, everything else fell into line."

"Oh, do tell all. You cannot leave me on tenterhooks."

"You husband, Lord Maynooth, and you had a very happy marriage, did you not?"

"We did, oh, did we ever. Jerry was so much fun to be with. In the clubs, at concerts, out racing our yacht, in Italy ... everywhere. I miss him awfully."

"And when he died, you learned that his estate was bankrupt."

"I'm afraid so. He was always welcomed at a card table. He kept the others laughing all night."

"While losing."

"Sadly, yes," she said and sighed.

"And if you wanted to continue to live in the manner to which you had become accustomed, you needed to find a wealthy and available man and do so quickly."

"I did, and there was dear old Lord Mount James. Crabbed and miserable and reputed to be one of the richest men in the country. It took some work, but I managed to reform his behavior and, to my delight, he began to act like a man half his age. Well, maybe two-thirds."

"And then," continued Holmes, "you learned that having put his money into disastrous investments in Argentine railroads and South African securities and the Bakerloo line, he was also nearly bankrupt. You did not put the Bechstein and the paintings in storage. You had to sell them. You laid off the household staff. You yourself prepared your meals. Most likely, you considered abandoning the old boy, but you could see your golden opportunity on the horizon in the person of Godfrey Staunton and the Home Nations Championship. You knew all about betting and gambling from your dear, departed husband, and you knew if you bet on long odds against Ireland and then manipulated the scores by threatening Godfrey, you would be rewarded with seventy-five thousand pounds."

"Seventy-eight. We mustn't be parsimonious."

"And you collected and immediately redeemed the piano back and restored some of the paintings or, shall I say, replaced them with those that are more to your taste."

"All very astute, Mr. Holmes. You truly are a delightfully clever man. But I am finally a wealthy woman in my own right. The accounts are all in my name."

"No, my dear lady, they are not. They are in the name of Mr. Elpis and the Chancellor of the Exchequer has been notified that they were opened under a false name with intent to deceive and evade taxes."

"I am not trying to evade taxes."

"Tell that to Number 11. They have been told that you are and are prepared to freeze all of your accounts for years perhaps. All it will take is a phone call to confirm that there is no Mr. Elpis in existence and you will be barred from those accounts within ten minutes. Might I borrow your telephone?"

"Fine. You won that round. What else do you want?"

"A portion of those funds must go to Godfrey and Millie. They are not only the rightful heirs, but they were the means you used to acquire your winnings."

"How much? Twenty-thousand has already gone recovering the plate, the piano, and His Lordship's furniture."

"Enough so that if invested, they should be able to count on a thousand a year."

Lady Maynooth picked up a notepad and pencil and appeared to be computing sums.

"I'm afraid that is a bit too rich. At today's rates of return, a well-balanced portfolio will not support that much and leave enough for Jim and me to live in the style similar to our neighbors. I could manage eight hundred. Can you live with that?"

Holmes nor closed his eyes and appeared to be computing sums inside his head.

"Eight hundred is accepted."

"Excellent. So, Mr. Holmes, are we finished?"

"No."

"Oh, good. I am quite enjoying our repartee. Go on. What next?"

"The Romanian girls. How were they obtained."

"Oh, really, Mr. Holmes, was that not obvious? When one is a director of the British Society for the Support of Indigent Immigrant Women from Troubled Lands, one meets no end of stunningly beautiful, exotic but desperate young woman. I have helped so many of the dears over the years. They quite adore me. Well, in their case, it was Perkins who recruited them."

Holmes grunted his disapproval but carried on.

"My last question. Explain how you co-opted the Office of the Privy Council."

"Oh, please, Mr. Holmes. I just answered that question."

"You mean—,"

"Of course, Mr. Holmes. Poor dear Clarence is married to an impossibly priggish woman who has denied him his rightful pleasures for decades. He was quite eager to have his needs met by a generous young lady from Russia and is now most accommodating to my requests."

"That is blackmail."

"Oh, please, Mr. Holmes, it nothing more than friends returning favors to each other. *Quid pro quo* as they say. You scratch my back; I will scratch yours. Only it applies to parts of the anatomy beyond one's back, if you know what I mean."

Holmes scowled his disapproval. "One final demand, my lady."

"Oh, only one more? Pity. And what might that be?"

"You will cease and desist from any future actions that are reasonably understood to be illegal or patently unethical."

"I shall never admit to having done anything illegal, Mr. Holmes, but will most certainly agree not to act in such a way in the future. As to unethical? Honestly, Mr. Holmes, what paragon of virtue do you know who enjoys the *crème de la crème* and salves their conscience by doing charity work for the *hoi polio* and who can be described, speaking charitably of course, as constantly ethical. I know them all, Mr. Homes and I cannot think of one. Can you?"

"Your point is granted, Madam. Illegal will have to do. Is that agreed? If I hear of you crossing that line again, I assure you that will be after you and pounce on you like a hound on a miserable fox."

"Please, Mr. Holmes, my sensibilities lead me to abhor blood sports, but yes, you have my agreement regarding the future, but you do understand that I cannot undo the past."

"And what do you mean by that, Madam?"

"That there are perhaps a hundred men—dukes, earls, bishops, captains of industry, scholars, deans—who owe me favors in return for favors bestowed in the past. And try as one might, one cannot change what has already taken place, can one, Mr. Holmes?"

Holmes had had enough. He stood up and did not so much as give a by-your-leave before turning to depart the room. Passing through the door, he turned back.

"I will honor my word, Madam. And you will honor yours."

"And all shall be well in this best of all possible worlds," she said … and laughed.

Chapter Fifty-Eight

In the cab on the way back to Baker Street, I looked at my unhappy friend.

"She did not best you. But I would have to say it was close to a draw."

He lit a cigarette and enjoyed several slow drafts.

"Those who killed Danny O'Hearn will go to jail. For that, I am satisfied."

"Don't forget that one of them will have a very sore leg for a long time."

That brought a smile to his face.

"No, I cannot forget that you have been the instrument of justice. And I must also take comfort in knowing that Mr. and Mrs. Staunton have been restored safely to each other. And at least one channel of illicit gambling on noble sporting events has been put out of business."

"Need I remind you—,"

"No, Watson, you need not remind me that there are many more such channels abounding throughout the country."

The cab dropped Sherlock Holmes off at 221B Baker Street and then carried on to deliver me to my home and wife. It would, in the best of all possible worlds, have been ideal if this story were to end at this juncture.

That was not to happen.

Chapter Fifty-Nine

April is beloved throughout Great Britain as it heralds the passing of winter and the coming of spring. Indeed, the spring of 1899 was every bit a splendid as those of the past. The crocuses had bloomed, followed by hosts of golden daffodils. The forsythia and quince bushes were in flower, the magnolias were about to burst open, and the trees through London's magnificent parks had emerged from their winter slumber and were now covered in a soft verdant hue. The populace of London, from the street urchin to the loftiest duke, had taken to the out-of-doors and were bathing their minds and bodies in the fragrant caresses of vernal breezes.

The world was getting along not badly at all. New inventions were appearing every week, it seemed. An Italian chap, Mr. Marconi, had just sent a wireless signal across the English Channel. The natives in India were making a few rumblings, but all agreed that the new Viceroy, Lord Curzon, would keep them under his thumb and the Raj would continue, as it had for over two centuries, to be the jewel in the crown of the British Empire.

On Baker Street, Sherlock Holmes had taken on a new case or two that promised to be acceptably challenging to his restless imagination. My medical practice was on an even keel. The English do not become nearly as ill come spring as they do in the winter. But that annual cycle gave me more time to write. I was busy scribbling my long account of *The Hound of the Baskervilles,* and my agent had agreed to submit it to the *Strand* as soon as he returned from his volunteer medical service in the Cape Provinces.

Godfrey Staunton had made a speedy recovery from his injury and was now attending practices of the Blackheath club, watching from beyond the touch lines and looking forward to scampering up and down the pitch. The Olympic Association had invited him to serve as a director, and he and Millie had enjoyed their first-class visit to Paris.

The lovely and radiant Mrs. Godfrey Staunton was in the bloom of expectancy and was starting to show, at least as seen by the eye of a doctor or the mothers of the land. Men would be oblivious for several more months.

Lord Mount James and his companion, Lady Maynooth appeared regularly in the society pages of the press as they attended endless charity functions and cut ribbons for no end of worthy causes. Her ladyship had kept her word, as had Sherlock Holmes.

All in all, life was good.

It was not unusual for Holmes to summon me to Baker Street when some unusual note had arrived or an appointment with a peculiar visitor scheduled. I looked forward to receiving his call and, I must confess, was somewhat despondent when there was a lapse for several weeks.

So, it was with some warm thrill that I opened and read his note of 26 April. It ran:

Kindly come here at 4:00 pm tomorrow. A gentleman is coming, and he has specifically requested that you be present.   Holmes.

The mystery of who it might be only enhanced the welcomed tingling in my heart and I shut down my medical office at 3:30 and made sure that I was ascending the stairs at 221B at precisely four o'clock.

Holmes stood to greet me, but the gentleman who was seated on the sofa did not. Dr. Leslie Armstrong had no very pleased expression upon his dour features.

"Good afternoon, Doctor," I said, trying to sound cheerful. "A pleasure to see you again."

He looked up at me and made no reply.

"Dr. Armstrong," said Holmes to me, "requested a meeting with both of us and has made no comments prior to your arrival. Now that you are with us, I turn the floor over to the good doctor."

He looked up at us, sternly glaring first at Holmes and then at me as if he were, in his severe mind, taking our measure.

"For ten years," he said, "I studied medicine here in England, briefly in America, and back and forth on the Continent. For the past thirty years, I have engaged in a medical practice as well as a growing involvement in medical research. I have published extensively not only in respected journals of medicine but in other disciplines that touch upon public health and the science of medical care. My diligent efforts have resulted in my enjoying some small reputation as a respected European thinker."

"We are aware," said Holmes, "of your accomplishments and we hold—,"

"Don't interrupt me!"

Holmes, looking uncharacteristically uncomfortable, accepted the rebuke and said no more.

"Throughout those forty years," continued Dr. Armstrong, "indeed since my days as a schoolboy, I have forced myself to act with the utmost integrity. Looking back, I cannot name a single instance when I compromised on what I knew to be the truth even when my stand caused me to lose lucrative offers, social invitations, and even friendships."

Here he paused, stood up, and began pacing the floor.

"Over the past fortnight, I have had very little sleep. I have been faced with the most difficult decision of my life. I have felt like Our Lord in the garden and wished that this cup might pass from me. Nevertheless, it is not my will, not my heart, but my resolve to act honorably that must be done, regardless of whatever suffering it might bring to myself and others."

He turned and glared down at Holmes.

"You are aware, Sir, that I have been an intimate friend to Godfrey Staunton. Indeed, I have loved him as a father would a son."

Holmes nodded, not daring to speak audibly. Now Dr. Armstrong turned to me.

"Dr. Watson, you have been in medical practice for many years now."

I nodded.

"You have treated men who were injured on the battlefield, in the factories, and on the sports fields."

I nodded again.

"You will have noticed that Godfrey Staunton has made an exceptionally rapid recovery from his injury and appears to be approaching full use again of his leg."

"I have," I said, not entirely confidently.

"Do you have any idea, any diagnosis, as to the nature of his injury?"

"Why no. I did not examine him. I assumed that it was another round of a slipped kneecap like he had before."

"It was not. What other injuries are you used to seeing from a rugby or football pitch?"

"The anterior cruciate ligament can suffer a tear. Godfrey's could not have been torn; otherwise, he would have required surgery."

"His ACL is just fine. Go on."

"Well, there are several other less common. A meniscal tear damaging the cartilage, a dislocation, a cracked kneecap or other bone, a posterior cruciate ligament. Any of those are possibilities. I have seen them all in the past.,"

"I agree. Those are all possible injuries. But none of them happened to Godfrey."

"Then what did?"

"Nothing."

Chapter Sixty

He paced the entire floor and returned to his chair and glared at Holmes and me again. The fearful implications of what he had just said were sinking in.

"Are you suggesting," said Holmes, "that—,"

"I am not *suggesting* anything, Mr. Holmes. I am telling you that when Godfrey was carried off the field, there was nothing whatsoever wrong with his knee or any other part of his body."

"But he was writhing in pain," I said.

"Yes, doctor. He was writhing. And no, it was not in pain."

After a long, horrible silence, Holmes stated the obvious.

"He threw the game."

"Yes, Mr. Holmes. The injury was fraudulent. His behavior was fraudulent. Now, understand this, I am not now nor ever have been given to contrafactual conjecture. It cannot be denied, however, that had he continued to play, the outcome of the game against Scotland and the final results of the Home Nations Championship *could* have been different. It is a distinct possibility that Ireland would not have won the Triple Crown. *That*, gentlemen, is what I am here to tell you."

"But why," I asked, "would he do that? He had made promises to his dying parents and to his first wife that he would do his utmost to win for England?"

"Yes, Doctor," said Dr. Armstrong, "he did. But unless your mind is of a less logical nature than I take it to be, you are fully aware that obligations to the dead are figments of one's imagination. The dead, if I may be blunt, are precisely that, *dead*. And gone. They are not leaning over the parapets of heaven cheering their favorite team on, and they cannot be disappointed if one does not keep one's promises to them. A man's wife, on the other hand, who is in mortal danger, is profoundly real. When one's imagined obligation to the dead, and one's compelling responsibility to the living come into conflict, one has no choice but to chose the living."

"But he knew that Holmes and I were on our way to rescue her."

"No, my friend," said Holmes, "he did not know that, not for certain. At the time Godfrey did what he did, all he knew was that Millie's life and well-being were still in grave danger. I had promised to rescue Millie and, to his knowledge, had not been able to do so. In order to protect her, he acceded to the demands of those who were threatening to do unspeakable horror."

"Yes, Mr. Holmes," said Dr. Armstrong, "That is my conclusion as well."

"And what, Sir, are you going to do about it?"

He stood up and again paced back and forth.

"Mr. Holmes, I know your reputation. I know not only of your brilliance as a detective, I know of your dedication to the cause of justice. I also know of your willingness, from time to time, to skirt the demands of the law and to take it into your own hands. I do not question your intent, although I suggest that in the long run doing so is not a wise course to follow. You are who you are. I, on the other hand, have never and will never behave in that manner. As a man of unassailable honor, I have no choice but to reveal what I know to the governors of the Rugby Union and let them perform their responsibilities as they see fit."

"Then why are you here?" said Holmes. He stood up and faced Dr. Armstrong. "You have now dirtied our hands with the knowledge of the fraud. Why not just go and do what you have to do?"

Dr. Armstrong reached out and placed a friendly hand on Holmes's shoulder.

"Sit down, please, Sir." He sat back in his chair as he spoke. After a moment of hesitation, Holmes did the same.

"I have come to request your help. I shall now go and confront Godfrey. I shall then request a meeting with the appropriate governors and reveal what I have learned. I am imploring the two of you to come with me to that meeting. You are far better able to give a detailed account of the litany of threats Godfrey endured and his behavior throughout those days. Having presented our case truthfully and honorably, we shall appeal to the governors to demonstrate mercy and show clemency. The ball will then be in their court, and we, having behaved with integrity, will hand over to them the responsibility to act justly."

Holmes and I gave each other a look and then a nod.

"We will do that," said Holmes. "Kindly inform us of the time and place of the hearing, and we shall do our best to speak the truth in love."

"Thank you, gentlemen," said the doctor. He pulled on his gloves and donned his hat, gave a shallow nod to us, and departed.

Chapter Sixty-One

A week later, I received a letter from the Rugby Union Secretariat requesting my presence at a hearing to be held on Friday, 26 May. It was signed by the Lord Bishop of Birmingham, a member of the Board of Governors and the Chairman of the Sub-Committee for Disciplinary Matters. The meeting would be held in Lambeth Palace.

That was quite clever, I thought. It would look as if it had some connection to religious concerns—matches played on Sunday, perhaps—and thus of little or no interest to a prurient press.

During the ensuing weeks, I dropped in several times to 221B Baker Street. Holmes seemed to enjoy my company provided I did not stay for an overly long time and interrupt his work either on a case or at his chemical table.

On my third such visit, there were some things I could not help but notice. Holmes had acquired some new items for his wardrobe. He had found himself a new hat and a full, new formal morning suit made of the most expensive Italian cloth. Several pieces of apparatus on the chemical table were shining new and of rather high quality. Two new sets of encyclopediae had appeared on his bookshelves. During the final week of May, a new sofa had replaced the threadbare one that had served him and countless clients for over twenty years.

Now, Sherlock Holmes was not one to deprive himself for the sake of flaunting asceticism and considered those who did so to be irredeemable charlatans. But he was nearer to being frugal than most figures in public life. Finally, my curiosity got the better of me, and I put it straight to him.

"Holmes, what is going on with all the money you are spending? I am seeing a degree of self-indulgence that I have not seen in all the time I have known you."

"I am getting on, Watson. No point in depriving myself any longer."

"Fine, but even looking around this room, I can see several hundred pounds of expense."

"I try to buy for lasting quality."

"No, you don't. You buy for efficiency."

"I must be slipping."

"Nonsense. Where did the money come from?"

"I came into some funds, quite unsuspected."

"From where? You don't have any family and certainly not any that have died in the past year."

"Quite true."

"One of your former clients was feeling guilty for not rewarding you?"

"I charge a standard fee and forward any such gifts to charity. I do not wish to let such inducements cloud my judgment."

"Well then, tell me. I might like to get in on it."

He lit up his pipe and ignored me whilst he puffed away.

"You could have. Pity that you failed to see the opportunity."

I glared at him as a thought slowly crept across my mind.

"Holmes, you bounder. You bet on the games."

"Of course, I did. So did you."

"But I bet on England. I bet out of loyalty."

"Which any gambler will tell you is a very foolish way to place wagers. I bet on Ireland to win the Triple Crown. You lost. I won."

"But … but why?"

"Elementary, my dear Watson. It was immediately apparent to me that we were up against a formidable foe who was intent on doing whatever was required to have Ireland win. That tipped the true odds heavily in favor of Ireland while the odds cited by the bookmakers were running opposite. It was as close to a sure thing as can be imagined in a sporting event."

"Holmes, you bet against your client."

"*Au contraire. Mon ami.* If Ireland won, Godfrey would get Millie back, and a position with the Olympic Association and I would win my bet. Our interests were entirely in line."

"How much did you bet."

"If I recall, it was £100."

"Which means that you won £3000."

"£3,200 to be precise."

I gave up. "Holmes, what am I going to do with you."

"I suggest that you go home and prepare for the hearing on Friday. My client needs both of us."

.

Chapter Sixty-Two

On that fateful Friday morning, I accompanied Holmes to the south side of the Thames, just upstream from Westminster Bridge, and we entered the grounds of the Lambeth Palace.

The dull, severe, sandstone buildings in which the Archbishop of Canterbury held sway—at least when he was in London and not in Canterbury, which was most of the time—seemed to me to be an excellent place for a disciplinary hearing.

We were greeted and led into a cloistered sitting room by two young seminarians and offered tea by a Vincentian nun. I heard the name of Sherlock Holmes being whispered out in the hallway and chuckled to myself, thinking that the young men and women of the cloth would be disappointed if they were to learn that our visit had nothing to do with nefarious activities in some questionable diocese and only with cheating at rugby.

At ten o'clock, we were summoned to the Guard Room on the second floor. It was a large open space with vaulted ceilings in which the bishops of the Anglican Communion met once a decade to advise

Almighty God as to how He might do a better job of running the world. At the front of the room were two rows of tables, each with chairs on one side of them and set up so that one row was facing the other. Each chair had a pad of paper and a pencil laid out in front of it.

Dr. Leslie Armstrong was already seated, as were Mr. and Mrs. Godfrey Staunton. The doctor appeared as severe as ever, but Godfrey was looking tanned and relaxed, and Millie was glowing as only a beautiful young woman, now well into her second trimester, is capable of doing.

We took our seats at the table and waited. At ten minutes past ten, five men, all formally dressed, and led by His Grace, the Lord Bishop entered the room. I recognized the third fellow. It was Baron Worthington, but he did not give any indication that he had met any of us previously.

I was about to stand up as a mark of respect, but I caught a glance for Dr. Armstrong that silently told me not to budge.

"I call this meeting to order," announced the bishop. "I will introduce the members of this Committee. On my far left is Lord Barbazon of Tara. Beside him is the Earl of Catheart. To my right is Baron Eccles of Moulton. Beside him is Baron Worthington of Wakefield. I am Bishop Edgecombe, the Lord Bishop of Birmingham and the Chairman of this Committee. Will the individuals across from us kindly introduce themselves?"

He pointed in the direction of Holmes.

"My name is Sherlock Holmes."

"Kindly state your occupation."

"It is my business to know things."

The Bishop did not appreciate Holmes's answer but let it go and pointed to me.

"I am Dr. John Watson. I am a medical practitioner and a writer."

"Thank you, Doctor. And you, Sir." He nodded toward Dr. Armstrong.

"You all know who I am, and you have a copy of my *Vitae*."

It is not an easy task to stare down a bishop, but Dr. Armstrong was in the habit of giving no quarter to any man. The bishop moved on.

"And you, young man," he said to Godfrey. "Kindly introduce yourself and the lady beside you who, we understand, is your wife."

"My name is Godfrey Staunton, I assist in the management of the estate of my uncle, Lord Mount James, and I play rugby. My wife will introduce herself."

"Good morning. Gentlemen," said Millie, quite cheerfully. "My name is Mrs. Millicent Staunton. I am a scientist. And I will happily answer any questions directed to me and not any directed by you through my husband."

Underneath the table, I could feel Holmes's fist pound lightly on my thigh. I returned the gesture and with the pencil nonchalantly scribbled a note back to him. *She's our Millie!* He responded with another bump on my thigh.

"We are here today," intoned Bishop Edgecombe, "on a grave matter and there is no place for frivolity—,"

"No one is being frivolous," barked Dr. Armstrong. "So don't you start."

There was another staring contest. It dawned on me that Dr. Armstrong had most likely not darkened the door of any church for at least the past two decades. The only bishops he was likely to have encountered during that time would have been those who were stark

314

naked on his examining table and being poked and prodded without any deference to their high calling.

"Dr. Armstrong, we have received your brief report and have, of necessity, called this hearing. I will turn the floor over to you to deliver a comprehensive account, to be followed by Mr. Sherlock Holmes, and then by Dr. Watson. Proceed, please, Sir."

We had agreed beforehand on the division of our presentations. Dr. Armstrong opened with his account of having first met Godfrey when he was a student at Eton and of having been impressed not only with his play of the rugby pitch but by his honesty and striving for academic excellence. He then moved on to speak of the loss of both his parents and the fortitude with which Godfrey had borne the tragedy. Without becoming the least bit maudlin, he then spoke of the devastating loss of the first Mrs. Staunton and Godfrey's devotion to her and the depths of his grief. He said many other things, citing examples, that confirmed the content of his character. He concluded by acknowledging that he had not been blessed with sons of his own but could not imagine any father who would not be proud and honored to have a son like Godfrey.

He put his report down and glared across to the Committee.

"Any questions?"

None were put forward. We moved on to Holmes.

He went on at some length concerning the criminal cabal who had threatened Godfrey and described in detail the murder of Danny O'Hearn. He emphasized Godfrey's refusal to bow before any threat made to himself, including the attempted beating and intent to lame him. Holmes then took on the role of a stern lecturer and accused the Rugby Union of having been soft on the vast undercurrent of wagering and demanded they take action to limit if not abolish the threats made by gambling to the integrity of games. Somewhat to my surprise, he ended by speaking quite highly of the care given to

Godfrey by Lord Mount James and the excellent example of the infectious optimism of Lady Maynooth. It struck me that he was going on far too long about the generous spirit of the Lady until I looked across to the other table and noted that while the bishop and three of their Lordships were looking intently at Holmes, Baron Worthington was intently regarding the blank pad of paper in front of him.

Then it was my turn.

I took out my report and slid my reading glasses down my nose and took on the dull, emotionless voice used by doctors when delivering monographs to medical conferences. However, I was not about to go easy on these fellows.

"Tell me, gentlemen, how many of you have sisters? A show of hands please."

All five raised a hand.

"Ah, as I suspected, in keeping with a normal demographic distribution. Now, tell me, whilst you were much younger and living in your parents' homes, did any of you ever come home to learn that your sister had been attacked by some monster who had systematically broken all of her fingers? You know, snapped he knuckles sideways until the fingers were pointing in every possible direction and left your sister screaming in pain."

Then in horrifying medical detail, I described what happens to mangled fingers and how they never heal properly. I looked across the table and thought that two of the chaps were looking a little peaked.

I moved on. "How many of you have either daughters or nieces?"

Again, four hands were raised.

"Have any of them ever been attacked ... brutally beaten ... raped ... sodomized?"

"Dr. Watson!" shouted the Earl. "where is your decency? There is a lady present."

Before I could say a word, Millie shouted right back at him.

"And the lady demands that Dr. Watson speak without holding anything back on my part. Please, continue, Dr. Watson."

In my practiced medical monotone, I described at length in sickening terms not only the lifelong damage to the psyche of a woman who has been forced to suffer such an attack but the damage it does to her body. Tears in her inner body can make urination and defecation painful for the rest of her life. The embarrassment of incontinence is seen in many cases. No end of nasty effects can go on for years. Nothing is ever forgotten.

I looked up at the panel. They were decidedly pale. Fine. They were about to be hit even harder with the same experiences that Godfrey had endured. I quickly reached down into my medical bag and pulled out a one-ounce vial. Then I stood up, walked around the end of our table and to the floor directly in front of the Chairman.

"This, gentlemen, is Vitriol."

Before any of them could stop me, I pulled the stopper from the vial and poured the contents on the floor. An immediate foaming took place when the liquid landed, accompanied by a loud sizzle. A flume of noxious vapor shot up toward the ceiling.

"Gentlemen, let me tell you what would have happened to your wives had a pint of this been thrown on her face and breasts a month after your wedding day."

I stated, again in wretched detail, the burning of eyeballs, the dissolving of the inner lining of nostrils, the scarring of lungs rendering one as if she were a consumptive for the rest of her life, the scarring of the face, sometimes beyond recognition, and the disfiguring and damaging of the breasts, often to make suckling a child impossible.

They had all gone pale. So, for that matter, had Holmes. Godfrey was drumming his fingers on the table in front of him, no doubt reciting the multiplication tables inside his head and trying not to hear me. Dr. Armstrong was utterly placid, nodding in affirmation, and Millie had her lovey hand clenched into a fist and was gently pounding the table is silent applause.

"What I have described, Gentlemen, is what these criminals told Godfrey Staunton they would do to his wife. I expect you to remember that when you consider whatever judgement you are about to visit upon him."

I sat down. The place stunk of sulfur. Perhaps I used a stronger concentration than was commercially available.

Dr. Armstrong resumed his commanding presence.

"Well, any questions? Speak up!"

"Yes, I have a question," said Baron Eccles. "Godfrey Staunton, looking back on the events of the past few months are you prepared to express any regrets, any remorse for your actions. Do you wish to make an apology to the Rugby Union?"

Godfrey sat up straight in his chair and squared his shoulders.

"No. None whatsoever. If I were faced today with what I was faced with since the New Year, I would do exactly as I have done. I can examine my soul and tell you that I could have done nothing else."

"Thank you, Mr. Staunton," said the Baron. "I thought that is what you would say."

A flicker of a warm smile passed over the Baron's face. It struck me that he admired the young man sitting across from him.

"Right," announced the bishop. "This is not the hearing we had expected and rather feels as if we have been in the dock and being charged. Nevertheless, we have heard what you have to say, and we shall now retire to discuss the matter and reach a decision. It will be rendered to you at one o'clock this afternoon. Now, we shall excuse ourselves and bid you a pleasant day."

He started to rise from his chair.

"Not so fast!" ordered Dr. Armstrong. "I am going to give you men one last instruction. You all need to ask yourselves if you could have displayed the intestinal fortitude that Godfrey Staunton has. You need to ask yourselves if you could have cared enough for your wives to have risked what he has risked, or are you so stuck on your precious game and its rules that it overrides all human compassion. Fine. Now you can go. Dismissed."

Good heavens, I thought to myself. That man can be intimidating like no one I have ever met.

The judges filed out of the room. Once they were gone, Dr. Armstrong turned to the rest of us.

Chapter Sixty-Three

"**L**unch, anyone? I don't know about you, but that made me hungry."

I looked at him, speechless. He smiled back.

"Good people, we have done our duty. We had a responsibility to report the truth, which we did, and we had a responsibility to deliver a robust defense, which we also did. The onus is gone from us and passed over to the governors of the sport. There is nothing further we can do. I suggest that we will ourselves to accept whatever verdict is rendered. And I am hungry."

"There is," said Holmes, "a decent old pub, The Windmill, a few minutes away. Might I suggest we continue our conversation there."

We walked south on the Lambeth High Street until we reached the pub. I could not help but notice that Mr. and Mrs. Staunton were walking arm in arm, holding on to each other rather tightly.

When we entered the pub, it was still before noon hour and the tables were mostly empty. Dr. Armstrong placed an order at the bar for five dishes of fish and chips and mushy peas. To that spread, he told the barkeep to add five glasses of a select whiskey.

"Are we celebrating?" I asked him.

"Of course, we did what we were supposed to do and did it well. That is reason to celebrate. Don't you agree?"

"Not entirely," said Millie.

"Indeed?" replied the doctor. "And how is that so?"

"I would have preferred that you had let me speak for myself rather than have three men speak about me."

"Darling," said Godfrey, "you are utterly correct but, dearest, could you tell us with a straight face that you could have spoken to those blokes without haranguing them for not having any women on the Board, none on their Committee, and not having a League of Women's Rugby? Now, your telling them so would be entirely justified but possibly somewhat distracting from the point of the hearing."

"Oh, very well. But that is something someone has to tell them. Next time you speak to any of them, let them know that I am going to start such a league next year."

We all laughed and tucked into our lunch.

"About their decision," mused Godfrey, as the last of the chips disappeared from his plate. "Do you think—,"

"No Godfrey," said Dr. Armstrong, cutting him off. "We do not think. Not right now. We wait until we hear what they have to say, and then we think how best to get on with our lives."

At one o'clock, we returned to the Guard Room and sat and waited for the panel to return. They did not appear until one-thirty.

"I am sorry to have kept you waiting," said the bishop. "We have been fully engaged in a very vigorous, perhaps even heated debate amongst ourselves. You have evoked quite strong feelings from us. However, we have reached our decision. Lord Barbazon, the Secretary of the Committee, will read it to you."

Lord Barbazon was known to anyone who had any involvement in the courts of justice over the past forty years. He had retired as a senior judge some five years ago and was now devoting his time to offering his experience and expertise to his favorite sports and hobbies. He was a tall, spare, distinguished fellow with thin, white hair and a neatly trimmed mustache. He remained seated to deliver the decision.

"The decision of the Sub-Committee for Disciplinary Matters on the situation regarding Mr. Godfrey Staunton. One: The Committee accepts the rebuke given to the Rugby Union by Mr. Sherlock Holmes regarding our failure to safeguard our sport from the influence of gambling and its attendant association with criminal elements. The Sub-Committee unanimously recommends to the governors of Rugby Union that effective immediately, any player, coach, or official shown beyond doubt to have placed a wager on a game, whether at an official gaming agent at a rugby grounds or with an unofficial bookmaker at any establishment of any kind at any time, shall receive a suspension of two years. A second offense shall result in a suspension of three additional years, and a third offense shall invoke suspension for life."

Here he looked up at the rest of us and added.

"What any rugby player does at the dog track is none of our business. What he does with respect to rugby is."

He resumed his delivery.

"Two: All matters related to this hearing shall be kept in strictest confidence both out of concern for the reputation of our sport and for those of the participants in this room. Provided that Mr. Staunton promises to abide but our rulings, it has been agreed that all records of this meeting shall be destroyed and any records related to it stricken from the minutes."

Again, he looked up.

"If news of this matter became available to the press, it could damage our sport for years to come. The entire Home Nations Championship series of matches might have to be played over. The implications for our sport could be devastating. Therefore, we shall treat this incident as if it never happened, subject to the terms I shall now deliver.

"Three: The appointment of Godfrey Staunton to the Olympic Association was directly connected to his illegal actions in the game against Scotland. Therefore, he is directed to resign his position so that it can be made available to another sportsman who has not been tainted by this affair.

"Godfrey, you cannot continue to enjoy that envied role. You did not deserve it in the first place, and it was offered to you as part of a criminal conspiracy."

Godfrey nodded his head. "I agree. It was fun while it lasted."

"Four:

He put his report on the table and looked up at us.

"All four of us acknowledge that our wives would be on their knees thanking God if we, their husbands, were to display the loving care for them that Godfrey Staunton has for his wife. Mrs. Staunton, you are a very fortunate young woman."

"I am," Millie replied, "and it is my hope for your wives that they will be as fortunate as I am."

"Yes, well, thank you. We also acknowledge Dr. Armstrong's parting challenge to us, and we admit that had any of us been placed in the situation that Godfrey was in that we would like to believe that we would have conducted ourselves as honorably as he had. Unfortunately, however, the role of the governors of Rugby Union is not to provide sterling moral examples to young men. Nor to give place of pre-eminence to the sanctity of marriage. We were elected by the members of Rugby Union to protect and promote the sport.

We serve in our roles as trustees and cannot divorce ourselves from the accompanying obligations; which brings me back to Number Four. We find that the actions of Godfrey Staunton seriously jeopardized the credibility of the results not merely of a single match between clubs but of the entire Home Nations Championship and regardless of his selfless motives, such behavior cannot be tolerated. Therefore, it is our decision that a fair penalty for your action is that you be suspended from serving as a player on any member club of Rugby Union and playing in any game held under the aegis of Rugby Union for a period of seven years. You may, should you wish to do so, serve as a coach or official. Provided you abide by this decision for the ensuing seven years, you will be welcomed back as a player for any club who wishes to have you on their roster. This ends the presentation of our decision. Mr. Godfrey Staunton, are you willing to accept the terms as stated?"

"Is there," asked Godfrey, "any avenue of appeal?"

"Yes, you may take your case to the overall membership and demand a vote by every player, official, coach, and director in the Union. The case would also then become fodder for the press. Your doing so would bring our sport, and your sport, into great disrepute and we would hope you do not choose that option."

"I believe," said Godfrey, "that I am being offered a Hobson's choice. I have no option but to accept. I will do so."

"Thank you, Sir," said Lord Barbazon. "Now that you have accepted, Baron Eccles has an opportunity to present to you and Mrs. Staunton."

I was confused by that statement. One is not usually given a punishment and immediately offered "an opportunity."

Baron Eccles took a telegram from out of his pocket.

"I do not believe, Godfrey, that you have met my younger son, Archibald."

"No, Sir, I have not."

"Archie is the headmaster at a very select boys' school. He sent me a telegram saying that they are in immediate need of a history master who can also serve as the coach of their school rugby team. He has asked me if I know of anyone who might be available. I am prepared to recommend that you fill that position."

"That is very kind of you, Baron, but I am confused, I am quite familiar with all of the better public schools in the country that have credible rugby programs for their boys. I do not know of any that are in immediate need of a rugby coach who can also serve as a history master."

"Of course not. He is Headmaster of the Auckland Grammar School."

"In New Zealand?"

"I know of no other Auckland, Mr. Staunton. The school has been in operation now for fifty years, has a brilliant reputation, and the entire country is mad about rugby."

"I'm not sure what to say, Sir, except that my wife and I come as a package. What opportunities would there be for her there?"

"Currently, the school is co-educational until such time as the new Girls' Grammar School is built. The girls' section requires an additional science teacher. The school has a generous benefit of maternity leave, and there are several fine and reliable Maori women who enjoy working as nannies for members of the faculty."

Chapter Sixty-Four

On the first of June, Godfrey and Millie Staunton boarded the *Oceania* in Southampton and set sail for the Antipodes. It was a long voyage, the longest undertaken by immigrants from Great Britain to any of its colonies or dominions. Holmes expressed some concerns for Millie's health, and I had to remind him that there were few things healthier in humankind than an athletic young woman who was in the middle of her pregnancy.

We received occasional picture postcards that the two of them had purchased and mailed from ports of call along the route. On the thirtieth of July, Holmes and I both received a copy of a telegram confirming that they had arrived safely in Auckland. Telegrams, however, were frightfully expensive and a very inadequate means of sharing abundant news.

Letters mailed from New Zealand, even when sent on the fleet of new steamships that traveled through the Suez Canal, took at least thirty days to arrive at their destination. As a result, we heard very little from Godfrey and Millie throughout the fall of 1899.

Then, during the first week of December, a note arrived at my door from Holmes. It ran:

Come around a pay a visit at your first opportunity. There is something here you would like to see. Holmes.

I came within the hour, and Holmes pointed to a letter lying open of the coffee table.

"It is addressed to both of us," he said. "Judging by the penmanship, it appears to have written by Godfrey."

I picked it up and read it. It was long and full of extensive descriptions of the natural phenomena and the culture of New Zealand. The parts which readers of this story might enjoy ran as follows:

Mr. Holmes and Dr. Watson:

Two weeks ago, on the 24th of October, Millie and I became the proud and blessed parents of a beautiful baby boy. The chunky little rascal tipped the scales at 8 lbs., 10 ounces. Both mother and son are doing well. We are calling our son James Leslie in honor of the two men who, in their own uniquely different ways, served in the place of my father.

The journey here was long but smooth ... [I have left out an extensive account of their voyage. It reads the same as every account of any ship that sailed through the Suez, past India, and on to Australia or New Zealand. J.W.]

We were not at all sure what to expect and on many evenings on board the ship we strolled arm in arm around the deck, holding very tightly on to each other, admitting that we were somewhat fearful and unprepared for what lay ahead.

We need not have worried. The school has excellent new buildings and as fine a rugby pitch as any school in England. When Baron Eccles said that the country was mad about rugby he was not joking. Not only are they bursting with enthusiasm, the boys here are outstanding, and the skill level of their men's clubs is every bit as good as Blackheath's.

... [description of the school omitted. J.W.}

The boys' team that I have started coaching is made of boys from all over Europe as well as a handful from a few of the better-off native families. They are well-behaved and have not a trace of the obnoxious arrogance of boys from Harrow or Eton.

Millie is looking forward to next term when she will start to teach science to the girls. Of course, she has been flabbergasted by the entirely different species of birds she sees here. Flightless birds are endemic to New Zealand, as are albatrosses, and penguins. She has acquired an excellent set of field glasses and has started putting James in his perambulator and taking walks along the coast of the ocean.

Not long after I arrived, the word went out about my having earned three international caps playing for England last winter. The governors of their national rugby association immediately approached me and asked if I would help train and coach the international team they are putting together. And what a team they are! Bigger, stronger, and faster than any of the teams I played on or against, and highly imaginative in the way they make and run their plays. My only complaint is their dull uniforms. Not a speck of color except black, but that adds to the fearsome feeling they create when they start every game with a terrifying Maori dance, the *Haka.* Lord willing, we are hoping to come on a tour of England in 1905, and I look forward to seeing the two of you at our games. I promise the time will be far happier than it was last year.

This was not the life I had expected to have, but I wake up every morning beside a woman who I love with all my heart and who loves me in return. Thank you for all you did so bravely to make this possible.

Yours very truly,

Godfrey Staunton

P.S. Millie sends her warmest regards.

"Nice to hear," I said, "that they are doing well. I can't help thinking, however, what a much more privileged life he would have had here in London had things not gone the way they did and the fates turned against him. He would be a sure-fire bet for this season's international team. By next year, he might have made captain."

"You feel," asked Holmes, "badly for him?"

"Well, yes. Don't you?"

"No, my dear Watson. Godfrey is the luckiest man on God's green earth."

Dear Sherlockian Readers:

The story is a tribute to the canonical *The Adventure of the Missing Three Quarter*. It is, therefore, focused on the game of rugby. The events are framed by the 1899 Home Nations Championship, a series of rugby matches between the national teams of England, Ireland, Scotland, and Wales that were played from January 7, 1899 to March 18, 1899.

The dates, locations of the matches, the teams that played against each other, the scores, the names of the individual scorers, and the names of any other players mentioned are historically accurate. The only exceptions are the names of Godfrey Staunton and Cyril Overton, who have been borrowed from the Canon.

The plays that took place as described in the story are fictional. The play-by-plays could not be found in the archives so I made them up.

The final results of the 1899 Championship were that Ireland won the Triple Crown and England was awarded the Wooden Spoon.

During the early 1900s, tobacco companies inserted picture cards of various people and places in their cigarette packages. Rugby players, including their statistics on the back of the cards, were among the collections available.

Readers who are familiar with literary criticism may recognize the journey on which I sent Godfrey Staunton. It was appropriated from Joseph Campbell's *The Hero with a Thousand Faces*. A similar pattern can be found in many of humanity's greatest novels, films, and epics.

The names and places mentioned and described throughout the British Isles are, with a few minor exceptions, accurate and were there in 1899.

The Severn Estuary is one of the major habitats of waterfowl in the UK. The birds named in the story are found there and it is the only place where a small colony of the Manx Shearwater (those who are too lazy to fly to the Southern Hemisphere) spend the winter.

I trust that readers will forgive me for what might be considered extraneous material inserted in the section with Holmes and Watson in Ireland. I am (not sure if this is a boast or a confession) one of the few people I know who has actually read James Joyce's *Ulysses* from cover to cover. Not only that, but I have been to Dublin and retraced the steps that Leopold Bloom walked on June 16, 1904. I could not resist sending Holmes and Watson to many that same places that Bloom visited.

Many readers will also note that the series of three temptations presented to Godfrey Staunton—the first to satisfy the physical appetites; the second to fame and fortune; and the final one to power—is not original. The temptations are recorded in three of the four Gospels and were faced by Christ in the wilderness.

In 1905 the national rugby team from New Zealand toured Great Britain and, with one exception, defeated every team they played. Their triumphal story, in historical fiction form, can be found in *The Book of Fame*, by Lloyd Jones.

Did you enjoy this story? Are there ways it could have been improved? Please help the author and future readers by leaving a constructive review on the site from which you purchased the book. Thanks. Much appreciated. CSC

About the Author

In May of 2014 the Sherlock Holmes Society of Canada – better known as The Bootmakers – announced a contest for a new Sherlock Holmes story. Although he had no experience writing fiction, the author submitted a short Sherlock Holmes mystery and was blessed to be declared one of the winners. Thus inspired, he has continued to write new Sherlock Holmes Mysteries since and is on a mission to write a new story as a tribute to each of the sixty stories in the original Canon. He currently writes from Buenos Aires, Toronto, the Okanagan, and Manhattan. Several readers of New Sherlock Holmes Mysteries have kindly sent him suggestions for future stories. You are welcome to do likewise at: craigstephencopland@gmail.com.

More Historical Mysteries
by Craig Stephen Copland

www.SherlockHolmesMystery.com

Copy the links to look inside and download

Studying Scarlet. Starlet O'Halloran, a fabulous mature woman, who reminds the reader of Scarlet O'Hara (but who, for copyright reasons cannot actually be her) has arrived in London looking for her long-lost husband, Brett (who resembles Rhett Butler, but who, for copyright reasons, cannot actually be him). She enlists the help of Sherlock Holmes. This is an unauthorized parody, inspired by Arthur Conan Doyle's *A Study in Scarlet* and Margaret Mitchell's *Gone with the Wind.*   http://authl.it/aic

The Sign of the Third. Fifteen hundred years ago the courageous Princess Hemamali smuggled the sacred tooth of the Buddha into Ceylon. Now, for the first time, it is being brought to London to be part of a magnificent exhibit at the British Museum. But what if something were to happen to it? It would be a disaster for the British Empire. Sherlock Holmes, Dr. Watson, and even Mycroft Holmes are called upon to prevent such a crisis. This novella is inspired by the Sherlock Holmes mystery, *The Sign of the Four.*   http://authl.it/aie

A Sandal from East Anglia. Archeological excavations at an old abbey unearth an ancient document that has the potential to change the course of the British Empire and all of Christendom. Holmes encounters some evil young men and a strikingly beautiful young Sister, with a curious double life. The mystery is inspired by the original Sherlock Holmes story, *A Scandal in Bohemia.*   http://authl.it/aif

The Bald-Headed Trust. Watson insists on taking Sherlock Holmes on a short vacation to the seaside in Plymouth. No sooner has Holmes arrived than he is needed to solve a double murder and prevent a massive fraud diabolically designed by the evil Professor himself. Who knew that a family of devout conservative churchgoers could come to the aid of Sherlock Holmes and bring enormous grief to evil doers? The story is inspired by *The Red-Headed League*. http://authl.it/aih

A Case of Identity Theft. It is the fall of 1888 and Jack the Ripper is terrorizing London. A young married couple is found, minus their heads. Sherlock Holmes, Dr. Watson, the couple's mothers, and Mycroft must join forces to find the murderer before he kills again and makes off with half a million pounds. The novella is a tribute to *A Case of Identity*. It will appeal both to devoted fans of Sherlock Holmes, as well as to those who love the great game of rugby. http://authl.it/aii

The Hudson Valley Mystery. A young man in New York went mad and murdered his father. His mother believes he is innocent and knows he is not crazy. She appeals to Sherlock Holmes and, together with Dr. and Mrs. Watson, he crosses the Atlantic to help this client in need. This new story was inspired by *The Boscombe Valley Mystery*. http://authl.it/aij

The Mystery of the Five Oranges. A desperate father enters 221B Baker Street. His daughter has been kidnapped and spirited off to North America. The evil network who have taken her has spies everywhere. There is only one hope – Sherlock Holmes. Sherlockians will enjoy this new adventure, inspired by *The Five Orange Pips* and *Anne of Green Gables* http://authl.it/aik

The Man Who Was Twisted But Hip. France is torn apart by The Dreyfus Affair. Westminster needs Sherlock Holmes so that the evil tide of anti-Semitism that has engulfed France will not spread. Sherlock and Watson go to Paris to solve the mystery and thwart Moriarty. This new mystery is inspired by, *The Man with the Twisted Lip,* as well as by *The Hunchback of Notre Dame.* http://authl.it/ail

The Adventure of the Blue Belt Buckle. A young street urchin discovers a man's belt and buckle under a bush in Hyde Park. A body is found in a hotel room in Mayfair. Scotland Yard seeks the help of Sherlock Holmes in solving the murder. The Queen's Jubilee could be ruined. Sherlock Holmes, Dr. Watson, Scotland Yard, and Her Majesty all team up to prevent a crime of unspeakable dimensions. A new mystery inspired by *The Blue Carbuncle.* http://authl.it/aim

The Adventure of the Spectred Bat. A beautiful young woman, just weeks away from giving birth, arrives at Baker Street in the middle of the night. Her sister was attacked by a bat and died, and now it is attacking her. A vampire? The story is a tribute to *The Adventure of the Speckled Band* and like the original, leaves the mind wondering and the heart racing. http://authl.it/ain

The Adventure of the Engineer's Mom. A brilliant young Cambridge University engineer is carrying out secret research for the Admiralty. It will lead to the building of the world's most powerful battleship, The Dreadnaught. His adventuress mother is kidnapped, and he seeks the help of Sherlock Holmes. This new mystery is a tribute to *The Engineer's Thumb.* http://authl.it/aio

The Adventure of the Notable Bachelorette. A snobbish nobleman enters 221B Baker Street demanding the help in finding his much younger wife – a beautiful and spirited American from the West. Three days later the wife is accused of a vile crime. Now she comes to Sherlock Holmes seeking to prove her innocence. This new mystery was inspired by *The Adventure of the Noble Bachelor.* http://authl.it/aip

The Adventure of the Beryl Anarchists. A deeply distressed banker enters 221B Baker St. His safe has been robbed, and he is certain that his motorcycle-riding sons have betrayed him. Highly incriminating and embarrassing records of the financial and personal affairs of England's nobility are now in the hands of blackmailers. Then a young girl is murdered. A tribute to *The Adventure of the Beryl Coronet.* http://authl.it/aiq

The Adventure of the Coiffured Bitches. A beautiful young woman will soon inherit a lot of money. She disappears. Another young woman finds out far too much and, in desperation seeks help. Sherlock Holmes, Dr. Watson and Miss Violet Hunter must solve the mystery of the coiffured bitches and avoid the massive mastiff that could tear their throats out. A tribute to *The Adventure of the Copper Beeches.* http://authl.it/air

The Silver Horse, Braised. The greatest horse race of the century will take place at Epsom Downs. Millions have been bet. Owners, jockeys, grooms, and gamblers from across England and America arrive. Jockeys and horses are killed. Holmes fails to solve the crime until… This mystery is a tribute to *Silver Blaze* and the great racetrack stories of Damon Runyon. http://authl.it/ais

The Box of Cards. A brother and a sister from a strict religious family disappear. The parents are alarmed, but Scotland Yard says they are just off sowing their wild oats. A horrific, gruesome package arrives in the post, and it becomes clear that a terrible crime is in process. Sherlock Holmes is called in to help. A tribute to *The Cardboard Box.* http://authl.it/ait

The Yellow Farce. Sherlock Holmes is sent to Japan. The war between Russia and Japan is raging. Alliances between countries in these years before World War I are fragile, and any misstep could plunge the world into Armageddon. The wife of the British ambassador is suspected of being a Russian agent. Join Holmes and Watson as they travel around the world to Japan. Inspired by *The Yellow Face.* http://authl.it/akp

The Stock Market Murders. A young man's friend has gone missing. Two more bodies of young men turn up. All are tied to The City and to one of the greatest frauds ever visited upon the citizens of England. The story is based on the true story of James Whitaker Wright and is inspired by, *The Stock Broker's Clerk.* Any resemblance of the villain to a certain American political figure is entirely coincidental. http://authl.it/akq

The Glorious Yacht. On the night of April 12, 1912, off the coast of Newfoundland, one of the greatest disasters of all time took place – the Unsinkable Titanic struck an iceberg and sank with a horrendous loss of life. The news of the disaster leads Holmes and Watson to reminisce about one of their earliest adventures. It began as a sailing race and ended as a tale of murder, kidnapping, piracy, and survival through a tempest. A tribute to *The Gloria Scott.* http://authl.it/akr

A Most Grave Ritual. In 1649, King Charles I escaped and made a desperate run for Continent. Did he leave behind a vast fortune? The patriarch of an ancient Royalist family dies in the courtyard, and the locals believe that the headless ghost of the king did him in. The police accuse his son of murder. Sherlock Holmes is hired to exonerate the lad. A tribute to *The Musgrave Ritual.* http://authl.it/aks

The Spy Gate Liars. Dr. Watson receives an urgent telegram telling him that Sherlock Holmes is in France and near death. He rushes to aid his dear friend, only to find that what began as a doctor's house call has turned into yet another adventure as Sherlock Holmes races to keep an unknown ruthless murderer from dispatching yet another former German army officer. A tribute to *The Reigate Squires.* http://authl.it/akt

The Cuckold Man Colonel James Barclay needs the help of Sherlock Holmes. His exceptionally beautiful, but much younger, wife has disappeared, and foul play is suspected. Has she been kidnapped and held for ransom? Or is she in the clutches of a deviant monster? The story is a tribute not only to the original mystery, *The Crooked Man,* but also to the biblical story of King David and Bathsheba. http://authl.it/akv

The Impatient Dissidents. In March 1881, the Czar of Russia was assassinated by anarchists. That summer, an attempt was made to murder his daughter, Maria, the wife of England's Prince Alfred. A Russian Count is found dead in a hospital in London. Scotland Yard and the Home Office arrive at 221B and enlist the help of Sherlock Holmes to track down the killers and stop them. This new mystery is a tribute to *The Resident Patient.* http://authl.it/akw

The Grecian, Earned. This story picks up where *The Greek Interpreter* left off. The villains of that story were murdered in Budapest, and so Holmes and Watson set off in search of "the Grecian girl" to solve the mystery. What they discover is a massive plot involving the re-birth of the Olympic games in 1896 and a colorful cast of characters at home and on the Continent. http://authl.it/aia

The Three Rhodes Not Taken. Oxford University is famous for its passionate pursuit of learning. The Rhodes Scholarship has been recently established, and some men are prepared to lie, steal, slander, and, maybe murder, in the pursuit of it. Sherlock Holmes is called upon to track down a thief who has stolen vital documents pertaining to the winner of the scholarship, but what will he do when the prime suspect is found dead? A tribute to *The Three Students.* http://authl.it/al8

The Naval Knaves. On September 15, 1894, an anarchist attempted to bomb the Greenwich Observatory. He failed, but the attempt led Sherlock Holmes into an intricate web of spies, foreign naval officers, and a beautiful princess. Once again, suspicion landed on poor Percy Phelps, now working in a senior position in the Admiralty, and once again Holmes has to use both his powers of deduction and raw courage to not only rescue Percy but to prevent an unspeakable disaster. A tribute to *The Naval Treaty.* http://authl.it/aia

A Scandal in Trumplandia. NOT a new mystery but a political satire. The story is a parody of the much-loved original story, *A Scandal in Bohemia*, with the character of the King of Bohemia replaced by you-know-who. If you enjoy both political satire and Sherlock Holmes, you will get a chuckle out of this new story. http://authl.it/aig

The Binomial Asteroid Problem. The deadly final encounter between Professor Moriarty and Sherlock Holmes took place at Reichenbach Falls. But when was their first encounter? This new story answers that question. What began a stolen Gladstone bag escalates into murder and more. This new story is a tribute to *The Adventure of the Final Problem.* http://authl.it/al1

The Adventure of Charlotte Europa Golderton. *Charles Augustus Milverton* was shot and sent to his just reward. But now another diabolical scheme of blackmail has emerged centered in the telegraph offices of the Royal Mail. It is linked to an archeological expedition whose director disappeared. Someone is prepared to murder to protect their ill-gotten gain and possibly steal a priceless treasure. Holmes is hired by not one but three women who need his help. http://authl.it/al7

The Mystery of 222 Baker Street. The body of a Scotland Yard inspector is found in a locked room in 222 Baker Street. There is no clue as to how he died, but he was murdered. Then another murder occurs in the very same room. Holmes and Watson might have to offer themselves as potential victims if the culprits are to be discovered. The story is a tribute to the original Sherlock Holmes story, *The Adventure of the Empty House.* http://authl.it/al3

The Adventure of the Norwood Rembrandt. A man facing execution appeals to Sherlock Holmes to save him. He claims that he is innocent. Holmes agrees to take on his case. Five years ago, he was convicted of the largest theft of art masterpieces in British history, and of murdering the butler who tried to stop him. Holmes and Watson have to find the real murderer and the missing works of art --- if the client is innocent after all. This new Sherlock Holmes mystery is a tribute to *The Adventure of the Norwood Builder* in the original Canon. http://authl.it/al4

The Horror of the Bastard's Villa. A Scottish clergyman and his faithful border collie visit 221B and tell a tale of a ghostly Banshee on the Isle of Skye. After the specter appeared, two people died. Holmes sends Watson on ahead to investigate and report. More terrifying horrors occur, and Sherlock Holmes must come and solve the awful mystery before more people are murdered. A tribute to the original story in the Canon, Arthur Conan Doyle's masterpiece, *The Hound of the Baskervilles.* http://authl.it/al2

The Dancer from the Dance. In 1909 the entire world of dance changed when Les Ballets Russes, under opened in Paris. They also made annual visits to the West End in London. Tragically, during their 1913 tour, two of their dancers are found murdered. Sherlock Holmes is brought into to find the murderer and prevent any more killings. The story adheres fairly closely to the history of ballet and is a tribute to the original story in the Canon, *The Adventure of the Dancing Men.* http://authl.it/al5

The Solitary Bicycle Thief. Remember Violet Smith, the beautiful young woman whom Sherlock Holmes and Dr. Watson rescued from a forced marriage, as recorded in *The Adventure of the Solitary Cyclist?* Ten years later she and Cyril reappear in 221B Baker Street with a strange tale of the theft of their bicycles. What on the surface seemed like a trifle turns out to be the door that leads Sherlock Holmes into a web of human trafficking, espionage, blackmail, and murder. A new and powerful cabal of master criminals has formed in London, and they will stop at nothing, not even the murder of an innocent foreign student, to extend the hold on the criminal underworld of London. http://authl.it/al6

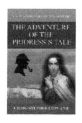

The Adventure of the Prioress's Tale. The senior field hockey team from an elite girls' school goes to Dover for a beach holiday ... and disappears. Have they been abducted into white slavery? Did they run off to Paris? Are they being held for ransom? Can Sherlock Holmes find them in time? Holmes, Watson, Lestrade, the Prioress of the school, and a new gang of Irregulars must find them before something terrible happens. A tribute to *The Adventure of the Priory School in the Canon.* http://authl.it/apv

The Adventure of Mrs. J.L. Heber. A mad woman is murdering London bachelors by driving a railway spike through their heads. Scotland Yard demands that Sherlock Holmes help them find and stop a crazed murderess who is re-enacting the biblical murders by Jael. Holmes agrees and finds that revenge is being taken for deeds treachery and betrayal that took place ten years ago in the Rocky Mountains of Canada. Holmes, Watson, and Lestrade must move quickly before more men and women lose their lives. The story is a tribute to the original Sherlock Holmes story, *The Adventure of Black Peter.* http://authl.it/arr

The Return of Napoleon. In October 1805, Napoleon's fleet was defeated in the Battle of Trafalgar. Now his ghost has returned to England for the centenary of the battle, intent on wreaking revenge on the descendants of Admiral Horatio Nelson and on all of England. The mother of the great-great-grandchildren of Admiral Nelson contacts Sherlock Holmes and asks him to come to her home, Victory Manor, in Gravesend to protect the Nelson Collection and the children. A tribute to *The Adventure of the Six Napoleons.* http://authl.it/at4

The Adventure of the Pinched Palimpsest. At Oxford University, a professor has been proselytizing for anarchism. Three naive students fall for his doctrines and decide to engage in direct action by stealing priceless artifacts from the British Museum, returning them to the oppressed people from whom their colonial masters stole them. In the midst of their caper, a museum guard is shot dead and they are charged with the murder. Sherlock Holmes agrees to take on the case and soon discovers that no one involved is telling the complete truth A tribute to *The Adventure of the Golden Pince Nez.* http://authl.it/ax0

Contributions to
The Great Game of
Sherlockian Scholarship

 ***Sherlock and Barack.*** This is NOT a new Sherlock Holmes Mystery. It is a Sherlockian research monograph. Why did Barack Obama win in November 2012? Why did Mitt Romney lose? Pundits and political scientists have offered countless reasons. This book reveals the truth - The Sherlock Holmes Factor. Had it not been for Sherlock Holmes, Mitt Romney would be president. http://authl.it/aid

 ***From The Beryl Coronet to Vimy Ridge***. This is NOT a New Sherlock Holmes Mystery. It is a monograph of Sherlockian research. This new monograph in the Great Game of Sherlockian scholarship argues that there was a Sherlock Holmes factor in the causes of World War I... and that it is secretly revealed in the *roman a clef* story that we know as *The Adventure of the Beryl Coronet*. http://authl.it/ali

Reverend Ezekiel Black—'The Sherlock Holmes of the American West'—Mystery Stories.

 ***A Scarlet Trail of Murder.*** At ten o'clock on Sunday morning, the twenty-second of October, 1882, in an abandoned house in the West Bottom of Kansas City, a fellow named Jasper Harrison did not wake up. His inability to do was the result of his having had his throat cut. The Reverend Mr. Ezekiel Black, a part-time Methodist minister, and an itinerant US Marshall is called in. This original western mystery was inspired by the great Sherlock Holmes classic, *A Study in Scarlet.* http://authl.it/alg

 ***The Brand of the Flying Four.*** This case all began one quiet evening in a room in Kansas City. A few weeks later, a gruesome murder, took place in Denver. By the time Rev. Black had solved the mystery, justice, of the frontier variety, not the courtroom, had been meted out. The story is inspired by *The Sign of the Four* by Arthur Conan Doyle, and like that story, it combines murder most foul, and romance most enticing. http://authl.it/alh

www.SherlockHolmesMystery.com

Collection Sets for eBooks and paperback are available at *40% off the price of buying them separately.*

Collection One http://authl.it/al9

The Sign of the Tooth
The Hudson Valley Mystery
A Case of Identity Theft
The Bald-Headed Trust
Studying Scarlet
The Mystery of the Five Oranges

Collection Two http://authl.it/ala

A Sandal from East Anglia

The Man Who Was Twisted But Hip

The Blue Belt Buckle

The Spectred Bat

Collection Three http://authl.it/alb

The Engineer's Mom

The Notable Bachelorette

The Beryl Anarchists

The Coiffured Bitches

Collection Four http://authl.it/alc

The Silver Horse, Braised

The Box of Cards

The Yellow Farce

The Three Rhodes Not Taken

Collection Five http://authl.it/ald

The Stock Market Murders

The Glorious Yacht

The Most Grave Ritual

The Spy Gate Liars

Collection Six http://authl.it/ale

The Cuckold Man
The Impatient Dissidents
The Grecian, Earned
The Naval Knaves

Collection Seven http://authl.it/alf

The Binomial Asteroid Problem
The Mystery of 222 Baker Street
The Adventure of Charlotte Europa Golderton
The Adventure of the Norwood Rembrandt

Collection Eight http://authl.it/at3

The Dancer from the Dance
The Adventure of the Prioress's Tale
The Adventure of Mrs. J. L. Heber
The Solitary Bicycle Thief

Super Collections A and B

30 New Sherlock Holmes Mysteries.

The perfect ebooks for readers who can only borrow one book a month from Amazon

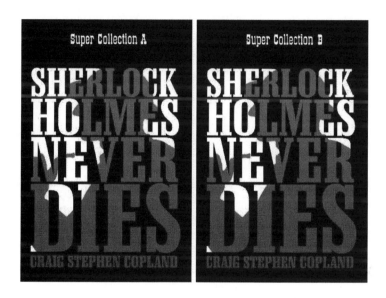

www.SherlockHolmesMystery.com

The Adventure of the Missing Three Quarter

The Original Sherlock Holmes Story

By Arthur Conan Doyle

The Adventure of the Missing Three Quarter

We were fairly accustomed to receive weird telegrams at Baker Street, but I have a particular recollection of one which reached us on a gloomy February morning some seven or eight years ago and gave Mr. Sherlock Holmes a puzzled quarter of an hour. It was addressed to him, and ran thus:—

"Please await me. Terrible misfortune. Right wing three-quarter missing; indispensable to morrow.—OVERTON."

"Strand post-mark and dispatched ten-thirty-six," said Holmes, reading it over and over. "Mr. Overton was evidently considerably excited when he sent it, and somewhat incoherent in consequence. Well, well, he will be here, I dare say, by the time I have looked through the TIMES, and then we shall know all about it. Even the most insignificant problem would be welcome in these stagnant days."

Things had indeed been very slow with us, and I had learned to dread such periods of inaction, for I knew by experience that my companion's brain was so abnormally active that it was dangerous to leave it without material upon which to work. For years I had gradually weaned him from that drug mania which had threatened once to check his remarkable career. Now I knew that under ordinary conditions he no longer craved for this artificial stimulus, but I was well aware that the fiend was not dead, but sleeping; and I have known that the sleep was a light one and the waking near when in periods of idleness I have seen the drawn look upon Holmes's ascetic face, and the brooding of his deep-set and inscrutable eyes. Therefore I blessed this Mr. Overton, whoever he might be, since he had come with his enigmatic message to break that dangerous calm which brought more peril to my friend than all the storms of his tempestuous life.

As we had expected, the telegram was soon followed by its sender, and the card of Mr. Cyril Overton, of Trinity College, Cambridge, announced the arrival of an enormous young man, sixteen stone of solid bone and muscle, who spanned the doorway with his broad shoulders and looked from one of us to the other with a comely face which was haggard with anxiety.

"Mr. Sherlock Holmes?"

My companion bowed.

"I've been down to Scotland Yard, Mr. Holmes. I saw Inspector Stanley Hopkins. He advised me to come to you. He said the case, so far as he could see, was more in your line than in that of the regular police."

"Pray sit down and tell me what is the matter."

"It's awful, Mr. Holmes, simply awful! I wonder my hair isn't grey. Godfrey Staunton—you've heard of him, of course? He's simply the hinge that the whole team turns on. I'd rather spare two from the pack and have Godfrey for my three-quarter line. Whether it's passing, or tackling, or dribbling, there's no one to touch him; and then, he's got the head and can hold us all together. What am I to do? That's what I ask you, Mr. Holmes. There's Moorhouse, first reserve, but he is trained as a half, and he always edges right in on to the scrum instead of keeping out on the touch-line. He's a fine place-kick, it's true, but, then, he has no judgment, and he can't sprint for nuts. Why, Morton or Johnson, the Oxford fliers, could romp round him. Stevenson is fast enough, but he couldn't drop from the twenty-five line, and a three-quarter who can't either punt or drop isn't worth a place for pace alone. No, Mr. Holmes, we are done unless you can help me to find Godfrey Staunton."

My friend had listened with amused surprise to this long speech, which was poured forth with extraordinary vigour and earnestness, every point being driven home by the slapping of a brawny hand upon the speaker's knee. When our visitor was silent Holmes stretched out his hand and took down letter "S" of his commonplace book. For once he dug in vain into that mine of varied information.

"There is Arthur H. Staunton, the rising young forger," said he, "and there was Henry Staunton, whom I helped to hang, but Godfrey Staunton is a new name to me."

It was our visitor's turn to look surprised.

"Why, Mr. Holmes, I thought you knew things," said he. "I suppose, then, if you have never heard of Godfrey Staunton you don't know Cyril Overton either?"

Holmes shook his head good-humouredly.

"Great Scot!" cried the athlete. "Why, I was first reserve for England against Wales, and I've skippered the 'Varsity all this year. But that's nothing! I didn't think there was a soul in England who didn't know Godfrey Staunton, the crack three-quarter, Cambridge, Blackheath, and five Internationals. Good Lord! Mr. Holmes, where HAVE you lived?"

Holmes laughed at the young giant's naive astonishment.

"You live in a different world to me, Mr. Overton, a sweeter and healthier one. My ramifications stretch out into many sections of society, but never, I am happy to say, into amateur sport, which is the best and soundest thing in England. However, your unexpected visit this morning shows me that even in that world of fresh air and fair play there may be work for me to do; so now, my good sir, I beg you to sit down and to tell me slowly and quietly exactly what it is that has occurred, and how you desire that I should help you."

Young Overton's face assumed the bothered look of the man who is more accustomed to using his muscles than his wits; but by degrees, with many repetitions and obscurities which I may omit from his narrative, he laid his strange story before us.

"It's this way, Mr. Holmes. As I have said, I am the skipper of the Rugger team of Cambridge 'Varsity, and Godfrey Staunton is my best man. To-morrow we play Oxford. Yesterday we all came up and we settled at Bentley's private hotel. At ten o'clock I went round and saw that all the fellows had gone to roost, for I believe in strict training and plenty of sleep to keep a team fit. I had a word or two with Godfrey before he turned in. He seemed to me to be pale and bothered. I asked him what was the matter. He said he was all right—just a touch of headache. I bade him good-night and left him. Half an hour later the porter tells me that a rough-looking man with a beard called with a note for Godfrey. He had not gone to bed and the note was taken to his room. Godfrey read it and fell back in a chair as if he had been pole-axed. The porter was so scared that he was going to fetch me, but Godfrey stopped him, had a drink of water, and pulled himself together. Then he went downstairs, said a few words to the man who was waiting in the hall, and the two of them went off together. The last that the porter saw of them, they were almost running down the street in the direction of the Strand. This morning Godfrey's room was empty, his bed had never been slept in, and his things were all just as I had seen them the night before. He had gone off at a moment's notice with this stranger, and no word has come from him since. I don't believe he will ever come back. He was a sportsman, was Godfrey, down to his marrow, and he wouldn't have stopped his training and let in his skipper if it were not for some cause that was too strong for him. No; I feel as if he were gone for good and we should never see him again."

Sherlock Holmes listened with the deepest attention to this singular narrative.

"What did you do?" he asked.

"I wired to Cambridge to learn if anything had been heard of him there. I have had an answer. No one has seen him."

"Could he have got back to Cambridge?"

"Yes, there is a late train—quarter-past eleven."

"But so far as you can ascertain he did not take it?"

"No, he has not been seen."

"What did you do next?"

"I wired to Lord Mount-James."

"Why to Lord Mount-James?"

"Godfrey is an orphan, and Lord Mount-James is his nearest relative—his uncle, I believe."

"Indeed. This throws new light upon the matter. Lord Mount-James is one of the richest men in England."

"So I've heard Godfrey say."

"And your friend was closely related?"

"Yes, he was his heir, and the old boy is nearly eighty— cram full of gout, too. They say he could chalk his billiard-cue with his knuckles. He never allowed Godfrey a shilling in his life, for he is an absolute miser, but it will all come to him right enough."

"Have you heard from Lord Mount-James?"

"No."

"What motive could your friend have in going to Lord Mount-James?"

"Well, something was worrying him the night before, and if it was to do with money it is possible that he would make for his nearest relative who had so much of it, though from all I have heard he would not have much chance of getting it. Godfrey was not fond of the old man. He would not go if he could help it."

"Well, we can soon determine that. If your friend was going to his relative, Lord Mount-James, you have then to explain the visit of this rough-looking fellow at so late an hour, and the agitation that was caused by his coming."

Cyril Overton pressed his hands to his head. "I can make nothing of it," said he.

"Well, well, I have a clear day, and I shall be happy to look into the matter," said Holmes. "I should strongly recommend you to make your preparations for your match without reference to this young gentleman. It must, as you say, have been an overpowering necessity which tore him away in such a fashion, and the same necessity is likely to hold him away. Let us step round together to this hotel, and see if the porter can throw any fresh light upon the matter."

Sherlock Holmes was a past-master in the art of putting a humble witness at his ease, and very soon, in the privacy of Godfrey Staunton's abandoned room, he had extracted all that the porter had to tell. The visitor of the night before was not a gentleman, neither was he a working man. He was simply what the porter described as a "medium-looking chap"; a man of fifty, beard grizzled, pale face, quietly dressed. He seemed himself to be agitated. The porter had observed his hand trembling when he had held out the note. Godfrey Staunton had crammed the note into his pocket. Staunton had not shaken hands with the man in the hall. They had exchanged a few sentences, of which the porter had only distinguished the one word "time." Then they had hurried off in the manner described. It was just half-past ten by the hall clock.

"Let me see," said Holmes, seating himself on Staunton's bed. "You are the day porter, are you not?"

"Yes, sir; I go off duty at eleven."

"The night porter saw nothing, I suppose?"

"No, sir; one theatre party came in late. No one else."

"Were you on duty all day yesterday?"

"Yes, sir."

"Did you take any messages to Mr. Staunton?"

"Yes, sir; one telegram."

"Ah! That's interesting. What o'clock was this?"

"About six."

"Where was Mr. Staunton when he received it?"

"Here in his room."

"Were you present when he opened it?"

"Yes, sir; I waited to see if there was an answer."

"Well, was there?"

"Yes, sir. He wrote an answer."

"Did you take it?"

"No; he took it himself."

"But he wrote it in your presence?"

"Yes, sir. I was standing by the door, and he with his back turned at that table. When he had written it he said, 'All right, porter, I will take this myself.'"

"What did he write it with?"

"A pen, sir."

"Was the telegraphic form one of these on the table?"

"Yes, sir; it was the top one."

Holmes rose. Taking the forms he carried them over to the window and carefully examined that which was uppermost.

"It is a pity he did not write in pencil," said he, throwing them down again with a shrug of disappointment. "As you have no doubt frequently observed, Watson, the impression usually goes through—a fact which has dissolved many a happy marriage. However, I can find no trace here. I rejoice, however, to perceive that he wrote with a broad-pointed quill pen, and I can hardly doubt that we will find some impression upon this blotting-pad. Ah, yes, surely this is the very thing!"

He tore off a strip of the blotting-paper and turned towards us the following hieroglyphic:—
some backwards writing

Cyril Overton was much excited. "Hold it to the glass!" he cried.

"That is unnecessary," said Holmes. "The paper is thin, and the reverse will give the message. Here it is." He turned it over and we read:—
Stand by us for God's sake!

"So that is the tail end of the telegram which Godfrey Staunton dispatched within a few hours of his disappearance. There are at least six words of the message which have escaped us; but what remains—'Stand by us for God's sake!'—proves that this young man saw a formidable danger which approached him, and from which someone else could protect him. 'US,' mark you! Another person was involved. Who should it be but the pale-faced, bearded man, who seemed himself in so nervous a state? What, then, is the connection between Godfrey Staunton and the bearded man? And what is the third source from which each of them sought for help against pressing danger? Our inquiry has already narrowed down to that."

"We have only to find to whom that telegram is addressed," I suggested.

"Exactly, my dear Watson. Your reflection, though profound, had already crossed my mind. But I dare say it may have come to your notice that if you walk into a post-office and demand to see the counterfoil of another man's message there may be some disinclination on the part of the officials to oblige you. There is so much red tape in these matters! However, I have no doubt that with a little delicacy and finesse the end may be attained. Meanwhile, I should like in your presence, Mr. Overton, to go through these papers which have been left upon the table."

There were a number of letters, bills, and note-books, which Holmes turned over and examined with quick, nervous fingers and darting, penetrating eyes. "Nothing here," he said, at last. "By the way, I suppose your friend was a healthy young fellow—nothing amiss with him?"

"Sound as a bell."

"Have you ever known him ill?"

"Not a day. He has been laid up with a hack, and once he slipped his knee-cap, but that was nothing."

"Perhaps he was not so strong as you suppose. I should think he may have had some secret trouble. With your assent I will put one or two of these papers in my pocket, in case they should bear upon our future inquiry."

"One moment! One moment!" cried a querulous voice, and we looked up to find a queer little old man, jerking and twitching in the doorway. He was dressed in rusty black, with a very broad brimmed top-hat and a loose white necktie—the whole effect being that of a very rustic parson or of an undertaker's mute. Yet, in spite of his shabby and even absurd appearance, his voice had a sharp crackle, and his manner a quick intensity which commanded attention.

"Who are you, sir, and by what right do you touch this gentleman's papers?" he asked.

"I am a private detective, and I am endeavouring to explain his disappearance."

"Oh, you are, are you? And who instructed you, eh?"

"This gentleman, Mr. Staunton's friend, was referred to me by Scotland Yard."

"Who are you, sir?"

"I am Cyril Overton."

"Then it is you who sent me a telegram. My name is Lord Mount-James. I came round as quickly as the Bayswater 'bus would bring me. So you have instructed a detective?"

"Yes, sir."

"And are you prepared to meet the cost?"

"I have no doubt, sir, that my friend Godfrey, when we find him, will be prepared to do that."

"But if he is never found, eh? Answer me that!"

"In that case no doubt his family—"

"Nothing of the sort, sir!" screamed the little man. "Don't look to me for a penny—not a penny! You understand that, Mr. Detective! I am all the family that this young man has got, and I tell you that I am not responsible. If he has any expectations it is due to the fact that I have never wasted money, and I do not propose to begin to do so now. As to those papers with which you are making so free, I may tell you that in case there should be anything of any value among them you will be held strictly to account for what you do with them."

"Very good, sir," said Sherlock Holmes. "May I ask in the meanwhile whether you have yourself any theory to account for this young man's disappearance?"

"No, sir, I have not. He is big enough and old enough to look after himself, and if he is so foolish as to lose himself I entirely refuse to accept the responsibility of hunting for him."

"I quite understand your position," said Holmes, with a mischievous twinkle in his eyes. "Perhaps you don't quite understand mine. Godfrey Staunton appears to have been a poor man. If he has been kidnapped it could not have been for anything which he himself possesses. The fame of your wealth has gone abroad, Lord Mount-James, and it is entirely possible that a gang of thieves have secured your nephew in order to gain from him some information as to your house, your habits, and your treasure."

The face of our unpleasant little visitor turned as white as his neckcloth.

"Heavens, sir, what an idea! I never thought of such villainy! What inhuman rogues there are in the world! But Godfrey is a fine lad—a staunch lad. Nothing would induce him to give his old uncle away. I'll have the plate moved over to the bank this evening. In the meantime spare no pains, Mr. Detective! I beg you to leave no stone unturned to bring him safely back. As to money, well, so far as a fiver, or even a tenner, goes, you can always look to me."

Even in his chastened frame of mind the noble miser could give us no information which could help us, for he knew little of the private life of his nephew. Our only clue lay in the truncated telegram, and with a copy of this in his hand Holmes set forth to find a second link for his chain. We had shaken off Lord Mount-James, and Overton had gone to consult with the other members of his team over the misfortune which had befallen them.

There was a telegraph-office at a short distance from the hotel. We halted outside it.

"It's worth trying, Watson," said Holmes. "Of course, with a warrant we could demand to see the counterfoils, but we have not reached that stage yet. I don't suppose they remember faces in so busy a place. Let us venture it."

"I am sorry to trouble you," said he, in his blandest manner, to the young woman behind the grating; "there is some small mistake about a telegram I sent yesterday. I have had no answer, and I very much fear that I must have omitted to put my name at the end. Could you tell me if this was so?"

The young woman turned over a sheaf of counterfoils.

"What o'clock was it?" she asked.

"A little after six."

"Whom was it to?"

Holmes put his finger to his lips and glanced at me. "The last words in it were 'for God's sake'," he whispered, confidentially; "I am very anxious at getting no answer."

The young woman separated one of the forms.

"This is it. There is no name," said she, smoothing it out upon the counter.

"Then that, of course, accounts for my getting no answer," said Holmes. "Dear me, how very stupid of me, to be sure! Good morning, miss, and many thanks for having relieved my mind." He chuckled and rubbed his hands when we found ourselves in the street once more.

"Well?" I asked.

"We progress, my dear Watson, we progress. I had seven different schemes for getting a glimpse of that telegram, but I could hardly hope to succeed the very first time."

"And what have you gained?"

"A starting-point for our investigation." He hailed a cab. "King's Cross Station," said he.

"We have a journey, then?"

"Yes; I think we must run down to Cambridge together. All the indications seem to me to point in that direction."

"Tell me," I asked, as we rattled up Gray's Inn Road, "have you any suspicion yet as to the cause of the disappearance? I don't think that among all our cases I have known one where the motives are more obscure. Surely you don't really imagine that he may be kidnapped in order to give information against his wealthy uncle?"

"I confess, my dear Watson, that that does not appeal to me as a very probable explanation. It struck me, however, as being the one which was most likely to interest that exceedingly unpleasant old person."

"It certainly did that. But what are your alternatives?"

"I could mention several. You must admit that it is curious and suggestive that this incident should occur on the eve of this important match, and should involve the only man whose presence seems essential to the success of the side. It may, of course, be coincidence, but it is interesting. Amateur sport is free from betting, but a good deal of outside betting goes on among the public, and it is possible that it might be worth someone's while to get at a player as the ruffians of the turf get at a race-horse. There is one explanation. A second very obvious one is that this young man really is the heir of a great property, however modest his means may at present be, and it is not impossible that a plot to hold him for ransom might be concocted."

"These theories take no account of the telegram."

"Quite true, Watson. The telegram still remains the only solid thing with which we have to deal, and we must not permit our attention to wander away from it. It is to gain light upon the purpose of this telegram that we are now upon our way to Cambridge. The path of our investigation is at present obscure, but I shall be very much surprised if before evening we have not cleared it up or made a considerable advance along it."
a university

It was already dark when we reached the old University city. Holmes took a cab at the station, and ordered the man to drive to the house of Dr. Leslie Armstrong. A few minutes later we had stopped at a large mansion in the busiest thoroughfare. We were shown in, and after a long wait were at last admitted into the consulting-room, where we found the doctor seated behind his table.

It argues the degree in which I had lost touch with my profession that the name of Leslie Armstrong was to me. Now I am aware that he is not only one of the heads of the medical school of the University, but a thinker of European reputation in more than one branch of science. Yet even without knowing his brilliant record one could not fail to be impressed by a mere glance at the man, the square, massive face, the brooding eyes under the thatched brows, and the granite moulding of the inflexible jaw. A man of deep character, a man with an alert mind, grim, ascetic, self-contained, formidable—so I read Dr. Leslie Armstrong. He held my friend's card in his hand, and he looked up with no very pleased expression upon his dour features.

"I have heard your name, Mr. Sherlock Holmes, and I am aware of your profession, one of which I by no means approve."

"In that, doctor, you will find yourself in agreement with every criminal in the country," said my friend, quietly.

"So far as your efforts are directed towards the suppression of crime, sir, they must have the support of every reasonable member of the community, though I cannot doubt that the official machinery is amply sufficient for the purpose. Where your calling is more open to criticism is when you pry into the secrets of private individuals, when you rake up family matters which are better hidden, and when you incidentally waste the time of men who are more busy than yourself. At the present moment, for example, I should be writing a treatise instead of conversing with you."

"No doubt, doctor; and yet the conversation may prove more important than the treatise. Incidentally I may tell you that we are doing the reverse of what you very justly blame, and that we are endeavouring to prevent anything like public exposure of private matters which must necessarily follow when once the case is fairly in the hands of the official police. You may look upon me simply as an irregular pioneer who goes in front of the regular forces of the country. I have come to ask you about Mr. Godfrey Staunton."

"What about him?"

"You know him, do you not?"

"He is an intimate friend of mine."

"You are aware that he has disappeared?"

"Ah, indeed!" There was no change of expression in the rugged features of the doctor.

"He left his hotel last night. He has not been heard of."

"No doubt he will return."

"To-morrow is the 'Varsity football match."

"I have no sympathy with these childish games. The young man's fate interests me deeply, since I know him and like him. The football match does not come within my horizon at all."

"I claim your sympathy, then, in my investigation of Mr. Staunton's fate. Do you know where he is?"

"Certainly not."

"You have not seen him since yesterday?"

"No, I have not."

"Was Mr. Staunton a healthy man?"

"Absolutely."

"Did you ever know him ill?"

"Never."

Holmes popped a sheet of paper before the doctor's eyes. "Then perhaps you will explain this receipted bill for thirteen guineas, paid by Mr. Godfrey Staunton last month to Dr. Leslie Armstrong of Cambridge. I picked it out from among the papers upon his desk."

The doctor flushed with anger.

"I do not feel that there is any reason why I should render an explanation to you, Mr. Holmes."

Holmes replaced the bill in his note-book. "If you prefer a public explanation it must come sooner or later," said he. "I have already told you that I can hush up that which others will be bound to publish, and you would really be wiser to take me into your complete confidence."

"I know nothing about it."

"Did you hear from Mr. Staunton in London?"

"Certainly not."

"Dear me, dear me; the post-office again!" Holmes sighed, wearily. "A most urgent telegram was dispatched to you from London by Godfrey Staunton at six-fifteen yesterday evening—a telegram which is undoubtedly associated with his disappearance—and yet you have not had it. It is most culpable. I shall certainly go down to the office here and register a complaint."

Dr. Leslie Armstrong sprang up from behind his desk, and his dark face was crimson with fury.

"I'll trouble you to walk out of my house, sir," said he. "You can tell your employer, Lord Mount-James, that I do not wish to have anything to do either with him or with his agents. No, sir, not another word!" He rang the bell furiously. "John, show these gentlemen out!" A pompous butler ushered us severely to the door, and we found ourselves in the street. Holmes burst out laughing.

"Dr. Leslie Armstrong is certainly a man of energy and character," said he. "I have not seen a man who, if he turned his talents that way, was more calculated to fill the gap left by the illustrious Moriarty. And now, my poor Watson, here we are, stranded and friendless in this inhospitable town, which we cannot leave without abandoning our case. This little inn just opposite Armstrong's house is singularly adapted to our needs. If you would engage a front room and purchase the necessaries for the night, I may have time to make a few inquiries."

These few inquiries proved, however, to be a more lengthy proceeding than Holmes had imagined, for he did not return to the inn until nearly nine o'clock. He was pale and dejected, stained with dust, and exhausted with hunger and fatigue. A cold supper was ready upon the table, and when his needs were satisfied and his pipe alight he was ready to take that half comic and wholly philosophic view which was natural to him when his affairs were going awry. The sound of carriage wheels caused him to rise and glance out of the window. A brougham and pair of greys under the glare of a gas-lamp stood before the doctor's door.

"It's been out three hours," said Holmes; "started at half-past six, and here it is back again. That gives a radius of ten or twelve miles, and he does it once, or sometimes twice, a day."

"No unusual thing for a doctor in practice."

"But Armstrong is not really a doctor in practice. He is a lecturer and a consultant, but he does not care for general practice, which distracts him from his literary work. Why, then, does he make these long journeys, which must be exceedingly irksome to him, and who is it that he visits?"

"His coachman—"

"My dear Watson, can you doubt that it was to him that I first applied? I do not know whether it came from his own innate depravity or from the promptings of his master, but he was rude enough to set a dog at me. Neither dog nor man liked the look of my stick, however, and the matter fell through. Relations were strained after that, and further inquiries out of the question. All that I have learned I got from a friendly native in the yard of our own inn. It was he who told me of the doctor's habits and of his daily journey. At that instant, to give point to his words, the carriage came round to the door."

"Could you not follow it?"

"Excellent, Watson! You are scintillating this evening. The idea did cross my mind. There is, as you may have observed, a bicycle shop next to our inn. Into this I rushed, engaged a bicycle, and was able to get started before the carriage was quite out of sight. I rapidly overtook it, and then, keeping at a discreet distance of a hundred yards or so, I followed its lights until we were clear of the town. We had got well out on the country road when a somewhat mortifying incident occurred. The carriage stopped, the doctor alighted, walked swiftly back to where I had also halted, and told me in an excellent sardonic fashion that he feared the road was narrow, and that he hoped his carriage did not impede the passage of my bicycle. Nothing could have been more admirable than his way of putting it. I at once rode past the carriage, and, keeping to the main road, I went on for a few miles, and then halted in a convenient place to see if the carriage passed. There was no sign of it, however, and so it became evident that it had turned down one of several side roads which I had observed. I rode back, but again saw nothing of the carriage, and now, as you perceive, it has returned after me. Of course, I had at the outset no particular reason to connect these journeys with the disappearance of Godfrey Staunton, and was only inclined to investigate them on the general grounds that everything which concerns Dr. Armstrong is at present of interest to us; but, now that I find he keeps so keen a look-out upon anyone who may follow him on these excursions, the affair appears more important, and I shall not be satisfied until I have made the matter clear."

"We can follow him to-morrow."

"Can we? It is not so easy as you seem to think. You are not familiar with Cambridgeshire scenery, are you? It does not lend itself to concealment. All this country that I passed over to-night is as flat and clean as the palm of your hand, and the man we are following is no fool, as he very clearly showed to-night. I have wired to Overton to let us know any fresh London developments at this address, and in the meantime we can only concentrate our attention upon Dr. Armstrong, whose name the obliging young lady at the office allowed me to read upon the counterfoil of Staunton's urgent message. He knows where the young man is— to that I'll swear—and if he knows, then it must be our own fault if we cannot manage to know also. At present it must be admitted that the odd trick is in his possession, and, as you are aware, Watson, it is not my habit to leave the game in that condition."

And yet the next day brought us no nearer to the solution of the mystery. A note was handed in after breakfast, which Holmes passed across to me with a smile.

"Sir," it ran, "I can assure you that you are wasting your time in dogging my movements. I have, as you discovered last night, a window at the back of my brougham, and if you desire a twenty-mile ride which will lead you to the spot from which you started, you have only to follow me. Meanwhile, I can inform you that no spying upon me can in any way help Mr. Godfrey Staunton, and I am convinced that the best service you can do to that gentleman is to return at once to London and to report to your employer that you are unable to trace him. Your time in Cambridge will certainly be wasted. "Yours faithfully, LESLIE ARMSTRONG."

"An outspoken, honest antagonist is the doctor," said Holmes. "Well, well, he excites my curiosity, and I must really know more before I leave him."

"His carriage is at his door now," said I. "There he is stepping into it. I saw him glance up at our window as he did so. Suppose I try my luck upon the bicycle?"

"No, no, my dear Watson! With all respect for your natural acumen I do not think that you are quite a match for the worthy doctor. I think that possibly I can attain our end by some independent explorations of my own. I am afraid that I must leave you to your own devices, as the appearance of TWO inquiring strangers upon a sleepy countryside might excite more gossip than I care for. No doubt you will find some sights to amuse you in this venerable city, and I hope to bring back a more favourable report to you before evening."

Once more, however, my friend was destined to be disappointed. He came back at night weary and unsuccessful.

"I have had a blank day, Watson. Having got the doctor's general direction, I spent the day in visiting all the villages upon that side of Cambridge, and comparing notes with publicans and other local news agencies. I have covered some ground: Chesterton, Histon, Waterbeach, and Oakington have each been explored and have each proved disappointing. The daily appearance of a brougham and pair could hardly have been overlooked in such Sleepy Hollows. The doctor has scored once more. Is there a telegram for me?"

"Yes; I opened it. Here it is: 'Ask for Pompey from Jeremy Dixon, Trinity College.' I don't understand it."

"Oh, it is clear enough. It is from our friend Overton, and is in answer to a question from me. I'll just send round a note to Mr. Jeremy Dixon, and then I have no doubt that our luck will turn. By the way, is there any news of the match?"

"Yes, the local evening paper has an excellent account in its last edition. Oxford won by a goal and two tries. The last sentences of the description say: 'The defeat of the Light Blues may be entirely attributed to the unfortunate absence of the crack International, Godfrey Staunton, whose want was felt at every instant of the game. The lack of combination in the three-quarter line and their weakness both in attack and defense more than neutralized the efforts of a heavy and hard-working pack.'"

"Then our friend Overton's forebodings have been justified," said Holmes. "Personally I am in agreement with Dr. Armstrong, and football does not come within my horizon. Early to bed to-night, Watson, for I foresee that to-morrow may be an eventful day."

I was horrified by my first glimpse of Holmes next morning, for he sat by the fire holding his tiny hypodermic syringe. I associated that instrument with the single weakness of his nature, and I feared the worst when I saw it glittering in his hand. He laughed at my expression of dismay, and laid it upon the table.

"No, no, my dear fellow, there is no cause for alarm. It is not upon this occasion the instrument of evil, but it will rather prove to be the key which will unlock our mystery. On this syringe I base all my hopes. I have just returned from a small scouting expedition and everything is favourable. Eat a good breakfast, Watson, for I propose to get upon Dr. Armstrong's trail to-day, and once on it I will not stop for rest or food until I run him to his burrow."

"In that case," said I, "we had best carry our breakfast with us, for he is making an early start. His carriage is at the door."

"Never mind. Let him go. He will be clever if he can drive where I cannot follow him. When you have finished come downstairs with me, and I will introduce you to a detective who is a very eminent specialist in the work that lies before us."

When we descended I followed Holmes into the stable yard, where he opened the door of a loose-box and led out a squat, lop-eared, white-and-tan dog, something between a beagle and a foxhound.

"Let me introduce you to Pompey," said he. "Pompey is the pride of the local draghounds, no very great flier, as his build will show, but a staunch hound on a scent. Well, Pompey, you may not be fast, but I expect you will be too fast for a couple of middle-aged London gentlemen, so I will take the liberty of fastening this leather leash to your collar. Now, boy, come along, and show what you can do." He led him across to the doctor's door. The dog sniffed round for an instant, and then with a shrill whine of excitement started off down the street, tugging at his leash in his efforts to go faster. In half an hour, we were clear of the town and hastening down a country road.

"What have you done, Holmes?" I asked.

"A threadbare and venerable device, but useful upon occasion. I walked into the doctor's yard this morning and shot my syringe full of aniseed over the hind wheel. A draghound will follow aniseed from here to John O' Groat's, and our friend Armstrong would have to drive through the Cam before he would shake Pompey off his trail. Oh, the cunning rascal! This is how he gave me the slip the other night."

The dog had suddenly turned out of the main road into a grass-grown lane. Half a mile farther this opened into another broad road, and the trail turned hard to the right in the direction of the town, which we had just quitted. The road took a sweep to the south of the town and continued in the opposite direction to that in which we started.

"This DETOUR has been entirely for our benefit, then?" said Holmes. "No wonder that my inquiries among those villages led to nothing. The doctor has certainly played the game for all it is worth, and one would like to know the reason for such elaborate deception. This should be the village of Trumpington to the right of us. And, by Jove! here is the brougham coming round the corner. Quick, Watson, quick, or we are done!"

He sprang through a gate into a field, dragging the reluctant Pompey after him. We had hardly got under the shelter of the hedge when the carriage rattled past. I caught a glimpse of Dr.

Armstrong within, his shoulders bowed, his head sunk on his hands, the very image of distress. I could tell by my companion's graver face that he also had seen.

"I fear there is some dark ending to our quest," said he. "It cannot be long before we know it. Come, Pompey! Ah, it is the cottage in the field!"

There could be no doubt that we had reached the end of our journey. Pompey ran about and whined eagerly outside the gate where the marks of the brougham's wheels were still to be seen. A footpath led across to the lonely cottage. Holmes tied the dog to the hedge, and we hastened onwards. My friend knocked at the little rustic door, and knocked again without response. And yet the cottage was not deserted, for a low sound came to our ears— a kind of drone of misery and despair, which was indescribably melancholy. Holmes paused irresolute, and then he glanced back at the road which we had just traversed. A brougham was coming down it, and there could be no mistaking those grey horses.

"By Jove, the doctor is coming back!" cried Holmes. "That settles it. We are bound to see what it means before he comes."

He opened the door and we stepped into the hall. The droning sound swelled louder upon our ears until it became one long, deep wail of distress. It came from upstairs. Holmes darted up and I followed him. He pushed open a half-closed door and we both stood appalled at the sight before us.

A woman, young and beautiful, was lying dead upon the bed. Her calm, pale face, with dim, wide-opened blue eyes, looked upward from amid a great tangle of golden hair. At the foot of the bed, half sitting, half kneeling, his face buried in the clothes, was a young man, whose frame was racked by his sobs. So absorbed was he by his bitter grief that he never looked up until Holmes's hand was on his shoulder.

"Are you Mr. Godfrey Staunton?"

"Yes, yes; I am—but you are too late. She is dead."

The man was so dazed that he could not be made to understand that we were anything but doctors who had been sent to his assistance. Holmes was endeavouring to utter a few words of consolation, and to explain the alarm which had been caused to his friends by his sudden disappearance, when there was a step upon the stairs, and there was the heavy, stern, questioning face of Dr. Armstrong at the door.

"So, gentlemen," said he, "you have attained your end, and have certainly chosen a particularly delicate moment for your intrusion. I would not brawl in the presence of death, but I can assure you that if I were a younger man your monstrous conduct would not pass with impunity."

"Excuse me, Dr. Armstrong, I think we are a little at cross-purposes," said my friend, with dignity. "If you could step downstairs with us we may each be able to give some light to the other upon this miserable affair."

A minute later the grim doctor and ourselves were in the sitting-room below.

"Well, sir?" said he.

"I wish you to understand, in the first place, that I am not employed by Lord Mount-James, and that my sympathies in this matter are entirely against that nobleman. When a man is lost it is my duty to ascertain his fate, but having done so the matter ends so far as I am concerned; and so long as there is nothing criminal, I am much more anxious to hush up private scandals than to give them publicity. If, as I imagine, there is no breach of the law in this matter, you can absolutely depend upon my discretion and my co-operation in keeping the facts out of the papers."

Dr. Armstrong took a quick step forward and wrung Holmes by the hand.

"You are a good fellow," said he. "I had misjudged you. I thank Heaven that my compunction at leaving poor Staunton all alone in this plight caused me to turn my carriage back, and so to make your acquaintance. Knowing as much as you do, the situation is very easily explained. A year ago Godfrey Staunton lodged in London for a time, and became passionately attached to his landlady's daughter, whom he married. She was as good as she was beautiful, and as intelligent as she was good. No man need be ashamed of such a wife. But Godfrey was the heir to this crabbed old nobleman, and it was quite certain that the news of his marriage would have been the end of his inheritance. I knew the lad well, and I loved him for his many excellent qualities. I did all I could to help him to keep things straight. We did our very best to keep the thing from everyone, for when once such a whisper gets about it is not long before everyone has heard it. Thanks to this lonely cottage and his own discretion, Godfrey has up to now succeeded. Their secret was known to no one save to me and to one excellent servant who has at present gone for assistance to Trumpington. But at last there came a terrible blow in the shape of dangerous illness to his wife. It was consumption of the most virulent kind. The poor boy was half crazed with grief, and yet he had to go to London to play this match, for he could not get out of it without explanations which would expose his secret. I tried to cheer him up by a wire, and he sent me one in reply imploring me to do all I could. This was the telegram which you appear in some inexplicable way to have seen. I did not tell him how urgent the danger was, for I knew that he could do no good here, but I sent the truth to the girl's father, and he very injudiciously communicated it to Godfrey. The result was that he came straight away in a state bordering on frenzy, and has remained in the same state, kneeling at the end of her bed, until this morning death put an end to her sufferings. That is all, Mr. Holmes, and I am sure that I can rely upon your discretion and that of your friend."

Holmes grasped the doctor's hand.

"Come, Watson," said he, and we passed from that house of grief into the pale sunlight of the winter day.

Manufactured by
Amazon.ca
Bolton, ON